elf-ish

A FAKE RELATIONSHIP, MILLIONAIRE-GRINCH, HOLIDAY ROMANCE.

L.B. DUNBAR

www.lbdunbar.com

Cover Design: Megan Dunbar
Cover Characters: Qambar Graphics
Editor: Nicole McCurdy/Emerald Edits
Editor: Gemma Brocato

Other Books by L.B. Dunbar

Sterling Falls
Sterling Heat
Sterling Brick
Sterling Streak
Sterling Clay
Sterling Fight
Sterling Touch
Sterling Stone

Chicago Anchors
Elevator Pitch
Catch the Kiss

Parentmoon

Holiday Hotties (Christmas novellas)
Scrooge-ish
Naughty-ish
Grouch-ish
Elf-ish

Hideaway Harbor
The Holiday Post

Road Trips & Romance
Hauling Ashe
Merging Wright
Rhode Trip

Lakeside Cottage
Living at 40
Loving at 40
Learning at 40
Letting Go at 40

Silver Foxes of Blue Ridge
Silver Brewer
Silver Player

Silver Mayor
Silver Biker

Sexy Silver Fox Collection
After Care
Midlife Crisis
Restored Dreams
Second Chance
Wine&Dine

Collision novellas
Collide
Caught

The Sex Education of M.E.

The Heart Collection
Speak from the Heart
Read with your Heart
Look with your Heart
Fight from the Heart
View with your Heart

A Heart Collection Spin-off
The Heart Remembers

BOOKS IN OTHER AUTHOR WORLDS
Smartypants Romance (an imprint of Penny Reid)

The World of True North (an imprint of Sarina Bowen)

THE EARLY YEARS
The Legendary Rock Star Series

Paradise Stories

The Island Duet

dedication

Marshall Field's, the department store.
Thanks for the memories.

chapter 1

[Angelica]

"Possible heart attack. Ashford's. Eighth floor."

When the call came through from dispatch, I was eager to take the ride. Alongside my ambulance driving partner, Maddix, I wiggle in my seat at the prospect of entering Ashford's iconic department store located in the middle of the pulsing beat of retail in downtown Chicago. Shopping at Ashford's is an experience, and I have fond memories of visiting the seven floors of retail heaven.

However, I understand my assignment.

I'll be entering the building to save the owner's life.

Jude Ashford is a bit of a novelty. At twenty-something, he inherited his great-grandfather's retail mecca, which had been reduced to one flagship store after decades of being a major department store chain with multiple locations throughout the world. Everyone knows how the old man left the family's heritage—the original store—out of any buyout arrangements and willed the place to his grandson, who by thirty-something had turned this historical landmark into a glorious shopping destination.

Not that the place hadn't been great prior to Jude's rule. As a child, my grandmother would make the entire family dress up in our church-going clothes for a special dinner in the Oak Room, where we'd sit underneath a two-story tree that sparkled and glittered beneath the low lights of the dark-paneled dining space. On other occasions, she'd take us to a formal breakfast with Santa, often themed with holiday bears or popular children's stories. A highlight of any visit was viewing the windows along State Street that told a story with automatons.

For me, I loved just standing on the bright red carpet on the first floor, staring up the middle of the store, where six higher floors were surrounded by shiny gilded railings, and the ceiling seven stories up offers a dream-like glass canopy.

Today, I wouldn't have time to stop and gaze.

Again—job to do—which was a job I loved. I wasn't some adrenaline junky or danger seeker, but more like an I-want-to-help-others kind of person.

Once parked beside the store, Maddix and I raced through the main floor, guiding a stretcher through the Black Friday doorbuster crowds, until we reached the elevator bank that would take us to the executive level.

A small group of employees is gathered outside the owner's office.

"Let us through," Maddix hollers, forcing people to part like the Red Sea.

Inside the office, we find a man, slumped in a high-backed office chair behind a massive wooden desk. With his white dress shirt unbuttoned to his waist, suit coat still on, and pants slung low at his hip, unbuttoned and unzipped, the hint of a tattoo along his side peeks out from the parted clothing.

His face is ashen and his eyes wide as his gaze pings from me to Maddix. "I'm having a heart attack."

His speech is slurred but still strong, which is a good sign.

"Can you tell me what your symptoms are?" I address the store's owner, who continues to ignore me and stares at Maddix.

Unfortunately, this kind of behavior comes with the job. Older gents can be bitter that women hold positions once predominantly held by men, such as first responders. Some men are threatened by the strength and confidence of a female in such roles. I might be average height, but I am solid and curvy. My uniform isn't flattering to my body, but it isn't meant to be.

"My chest. My heart is racing." Jude weakly slaps his hand over a firm looking pec, while still looking at Maddix. "I feel like a vise is squeezing my ribs. I can't take a deep breath."

Sounds like a panic attack, but I don't mention it.

"Any other symptoms?" I question.

The patient keeps his focus on Maddix as if I haven't spoken.

"Don't look at me. I'm just here for the muscle," Maddix teases.

I snort, knowing my partner is kidding.

With a glove-covered hand, I check Jude's pulse at his wrist. He flinches beneath my touch, and our gazes clash a second before he yanks his eyes away from me. Then tugs his wrist free from my fingers.

Maddix stands behind the large, leather office chair while I move to Jude's ankles.

"On three," Maddix states before counting down, and we lift Jude onto the stretcher.

With a quick glance at a woman standing just off the corner of the oversized desk, my earlier suspicions about what caused his heart palpitations appear confirmed. Being an EMT, we encounter the strangest things. Heart attacks induced by sex are not a novelty.

A mix of guilt and concern dust the sharp cheekbones of the lithe raven-haired beauty while she chews a polished fingernail.

"I'll be right behind the ambulance," she eventually states.

"No," Jude grunts, a little too strongly. He closes his eyes and rolls his head on the pillow. He doesn't want her to follow him.

Maddix and I meet eyes only briefly, speaking a silent conversation we've mastered after years of being partners. Then, we hastily get to work administering oxygen, which our patient sluggishly attempts to remove while shaking his head back and forth in agitation.

"Sir, I need you to remain calm." Yet I understand the oxygen mask can cause feelings of claustrophobia in some patients, and the last thing I want is to further exacerbate his panic.

With the cantilever eventually over his mouth and nose, any additional grumblings are muffled.

Next, heart monitors are placed on his chest. I typically don't notice the physical features of a patient. The human body is an incredible machine, and I've been conditioned to remove salacious thoughts about the flesh and bones making up a person.

But the beauty of Jude cannot be denied. Ripped abs. Smooth pecs. That side tattoo. And a smattering of hair on his chest. Not to mention a trail of darkness that leads below his dipping suit pants.

"You might have some drool there, Angie," Maddix quietly mocks me, despite the severity of our position, which is wheeling a patient to the elevator bank.

"Shut up."

Once locked and loaded in the ambulance, the lights flash, but the siren doesn't blare, as the noise can increase the anxiety of patients within the bank.

I sit in the back with Jude on a stretcher while Maddix drives the rig. Raising his voice because of our proximity to each other, Maddix picks up on a conversation we'd been having when the original call came through.

"So, you still don't have a date?"

"Now isn't the time for this," I groan, checking Jude's vitals, when his eyes open quickly before closing again. His coloring still isn't right. He's more putrid-green than ashen. I don't know if I've ever seen this shade on someone's skin, but there's always a first.

"I told ya, I'd go with ya," Maddix continues, skillfully maneuvering the ambulance through the day after Thanksgiving, early-morning traffic in downtown Chicago.

"And I told you thanks but no thanks." Genuine gratitude mingles with my rejection.

Trey Maddix is a great guy and hot in the way best friends are *not*. He's good-looking to a multitude of women, which makes him physically unattractive to me. He's my friend, honest and true, and generously offering to ease my suffering.

My *younger* brother is getting married in a few weeks during the holiday season.

Santa, stab me with a peppermint stick.

I love Christmas, but I don't have time for a family wedding, especially when the announcement triggered my well-meaning grandmother and great aunt to ask when I'm getting married. Why don't I have a fella, or a baby, or three, while at the same time, preaching independence for women and keeping your man in line. I can't keep up.

It isn't that I don't want marriage or babies. It just hasn't happened for me. I haven't experienced that all-consuming, can't-live-without-you feeling that leads to happily-ever-after and babies in a carriage. The kind of love my parents had.

I swallow thickly at the brief thought of my parents and return to the business at hand.

As the heart monitor begins to erratically beat, a wave of panic sets in *for me*. That niggling sensation I have within me right before things go bad.

And my patient crashes.

"Shit." On automatic, I react, ripping the cantilever off his mouth and start chest compressions, then check for his breath. Repeating the motions one more time, I'm prepared to reach for the defibrillator if I can't revive him after my next compression pass.

Leaning over Jude, I lower inches from his face, determined to save him.

"Don't you leave me, Jude."

My jaw is clenched while the words aren't anything more than a whisper. A desperate plea.

With another series of rhythmic pressure against his firm chest, Jude gasps.

Relief instantly fills me.

His eyes fling open, wild and icy. The coolest blue I've ever seen latches onto mine. While I often find tear-filled appreciation in a gaze, these eyes are like icicles, sharp and pointed, and glaring at me like saving his life was the devil's work instead of an angelic calling. A certain something deep within me that likes to help others.

I reach for the cantilever, intending to return it to his nose and mouth region, but Jude lifts his arm, limp and jerkily, before catching my hand.

"Don't move," I warn, attempting to remove my hand from his grasp.

He's surprisingly strong and ignores my request, dragging my hand to his bare chest and flattening my palm over his heart. Then he grouses, "You shouldn't have. . ."

I shouldn't have what? Saved his life?

"But I did," I counter, without pride. This is what I do.

With my hand plastered beneath his larger one, pressed firmly against his chest, the coolness of his skin prickles through my latex glove. My arm strangely tingles from the sensation.

A beat passes before I ask him, "Is there anyone I can call for you? Let them know which hospital we are taking you to?"

Those cold eyes shift away, looking confused, almost lost. He rolls his head once before he states low, “There’s . . . no one.”

The quiet admission pierces my soft heart. This big, powerful, wealthy man has no one to call in the case of an emergency? The thought makes me feel sorry for him.

He closes his eyes while his frigid hand remains over mine, like he’s afraid to let go of me. Despite the inappropriateness, I allow our position—my hand over his heart—assuming this is a rare gesture of gratitude from Jude Ashford.

The well-known millionaire. The society playboy. The retail tycoon.

Who, at the end of the day, is only a man, albeit probably a selfish one.

chapter 2

[Angelica]

The truth about Jude Ashford is that I knew him in a previous life where scholarship kids got free rides to private high schools. I was the scholarship kid. And Jude was *that* guy. The one too slick for high school hallways; too smooth for classrooms. And the one driving a fancy sports car at sixteen.

He wasn't just part of the upper crust; he was the decoration on the top layer of icing. Like the bride and groom on a wedding cake, only Jude stood alone, apart from the rest.

Oh, he had friends. Followers more like it.

He was mean and cruel and defined the slur *dick*.

But there was also something about his aloofness that always seemed lonely to me. Like he wasn't set apart from the crowd as much as playing a role to disappear within the *populars*. Like he was an outlier and a leader when he might not have wanted to be either.

His family was picture perfect. Just check out his mom's Instagram from back then. She had been a major influencer promoting lifestyle perfection with so-called candid images of their family and their magazine-worthy home. Personally, I always thought their smiles looked a little forced. Especially Jude's, where dullness lingered in his icy eyes.

Our history—his and mine—is the excuse I tell myself to check on the patient I'd brought to the ER yesterday morning. Not that Jude and I have any history, per se. We went to the same high school, and that's the closest proximity we've ever shared.

I shouldn't be here. I don't have any business checking up on someone. *Get in, do my job, and move on.* There were always more casualties and tragedies. Jude Ashford should have been no different than any other emergency call.

Still, I wander through the telemetry unit seeking Jude's private room. The hospital kept him overnight for observation.

The panic attack I'd misdiagnosed turned out to be stress cardiomyopathy.

Broken heart syndrome.

The condition happens when the heart muscles weaken as a result of rapid and sudden surges of adrenaline, often caused by the onset of a stressful event. However, up to thirty percent of people who experience this condition have no triggers prior to the instant symptoms.

Not surprisingly, this condition happens more often in women.

Why Jude flatlined is beyond me and my medical training level. Checking on him is above my pay grade, yet here I am opening the door to his private hospital room because something in his voice yesterday spoke to me when he told me he had no one.

Invisible string theory perhaps. Or maybe just a thread of holiday good intention.

"Knock, knock," I cheerfully call out.

"What now?" he grumbles, tossing his head back on the pillow against the elevated back of the hospital bed. He's glaring at the ceiling like it offends him. Even with severe bed-head and pale skin, Jude is stunning.

"Hi." I swallow around the croak in my throat, although I don't know why my throat is thick. I'm no longer that average girl, hanging out with the STEM kids and winning Science Olympiad tournaments, while guys like Jude rule football fields and celebrate weekend conquests. I'm a successful, confident woman, and I hold my head a little higher as I approach the side of his bed.

"I just wanted to see how you were feeling."

His head swivels in my direction, mouth popping open like he's ready to bite *my* head off. But his lips instantly clamp shut as he uses his fists to push himself more upright on the raised bed.

"Hey." His voice is tight, straining to hold back that original gruffness I suspect lies against his tongue right now. He swipes a hand over his hair, eyes wide as he looks at me.

Then those icy orbs narrow, and his expression turns sour. "What do you want?"

I could be offended by the abrupt change in his tone, the sharp edge to his words, but being that this is the most wonderful time of the year, I paste on a cheerful smile and lift my hand.

"I brought you something." Stepping even closer to the bed, I hold out the white bakery bag.

Jude cautiously takes the bag from me and peers inside before glancing up at me again. "You brought me candy?"

"Not *candy*," I mock, leaning my hip against the railing raised to prevent patients from falling out of bed. "Angelica's chocolate mints."

"Who?" He arches a perfectly-shaped brow. Men shouldn't have eyebrows that immaculate.

"Me." I point to my chest. "Angelica." Then I hold out my hand. "Angelica Winter."

I look a bit different than I did in high school, so Jude not recognizing me isn't a surprise.

He scoffs, ignores my hand, and glances back in the bag. "Hasn't anyone ever told you, you can't give sweets to a heart attack victim?"

"You didn't have a heart attack," I remind him. "And a single chocolate truffle isn't going to hurt you." The perfect combination of dark chocolate and mint flavor might even refresh his stinky attitude.

He harumphs again and crumples the top of the delicate bag to close it before lowering the sack beside him.

"Should I know you?" he questions, staring at me a long minute, taking in the wild, curly red hair my family likes to compare to a lion's mane, although it's currently in a thick braid. He can't miss the smattering of freckles over my nose and cheeks, giving away my Irish heritage. But he fixates on my eyes, the ones that are blue like my grandmother's.

I shrug. "Well, I did save your life yesterday."

At that, his eyes open wider, darkening a bit from icicles to something warmer. His hand fists beside his hip.

"That was . . ." He licks his lips, pausing for a breath while he continues to stare at me. "Thank you."

Not a drop of sincerity mingles in his spoken gratitude. He'd mentioned yesterday I shouldn't have done something, and a teeny-tiny niggle inside me worries he wishes I hadn't saved him. The holidays can be the most depressing time of the year for some. Suicide rates run high, but they are actually higher in late spring and early summer compared to the cold, bleak winter months, which are facts I'd rather not think about during any season.

Keeping a smile plastered on my face, I offer Jude all the compassion I can muster.

"Just doing my job," I remark, like I'm unworthy of his thanks while knowing I'm a daily superhero.

Jude snorts, proving he's mastered a variety of dismissive sounds. "Thank you for doing your *job*." Again, a derisive twist in his tone. "I'm happy to give you any item you'd wish from my department store to express my gratitude for your service."

He still doesn't sound very appreciative nor overly willing to depart with something from his store—Ashford's, the dreamy, shopping experience.

Plus, there isn't anything material I'd want from this man, anyway, especially with his attitude.

Still, I can't seem to help myself and counter his unwitting offer with my own snark. "You don't happen to sell dates, do ya?"

"We aren't that kind of establishment." He smirks, narrowing those icicle eyes once more, but the corner of his mouth ticks. Twitches more like. Like he might have found something humorous in my retort.

The other thing about that smirk—a tiny dimple pops on his barely-stubbled face, like a punctuation symbol. A single quotation mark near his lip, or an apostrophe on his attempt to smile.

I chuff, the sound light and bright, knowing, *of course*, he didn't sell dates at his fancy store.

"Anyway . . ." I wave my hand in the air, but Jude catches my wrist, holding it with tender strength in his chilled hand.

That cool sensation that seeped through my glove-covered hand yesterday intensifies with our skin-to-skin contact. His touch feels like the explosion of ice crystals against glass, beautiful while potentially dangerous. The effect should be chilly, but it's more like a white-hot heat, tickling my flesh, melting me.

Whoa.

Those eyes of his narrow once more as he scans over my face. "You were serious, weren't you?"

I mean, I was kind of serious. Not that I want a date with him, but I could still use a date for my brother's spontaneous wedding. The engagement he sprung on the family during Thanksgiving dinner. The way he announced the wedding would take place on December twenty-third. The day before the holiday.

"*Christmas Eve Eve*," his sweet but silly girlfriend, *er*, fiancée, added with a childlike giggle because she's all of twenty-three compared to my younger brother's thirty-five years of age.

"*It's the night we met*," Beau simpered, staring at his pretty little bride-to-be with heart emojis in his eyes.

Then they proceeded to make out at the dinner table like porn stars warming up for the first act in a film.

Not that I have any experience with watching porn, but . . . Aunt Gertie took out her phone for a picture while Gran covered the eyes of my youngest nephew sitting beside her. My sister, Christmas, clapped her hands, like a movie clapboard, to break up the scene.

"It's nothing." I shake my head, not willing to discuss my non-existent love life with a man who wouldn't understand *lack* or *love*. He could have almost any girl he wanted twenty-years ago, and according to local tabloids, he still does. Case in point, the woman in his office yesterday. He is not a man who struggles to find company.

Tugging at my wrist, Jude only tightens his grip. His larger hand is cool against my suddenly too-hot skin.

"Wait—" He counters the force of my leaning away by pulling me forward, only the door to his room opens at the same time.

I turn my head like the guilty party in a tryst, and Jude drops my wrist as a beautiful raven-haired woman in a hip-hugging skirt and cute little blazer enters the room. The same woman who'd been standing beside Jude's desk, looking not-so-innocent in relation to Jude's condition yesterday.

"Oh, Jude," she cries, rushing to the opposite side of his bed and leaning over him. Gripping his shoulders, she lowers over him in an awkward attempt to hug him.

Jude doesn't raise his arms.

Instead, he watches me, those icy eyes suddenly wild, shifting side to side like he's been caught in a compromising position. Almost like he isn't comfortable being hugged.

Strange.

Still, I'm the odd woman out in this reunion. Taking a giant step back from the bed, I mutter, "I'm glad you're feeling better."

Our eyes are locked on one another's as the dark brunette slowly pulls away from Jude, glancing at me like she didn't even notice I was standing here upon her entrance.

With another forced smile, I shake my head, ridding it of images of what she might have been doing with Jude yesterday when his heart broke.

Doesn't matter.

In no time at all, this man will be up and at it with her again. His heart fully restored, whatever size a grinchy man's heart is.

On that note, I see myself out.

chapter 3

[Angelica]

Standing in the middle of Ashford's on a Sunday was the last place I wanted to be on my day off. But seeing as I had a Christmas list a mile long, and I'd do anything for Aunt Gertie and Gran, I'm here.

The retail destination is dripping with holiday decor. Vibrant red carpet covers the classic tile. Dozens upon dozens of evergreens decked out in silver and gold ornaments are on raised daises. Garland drapes around register counters. Giant brass trumpets line the ceiling in the entry and practically bleat a holiday greeting despite being ornamentation. The glitter and glitz are almost spellbinding.

And I'm taking that moment I didn't get the other day when I entered the iconic store to stand in the exact center of the first floor, looking up at the glass-domed ceiling, some eight stories above me.

It might be dangerous to stand still in the middle of a busy location, people bustling by me with bags hanging off wrists and phones in hands, oblivious to others with their minds focused on their own holiday lists . . . but I take this minute for myself.

The intricately designed gold railings surround each level as the store climbs higher and higher are mesmerizing. Their color is reminiscent of a long-gone time. The sensation is almost dizzying, and my body sways a bit, but I don't stop staring once I reach the almost crystal-like dome, highlighted by the winter sunshine outside. Rays beam down toward me like being here is a religious experience, not a shopping nightmare.

"If you get trampled in my store, I'm not footing the bill for an ambulance trip."

My head snaps forward, causing my neck to crack as I spin to face Jude Ashford, upright and dressed in a suit certain to cost more than six months of my salary. No man should look so good in a bright blue suit and simple white dress shirt minus a tie. A slight dusting of hair along his jaw appears artistically designed and not naturally grown.

"What are *you* doing here?" I can't seem to help my smile at his sudden presence, nor the surprise in my voice when I say, "You shouldn't be out of bed."

My statement shouldn't sound as breathless as it does.

Jude pats over his heart. "Doc says I'm as strong as an ox."

"Are you certain he didn't say, as stubborn as one? Because you should still be resting."

The corner of his mouth twitches again. Sadly, the dimple isn't as prevalent with another day's growth of facial hair in the way.

"You know, not many people can get away with talking to me like that."

I tilt my head, cock my hip, and place my fist there, like I'm prepared to throw down with the man.

"Good thing I'm not *many* people." I don't know where the confidence or sass comes from, but something about this man has me on edge. Not a negative one, but more like a teetering one, like I'm standing on the tip of ballet pointe shoes, my ankles wobbling. Any minute, I might topple over.

After all these years, I'd like to believe Jude has grown up, changed a bit from the spoiled, rich kid act, he'd once been. The man once ruling high school hallways has a more meaningful position amid the levels of his department store after all. Yet, I don't have any proof that he's matured emotionally.

My foundation for change comes from me. *I'm* not that girl anymore who might have stepped out of his way when I was seventeen. A girl who might have stared at someone like Jude and wondered what it would be like to be near him. At thirty-seven, I'm made of stronger stuff.

And Jude Ashford cannot intimidate me.

Still watching me, he finally states, "Actually, I just needed a few things from my office."

"And you needed to wear a suit for that?" I arch a brow, scanning down the fit of a one-button suit jacket and the slim pants cropped at his ankles, in the modern style.

He's almost too pretty.

He scoffs, the sound becoming familiar. "I have a reputation to uphold."

"So, no sweatpants for you," I tease, glancing down at myself wearing black leggings with a rip in the knee and an oversized, holiday-green sweatshirt that reads: HO-HO-Oh No!

Dammit, why didn't I dress up like Gran used to make us do as kids?

Then again, I'm not here to impress a man I didn't know would be present. This outfit is my day-off uniform.

"Anyway, don't you have an assistant for that?" The pretty raven-haired woman comes to mind. "Or a courier service could have brought you your things."

This busy city is teeming with service providers. If only I was comfortable enough to take up the service of hiring a date. Which I'm not. And reminds me I have a shopping list to complete.

I'm distracted once again when Jude runs a practiced hand through his dark hair that has the smallest hint of gray, like snowflakes randomly sprinkled among the dark strands.

He, on the other hand, avoids looking at me, eyes pinched while his head is turned away from me. For a second, he almost looks . . . lost. He could be any average shopper. Someone popping in during a weekday lunch break to quickly pick up a gift. Only it isn't during the middle of the week or lunchtime, and he is anything but average.

"What were you looking at?" he abruptly asks.

I flinch like I've been caught gawking at him, which I had been doing. He tips his chin toward the ceiling, and I spin a little before glancing upward once more.

"I love that ceiling." My voice is a little strained due to the awkward angle of my tilted head. "There is something magical about it, almost mystical," I admit, dreamily. "Like the Sistine Chapel's greatness, even if it's only a glass ceiling in a department store."

I risk a glance at Jude, who has stepped closer to me to avoid the path of a harried shopper not watching where he walks. With Jude this close, I catch a whiff of something expensive and sharp coming off him.

He stares up at the ceiling as well, as if he hasn't seen it a thousand times already in his lifetime. He *is* Ashford's royalty. Heir to this shopping kingdom that his great-something-grandfather began. But maybe he no longer notices the majesty of the dome.

Gazing back up at the ceiling, sun beams pierce the glass, making a kaleidoscope pattern on the upper levels.

Eventually, Jude says, "Ever find that date you needed?"

My head snaps forward again, cracking my neck one more time. Any more whip flashes in this store and I might need medical assistance after all.

I scowl at him.

"When you mentioned picking a date from Ashford's, I vaguely remembered a conversation in the ambulance. Or maybe I dreamt it." His brows pinch, questioning his own memory. "Another man was asking you out, but you declined."

His typically cold eyes focus on my face, causing my cheeks to heat, certain to be turning as red as the carpet beneath our feet.

"That was Trey Maddix, my partner. He was driving the ambulance."

Jude glowers. "Seems inappropriate for an ambulance conversation." He shifts again to avoid another frantic holiday shopper, bringing him closer to me. "I could have you fired for such behavior."

"You wouldn't." My eyes widen with shock, before narrowing with reality. I can't get fired for an innocent discussion. And my hope for transformation within Jude Ashford is suddenly dashed with disappointment.

"Wouldn't I?" Those damn eyes of his instantly shift back to cold and dangerous.

"Why would you?" I argue, then decide I don't need an answer. Sparring with this man feels like trying to shovel snow in a snowstorm . . . unproductive, and I have a list of things to do today.

"Anyway, I should prob—"

"I have an offer for you." Those eerie eyes focus on mine, pinning me to the red carpet like the North Pole itself. Or Jack Frost wielding some wicked winter spell.

"I promised you anything from the store yesterday." He hesitates for a second but doesn't look away from my face. "How about you pick me . . . for your date?"

I snort, the sound sharp and loud, and totally unladylike. "I couldn't afford you."

He wrinkles his nose. "You aren't purchasing me."

Still, I continue, "What's the going rate for a millionaire anyway?" I mean, he makes millions, right? And my brain drifts to all the ways those millions could help people. Libraries. Hospital wings. Homeless shelters. All the toys for tots . . .

"I'm free." He straightens his shoulders and holds his head high.

I blink. Then blink again, processing his word choice.

Pick him. Not purchase.

Somehow, I doubt anything about Jude comes without a cost.

He clarifies as if he read my mind. "I'm available."

"You don't even know the date," I counter. *Nor why I need a partner for the evening.*

Jude arches a brow, hinting I should enlighten him.

"My younger brother is getting married on December twenty-third." Which will totally eclipse Christmas, which is so like Beau.

Like Sam's sister in *Sixteen Candles*, planning her wedding on Sam's sixteenth birthday.

A salacious grin curls Jude's lips. "I'm your man."

The statement should not do funny things to me, like bring on the joy of twinkling lights beneath dark winter skies.

"How would that even work?" I counter, knowing the idea of him being my date is preposterous. I could never explain *him* to my family.

"I need a favor in return," he replies, ignoring my question.

And here it is. The price tag.

"A Christmas party. My board expects me to bring someone, but I need someone . . . respectable."

He eyes me up and down, taking in my slightly inappropriate sweatshirt.

"Someone without ties to me," he adds.

"Like no strings attached." I smile at my own joke, but Jude's face hardens, like I've hit a nerve.

"I recall a certain dark-haired woman cooing over you beside your hospital bed." I hitch a brow, suggesting it's his turn for more details. "She'd look pretty on your arm, all wrapped up with a bow."

Jude digs his teeth into his lower lip and slowly rolls his gaze down my body again. "You would look pretty in ribbon."

With my curves and flatter chest, there isn't a spot on my body a ribbon could cover.

I'm not the buxom bombshell he had draped over him in the hospital. The same woman whom I'm certain was doing nefarious things to his body before he went into cardiac upheaval. A woman who apparently came with strings.

On that note, I've lost my desire to be standing in Ashford's. I'll find another store to shop in. State Street is full of them.

"You should be home in bed, and I have gifts to purchase." I hold up my phone, which contains my list.

"Would you come be my nurse?" The corner of his mouth twitches again, reminding me that a dimple exists, but this isn't a smile. He isn't being playful, even if he sounds flirtatious.

If anything, his question almost hurts my feelings.

"Now you're just being rude. I'm not a nurse. I'm an emergency medical technician." And he's a casualty my heart cannot handle. I don't need some prissy, pretty man thumbing his nose at me while tossing out flirty comments and suggesting I accompany him to a Christmas party.

He tilts his head, practically admitting he doesn't know the difference between medical positions. As for me, I'm just done with this conversation.

"Have a nice life, Mr. Ashford. It was my pleasure to save it for you." I brush past him, preparing to exit Ashford's, hoping this interaction doesn't tarnish all the golden memories I have of being here as a kid.

However, Jude catches my wrist, causing me to spin and face him again.

"Wait." One singular word and I'm stalled, because his voice has reached a new pitch. Desperate.

He swallows thickly. "Please."

I doubt that word has ever graced his vocabulary. Not when his eyes pinch closed, and his chin tips upward. A pained expression etches into his chiseled cheeks.

"Why?" I whisper, my gaze flitting around his face, equally desperate to understand him. Just a sliver of a bit.

He lowers his head and opens his eyes, shocking me again with their coldness. "Because you saved my life."

I chuckle, acidic and rough, tugging at my wrist, which only ends with me being pulled closer to him. His breath mingles with mine. My gaze falls to his lips, parted and too close. I lick my own and notice him watching the motion.

"It doesn't work like that." My voice hardly sounds like mine. "I save your life, and now I owe you a favor?"

"You saved my life." He pauses, glancing back at my mouth a second before meeting my eyes. "And now I need your help to live it."

With those icy eyes and the divot to one side of his mouth, he has me stunned, like a snake in summer grass.

Because my Rikki-Tikki heart wants to help him somehow, and protect his fragile, broken one.

chapter 4

[Jude]

There was something about her I couldn't place. It was more than just her being the EMT who saved my life. Something deeper. I could feel it in my cold, hollow heart, but I could not recognize the sensation. Or her.

Still, I wasn't ready for her to depart.

She was right. I shouldn't be at Ashford's, but I didn't have anywhere else to go. Lounging around my condo wasn't an option. I was going stir crazy alone there. I needed to get out, be among people, even if it is a faceless crowd.

Imagine my surprise to find the woman with a wild mane of hair, glistening various shades of sienna and auburn, standing in a ray of sunlight shining down to the first floor of Ashford's. Her eyes are blue, but everything opposite the color of mine. Hers are wide and expressive, telling me things I unfortunately cannot read. Their openness is welcoming, almost inviting, although I don't have the foggiest idea what she would invite me to do for her. Other than be her one-time date.

And she was focused on that old ceiling, staring up at it with awe, like she'd never seen anything so beautiful.

What the hell does she see up there that I don't?

I've looked at that domed glass a thousand times in my life. It wasn't special.

"You mentioned you have a shopping list." I clear my throat, swallowing down her initial rejection. The corner of my mouth ticks upward. "I could help you with that."

Shopping isn't my thing, although it's how I've made a living. A lucrative living that's afforded me a pricy condo on Lake Shore Drive, fancy sports cars, and lavish trips around the world, most of which I write off as a business expense.

Angelica glances at the phone in her hand.

I shouldn't have grabbed her wrist, but I'd been desperate not to lose her again. She'd introduced herself yesterday, but I'd wanted to know more about her. Then Sabrina interrupted us. Eventually, a flustered nurse was able to tell me which firehouse Angelica worked for. The information wasn't enough.

"What's on the list?" I nod toward her phone, slowly releasing her wrist, which was warm and strong beneath my grip. Touching her was like holding my hand over a flame—dangerous while awe-inspiring.

"Just . . . things."

I chuff. "Well, which *things* should we start with?" I square my shoulders, straighten my suit jacket, and nod again at the device holding her holiday wish list. I'm not a personal shopper, never have been, but I know this store like I know my name, and I'll find her whatever she needs.

Hell, I'll even look outside Ashford's if we don't have it.

Anything she wants, because something happened to me the other day. Something strange and unexplainable. Something rare and unfamiliar.

I feel . . . different.

Don't you leave me, Jude.

The angelic whisper in my head causes my back to stiffen. Since Friday, I've been restless, anxious even, in a very unsettling way. Like something, or rather someone, is waiting on me, and I'm compelled to turn over a new leaf. A holly one for the season.

Which meant proving my worth to my board of directors.

The same board that's questioning business trips and expensive dinners. The ones doubting my leadership ability because they question my morals. My behavior. My attention.

Did I even care about Ashford's anymore?

Of course I cared. I've worked here since I was a teen.

I inherited the place when I was in my twenties, and I've devoted my entire life to it. *Alone*.

Without my great-grandfather dictating direction. Without my father by my side.

And I was fucking tired.

That was my explanation for what happened the other day. The near heart attack. I refuse to accept the doctor's explanation of a broken heart. Stress cardiomyopathy.

I wasn't stressed, dammit.

I glance at Angelica and take a calming breath. A breathing exercise a nurse instructed me to practice when my heart began to race and my skin grew clammy. A second *episode* was highly unlikely, she'd assured me. Still, the nurses made me practice the deep inhale and slow exhale, counting to four with each pass.

Concentrating on Angelica seemed to help.

Inhale. One, two, three, four freckles on the right cheek.

Exhale, one, two, three on the left. *Oh wait*, she has one near the corner of her mouth.

"You okay?" Angelica asks, her eyes full of concern. She almost looks like a cartoon character. A popular Irish princess doll Ashford's had sold years ago.

"I'm fine." However, my reply is terse; my jaw still too tight. I concentrate on her again. The warmth in her eyes. The soft mix of red in her hair. The freckles that decorate her nose and cheeks.

"Where should we begin?" I ask again, clenching my back teeth to keep me calm. I need something to distract me, and shopping appears to be the immediate answer.

Angelica sighs. The slump of her shoulders and hanging of her head suggest I've ensnared her. Acquiescing, she opens the Notes app on her phone.

"Toys." She glances back at me. "I need lots of toys."

"Level five, it is, then." I wave my hand, implying I'll follow her lead, and she spins for the . . . escalators.

"We have elevators," I snark.

Glancing over her shoulder, she says, "Yeah, but the escalators are more fun."

As she walks in front of me, I shamelessly admire the curve of her hips. The way that hideous Christmas sweatshirt covers her ass but does nothing to disguise the shape of it. She'd be a handful, and I want my hands on her.

Quickly, I dismiss the thought. She's not here to get me off. I need a date. A wholesome, respectable, board-unknown woman who can play the part of a doting girlfriend, albeit a temporary one. Just enough of one to draw attention away from my past and their doubts about my future.

We begin the laborious ride up one floor in silence. The holidays are still weeks away, but everyone wants a deal. This weekend, our Black Friday sales attempt to capture as much profit as we can. December is always our best month, and I need this year to end with a bang.

Retail shopping is on the downswing, even if coming to Ashford's is considered an experience. A popular destination when visiting Chicago. I pride myself on the fact we pulled it off. We flipped our flagship store from one of many in a chain to a sole destination.

Think Liberty in London. We have Ashford's in Chicago.

I am Ashford's.

We exit one set of moving stairs and immediately round to the next, and my gaze falls to Angelica's backside again as she stands two steps higher than me. Her name suits her, only she looks like a wild angel. One who would be both a blessing and a curse.

When we exit the final set of escalators, I reach for Angelica's lower back, then pause, not allowing myself to touch her. Strangely, I want to show possession of her. Like that girl in *The Nutcracker,* obsessed with her new toy.

Angelica is mine.

I can admit I'm a selfish man.

When we reach the cashier counter, I greet the young salesclerk.

"Hello . . . Jennifer." I read her nametag. "This is Angel."

"Angelica," she corrects.

With the sternness in her voice, I realize—that's it. She's *my* angel. The whisper pulling me back from death.

But that couldn't be right.

"Angelica here is shopping for . . ." I arch a brow, pushing aside my reckless thoughts and flipping them to more concerning ones. "Her children?"

Fuck. Is she married? I hadn't seen a ring. But she could still be a mother.

"Nieces and nephews," she clarifies.

I relax a little. I have nothing against kids; I just don't have any nor want any. Children are messy, both physically and emotionally.

However, Angelica smiles warmly at the mention of her young relatives.

"And we need to complete her shopping list." I address Jennifer while nodding toward Angelica's phone, still in her hand. "Anything she needs, let's find it for her."

Jennifer jumps at the chance, knowing her commission is about to soar. We offer extra compensation in the form of bonuses for our salespeople, in addition to their hourly pay, and Jennifer looks eager to score some points.

But, while I listen to Angelica's requests, I try not to explode when Jennifer isn't certain where to find the toys mentioned or if we even carry them. We might not be *the* internet shopping mogul, but we still offer a variety of items. Ones not easily found in big box stores.

Unfortunately, Angelica doesn't find any of what she wants.

"It's fine. I'll just shop on Am—"

I hold up a hand to stop her. "Don't even mention their name. That's sacrilegious in here."

I offer Jennifer a tight wink. More like an eye twitch, as I attempt to contain my irritation.

Why don't we have the things Angelica wants? I remind myself Ashford's has become more of a specialty store, reverting back to our original departments with unique offerings.

Dismissing Jennifer, I place my hand on Angelica's back and lead her toward a display with stuffed animals and wooden puzzles. Classic games and craft items.

I'm pleased with myself when Angelica finds options for her nieces and nephews.

"What's next?"

We travel down to the men's department, for her brothers, I quickly learn.

Then into housewares, where we stall in front of the candy section when Angelica stands in front of a glass display case, admiring the carefully stacked chocolates and old-fashioned candy shaped like fruit slices.

"Would you like something?" I offer. "My treat."

She's already shaking her head as she stares at the arrangement. Her eyes are wide, quite literally like a kid in a candy store. Like she can't decide, because there are so many tantalizing options.

"I never thanked you for the chocolates you brought me," I say, recalling the treat that was an explosion of mint in my mouth. "What were they called again?"

"Angelica's chocolate mints. Not very original, I know. I'm still working on a name."

A second passes before her explanation registers. "You mean you made those chocolates? For me?"

She shrugs, still looking with appreciation into the candy case. "Well, I didn't exactly make them *for you*, but I did make them and gathered a small sample to give you. I thought you could use something sweet."

She glances over at me, offering a soft smile. One that could dismantle my hard edges.

Our eyes remain locked on one another for a long second before I clear my throat. *I don't need to be softened.* I force my gaze from her and address the chocolate display. "Anywhere else to visit today?"

"Just one more place, but I can handle it on my own.

"What is it?" I question, concerned that her day hasn't been as productive as she'd like. And like I told her, Ashford's has a reputation to uphold.

"Lingerie."

chapter 5

[Angelica]

I shouldn't be embarrassed by the mention of the ladies' intimate department, as Gran calls it. I wasn't even entering the section for myself. But admitting that I was shopping for my great Aunt Gertie would be awkward.

For the adult gift exchange within my family, which reduces the number of presents to be purchased per person, I'd gotten Aunt Gertie. I *always* get Aunt Gertie. The rule for presents is fifty dollars or less, and the gift can be anything. Aunt Gertie takes the option literally, and every year she requests an item I'd rather not purchase in front of Jude.

"I can help you find the right item," Jude suggests. That dimple of his pops out, a little more playfully this time.

"I think I got it."

"Angelica," he counters.

"Jude," I snipe back.

We eye one another before he finally breaks, scanning down my body with those cool eyes. "I'm very good at selecting a perfect fit."

"I just bet you are," I mutter. And the last thing I want to think about is Jude Ashford picking out lingerie *for me*.

After another awkward minute, where Jude refuses to leave me alone, he states, "Maybe we should head to the evening wear department first anyway. You'll need to know what your dress is like before you pick something from the intimate persuasion."

"Evening wear?" I question.

"Yes. The company Christmas party is a formal affair."

What the Christmas trees?

"I didn't agree to the date exchange," I remind him.

"But you will." He winks. Pure devil-don't-care is in that flinch of his eyelid. Like he's a man used to getting what he wants, and he strangely wants me to agree to a date with him.

Me and my sassy mouth. I should have known Jude didn't have a sense of humor when I was *joking* that Ashford's had dates as a commodity.

Plus, does he not see me? I glance down at my outfit to notice the smear of toothpaste near one of the HOs and the widening of the hole in my leggings. I can't afford an evening gown. I'm already sweating over all the items he piled up from the various departments we visited and had sent down to gift wrap, where I will cash out later.

"Jude," I groan, like his name says everything; *No*, and *never happening*, and *get over yourself* with this idea.

"Look, you need a date and so do I," he attempts to reason. "It's equally beneficial, and I'm an equal opportunity employer." He smooths his hand down the front of his crisp shirt, as if proud.

"Well, I don't work for you. And *if* I agreed, it would only be because it also benefits me. You aren't the boss of me. I'd be cooperating, not submitting to you."

"So, is that a yes?" A flare of something bright sparks in those cold eyes, lessening the icy effect of them. The corner of his mouth twitches once again, the flash of that dimple whipping out like a rare beam of light in a dark night.

"Maybe." I sigh, knowing I don't need a date, but it still would be nice to have one for Beau's wedding. A little buffer from the family and their well-meaning but incessant questions about my lack of a love life.

"Fine," I groan. I cannot believe I'm agreeing to this exchange.

"Excellent." The excitement in Jude's voice is surprising and a bit alarming. He's a child who has gotten exactly what he wanted from Santa. "And, as it's my party, I'll pay for your dress."

"You don't have to do that." As an EMT, I make decent money, but not money to purchase *an evening gown* that I'll only wear once in my entire life. Still, I can pay for my own things.

"I insist. And you'll need to tell me what to wear for your brother's wedding."

Beau's shindig is being thrown together by me because I couldn't keep my mouth shut and volunteered to help the newly engaged couple in their rush to wed. Which means, I'll be put in charge because Beau is lazy like that.

"I'll have to get back to you on that," I admit.

"Formal wear department, then?" he arches one of those perfectly sculpted brows, and I nod, relieved to leave the lingerie section behind. I can always get Aunt Gertie something from the retail site that shall not be named.

Following Jude into the evening wear section, he enters like the boss he is. The women, one young and one older, simper a little at his appearance.

"Ladies," he greets them, and I swear they sigh in unison. "This is Angelica. She'll be needing a dress for a holiday affair. When she's finished, send the bill to my office."

This causes an arched brow from the younger woman, and a scowl from the older one.

Jude then turns toward me. "Angelica. The day has been a pleasure. I'll be in touch."

He bows—freaking bows—and steps back, retreating like he can't get away from me fast enough.

What the hell was that?

A pleasure? *Ha!*

I don't know how to describe this morning, other than a mental rush. With every gift option he suggested, I grew more excited for the holidays, envisioning the expressions on my nieces' and nephews' faces. The puzzles and games. The stuffies and crafts. The kids did not need the electronics on the list. They needed the unique and unusual. I wanted something special for each of them.

My sister, ironically named Christmas, has three boys, and my older brother, Dane, has twin girls. Gran's apartment will be bursting with excitement come the morning of December twenty-fifth.

This moment, however, is apparently about me, and I turn toward the older woman, who offers me a warm smile.

"Guess you'll be helping me doll up."

"Honey, you don't need any help looking special."

Her comment alone makes me feel exceptional, and I smile as she asks me about size, cut, and colors for a dress.

When I finally enter the gift wrap section roughly two hours later, I'm sweaty from taking my clothes on and off, and suddenly worried about the exorbitant bill I'm certain to have accrued.

Sticker shock. It's real.

The dress I picked out cost more than my paycheck, and I'm still not certain it's right for me, but Zaleya, the older woman, insisted the gown would make men worship at my feet.

I didn't really need a man to worship my toes, which are in serious need of a pedicure, but the compliment was still nice.

I'm fumbling for my wallet, hands still trembling for some reason, when the gift wrap clerk says, "It's all taken care of. Happy holidays."

She gives me a knowing look, because she clearly knows something I don't.

"I'm sorry. I haven't paid for anything yet." While I'd love to believe there's a mix-up that doesn't cost me thousands of dollars, I'm honest to a fault. I find a penny on the street, and I look around to see if someone dropped it.

The older woman with a cute bob cut tips up her shoulder and tilts her head. "Santa took care of it."

"Santa?" I choke before realizing Santa isn't the jolly man dressed in red velvet, but a grumpy one wearing a blue suit.

"Oh, hell, no," I mutter, taking the gift receipt from the clerk.

As a former scholarship kid, I take pride in being able to afford things now. I'm grateful for that step up back then which led me to being to the independent woman I am today. Which means, I pay my own way, and I don't need some man whipping out his credit card, aiming to lure my affection because I saved his life. Plus, I'm not one of *those* women. The ones who want a man to fund their lives. Jude has a reputation for aligning himself with such women, and I am not like that.

Leaving my packages behind, I head for the elevators, which will take me to the seventh floor. Offices are on the eighth, and we had privileged access when we arrived for Jude's medical emergency the other day. Today, I need to exit on the seventh floor and take the stairs to the next level.

By the time I slam through the emergency exit on floor eight, I'm out of breath. Without a receptionist in sight, I help myself to wander the narrow hall leading to a final set of doors.

The same doors Maddix and I entered on Friday.

"What is this?" I rattle the pile of gift receipts in my hand, shaking my fist at Jude, who is seated smugly behind his large wooden desk that looks as old as this building but in pristine condition.

"You're welcome?" he counters, tipping his head to the side.

"You can't pay for my Christmas presents."

"Consider me Santa's helper." The corner of his mouth quirks, more mockery than generosity.

"I don't want Santa's help." I sound ungrateful and ridiculous, but I'm pissed. "Look. I can pay for my own Christmas presents."

"And while I'm certain you can, I'd still like to cover the cost. As a thank you."

"I already agreed to a date," I fire back at him.

"Because I agreed to date you," he counters.

"What?"

I spin at the sudden gasp from a female voice and face the raven-haired beauty who'd been in Jude's office and then by his bedside in the hospital.

"Sabrina," Jude groans, pressing his fingers against his forehead.

My heart crashes to the floor like a broken vase. Even her name is beautiful. And there is clearly something going on between them. Why isn't he taking her to the company party?

Respectable, he'd said. Not exactly a glowing compliment, and standing next to this lovely creature in her crisp pant suit, I don't feel like anything other than a hole-y mess.

"I need to go." I tip my chin at Jude and smile at Sabrina. *Let Jude fix this disaster*. I don't need a date bad enough to ruin someone else's relationship. And I definitely don't need a date with Jude.

Turning in a rush for the door, I then fly to the exit stairs, taking them in record time to the seventh floor. The elevator line is long, and I search for the escalator instead of waiting for the lift.

"Angelica, wait."

Spinning around, I catch Jude racing after me. He appears only slightly winded, and for half a second, I worry about his heart.

"You shouldn't be running."

"I wasn't running. I was chasing."

"Chasing?" I counter. *Chasing after me?*

Jude is already waving his hand. "Look, I can explain Sabrina."

"*Look,*" I snap back at him. "I don't need an explanation. I'm not into OWD, and I'm not interested in breaking girl code." I don't steal other women's men.

"OWD?"

"Other woman drama."

Jude snorts. The sound is dismissive and unattractive, and I turn away from him again.

"She isn't my woman. She isn't even my girlfriend."

Spinning back for him, my lips flatline. "That's awful, Jude." I remember how he casually dated when we were younger. More like carelessly dated. The whispers in the high school hallway. The tears of innocent girls.

And I recall the woman in his office staring at him with genuine fear during our medical visit and deep concern during her hospital entrance.

Jude swipes a hand through his thick locks and glances away from me before leveling me with a hard stare. "We only went out like three times. The other day, her visit surprised me, and I had that panic attack."

"Broken heart," I remind him.

"I don't have a broken heart," he argues, his voice rising. Then he exhales heavily. "She . . ." He pauses. "It just isn't going to happen between us ever again."

As in, he is never, ever getting back together with her? Doubtful. She's a beauty, and she obviously cares about him.

"She worked for me, and that's a line I can't cross again."

"She works here?" I shriek. He sees her every day. You cannot ignore *that*.

"She *worked* here, past tense. I made a mistake." He swallows hard like the admission is acid in his mouth. "I didn't know she was a perfume counter girl when I met her, but once I knew, I stopped everything. She quit in hopes we could be together, but it's not going to happen."

Another thought hits me. "What do you mean *a line you can't cross again*?"

Jude scratches at the back of his neck and looks away from me. "I had an incident a few years back with the head of HR, but that won't happen again either."

"Can't? Or won't?"

"Can't or won't what?"

"Date another employee."

"Won't," he states, holding his head high, but his gaze dips down to my mouth. His eyes narrow as he stares at my lips.

The sternness in his body language should convince me of his conviction, but I cannot read Jude Ashford. He's a book I'm certain needs to be DNF'd—*do not finish*—even if I'm a teeny bit curious how it might end.

Nope. Don't be curious. It harms cats. And I'm shopped out, and over Jude.

"I need to go."

"Where are you going?" His question shouldn't sound so worrisome, almost . . . paranoid. Like he's afraid I'm running away, never to return. Ridiculous.

"Right now. The escalator."

"Take the elevator," Jude sighs. "There's a back one." He steps toward me, but I turn for the sign that reads ESCALATOR.

"What are you doing?" he snaps.

"Escalator." I point in the general direction. "It's more fun," I remind him of our earlier ride up five floors, then down two and three more.

Jude follows behind me, his hard-soled heels clacking until we reach the automatic staircase leading down a level.

"Shouldn't you be getting back to Sabrina?" Her name is musical, while mine is just a mouthful.

"There's no going back." He narrows his eyes and glances over the top of my head as we descend.

I can't tell if he's sad about their separation, or remorseful, maybe, or relieved. Either way, the discussion feels closed, and I'm too tired to continue arguing with him.

Shoveling in a snowstorm again. No benefit.

We hit the next level, and I instantly spin for the escalator again.

"You aren't seriously taking these down all seven floors."

"Only five more to go," I admit, holding up my hand and spreading my fingers to confirm my excitement, before continuing my journey, *down, down, down*. The slow pace is calming. The descent gives me time to reflect. Shopping with Jude has been weirdly . . . fun. He was excited, almost animated, as he pulled toys off the shelf and clothes off the rack. He seemed to know just the right thing for every age group for my nieces and nephews, and the two men in my life, my brothers.

"Where are your packages?" Jude eventually asks, as we near the lowest level, like he's finally realized I'm empty-handed.

"I need to pick them up." In my anger, I'd left them all behind, but now the steam has seeped out of me. Like a holiday bag void of tissue paper and its contents, I'm empty.

Jude continues to follow me in silence until we reach the counter where my presents are stacked, wrapped in pretty paper, and tucked into giant sacks, along with a dress bag hanging from a hook.

For our date.

How did everything get so turned around?

Jude reaches for the dress, carrying it like a bride, while I collect the shopping bags bursting with packages.

"I'll walk you to your car."

"I took the train." And I'll figure out how to pay for my purchases on another day.

"Let me order you an Uber." Jude glances at the numerous bags in my hands and the dress in his. He retrieves his phone from the inside of his suit jacket, and one-handedly connects to the car service app.

"What's your address?"

I groan and begrudgingly give it to him.

Slowly, he smiles after ordering the paid service. "Good. Now, I know where you live. I just need your phone number."

He holds out his phone for me to type in my number. I set down all the shopping bags and take the device.

"Oh, are we still doing this?" I mock.

"Yes, Angelica. We are still exchanging dates." He pauses a second. "They have a strict no-return policy."

I snort, and it isn't until I'm in the hired car that I realize Jude Ashford might have made a joke.

A sense of humor is even more attractive than the outer shell of a man.

chapter 6

[Angelica]

"Where are your bags?" Jude asks when he arrives at my apartment a few minutes before four-thirty on Friday. He's early and I'm running late.

My one-bedroom apartment is in a quaint three-story, three-sided, brown brick building that surrounds a courtyard with a small fountain. Of course, the fountain is off in the winter months, so the landlord stuffs it with festive greenery, redwood twigs, and glittery silver swirls. One day, I hope to have a house. For now, I'm just grateful I no longer live in Gran and Aunt Gertie's three-flat, and we are stuck in my narrow entryway because I haven't invited him further into my place.

He hasn't mentioned how I'm not dressed for the party yet. However, he is wearing another deep blue suit with a patterned shirt minus a tie, looking a little too casual for a formal affair. Still, my darn curiosity wonders if he owns clothes other than suits.

"Why would I need a bag?"

"Because the party is out of town?" Jude gives me a puzzled look like I should know this fact when I clearly do not.

"What?"

"The party is in Wisconsin," Jude clarifies. He's acting like he told me this information when he only sent me one text confirming my address and telling me when he'd pick me up.

"Wisconsin," I grouse. "What's in Wisconsin?"

"An inn."

"Wait a minute." *Just wait one cheesehead minute*. "An inn?"

"Yes. We'll be staying overnight." He flips his wrist, glancing at a silver watch that probably cost four times my paycheck, and then states, "We have a few minutes. I'll wait while you grab some things."

"For what exactly?" Not the first question I should be asking, but I'm curiosity jumped the line.

"Casual drinks. Maybe a walk outside. Hot tubbing."

It's thirty degrees with the threat of snow, and Wisconsin is at least ninety minutes from here.

"Sleepwear optional," he deadpans, because he knows as well as I do we are not having sex.

"This was not part of our deal," I remind him. "One night for one night. Not an overnight," I emphasize.

"Well, I need two nights," he counters, not looking the least bit chagrined.

"Look," I sigh, biting back the irritation tickling my throat. "I get that you are a man who evidently gets his way easily and often, but I've had a week."

My brother's wedding is not coming together as easily as he'd hoped, which shouldn't be surprising because he doesn't have a plan. Plus, I'm hosting the breakfast with Santa at my Gran's church. And, I have copious lists of random holiday responsibilities, like cookie baking, Christmas decorating, and more gift shopping. Not to mention, I worked my typical schedule this week and took an extra shift to cover one expensively lavish evening gown.

I'm determined to pay Jude back for the purchase, and that extra shift is why I'm running late.

But this . . . this business about an inn and two nights . . .

"I'm tired," I admit. All I wanted to do was make an appearance at Jude's party and then snuggle up with peppermint ice cream and a decent holiday rom-com afterward.

"You can nap in the car." At least, he looks a teeny bit chagrined by this suggestion.

"What if I have to work tomorrow?"

"Do you?" His brows lift, those chilly eyes looking only slightly innocent, almost apologetic, like he hadn't considered my job. Which means he hadn't thought of me.

Even if I fortunately have tomorrow off, spending the night in Wisconsin is not on my Christmas bucket list, let alone two nights there. And I don't have the patience for a man-child thinking he can get his way without giving me all the details.

"Maybe you should call someone else." He probably has a list of women on speed dial.

Jude steps closer to me, sending me a step back into my apartment. "I don't *want* someone else."

The words should have no effect on me. He doesn't intend them the way they sound, like I'm the only person he wants by his side. The thought is ridiculous.

"I don't think I'd be a very convincing date." Even though everything between us would be pretend, I'm not certain I even like Jude right now. I'm not sure I could fake my way through a date with him.

"You're perfect." His eyes drop down to my mouth for a second and then flick back to my eyes, holding firm.

Again, the compliment should not sneak into my bloodstream, slinking toward my heart. He's only spewing words. He's a charmer. I know this about him. I remember him.

"Why do you even need a *respectable* date?" The question feels a little too late to ask, considering we've had a week to discuss this situation.

And that word, respectable. It's like saying someone has a nice personality to cover for lacking looks.

Jude sighs, swipes a hand through his hair, and glances toward my front door, which is still open but somehow a barrier between us. He hasn't made it further than the entryway because I haven't invited him further inside my place.

"The Ashford's board of directors thinks I'm reckless. A wild card. Bad for the company. And I need to show them I'm settling down. I'm . . . different." He hangs on the word before he sighs and lowers his head a little bit. "Something happened to me with the heart attack."

"Stress cardiomyopathy incident," I clarify for him. "A broken heart."

He shakes his head, dismissing the concept. "I want them to see that I've changed. I'm turning over a new leaf." His tone lightens as he lifts his head, and he almost convinces me, but a man in sales is a persuasive man.

I refuse to be duped.

"If I don't convince them I've transformed, they'll vote me out of the company. The one with *my name* etched on a historical landmark placard on the side of the building." He slaps his hand against his chest and pauses.

Recalling his teenage behavior, Jude is good at acting, but this doesn't sound like something in a play. Jude looks seriously concerned about his name and his company. His life is on the line in another manner here. Proving himself to his board members sounds urgent.

And when I'd asked Jude before who was there for him during an emergency, I remember his answer.

There's no one.

With a heavy sigh, I state, "I have to be home Sunday morning for a breakfast with Santa."

I'm still put out and upset, but I can also be reasonable. *Or stupid.*

"Ashford's isn't hosting their annual holiday brunch until next weekend," Jude states, looking a little stunned. Whether that's over my agreement to give him two nights or the idea of attending a breakfast for the man in red is to be determined.

"But I'll have my assistant call you and reserve tickets for whomever you'd like to attend."

I'd call bullshit because I know for a fact that the Ashford's breakfast with Santa books up almost the day after the previous year's event. But I'm not talking about an Ashford's activity.

"It's at my Gran's church. I'm *hosting* it." *Two nights?* I want to remind him. I don't conveniently have two nights, and I have plans Sunday morning.

"What?" Jude's brows lift before he narrows his eyes.

Glowering back at him, I hold my ground. "And if you get two nights, I want the rehearsal dinner tossed in as well."

Then again, maybe this date for a date isn't such a good idea after all. I'd never be able to explain Jude to my family. I simply wanted a companion for Beau's wedding, so I didn't look like the loser sister for the evening while my younger brother dry humps his new wife on a dance floor. If we can even find a dance floor, because everywhere I've called has been booked for years because of the holiday timing.

"Done," Jude announces, surprising me and extending his hand.

I'm reminded of how he refused to shake mine when I first visited him in the hospital. Still, I slap my hand against his, and he firmly grips mine, holding on a little longer than necessary, causing that cold crackling sensation over my skin again. The odd combination of ice and heat collides once more.

"Deal."

With the devil, probably. Or more like a holiday grinch.

+++

Our drive to the inn in Jude's sporty car is quiet at first as we muddle through Friday evening traffic out of a city with constant construction on its surrounding highways. When we finally pick up speed, my eyelids lose their fight to stay open.

"Set the seat back a little bit. Take that nap," Jude suggests, sounding surprisingly considerate, and I give in to sixty restless minutes.

When I finally rouse myself, I straighten and stretch in the comfort of his heated, leather bucket seats.

"Warm enough?" Jude asks when I rub my hands up and down my arms.

I nod, while staring out the window, and ask, "Where are we?" We've definitely moved away from cities into what appears to be flat, empty farm fields blanketed by the cold, winter night. However, the stars are abundant and bright in the sky.

"We have another half-hour before we get there."

I nod again, then turn my gaze toward Jude. "So how will this work? Am I a date for hire?" I wiggle my brows at the salacious thought, then remember I'm supposed to be *respectable*. "Or your new girlfriend?"

Jude rolls his head in my direction and gives me a tight smirk. "Girlfriend works."

He pauses another second while returning his attention to the dark highway in front of us.

"What does being your girlfriend mean?" Has he ever had one? A meaningful one, not the on again off again woman in his office.

"I don't know. I've never had one."

The answer should surprise me, but it strangely doesn't. It also makes me a bit sad for him. There's an aloofness to Jude, suggesting he doesn't allow people to get too close. A girlfriend would definitely want in his space.

"But in this case, it means . . ." He clears his throat. "That I might have to touch you."

What? Imagine my foot hitting the brakes on this moving vehicle.

"Maybe a hand on your back or an arm over your shoulder."

"Okay," I whisper, drawing out the word. *Okay*. Maybe. *I guess*. I mean, I can handle that. Casual touching is acceptable. It won't mean anything.

"And maybe a kiss or two . . . on the cheek," he clarifies. He glances toward me, but his gaze stalls on my lips. Quickly, he yanks his attention back to the road, and he rolls his tight grip over the steering wheel.

Jude does not strike me as a cheek-kisser.

"Okay." Still, my voice quivers and hesitates. How difficult can it be?

But a glance over at Jude, his features highlighted by the lights on the dashboard, has me swallowing hard.

That sharp nose. The smattering of facial hair. The glow of those luminescent eyes.

I've definitely sparked a deal with a devil.

+++

When we finally arrive at the quaint inn, we're met by the soft glow of a million lights. One minute we are in complete darkness other than the headlights of Jude's sports car and the stars overhead, and then, like an oasis in the desert, this beacon of brightness illuminates. The inn looks like something one might find in the French Alps, not amid Wisconsin farmlands. The sprawling chalet-like structure is a combination of Old World and modern flair with its white stucco and dark timbered accents.

Inside, the lobby features rich, walnut paneling and antique furniture that looks plush, facing a large fireplace where welcoming flames crackle. Large lit candles decorate the wide, stone hearth. A large circular table fills the center of the lobby near the registration counter, and a giant winter floral arrangement of pine boughs, redwood twigs, and berries on branches explodes out of a low-bowl container. The place is inviting and cozy, bordering on romantic, and standing here, we encounter another dilemma in our dating exchange.

"There must be a mistake," Jude argues with the front desk clerk, a young man no more than twenty.

"I'm sorry, sir. Only one room was booked."

I sigh and hang my head. This cannot be happening. I cannot stay in the same room with Jude.

"And there's only one bed?" Jude confirms.

My head snaps upright. *No*. Absolutely not.

"Jude." The deep masculine call of his name causes Jude and me to spin toward an older gentleman with a wet smile. "So glad you could make it."

He holds out his hand to shake Jude's, clapping him on the shoulder for extra effect before he turns toward me.

"And who do we have here?" the man addresses me. His white hair is cut short, and his eyes are bloodshot and watery.

"Walt. This is . . . my girlfriend, Angelica."

"Angelica." Walt raises his brows. "What a lovely name for a lovely woman."

"Thank you, sir," I answer.

He leans forward, placing a clammy kiss on my cheek. "Pleasure to meet you."

Fighting a shudder, I simply respond, "Oh."

When Walt stands upright again, he claps Jude one more time on the shoulder, visibly squeezing tight. "Looking forward to a drink later this evening."

Walt nods at me, then looks at the clerk who has been standing still, watching our introductions.

"Is there a problem, Mickey?"

"No, sir, I was just assisting Mr. Ashford with his reservation and the issue with—"

"No issue," Jude interjects, sharply cutting him off. "My *girlfriend* and I are happy to take our room keys now."

Mickey looks from Jude to me and back before finishing our registration.

For one room with one bed.

chapter 7

[Jude]

I might have left out a teeny-tiny detail like the party being held three hours from Chicago in a small Wisconsin village. I also might have purposely held back that information until the last minute because I was afraid she'd back out. Other than one text exchange confirming her address and the time I'd pick her up, we haven't spoken for the last week, which has been strangely unsettling for me. Because I'd wanted to talk to her even though I couldn't think of a single thing to discuss. I'm not even a talker, but still, I'd wanted to hear her voice. The concept was fucking with my head.

The inn is practically suffocating in holiday garb. Twinkling tinsel and chiming bells. Lights and crackling logs. Evergreen fragrance everywhere, including our hotel room.

The one room. With one bed.

Heads will roll come Monday for this practical joke, although I'm certain my assistant will have an excuse, claiming the situation is my fault.

"*You requested one room, sir.*" I can already hear the sarcasm in her sixty-something-year-old voice. The same voice that knows I probably did request a single room, without knowing if I'd have a date or not.

Maxine Kelsey knows me better than anyone. She should. She's been assisting me for over a decade. Working with her is the longest relationship I've ever had. Pathetic but true.

As I told Angelica in the car, I've never had an official girlfriend.

And under any other circumstances, I wouldn't balk at sharing a room with a beautiful woman, but this is Angelica.

I'm trying to be a new man.

Not only is she beautiful in her EMT uniform and dorm-room drab shopping attire, but she's stunning in a pair of jeans that perfectly sculpt her hourglass shape and a sweater that drops off her shoulder, exposing the thin strap of a tank top underneath the soft, white material. A *red* tank top that suggests there might be a little naughty beneath the nice.

Then again, I'm not here to corrupt Angelica. I need a date to impress Walt and his cronies on the board. Angelica feels like the right fit. In fact, I'd go so far as to blame her for my harebrained idea. She suggested needing a date first. I just took the wish-list request and ran with it, adding my own holiday desire alongside hers.

I wouldn't say we are tit-for-tat, but I am petty enough to request that we be one for one on our deal.

I'd also like to see her tits. I keep wondering how she'd look bare to me. If a constellation of freckles highlights the curve of each breast, and if her nipples match the color of each rusty dot on her skin.

Whoa! Not happening. Internally, I scold my dick as it stiffens. *Down boy.*

We are not here for *that* this weekend. I've promised myself, the board, Santa, and anyone else who wants to listen that I will behave. I will be the model boyfriend, even though I have no idea how to act like one.

My entire life, I've dated at random but never long-term. If anything, watching my parents' relationship taught me to distrust the term *commitment.* Actually, the concept became most confusing in my late twenties, when I learned just how committed my dad, Tucker, had been to my mother. To the family. To the Ashford name.

Unfortunately, it took me almost another decade to recognize the sacrifice Tucker made for me. And still, I haven't always been grateful.

Selfish. That's the term best used to describe me. My younger sister, Julia, says it all the time, even if her tone is teasing. Underneath the humor is the truth. I'm a bastard, and that's in the truest sense of the word.

As much as I portray a tough skin, with a side of don't-approach-me, I recognize the defensiveness of my ways. If someone got too close, they'd see my faults, and they were pointed out to me often enough as a child by my mother. Of course, I thought her criticism was constructive, only to later realize how destructive her words really were. Peeling back a layer of the spoiled, entitled, selfish man I've become would only reveal a hollow layer within me that no one wants to see.

"So, what should I expect for *drinks*?" Angelica plops on the edge of the queen-sized sleigh bed and huffs while hooking her fingers in air-quotes.

"Boring conversation. You're typical my-dick-is-bigger-than-yours bullshit."

Her eyebrows lift. The red in them almost brightens. "That's rather direct. And I don't have a dick." She glances down at her thighs, like she's double-checking.

I almost laugh. This woman has been a breath of fresh air. Quirky and quick. Mouthy, too. She isn't like anyone else I've ever dated. Not that we *are* dating, because she is only doing me a favor, and I think . . . I hope . . . we can pull this off.

"Stand there and look pretty, is that the memo?" She folds her hands underneath her chin and bats her eyelashes, and I want to tackle her to the bed.

I'll tell her how she can be pretty. With that vibrant red hair spread against the white pillow. And her alabaster skin exposed, letting me count every freckle on her body. *Are her nipples bright red or a dusty pink tone?*

These are questions I should not be considering, and I slip my hands into my pants' pockets, attempting to subtly adjust myself. Sighing, I focus on the freckles on her cheeks. One, two, three, and that fourth near her mouth.

"Look," I swipe a hand through my hair and tug my gaze from those marks on her face. "This is really important to me, and I know you're doing me a solid by being here. Just—"

"Doing you a solid?" she scoffs. "Okay, bro. We aren't in high school anymore, dude." Her tone mocks me and our arrangement.

Maybe we can't pull this off after all.

Angelica abruptly stands, forcing me back a step at her sudden nearness. "How long do I have?"

I glance down at the watch my great-grandfather gave me. The same man who left me Ashford's, hoping I could bring the family vision into a new era. The last decade has been a struggle, but we're doing it. His dream is my reality, but I'm slipping. And I need Angelica to help me.

"Twenty minutes."

She nods. "Okay, then. I'm going to freshen up."

We stare at one another for a minute. Her welcoming eyes have more definition than I'd initially thought. The coloring is almost two-tone, vibrant cool and softer blue, reminding me of a brilliant flame. One that might burn if I got too close.

Her mentioning time to freshen up is my cue to exit the room. There is only so much close proximity a guy can take, and knowing she's changing her clothes on the other side of the bathroom door is more than I can bear to imagine.

My imagination and I need a drink.

"I'll be at the bar," I call out toward the closed bathroom door. The inn only has one watering hole.

"Be right on it," she hollers back.

I close my eyes for a second, wondering if she knows she's torturing me, or if she's sweetly unaware of how incredibly enticing she is.

+++

The bar looks more like an English pub with dark panels and tons of plaid accents, and while I sit on a stool at the thick wooden counter, I'm approached by Walt.

Fucking Walt Witticker, whom I've jokingly called dick-icker behind his back.

The seventy-something man with snow-white hair and a paunch belly is old school, preaching family first while occasionally dipping his wick on the side. He's another example of my resentment toward commitment. His behavior matches my mother's past actions.

On that note, I take a sip of my whiskey neat and brace for Walt's onslaught of questions.

What's your vision, Jude? Where's your head lately? What would your great-grandfather think?

I don't know what he'd think. He was an old man when I was young and an even older one when he died, leaving me too young to run a company. By then, my father had stepped away from

Ashford's, finding his own footing in marketing and branding with his half-brother.

Impact Media is proudly owned by Tucker Ashford and Machlan Wright.

I'd like to tell Walt what I really think about my great-grandfather. As for where my head is at . . . I just don't know anymore.

The one thing I do know is I fucking hate Christmas and—

My thoughts screech to a halt like Santa's sleigh skidding on a rooftop when I catch a glimpse of a vision in the reflection of the bar mirror. Needing to see for myself if I'm imagining her, I spin on my stool, continuing to ignore Walt's questions, and take in the lady in red.

I swear a tune plays in my head, accentuated by trumpets blaring like announcing royalty.

Holy . . . "Angelica?" My mouth gapes as I take in her red hair, folded around itself and pinned against the back of her neck. The same place I want to cup my hand to pull her closer to me. I want to breathe in that cherry-red lipstick on her lips and inhale whatever that sweet scent is she wears. An odd combination of sugar and spice.

Walt's voice drowns out, or maybe he's as gobsmacked as I am.

Slowly, I slip off my bar stool and approach my date, who is wearing a form-fitting, garnet-red dress that accentuates the paleness of her skin and the heat in her eyes.

"Angel," I whisper as I approach her, like she's a mythical creature, but she's made me a believer.

"Jude." The sharpness in her voice is like someone snapped their fingers, and I flip out of hypnosis. At the same time, I blink, wondering what the attitude is all about, while Walt approaches behind me.

"Angelica, you are a vision," Walt mutters while I'm coming out of my stupor. Without looking at the old man, I sense his eyes wandering over her form. Her breasts, emphasized by the slight dip in the top of her dress. Her hips are the perfect curve for my hands.

Instantly, I feel obsessed. That Clara sensation returns. This new toy is mine, only I'm the toy soldier, and she's my human.

I slip my hand around Angelica's back.

"Baby, you look beautiful," I mutter to her, pressing a kiss to her temple.

"*Baby*," she mocks. "I wish you'd told me you wouldn't be coming back to the room. I've been waiting for you."

Shit. Walt misinterprets what Angelica means while I surmise more than twenty minutes have passed. I hadn't mentioned coming back to the room. Nor had I specifically suggested she meet me here. I'm already failing at boyfriend material.

Still, Walt hammers on my shoulder blade. "Now, now. Plenty of time for that later."

"We—" Angelica begins, but I squeeze her side where my hand rests just above her hip, tugging her closer to me.

"Angel, *baby*," I counter, dipping my tone to match the edge in hers. "Walt doesn't want to hear about how I can't keep my hands off you."

The comment is lewd and a little too much, but I want Walt to know one thing—hands off. Eyes too. Actually, don't even breathe in her direction.

Walt chuckles, the sound like a cymbal, a clang of camaraderie, like we're both part of that good ol' boys club I'm getting sick of participating in. Playing a game with their attitudes and their threats like I'm still a teenager. Always acting a part. Always trying to prove myself.

"Actually, what I'd like to know is how you two met? And why haven't we heard about you before today?" Walt lifts his glass, which he must have dragged off the bar while I left my drink behind. His distrustful eyes narrow as he takes a sip.

"It's a funny story . . ." I begin, like my great-grandfather taught me when I needed a moment to think of an answer. *Pause for effect*, he'd said.

"We met in high school," Angelica completes for me, turning her head in my direction and causing me to focus on her face. With those sapphire eyes on mine, she continues. "He was part of the in-crowd. You know, the popular kids."

What? That can't be true. How could I have missed her?

Angelica turns toward Walt. "And I was a scholarship one."

Walt slowly lowers his glass. If he's empathetic, he doesn't show it, but his eyes don't meet hers.

"And we recently reconnected. At Ashford's."

Walt's head slowly lifts, and I hold my breath, wondering two things: How did I miss her in high school, and what will she say next? The board knows I had *an incident*, and I should be on medical leave, but I returned to work the day after I was discharged, and I'm standing here a week later.

"I love that store," Angelica leans toward Walt like she's sharing a secret.

"Oh really?" He tips a bushy white brow, pleased with her comment. "And what do you love about the place/"

She sighs, like Ashford's is Disneyland and not a department store.

"The red carpet when you enter. You instantly know you are someplace special." She clasps her hands in front of her. "And when you stand in the center of the first floor, you look up and those gold railings are like something straight out of the Gilded Age."

Oh, she's good. This is exactly what a man in Walt's position likes to hear.

"Then you see that ceiling. Domed and magnificent."

I remember her calling it a Sistine Chapel effect, but I still don't get it. However, Walt is eating up her dreamy eyes and praising words, and I squeeze her side again, hoping it encourages her to continue.

Then Walt's eyes shift, like he quickly reflected on Angelica's assessment and changed his mind about something.

"So, you like all the money it represents, huh?"

"Pardon me?" she blinks at the old man, her tone instantly hurt while hard.

"Ashford's. We represent money. Wealth. The privilege to spend, spend, spend on material goods." Shopping at Ashford's suggests excess. More shoes. More shirts. More housewares. Just more, more, more, and I suddenly don't like what Walt is implying about Angelica.

"Do you shop at Ashford's often?" Walt counters.

Again, I hold my breath, wondering how many times this beautiful woman has entered my store, and I haven't seen her. Had no cause to notice her from my office on the top floor.

"Actually, I don't. It's a once-a-year occasion." She offers me a quick glance. "When I was a child, my grandmother would dress us all up near the holidays and bring us to the Oak Room for dinner. Then she'd encourage us to wander the toy department and point to all the things we'd like from Santa."

Her gaze lowers, brows pinching for a second. "We didn't always get what we asked for, but it was fun to wish."

"And what did you wish for most?" Walt asks, his tone bordering on insensitive, like the man he is.

Angelica slowly lifts her head and weakly smiles. "For my parents to come back."

"Run off, did they?" Walt mutters, lifting his glass for another sip.

"They're dead, sir."

My head whips in Angelica's direction before I snap a glare at Walt.

He swallows hard and finally has an appropriate response. "I'm sorry to hear that, dear." Shame blanches his pasty cheeks.

Angelica shakes her shoulders. "It was a long time ago." She glances around Walt at the bar, lit by softly glowing pendant lamps, accented by white Christmas lights wrapped around looping garland.

"And now we are here in this beautiful place to celebrate Ashford's." She offers him a final smile. One tight but strong before she glances at me. "And I'd like a drink."

Taking my cue, I nod at Walt. "What the lady wants . . ." I whisk her around him, placing myself between Walt and her before guiding Angelica to the bar with my hand still on her side.

However, I'm not certain if I'm holding onto her to keep her away from Walt or clutching her because I don't want to let her go.

chapter 8

[Angelica]

"That was brilliant," Jude says, the second we approach the bar, where he pulls out a stool for me and holds my hand as I try to slip elegantly onto the raised seat while wearing a dress with a big slit up the front of the skirt. The material folds over itself, but when I take a seat, the folds gape a bit. When I cross my legs, the fabric separates, and most of my thigh is on display.

Jude appears to falter a second before looking at my face. "What would you like to drink?"

"What was brilliant?" I counter.

"That story about us meeting in high school."

"It isn't a story. We went to Immaculate Academy at the same time." I point at him. "Popular jock." Then point at myself. "Science geek."

His eyes flick to mine, then away, for a breath. Long enough to register something like shame, before he chuckles, the sound almost bitter, definitely off-kilter. "Well, that explains it."

"Explains what?"

"How I never saw you?"

"Has anyone ever told you you are a snob?"

"Yes. And often." He offers a blinding smile. One clearly practiced and plastic, but holy elf on a shelf, the effect is dazzling as I'm certain he intended it to be.

"Now. Drink?" He arches a brow and tilts his head toward the bar. He hasn't taken a seat but stands close enough that his front brushes against my hip on the edge of the stool. He holds up a hand to capture the bartender's attention, who quickly appears as if sensing the authority in Jude's presence. Or a large tip because that silver watch is on display.

I quickly scan the cocktail menu and pick a drink with cranberries and vodka plus a splash of Christmas, according to the description.

Once our order is placed, Jude leans against the bar and sets his foot on the rail near the floor. His side presses into the counter in a pose he's performed a few times in his life. Only I'm not a conquest. He doesn't need to try to pick me up because I'm already here with him.

"Stop acting," I say.

Jude straightens his body, then smooths down his tie. "I'm not acting." He pauses a second, glancing to his side before looking directly at me again and waving between us. "Actually . . . *we* are an act."

"For them?" I glance toward that weaselly old man with his condescending attitude, currently giving me a leering look. "But not with each other."

I'm not pretending around Jude.

"Okay." He anxiously smooths down his tie again and gazes toward a group of older men gathered near the bar entrance. When he looks back at me, something settles on his face.

"So, science girl, huh? Is that why you are an EMT?"

"I'm an EMT because my mother was killed by a drunk driver, and I never wanted another little girl to lose her mom like that."

The truth is hard and socks a punch when spoken so directly, but I'm not liking the vibe coming off Jude. If he can't have sympathy for my loss, like that dickhead Walt, I'm going to have a tough time *acting* like I even like Jude, let alone date him.

My truth is difficult to share because I haven't been able to save every victim I've encountered.

"My father died in a building fire. He was a fireman."

Jude gives me his first honest look of the evening. One where those cold eyes melt a little bit, and I dare say compassion fills them.

"Okay." Jude exhales, concentrating on my cheek for a beat too long. Then he sucks in a breath. "Let's get the sad stories out of the way. My mother died in a plane crash, which is public knowledge."

I didn't know that.

"She was leaving my father, running off with her *lover*." His tongue sarcastically rolls over the term. "I learned a few years ago my father had intended to leave her first . . ."

Our drinks arrive, so Jude pauses a second before picking up his glass. "And—"

He abruptly halts, leaving me on the edge of my seat. His life sounds worse than Aunt Gertie's soap operas.

"You'll need to sign an NDA before I can tell you the rest of the story."

I playfully swat at him. "You're mean."

"I've heard that a time or two hundred as well." He sips his drink while gazing at me over the edge of the glass.

While I understand where his walls come from and why he insisted on fitting in, carrying on his family's legacy, and living life to the max, tragedy and heartbreak have two paths. I didn't travel the road he has after losing my parents, or the man I thought should have been the love of my life. If anything, my heart might have softened to tragic moments and deep loss.

Jude, however, has taken the callouses on his heart and hardened them, molding a glamorous but empty shell.

Jude sips his drink, but I still haven't raised my glass despite my throat suddenly going dry.

"Let's see, what else?" he continues. "My father always loved my younger sister more than me. Hell, *I* love my younger sister more than anyone. And she worships me, for obvious reasons."

He winks, laying on that charm like people layer a cake, but I accept the twitch of a smile. The quotation mark at the corner of his mouth digs a little deeper, a little more pronounced.

"Obviously." I scan down his form. Jude wears business suits like a second skin, powerful and attractive. Or are they a protective layer?

"She's married with a few rugrats and lives in California."

"That's a long way from home, Toto," I tease.

"Don't I know it," Jude mutters, lifting his glass but then notices I haven't raised mine. He glances into the container in his hand and lowers it. "I'm really sorry about your parents." He continues to stare at the amber liquid inside his crystal glass.

"Thank you, Jude. I'm sorry about your mom." Finally, I lift my slim glass, salute him, and sip the drink that bursts on my tongue like the Christmas promised. Something minty while pine. Spicy and sweet all at once.

"Oh God," I close my eyes and tip back my head. "That's so good."

When I lower my head, I meet Jude's icy eyes, nearly crystallized, piercing and focused intently on me.

For some reason, I want to uncross my legs, spread my knees, and beg him to step between my thighs. The thought is so instant, heat creeps over my body, starting at my ankles and licking up my skin, swirling at my center, which I clench tighter because my legs remain crossed.

Jude's gaze drops to my lap, where I've shifted from one butt cheek to the other.

He slowly gazes up my body, taking his time over my belly and along the V between my breasts.

"Let's get—"

"Ashford." The sharp bite of Jude's last name, along with a firm hand squeezing at his shoulder, breaks the spell between us and cuts off his suggestion.

A suggestion I'm certain would have finished as an invitation to leave this bar. If only I didn't need an NDA to get more truths from Jude.

He's sex on a peppermint stick in the physically attractive column, but he has miles of question marks in the attitude department.

Naughty versus nice list. He's fine to look at but his heart is still black and that's just not enticing to me.

chapter 9

[Angelica]

Sharing a room with a stranger should not be this complicated. Especially when Jude isn't entirely a stranger, although I still know very little about him.

The rest of the evening passed with me sitting on the barstool, looking pretty, smiling at creepy old men, and nodding at the wives who were talking about other wives who were absent. To Jude's credit, he never left my side. Those necessary, occasional touches he mentioned in the car were constant, almost as if he needed the reassurance that I was here for him.

His hand on my back. Or the backs of his knuckles tickling down my arm. And once, he even reached for my hand, giving it a squeeze and then holding tight.

That perfected smile was in full bloom, and I wondered a time or two if his cheeks ever grew tired. Or if his soul did, because keeping up appearances developed a whole new meaning after watching Jude interact with the people affiliated with his company.

Hell, I was exhausted for him.

The entire evening reiterates how Jude and I are so different. He is all social media and flashing cameras. False smiles and big words, and I just wanted a cheeseburger and the fireplace in our room.

"Thanks for putting up with everything tonight," Jude says once I exit the bathroom. He graciously offered me the bed and suggested he'd take the floor. Something tells me Jude has never willingly slept on carpeting in his life, but I don't argue with him.

I don't suggest we share the bed like grown adults who have silently agreed not to touch one another.

Because Jude had a difficult time keeping his hands off me tonight, which was confusing. Every movement made by me was countered by him. His hand on my back or his arm wrapped around me. He tugged me closer if one of his board members came near us, like he was afraid I'd be snatched up like the Heat Miser hunting for forbidden toys.

"Of course," I say, rubbing in the hand cream I put on every night before I sleep. The vanilla and citrus lotion reminds me of my mother somehow. Her absence hits profoundly at this time of year. Especially as Gran has grown older and more of the holiday responsibilities fall on me.

I tug back the covers on the king-sized bed while Jude stands in front of the built-in fireplace. The soft crackle of flames behind the protective glass casts a romantic glow around the room.

Ignoring the pinch in my chest, because this is not a romantic getaway, I slip beneath the blankets while Jude continues to stare at the flames.

"What did you miss out on this evening?" he asks, his concentration focused away from me.

"What do you mean?"

"A date, maybe."

I scoff. "If I had a date, I wouldn't be attending my brother's wedding with you." Or be tucking into this bed with him in the room.

He shifts his upper body to glance at me. "Seriously, then. What would you have been doing tonight instead?"

"Actually, I missed out on a fundraiser. It's called A Snowball's Chance. One of the guys at the firehouse has a daughter with a congenital limb defect."

"What does that mean?" Jude shifts to fully face me, while his hands slip into his pockets. He removed his jacket earlier and unbuttoned a few buttons on his shirt.

"Her legs didn't fully develop while she was inside her mom." I smile softly. "But she's amazing." I wave a hand and swallow hard, thinking about how fun Tamarra Scroggs is when she comes around the firehouse. "Her dad is a former pro football player turned firefighter, and he started this annual fundraiser to raise money for families who might need financial assistance if their child has a long-term medical condition. A snowball's chance—"

"In the hell of their life," Jude finishes.

I sit straighter, defensive and prickly. "Her life isn't hell, Jude. In fact, I bet her life is more fulfilling than yours or mine. Richer even. And not because she has money or can spend, spend, spend," I mock Walt's tone and his accusation, like I'm interested in Jude for money reasons.

Say gold digger much?

"She's well-loved, adored, even admired, for her spirit and spunk, and she's only eleven. She's going to do great things in this world."

Jude's mouth falls open, hopefully not misinterpreting the chastising I've given him, because I am scolding him. Shame on him.

"Don't be *that* guy, Jude."

"What guy?" He asks, slowly lifting his head. His shoulders stiffening.

"The mean guy in the room." Maybe he was like that in high school. Not a bully so much as just condescending with a comment and demeaning with a glance. We should be past the point in our lives where others need to be put down to bring ourselves up.

Jude scoffs and glances back toward the fire. "The problem is, I've always been *that* guy. I get what I want when I want it."

I don't feel threatened by his statement. I'm confident Jude Ashford does *not* want a bite of me. He's playing an act. I'm his fake girlfriend. He was handsy, protective even, but it's all pretend. For show only. At least, in front of the others.

In here . . . it's getting a little too real.

"Well, you can always change that," I state, flinching a little bit as I look down my nose at him. "'Tis the season for transformation. Haven't you ever seen *A Christmas Carol*?"

Jude chuffs and points at his chest. "Scrooge here. I don't watch that shit."

"You cannot hate Christmas." My mouth falls open. "It's the most wonderful time of the year." I practically sing but then I lower my voice. "Seriously, Jude, isn't this your season? Spend, spend, spend," I mock again.

Cha-ching, cha-ching. Although cash registers now make more of a *beep-beep-beep.*

"Yeah. Spend." He finishes unbuttoning his shirt, tugging it loose from his pants before slipping his hands back into his pockets. He pauses another second, staring into the fireplace. His head dips forward, reflective almost, and his voice is low when he asks, "Ever think there's more to Christmas than boxes and bows, ribbons and gift bags?"

"Of course there's more." My accompanying laugh is sharp and puzzled.

"Like what?" Jude faces me full-on once more.

Another bitter laugh almost escapes but the earnestness in his face freezes the sound on my tongue. The deep well of his eyes honestly questions what all the excitement is about.

The other thing tying my tongue is the expanse of Jude's chest revealed by the two halves of his shirt spread wide because of the way his hands rest in his pockets. That side tattoo is peeking out at me again like it did the day we were called to his office.

Finally, words filter forth. "It's about love, Jude. Not just romantic love but love of family and friends. Compassion for others. Hope for the future. Christmas is simply . . . believing in magic."

"So, it's pretend, too? Santa. Angels on high." He tilts his head, like I've only proven his point.

"No, Jude. It's not pretend. Maybe it's make-believe, but that's different than pretending. Pretending covers up something false. Believing is faith in the unknown."

Jude stares at me. I don't think I've argued my thoughts well, and I'm about to offer more explanation when he lowers his head and steps around the foot of the bed.

"I'm going to use the bathroom quick. Then I'll turn the fireplace off before hitting the floor."

I'm too stunned by the ripples on his chest and the abrupt end to this discussion to realize he made a joke before he disappears into the bathroom. I'm left wondering what else I'm missing.

Who is the real Jude Ashford?

When he returns to the bedroom, he wears only his boxer briefs. My mouth falls open at the walking underwear commercial. His name is a whisper from my lips, but Jude doesn't hear me.

Instead, he says, "Going down." Then he lowers his body in increments like he's actually riding down an escalator. He disappears at the foot of the bed before I register what he's done.

"Oh my God." I laugh, covering my mouth. "How did you do that?"

"Do what?" His voice travels up to me from the gap between the foot of the bed and the fireplace, which he hasn't turned off.

"Did you just take an escalator ride to the floor?"

"The escalators are always more fun."

I lunge toward the end of the bed, glancing over the curved footboard. "Jude Ashford, do not tell me you have a sense of humor."

"What's wrong with a sense of humor?" he counters, staring up at me from his nest of blankets on the floor.

I shift and cross my arms over the rail across the bottom of the bed. "Depends. You trying to be funny or charming?"

Jude tilts his head, that apostrophe by his mouth twitching, spreading deeper. "Whichever gets me up there."

Laughing in earnest, I tug at the blanket loosely covering him from the waist down, exposing that firm chest and the unidentified tattoo on his side. "You might need to work on both, Mr. Grinch."

Jude captures my fingers as I pull them back from his blanket, stroking the pad of his thumb down the length of my middle finger. That cool sensation spreads over my hand yet surprisingly warms me. This touch isn't accidental or an act for the board members. This feels real.

He holds just a little too long, but then not long enough before slipping down my hand and dropping his to his belly.

"I'm good under pressure," he murmurs, tucking his other arm beneath his head.

I raise a brow, ignoring the skip in my pulse. "Is that what this is? Are you trying to seduce me from the floor?"

He scoffs, like it's the most ridiculous notion he's ever heard. "Of course not."

"Good," I state, swallowing down the pinch of hurt and disappointment.

Then I scramble back to the top of the bed, grab one of the extra pillows, and toss it toward Jude, pleased when I hear him emit a small *oof*.

"But . . ." Jude pauses a second, his voice lowering, but still reaching me. "If I were going to seduce you? You wouldn't have to question if I was or not."

chapter 10

[Jude]

In the morning, I wake to knocking on the hotel room door.

"Hang on," I mutter, standing to my full height, adjusting my morning wood, which could not be prevented as I'd been dreaming about a certain redhead in my hotel bed. The bed I did *not* share with her.

Giving the bed a quick glance, Angelica's hair is sprawled in all directions as she lies on her front with her cheek against a pillow. Her arms are tucked underneath the firm pillow. Her legs obviously splayed outward like she's a giant starfish in the oversized bed.

"Lucky," I mumble as the hammering continues and I reach inside the closet for a robe, quickly covering myself and loosely tying the sash at my waist.

Considering my roommate is dead asleep despite the racket, I don't think she's ordered room service.

"What?" I snap, opening the door and registering that my prediction was correct. Angelica did not order breakfast.

Instead, Walt stands in the hallway.

"Mornin'." He tips up his chin, looking a little rough. Bloodshot eyes. Pale cheeks. "You didn't respond to the text I sent you, so I thought I'd just stop by. Breakfast?"

He gazes around the shield I've made of my body, and I swallow thickly, hoping he doesn't—

"Were you sleeping on the floor?" His eyes come back to my face, pinching with the question.

"He has a bad back." The headless voice echoes from behind me, and I shift, thankful Walt isn't getting a view of Angelica this morning.

"Bad back or not, you shouldn't be sleeping on the floor with your condition."

My heart. "I'm fine," I counter, turning in a way to block Walt's view of my room again.

"Angelica," Walt hollers into the room. "I expect you to be taking care of our boy here." Walt winks at me. The movement was slow, almost like his eyelid had trouble lowering then lifting again.

Boy. That's been the issue. These older men all think I'm a child. The kid racing around my great-grandfather's office or hiding beneath clothing racks. A young lad who stole a toy from a store with my name on it before I was an actual owner. A teen who lost his virginity in a fitting room.

"Yes, sir," Angelica calls back, still not visible, thanks to the wall blocking off the bed.

"Jude." Walt appraises my attire. "I'll give you fifteen minutes."

"I'll see you downstairs." After a sharp head nod and a quick shutting of the door, I lean against it and tip back my head.

"Fuck," I groan, swiping a hand down my face, closing my eyes a second as I do, and then opening them to an angelic mirage in front of me.

Hair wild like she had a restless night in bed, I've never seen those curls so untamed. She wore a braid all the times I've seen her, other than last night when she had the low twist at her nape.

But this version of her? This vision . . . *fuck!*

"How did you sleep?" Her voice expresses concern, but I'm stuck on her lips. The way her mouth curls. That damn freckle just below the corner on the left.

"Okay, I guess," I mutter, realizing the truth. Despite spending the night on the floor, I actually did sleep pretty well. The night was full of dreams. High school hallways. Faceless girls. And searching for one with wild red hair. "You?" Had she dreamt of me? Sought me out?

"I slept amazing." She tucks her hands beneath the mass of curls and lifts them upward.

My mouth falls open as the strands flare out in all directions, and I want to slip my fingers through the explosion. Then wrap as much as I can around my fists and tug her head back so I can suck on her neck and lick that sacred freckle.

Jesus. I swipe my hand down my face again. "I need a shower." I need to fucking jack off and get these visions of her out of my head.

"I'm going to hit the gym," she says.

"Yep." I nod. "Need the bathroom before I jump in?"

Angelica nods like a bobblehead and skips into the bathroom while I cross the space to the bed and toss myself on my back, staring up at the ceiling.

It's going to be a long day.

+ + +

Thankfully, Walt wasn't up for more conversation than idle chit-chat, which I hate almost as much as a profit and loss discussion. However, the short conversation allows me to get back to my hotel room sooner than I expected.

As I enter the room, I hear the shower running, the door cracked open to allow the steam to filter out into the main room.

The deep tenor of a male voice echoes against the tile wall.

"You like that, baby girl? You like me touching you there? You want my cock inside you?"

What the fuck?

I press at the bathroom door, allowing me a full view of the small room, where Angelica stands alone in the glass-enclosed shower. A quick assessment of the room confirms she's the only one present, and my gaze lands on her phone, screen face up, volume maxed.

"That's it, take it like you want it," the male voice encourages.

My attention flips back toward Angelica. Is she *listening* to porn? But as additional words filter through my head, I realize the narration is an audiobook. A very steamy one.

The continuation of the story is lost to me as I watch Angelica. Her hand on the tile wall. A washcloth between her thighs with her other hand. Her head tipped forward.

Sweet Santa, I'm permanently going to be on the bad boy list.

Because for another half a second, I'm frozen as I watch her arm move, imagining the rhythmic circles she's making where she's most sensitive.

Everything in me wants to strip out of my clothes and step into that shower with her. Be that washcloth giving her pleasure.

Instead, I take a giant step back, leaving the door suddenly wide open, confident she hasn't noticed me. Pressing my back to the short hallway wall at the edge of the door frame, I tip back my head and listen as the male voice continues his narration and Angelica adds her own response.

"Yes," she mutters as the voice-actor asks more heated questions, followed by a description of what he's doing to the female character, filling in the space between the dialogue.

"Yes, Jude, yes," Angelica's voice rises, and I make a fist, bringing it to my mouth and digging my teeth into my knuckles.

What the fuck? And I mean that in the most eloquent *what the fuck is happening* way? My name on her tongue in that breathy plea compares to finding gold coins in my stocking.

I'm so tempted to pop the button on my pants and work myself within them, but this is Angelica's moment, and I'm a fucking auditory voyeur.

"Jude," she hums.

My dick leaps, as if he heard her call out my name, begging for me.

What does she want from me? This moment is nothing more than pure lust and longing, right?

As a final gasp leaves Angelica's mouth, silence follows a beat. Even her phone has gone quiet, and I hold my breath.

I glance at the hotel door and peek over my shoulder at the open space leading into the bathroom.

I need to get out of here. Need to act like I never heard her call out my name while she touched herself, but I'm trapped.

I don't think I can reach the bathroom door and restore it to its original position without Angelica noticing me. And I don't think I can make it through the room door . . . without her noticing me.

As the shower shuts off, I race for the middle of the bedroom, noting Angelica has picked up the blankets I slept on, folded them, and neatly stacked them on the boudoir chair. I swipe my phone from my pocket, hold it up to my ear, and stare at the slightly open curtain.

Speaking louder than necessary, I say, "Okay, great. Yep. I'll get right on her . . . I mean, it."

Idiot. I close my eyes and give a quick glance over my shoulder.

With the shower off, the silence in the room is an eerie echo of nothing.

"Okay. Yep." I state again, rather too strongly.

Angelica pops her head through the bathroom door. Her wide eyes land on me, and I point to the phone by my ear before turning back toward the window.

"Okay. Good idea. We'll talk later." I pretend to snap off the device and hang my head for a second.

"Why are you in here?" I can almost hear Angelica's voice in my head.

"It's a funny story . . ." my thoughts counter like my great-grandfather taught me as a stall tactic.

"Jude?"

I spin on my heels. Her hair is covered by the massive twist of a white towel. The robe she'd been wearing earlier now covers what I'm certain is a still naked body underneath the lush cloth.

I've never been so jealous of a robe. The pleasure of that material touching her skin.

Her eyes avoid mine. "I didn't hear you come in." She swallows while her gaze aims away from me.

"I was on the phone," I lie.

"Oh. I had my audiobook on kind of loud to be heard over the shower." She pauses, eyes shifting in my direction and then quickly flicking away. "Did you . . . I mean, did it . . . was it too loud?"

I bet I could make you cry out louder.

"You had an audiobook running? I didn't hear it." I lift my hand holding the phone, but it feels like the heaviest weight I've ever pressed. I shake the device. "On the phone," I remind her. "Focused on the conversation."

"Oh." Her mouth pinches, her eyes still avoid mine.

I could give you something to unpucker those lips. Would you like that, baby girl*?*

The montage in my head isn't helping me downplay the truth.

I fucking heard every word that narrator said and every moan and plea from Angelica in response.

She looks thoroughly embarrassed. Hand caught in the cookie jar, or rather, between her thighs.

The thought forces my gaze to where the folds of the robe cover her legs. Last night, when she took a seat on the barstool, her dress slid to the side, exposing one lush thigh crossed over the other, and the struggle to pull my gaze from her was real.

She is temptation at every turn. An angelic devil, if there ever was such a thing.

"I'm going for a walk. Head outside for a little bit." I need to clear my head, and some cold, crisp country air will do the trick.

"It's cold outside," Angelica counters.

What does that ice queen say: *the cold never bothered her anyway?* I rush for my suitcase and flip up the lid.

Angelica watches as I rummage through my bag for a base layer to put beneath my jeans and sweater.

"I could come with you," she offers, which causes me to spin and face her.

"Yeah?" I shouldn't be encouraging her. We need some distance. I need space.

"Yeah." She shrugs, leaning against the corner where the short hall meets the larger room. She tips her head against the hard edge. "But I don't want to be in your way, if you need to make more phone calls or want some time alone."

Alone. Nope. That's the last thing I really want, but I also don't know if I can spend another minute near her without exploding.

Still, having her as a companion might also be nice. I don't typically take walks with someone else.

Eventually, I offer her some truth. "I don't think you'd ever be in the way, Angelica." And while I mean that she'd be a welcome distraction, her face falls, somehow misinterpreting my comment.

"Oh. Okay, well, I'll let you—"

"Come with me," I counter as she rolls against the corner and presses off the wall.

We could come together, baby.

Fuckity-fuck. I shake my head, ignoring the sudden narration in there.

Straightening, I admit, "I'd enjoy the company. *Your* company. Let's take a walk together."

While her eyes still look askance, her lips slowly curl into a soft smile.

Inhale. One, two, three, and four at the corner of that mouth.

Exhale.

"Okay, I'd like that," she says. "Just let me get dressed."

And there goes all my good intentions, because I'm thinking about her naked again.

Quickly, I shut down the narrator in my brain that wants to beg her to stay undressed, and I change my clothes instead.

chapter 11

[Angelica]

I was so busted, and embarrassed. There was no way Jude didn't hear my audiobook, or me, unless he really was oblivious to others around him.

Like he said last night, being the science girl in high school explained why he never noticed me. I didn't stand out in a crowd, even if I did have wild red hair.

As for that hair, I had to dry it as best I could before we went outside, but it was still damp underneath the knit cap I wore. Bundled up in a layer of long underwear beneath my jeans and sweater, plus my long puffy jacket, a thick scarf, and mittens, I was as covered as I was going to be. Despite the initial nip of sharp, cold air, the layers do the trick as we wander out of the resort into brilliant winter sunshine.

"The concierge said there is a small pop-up shop nearby. Let's get some fresh air and then we can wander over there."

"You can leave the shop, but can't take the shop out of the man," I tease.

He chuckles, the sound more like he's strangling. "Yeah, something like that." His eyes slit in the blinding sun, and he sets Aviator sunglasses on his face, making him look like a runway model as he leads us toward a paved trail that's been shoveled and salted for guests to travel.

We walk in silence a few feet before I slip my arm into his. Jude stumbles and stares down at my hand tucked into the crook of his elbow.

"Mr. Marksman." I nod in the direction of one of his board directors approaching us with his wife.

Jude's head whips upward before he blows out a breath. "I'm really not in the mood for more small talk."

I don't answer as I try to think of an excuse for us not to stop and chat. Thankfully, Mr. Marksman and his wife only pass by us with a pleasant greeting, apparently having no interest in talking to us either.

After a few more steps, I peek over our shoulders. "Okay, they're out of range," I say, while tugging my hand from Jude's elbow, but he tightens his hold, trapping my hand against his side.

"Maybe . . . maybe you should keep holding onto me just in case."

When I glance at him, he doesn't meet my eyes, keeping his eyes hidden behind those dark lenses while he faces forward.

Deciding he might be right, I settle in, looping my arm with his.

"Last night you mentioned you had a sister, Julia." I don't remember her from high school. "Do I need to sign an NDA to learn if you have more siblings?"

Jude lets out a huff. "My sibling situation is complicated." He doesn't expound, firmly closing out the topic. More quiet seconds pass before he says, "What about you? Do you have siblings?"

I laugh, squinting into the bright sunlight. "Three. My older brother Dane, a younger sister, named Christmas."

"Christmas? You're kidding me."

"I kid you not," I counter, imparting a poor British accent. "And then my youngest brother, Beau."

"So Dane, Angelica, Christmas, Beau. Sounds a little like a theme." His lip crooks.

"My last name is Winter. There's definitely a theme."

Jude nods. Since he doesn't want to talk, I can't seem to help myself. "Our parents died within a few years of each other. Our Gran and Gramps took us in." Narrowing my eyes beneath the glare of the sunshine, I add, "Gramps died a few years ago."

I sense Jude glance at me but move on to the happier points about my family. "We also lived with my Aunt Gertie, who's a bit of a Mrs. Havisham. Jilted lover. Proud fornicator."

Jude snorts.

"She's the reason I needed to go to the lingerie department at Ashford's. Every year we do an adult gift exchange, and every year I get her." I tilt my head. "Highly suspicious, if you ask me. But also every year, she asks for something provocative . . . her word, not mine." I chuckle.

Who am I to judge if an older woman wants to feel sexy and provide herself *special time*?

"Anyway, they live in a three-flat. The bottom is a garden apartment for Gertie. The middle is our grandparents. The top was ours." Talk about a close-knit, extended family.

"But the entire building was our home." And a cramped one at that. "Now my sister lives on the top floor with her three kids."

Jude remains quiet another second before stating, "My grandparents had a place on Prairie Avenue."

"Fancy," I remark about the historical millionaire's row.

"But we had a place in the Gold Coast neighborhood," he adds.

Equally swanky.

"My mom was an influencer before the term was born, and Tucker had been in a band."

"That's cool," I interject, noting this is the second or third time he's called his dad by his first name.

Jude scoffs. "Yeah, but he gave it up to marry my mom." Jude squints, the corners of his eyes crinkling. "I was always closer to her than him. And Julia, my younger sister, was always the apple of my dad's eye."

"That's how it is with girls," I smile, recalling how Christmas and I were close to our dad, especially after he took on the role of both parents for a few years.

"That's how it is when she's his, and I wasn't."

My feet falter, and Jude tightens his elbow to hold me steady.

"My family is complicated, like I said." He purses his lips a bit.

I quietly ask, "Did he take that out on you? The not-being-his part." The situation certainly sounds complex and difficult.

"No. *I* resented him. Like it was his fault I wasn't his."

My brows pinch. I'm puzzled by this statement as well as the relationship.

"So, you aren't close with your father?" I clarify, which is all kinds of sad.

"My father . . . is dead. Tucker and I aren't close." Sadness layers his tone.

Maybe he could rectify the distance. He could open communication. Be the first to express a desire to connect. However, the tightness of his lips causes me to keep my advice to myself.

I'm not here to judge Jude's upbringing. I don't even need to understand it, but I'd like to understand him, and I often find that the root of a person's personality stems from their childhood.

Love or loss. Appreciation or abuse. Novelty or neglect.

"I guess you could say I'm a bit of a lone wolf." The admission expresses deeper sadness, a gut-wrenching melancholy.

"Well, if you're a lone wolf, I'm the leader of my pack, because I am involved in everything."

Jude turns his head. "Like what?"

"The holidays, for instance. You already know I had a shopping list a mile long, and it wasn't even my list. Beau's wedding. Breakfast with Santa. Cookie exchanges. Cocktails. Kids' concerts—"

"You don't even have children," he cuts me off as we weave around a curve in the trail.

"My nieces and nephews." I clarify. "I attend their holiday program."

He nods slowly. "What do you have to do for your brother's wedding?"

"Plan it." I chuckle, the sound laced with bitterness I don't want to admit. I'm not upset that Beau is getting married, but I am a bit put out that he's asked me to do the hard work, like find a place to host the wedding.

"Why? You aren't the one getting married."

"His fiancée has finals."

"Finals?" Jude barks.

"She's finishing her first semester of graduate school. They are a classic age gap. Older man. Younger woman." Only Beau and his future wife really are cute together, if a bit nauseating.

Jude's mouth pops open but then clamps shut. "What's her name?"

"Belle."

Jude's brows crease severely before he says, "Beau and Belle."

"Yep." I pop the *-p* and stare at the copse of trees we are walking toward.

Jude doesn't ask for more details, and I don't offer any. Even their names together are sickeningly cute.

"Julia lives in California?" I prompt.

"She's a baker. Part owner in a business called Because Cupcakes." For the first time ever, a genuine smile graces Jude's lips. A small one but a distinct one. He's proud of his sister. "She has red hair like you," he adds, turning to look at me. But then his brows pinch again. "But also, not like you. I mean, you don't look anything like my sister."

I bet I don't. I bet she's beautiful if she looks anything like him, same father or not. And with that, I note that even though Jude told me I was beautiful last night, he said it in front of Walt. For our act.

With that thought, I pull my arm free from his. We haven't seen anyone else on our stroll, and if we do near someone else, I can always slip my arm through his again.

For now, I need the slight distance as a reminder of my place.

"Do you do anything special for the holidays?" I ask next, needing something to fill the suddenly awkward silence. Our walk continues beneath a set of trees, which act as a canopy from the bright blue winter sky. Lights are strung limb to limb over the walkway versus being wrapped around each tree, giving the suddenly darker space a cozy, intimate feel.

With anyone else, the space would feel romantic. Out of view from the resort, it's the perfect place to steal a kiss, but that's the historical romance lover inside me wanting to toss her petticoat.

"I don't celebrate Christmas."

Recalling he told me he doesn't *like* the holiday, I stop short. "What?"

Jude takes another step forward before spinning to face me. With his hands in his coat pockets, and those glasses on his face, he looks like a bodyguard.

"Surely, you must celebrate somehow."

"I don't. Celebrate, that is."

"Because you're an atheist? Or an agnostic?"

Jude shrugs, looking off toward the trees. "I just don't get the big deal."

"The big deal?" I choke. "It's Christmas."

"But why is it important?" He turns his head back toward me, asking the same question he asked last night.

"Besides the presents and packages? The things bought from a store?"

Jude remains silent, pursing his lips and twisting them in that way he does, like he's angered, maybe anxious. He's waiting on an answer, and he wants it now.

"Christmas is about faith in the un—"

"Give me a real answer." He reaches for his sunglasses, tugging them free from his face so he can look at mine with those icy eyes.

"Fine. There is something special about winter, almost magical. The snow and the silence. The cold that forces you to sit by a fire. The comfort of hot chocolate. The lights." I wave at the ones over our heads. "The peace in them. The beauty of them. The promise that sunshine always follows darkness."

Life goes on even when your parent dies in a drunk driving accident, a burning building, or a plane crash. Yet somehow, I'm not certain Jude has moved on. Or maybe he's always been stuck in a role. An image. An act.

Slowly, my shoulders lower and I exhale. The Instagram images of his family flash through my head. The coordinated outfits. The false smiles.

"Who hurt you?" I whisper. Who made him so cynical? What happened to him to make him hate Christmas?

"Everyone," he says, lowering his head. Then he pops it back up, slips on his sunglasses, and spins toward the remaining path, taking quicker steps, which force me to walk double time to keep up with him.

There is so much to say and so much to ask, and yet silence feels simpler. I don't want to push Jude. I don't need to know more about him.

He's a man with a boy trapped inside him, who has lived with a life of disappointment. He's conjured the belief that he wasn't wanted, because he hadn't been wanted by his father, and his mother sounds like a mess, having an affair and running off, as he said, to be with her lover, only to perish in a plane crash. I surmise his great-grandfather was long gone by then, and his dad had started a separate business.

Jude had Ashford's, but who had Jude?

When I finally catch up to him, we only have a few additional feet before we exit the tunnel of trees, stepping back into the brilliant winter daylight. Music fills the air, and to my surprise, a skating rink is before us.

"We should ice skate," I blurt. The rink looks like a frozen pond, complete with a portable wood hut for skate rentals, and a cart with roasting chestnuts. The strong, nutty aroma mingles with cinnamon and wafts toward us. Another cart distributes coffee or hot cocoa to the skaters.

This is straight out of a historical romance, and I'm not passing up the chance to ice skate on an actual pond.

I reach for Jude's arm, tugging at his sleeve. "Please." I pout, pressing out my lower lip and batting my eyelashes, which probably makes me look more like a Furby than the coquettish expression I wish to portray.

"An Ashford skis and snowboards, but they do not skate." His tone is almost sarcastic while sounding overly aristocratic.

"Well, we're going to change that, starting today."

Jude lets his head drop back a second, then rolls his neck. "Fine," he grunts, but the tone isn't quite so dismissive as the word intends. He might even be smiling, if that grimace can be mistaken for one.

Perhaps Jude doesn't know how to grin, other than when mentioning his sister.

Maybe smiles are as absent as Christmas for him.

And my new wish for the season is to make Jude find a reason to curl those lips in happiness.

chapter 12

[Jude]

I cannot believe we are doing this. Putting our lives at risk, balancing on a thin steel blade against thick ice. I can't remember the last time I ice-skated. I also don't think I can remember how to skate, and I was about to make the biggest fool of myself.

I think back to last night when I did that silly trick my great-grandfather taught me. The one where you walk forward while squatting lower and lower like you're descending a staircase. Only I'd perfected the move in a way it looked like I was lowering on an escalator. I hadn't done that trick in decades.

And when Angelica laughed, the sound was pure glee. Tinkling bells and angels singing. The noise was so playful, so pleasant, I was stunned for a minute. That I'd caused that joyful noise to escape from her was puzzling.

Don't tell me you have a sense of humor? No one would ever accuse me of such a thing. I was serious and intense. Edgy. Aloof. Standoffish.

Mean.

And I honestly didn't know where my attitude came from. My mother? My father? My regrets? Their regrets?

"Jude?" Angelica saying my name pulls me from the darkening thoughts, and I blink at the man inside the wood hut.

"What size shoe?" Angelica states like she's already asked the question.

"Fourteen."

For some reason, Angelica's gaze drops to my boot-covered feet and then flits higher. Is she wondering if the shoe size compares to the length of something else? The bigger the feet . . . the bigger the . . . Yeah, she'd never have to worry about me in that department.

But another thought comes just as quickly—would she be curious?

After her earlier activity, I'd say she's interested. I consider what Walt implied last night. Angelica is after the money. What a dickhead. If he only knew I'm using her, and she isn't even getting paid. We've wagered the old-fashioned way. A fair trade.

However, I didn't expect that trade to mean slipping my feet into a boot on a blade that probably hasn't been properly sanitized from the last guy.

I also didn't expect it to mean I'd open up and tell her how I don't celebrate the holidays. I'm typically over the season by the time the official date arrives, but that isn't the real reason for my lack of celebration.

"Are you sure you want to do this?" I hitch my thumb toward the path. "We still have that shop to visit."

Angelica waves her hand. "I don't need to see the shop."

"You don't?"

She straightens, giving a longing glance at the ice rink. "Well, I mean, not unless you need to see it."

I don't need to visit the pop-up, I just used the destination as an excuse. But, don't all women love to shop? *Spend, spend, spend.* At least, most of the women I've encountered do.

Then I consider my sister, who has always been an anomaly in my head.

And Tucker's new wife, Mae, who'd rather dig in the dirt than scavenge through dress racks.

And clearly, Angelica is different. Not just in her looks but in her attitude. In her nature. She hasn't complained about the cold. Didn't decline a walk outdoors. And now, she'd rather ice skate than go shopping.

"No, I don't need to see the store." I visit one every day of my life. While that store is essential to my livelihood, being there has become claustrophobic at times. My office is like a solitary cave on a mountain top, high above a village. I'm an outlier of the community. The lone man out.

With that thought, the skate attendant slaps two pairs on his countertop, and Angelica reaches for hers before I can grab both sets. She practically skips over to a bench where she takes a seat and slips off her boots, easily sliding her feet into the rented skates and lacing them up. I follow, while not as thrilled as she is about this experience.

"This is going to be so fun," she says, her voice rising with glee.

"Fun?" I scrunch my nose, leaning down to remove my boots.

"Yeah. This thing people do when they enjoy activities. Or enjoy themselves with simple things like hot chocolate and roasted chestnuts." She nods toward the carts. "It's when someone enjoys life."

I shake my head. "People would never describe me as fun." In fact, I'm not certain when the last time was that I truly enjoyed myself.

"Then don't be the thief of joy, Jude. Live in the moment."

Don't you leave me, Jude.

I'd promised myself I'd change. Still, I chuckle bitterly. "If you tell me to live, love, laugh, we can no longer be friends."

"Are we friends?" Her summer sky-colored eyes meet mine and hold a second, warming my insides.

We might be pretending we are boyfriend and girlfriend, but are we becoming friends? I didn't know. I didn't have many of those either.

I must scowl or give her a strange look because she quickly looks away from me and stands on her skates.

Eventually, I follow her lead but instantly teeter.

"Whoa," Angelica says, holding out her hands like she'd catch me if I fall.

"I got it," I snap, never wanting to look unsteady around her.

She clamps her lips tight and nods once before taking a step back. Then another and another, before spinning toward the icy pond.

Dammit. I'm frozen in place and not just from the cold. I'm afraid to move. Afraid I'll tip over. Afraid I'll look incompetent.

"You should waddle."

I turn my head toward the smart mouth of a young boy.

I am not fucking waddling.

"Like this." He spreads his arms, widens his legs, and softens his knees, then steps forward. "Waddle."

Not happen— But the second I start to wobble, my arms stretch outward, and I bend my knees for stability. Then I waddle like a goddamn penguin before dipping my toe against the ice like I'm afraid to get in the water.

"You got this, Jude," Angelica says as she whizzes past me, her smile wide, and beaming almost as bright as the sunlight overhead.

Why does she have to be a ray of sunshine and as pretty as one with that red hair? Her head is covered by her knit hat, a ball bouncing on the top, but the long length of her hair is braided and hangs over her scarf and shoulders. She giggles as my feet slip, and she travels against the flow of the skaters to double back to me.

"Here." She holds out both her hands.

I'd like to refuse. I'd like to tell her I don't need her. I'd also like to say I'll sit this activity out, but she looks so happy standing on those shaky skates.

"I don't want to hold you back." She should go off, have her fun, and not wait on me.

"You won't." Her voice is strong.

Hesitantly, I hold out my hands, setting my glove-covered ones against her woolen mittens. Slowly, I feel Angelica pulling me forward, my body stretching.

"Move your feet, Jude," she coaches, her voice calm, encouraging.

At first, my feet shuffle like I don't have conscious willpower over them.

"Push off to the side a little bit. Like this." While standing opposite me, Angelica motions with her foot how to work the blade at a slight angle instead of straight on.

I could snap again. *I know how to do this*. But I'm not certain how to fake ice skating. With Angelica holding onto me, I'm also not certain I want her to let go.

When she tucked her arm into mine earlier, the move had been a shock. She quickly explained away the touch because of the Marksmans, which strangely caused the pit of my stomach to drop. She hadn't touched me voluntarily. Then again, why would she? Calling out my name meant she only had fantasies of me touching her. I don't think Angelica would act on such fantasies. She doesn't seem like a woman who would throw herself at a man. Why would she need to? She's fucking funny and gorgeous and outgoing.

And she's giving me a dazzling smile.

So dazzling, my feet shuffle and I tighten my grip, sensing impending failure.

Angelica strengthens her grasp in response.

"Don't," I snap. "Don't let me drag you down."

"You won't," she states again, confident that I wouldn't pull her down. At least not during ice skating.

With strength in her small arms, she tugs me forward again, and I follow her lead, letting her take the reins and guide me. Her hips swish from side to side to keep her own balance steady as my wobbly legs gain confidence. Eventually, she loosens her grip, then removes her hands, holding them only inches above mine.

"You got it, Jude. You're doing it, baby." The coo is sweeter than her echo last night. The term is more endearing, special even. Pride fills her voice.

Like I'm a child, not a man.

The thought tosses off my concentration, and my arms begin to flail. Angelica leans toward me. Too fast. Too close. My feet tangle with hers, and I fall backward, taking her down with me. Landing flat on my back, she tumbles against my chest, and I let out a sharp, "Oof."

"Are you alright?"

With my back on the hard ice, I could snap: *Do I look alright?*

Instead, the weight of her body blanketing mine does strange things to my head, freezing my retort.

"Just . . . give me a minute," I grunt, needing a second to catch my breath.

Angelica tries to move off me, roll to the side perhaps, but my hands are on her hips, and I hold tighter, keeping her in place over me. Our legs are entwined.

Hers. Mine. Hers. Mine.

One, two, three . . . I seek that freckle at the corner of her mouth. Four.

Slowly, I nod. "Okay. I'm . . . good." I'd like to stay here all afternoon despite the solid ice at my back, and the cold suddenly seeping through my jacket, because Angelica is lying on top of me. However, our position is hardly intimate with skaters racing around us and broad daylight glaring down on us.

Angelica slowly presses off my chest and kneels. "You're going to need to frog it."

"Frog it?" I croak as if I am the creature.

"One foot up and one foot out while your hands remain on the ice. Then one hand up and one hand out." She imitates the motions, sticking her butt in the air a second before she stands upright.

I do as she did, no longer caring what I look like. I look like more of a fool lying on the ice. When I'm finally standing, Angelica takes my hand again, this time skating by my side, and slowly, I copy her movements.

Left. Right. Slide. Glide.

Repeat. Repeat. Until I'm moving in rhythm with her. Our timing is slow, patient even.

And I wonder if she'd be patient with me in other ways.

chapter 13

[Angelica]

To my surprise, Jude and I skated for nearly ninety minutes before our legs grew tired, and the cold seeped in despite the heat of exertion. We took a break on wobbly legs and walked faster than our original stroll back to the main resort for lunch.

I was so hungry I ordered a cheeseburger despite knowing it would ruin my appetite for dinner. Jude had shared the evening's menu with me. Beef tenderloin. A true feast.

Our conversation got a little heavy during our walk to the rink, so I stick to more casual topics while we eat lunch. Sports.

Jude loves hockey, despite his personal struggles on the ice. I prefer baseball, but I wouldn't balk at tickets to a professional game on the ice.

We also cover music. Jude likes techno. Club music, as I call it. I'm a country girl despite having lived in a major city my entire life.

We don't really agree on much, but the meal passes with ease . . . until we stand.

"Oh." Jude clutches at his back. "Fuck."

"Are you alright?" With sudden alarm, I rush to his side.

"Yeah, I just feel like I pinched something." He stands taller, wincing as he attempts to stretch.

"You did fall on the ice pretty hard, and I fell on top of you."

"Well, you can fall on me anytime you want." He says it with such a straight face I can't tell if he's deadpanning. His tone is definitely not flirtatious, though.

"Maybe you need a massage." Or a medic. *Me*. I could take a better look at him, but after this morning's activity in the shower, where I was hoping to relieve the sexual tension humming inside me, I don't think placing my hands on Jude is a good idea.

Especially since I'm certain he heard me, even though he's politely ignoring the topic. The last thing he probably wants is a horny woman he caught helping herself to get off with visions of him touching her for real.

Then again, he didn't seem to mind earlier when I kept my arm tucked into his for longer than necessary. And he held my hand most of the time we skated, but that was for his stability.

"I don't think I can get a massage on such short notice." His voice remains tight.

"What about the hot tub?" I suggest before thoughts of Jude in a sporty Speedo come to mind. Something similar to the boxer briefs he so casually wore last night.

"Great idea." He grunts, clutching at his back again. "Am I getting old?" He grimaces. "Those words did not just come out of my mouth. I'm not even forty."

"You aren't even in your prime," I tease. Something tells me when Jude hits his forties, he's still going to be *mighty fine* to look at.

When he places his other hand on my lower back, I lead us from the dining room to our shared hotel room where we quickly change and head to the indoor pool area.

The last thing I want to do is show off my pale skin in the bleak winter. At least I opted for a one-piece for our dip, and I wait until the very last minute before slipping off the robe that covers me.

Jude has already lowered into the small, heated pool and crossed the space to the seat opposite me. The hot tub probably holds up to ten, but I'm grateful it's only Jude and me. His icy eyes fixate on me as I glide into the pool, catching my breath on both the heat of the water and the comfort. Lowering as quickly as I can, I dip down until only my shoulders crest the surface, keeping most of my body hidden beneath the gurgling bubbles.

"Feel good?" Jude's voice drops, deep and almost dirty. Like he knows what I did this morning, although neither of us will bring up the subject. A secret best unspoken. We're already pretending we're dating. We can pretend this morning never happened as well.

"Yeah, it feels nice." I swish my arms along the surface and Jude tips back his head. The rumbling of the water is the only sound between us for several minutes.

"There the love birds are." The older male voice pops our solitude, and I spin, catching a sight I don't think I can scrub from my brain.

Walt, in a speedo.

Quickly, I glance away, catching on Jude's eyes, which are glaring at Walt behind me. As Walt helps himself into the hot tub, he slips in a little too close for my comfort. Surprisingly, Jude rushes across the pool, wraps his arm around my back, and tugs me toward him.

We almost knock heads. "What the . . ."

He drags me across the small pool, returning to his seated position, and spinning me so I sit on his lap.

Thankfully, Walt's wife enters the area, and I'm grateful there will be safety in two couples in the pool, not just me and two men.

I watch as Walt's wife steps into the hot tub, while Walt keeps his eyes on Jude and me.

Jude spreads his legs, and my backside drops between his thighs. His arm remains around my belly, and he dips his head into my neck. He brushes his lips below my ear.

"Don't look at him." He isn't threatening me as much as warning me. Against Walt.

I'd like to say I'm not afraid of the big and bad who thinks he's a wolf, but I don't argue and twist my neck so I can look at Jude better over my shoulder.

"Forgive me," he mutters, before his lips brush against mine. The swipe is nothing more than a whisper. The light dusting of the first snowfall.

Then, Jude releases my waist and slides his hand up my back. With my hair piled on top of my head so it doesn't get wet, he easily cups my nape and brings our mouths together again.

The initial taste is a sip, although a hearty one. Jude draws my lower lip between his and leans away, dragging out the kiss. But then I'm cupping the side of his face, and his mouth opens wider, taking more from me. I tilt my head, deepening the connection.

My body is on fire, and it is not because of the bubbling water around me. My heart races. My clit pulses. I'd give anything to spin and straddle Jude's lap, but at the same time, this kiss is perfection. His fingers squeeze the back of my neck. His other hand is on my thigh beneath the water. My palm is against the stubble on his jaw.

And his mouth . . . *holy Christmas trees*, Jude kisses like he has all day. Like this is all he wants to do for the next hour or two or five.

When he slips his tongue forward, gently tracing along the seam of my lips, like asking permission to enter, I greedily open, meeting him halfway, instantly enjoying the swirl and twirl, like the way chocolate and mint melt together.

Our lips tangle. The kiss deepens.

"Ah-hmm." The throat clearing is like a sharp punctuation on the moment, and quickly Jude and I break apart. My face heats for a new reason.

I was just kissing Jude Ashford in front of his top board member.

With my mouth still tingling, the impression of his on mine lingering, my lips are certain to be swollen and red. When I remove my hand from Jude's face, I'm afraid to meet his eyes. Afraid to see I've had no effect on him when I'm suddenly all twisted up inside.

Instead, I spin in the direction of Walt and his wife, but I don't look at them either. Guilt collides with the rush of arousal. I'm almost as bad as Beau and Belle, making out at the Thanksgiving dinner table.

Only this isn't real. Jude apologized before he even kissed me. Like he knew it wasn't right, but he had to do the wrong.

Still, his arm wraps around my waist again, and he tugs me back, bringing me against his chest again. He surprises me further by pressing his lips to my temple and lingering there while whispering, "Thank you."

My gaze briefly connects with Walt's wife. When I glance away from her, the weight of Walt's attention presses on the other side of my head.

All four of us remain silent for a few minutes, and I'm hyper aware of Jude's fingers tickling up and down my arm underneath the surface of the bubbling water. When he places another kiss on my shoulder, Walt's wife asks me what we did today, as if determined to distract us from another mini-make out session.

I tell her about ice skating.

She tells me how they went shopping.

And all the while Jude's fingers dance up the side of my arm and then back down to the crease of my elbow. He drops an occasional kiss on my shoulder to further rile me.

While small talk volleys across the small pool, my nipples are hard, and my center clenches. My flesh is goose-bumped despite the heat of the water, and the effect of our kiss on Jude is apparent as his thickness is trapped against my backside because I remain seated between this spread thighs. He's long and hard and very erect.

Try as I might to focus on Walt's wife, I fail at recalling her name. Hell, I struggle as well to remember my own. Because Jude continues his tender assault with soft kisses to the side of my neck or another swipe of those fingers down my arm to my wrist to link our hands together. He even brings our collective grip up to his mouth once to delicately scrape his teeth over my knuckles. I watch the entire display with bated breath.

I'm a roaring inferno of rising hormones, and I'm going to strangle Jude the second this couple leaves us alone.

Or kiss him again.

The jury is still out on this one.

One conviction that's firm is the pressure of Walt watching us, and I start to wonder what game Jude is playing with this other couple present.

Eventually, Jude twists my head to give me one more soft kiss, and then he hops out of the hot tub, taking a seat on the thick edge directly behind me. My gaze follows his retreat, and my view is of him in sporty European trunks that outline every detail of his length and girth.

He leans forward one more time, cups my jaw again, and brings his mouth close to mine. "Getting a good look?"

I don't answer. I can't find words. I try to hold Jude's gaze. I really, really try, but my eyes dip, catching another sneaky peek at that solid bulge, angled sideways because that is the only way his dick won't burst out the top of his trunks.

Placing his hands on my shoulders, Jude chuckles and spins me to face the other couple. I still cannot meet their eyes.

Jude massages my shoulders and neck, but the tension coming off me is too great to relieve. His touch is only making matters worse.

"Walt, you probably shouldn't be in the pool too long with your high blood pressure," Jude warns, digging his thumb along my nape. I need to bite the inside of my cheek to prevent moaning.

"And you have a heart condition," Walt counters, glaring over my head at Jude behind me. "A hot tub isn't good for you either."

"My heart is as strong as ever. Plus, I have Angelica to take care of me." He cups the back of my neck and runs his thumb up the side, pausing as if feeling for my pulse, which is rapid.

Just what is he doing to me?

"And you have Sandy to take care of you." At the mention of her name, Walt's wife seems to pop from a daydream, most likely of the man behind me and what he's hardly hiding in his saturated swim briefs. She shakes her head and glances at her husband.

"Oh my. Jude is correct. We need to get out of here, Walty. We've been in here long enough." She lifts her hands, holding her palms toward us. "My fingers are already raisins."

Walt glances at what must be a waterproof watch on his wrist. "We have forty-five minutes before cocktails, Jude," he warns.

"Plenty of time to get things done," Jude counters.

I close my eyes. No doubt this is a sparring match filled with sexual undertones meant to build the impression Jude and I are together. Like *together*.

The thought is a good reminder of what we truly are, and where I really stand, or rather sit, with Jude.

Pretend.

As Walt and his wife exit the pool, I watch him unfortunately *not* assist his wife and she stumbles. I rush forward to assist her, but she finds her footing before my help is necessary. They grab their towels, do a hasty swipe over their wet skin, and cover themselves in robes before exiting the pool area.

When they leave, I spin and shove water at Jude.

"Hey." He laughs, the sound strange as it echoes off the fake boulders around us. He lifts his hand as if that will shield him from the onslaught of water.

"That was so mean," I mutter, sending another wave in his direction.

Jude is fast to react, reentering the hot tub and capturing my wrists, tugging my hands behind my back, which brings my front flush against his. The weight of his dick wedges between us, although it has softened a little bit. However, my nipples could cut glass, and Jude glances down at where my small breasts flatten against his firm pecs.

Slowly, he lifts his head. "Just tell me one thing. How long would it have taken to get you off, if I'd really touched you?"

My mouth falls open.

"Longer or shorter than that narrator this morning?"

"Oh my God, I knew you heard me."

"A little difficult to miss when my name was coming out of your mouth . . . while you were coming."

I close my eyes, wanting to die a million deaths, and willing to let this hot tub drown me. Only I feel Jude lean closer to me, the scruff on his jaw gently brushing against my cheek.

"The next time you want to come with my name on your sweet lips, it better be my hands between those lush thighs and my fingers against that—"

My mouth crashes against his to shut him up. I can't listen to him tell me what he'd do, like a seductive narrator, or I'll be making a mess right here in this pool.

The kiss isn't pretty. Our lips coming together a second time is harsher than our earlier connection. His tongue is an invasion. His mouth pillaging before he abruptly pulls away.

"Like Walt said, we only have forty-five minutes until cocktails, and I definitely need a shower. A cold one." He tilts his head. "Unless you want to join me."

Sweet baby Jesus in a manger. That's a proposition if I've ever heard one, and as much as my body is screaming, *yes, yes, yes*, my heart is saying *ho, ho, hold the phone*.

When I don't answer Jude, he releases my wrists and steps back while blatantly glancing down at my chest. As we're both standing, from the waist up we are exposed to one another, and he can't miss the sharpness of my nipples poking my wet swimsuit.

He bites his lower lip again. The white of his teeth visible as he hums, "That's what I thought."

Then the arrogant man steps around me and exits the pool. I spin and get another full look at his complete package as he proudly stands on the pool's edge.

My body weeps, but my head knows I've done the right thing.

Sometimes, it sucks to be on the good girl list.

chapter 14

[Jude]

As I make it to our room first, I steal into the bathroom and jerk off in the shower in record time.

Although I want to blame the heat of the hot tub for the dizzying sensation that occurred while seated in it, that fucking kiss jacked up my heart rate, forcing me to slip out of the pool behind Angelica.

I didn't need a second heart attack.

And fucking Walt was eyeing her like he does every other new, young woman around Ashford's. He's a damn lawsuit waiting to happen.

He can't have my Angelica. If I had to fuck her in front of him to claim her, I would have, only that would probably excite Walt further. My damn kiss backfired, turning Walt on. Fucker.

My initial intention was to give Angelica a chaste kiss. Keep it innocent, but make a statement.

However, the second my mouth whispered over hers, it wasn't enough. The hint of sugar and spice was elevated by the heat of the pool. Her body wedged between mine. Her eyes saying yes and then echoed by her mouth.

She is everything that would earn me a lifetime of coal in my stocking. And I'd excavate an entire mine myself to kiss her again.

With my heavy dick in my hand, I came in two strokes and hung my head, trying to erase thoughts of the way Walt's eyes were devouring Angelica.

The Clara effect hit again. *Mine*.

When I exit the bathroom wearing only a towel around my waist, Angelica doesn't meet my eyes. She also doesn't look at my body. Instead, she stares at her phone like the screen is more interesting than me, only I notice her thumb isn't scrolling.

Because we don't have much time, and technically I'm the host of the party, I swipe right on thoughts of crawling up the bed and begging her for more.

That fucking kiss.

She wants me. And I want her.

But that's not what this is about. I cannot have one night with her and walk away.

I clear my throat. "Bathroom's free."

She nods, tossing down her phone and slipping off the edge of the bed.

"If you don't need me for anything, I'm going to head out early. Make sure everything is all set." It's a lie. I don't need to check on any nonsense.

Angelica gives me only a quick glance before averting her eyes again. "I can take care of myself."

With that sassy comment, I cannot help myself. I stretch across the bed and pick up her phone, then hold it out toward her.

"You might need this again."

Aggressively snatching her phone from my hand, she shakes her head, then taps her temple. "I have an excellent imagination. And a photographic memory."

She spins for the bathroom, implying she'll be imagining me and what she remembers about how she affected me earlier. I was as hard as the frozen skating pond.

I scrub both hands over my face and fall back on the bed, wincing as my back pinches but chuckling into my palms.

Score Angelica.

She's besting me at my own game.

+ + +

Angelica is late, and I'm prepared to chastise her. Remind her how important this night is to me. How important it is to fool these *fools* into thinking I've changed my ways. Dedicated. Committed. The doting boyfriend.

But when Angelica finally enters the private dining room, irritation exits my head.

Because my girl is fucking gorgeous.

While her dress is stunning on her, I want to see it pooled around her ankles and the rest of her on display because that dress doesn't leave much to the imagination. The curve of her hips. The solid shape of her thighs. The collar that drapes wide over her shoulders, and points like an arrow at the divot between her pert little breasts. Swells that stood at attention earlier with sharp nipples begging me to bite them.

With heavy feet, I approach my late date. My legs take their time to cross the room while my heart races a mile ahead of me. Hell, I'd be running toward her if I didn't think I'd cause a scene. I'd have her back against a wall, and my tongue down her throat in record time.

Instead, I slowly prowl toward her, cataloging every inch of that dress. Velvet and dark green. Her hair is down and wild. She looks like a Celtic princess, and I want to bend a knee before her.

Then I want to lift the skirt of that dress and bury my head between her thighs.

With my fist near my mouth, I stroke over my lower lip with my thumb, like I can still taste our kiss. Her eagerness. Her reciprocation. Her desire.

Once I stand in front of her, my mouth falls open, but I can't conjure a compliment.

Breathtaking isn't a strong enough word.

"Angel," I squeak instead, the sound like a pre-pubescent teen.

"I'm sorry I'm late." She smiles sheepishly. "I got lost."

My brow arches, uncertain how she could have gotten tangled up in this rather straightforward hotel layout, but guilt hits me harder. For the second time, I've left her to find her own way to the party. *My* party. I swear I have better manners than I've exhibited, and I mentally promise to do better.

For now, I'm grateful she's here. She's my date. My fake girlfriend.

With her presence, a strange sense of relief washes over me. Like the warmth of that hot tub earlier, and the weight of her mouth against mine.

I can't describe it. How strange and right, or strangely right, kissing her felt. Like I've been longing all these years for some Christmas present, and I've finally received the gift. It was even better than I expected.

Late. Lost. But finally, here.

Placing my hand on her shoulder, I swipe over the notch of bare skin and then along the velvety material covering her arm.

"You look like . . . a queen," I state, still sounding like a bumbling teenager—tongue-tied, star-struck, horny as fuck.

"Thank you." Her face pinkens, accentuating the freckles I've come to adore.

One, two, three, and that sacred fourth one, that I want to lick and nip before taking her lips with mine again.

Instead, I lean forward and press a kiss there, right at the corner of her mouth where that freckle almost meets her lip. The kiss is a stamp. She belongs to me.

Angelica's breath hitches as I pull away, almost like she expected more from me, but I can contain myself. For a little while.

Slipping her arm into the crook of my elbow, like she did earlier, I lead her around the room, re-introducing her to board members from last night's drinks and other important executive staff who were not present.

"Angelica, I'd like you to meet Maxine Kelsey, my personal assistant." I offer Maxine a tight smile. "Maxine, this is—"

"The EMT who saved you," Maxine cuts me off before I finish my explanation.

"Yes, ma'am," Angelica offers Maxine a warm grin before leaning toward her and whispering, "Although I think his heart might still be a little broken."

Maxine puffs out her lower lip like she agrees, but she's shocked by Angelica's assessment. "Jude? A broken heart? Nothing penetrates that frozen tundra." Maxine offers a teasing laugh. If anyone knows I have an erratic heartbeat, it's her. As my faithful assistant, she's seen the ups and downs of my wrath.

"He's all work, and then equal amounts of pay."

"Pay?" Angelica tips a brow, looking from Maxine to me and back.

"Did I say pay? Slip of the tongue. The only one making a decent wage at Ashford's is this one." She hitches a crooked thumb in my direction like I'm not standing here, listening to my top employee complain about her paycheck.

"I meant play," Maxine corrects. "I'd say he plays as hard as he works, but he hardly works. Sits behind that mammoth desk all day and shuffles papers."

Maxine winks at Angelica, and I assume she's joking.

"I bet he doesn't just push papers," Angelica states. "Sometimes, he probably stacks them. Neatly." She laughs at her own joke. The sound is a riot among the quieter tones of the room.

Maxine smiles deeply at my date before turning to me. "I wouldn't let this one get away," my assistant says, hitching her thumb in Angelica's direction now, like *she* isn't standing there.

Wrapping my arm around Angelica, I tug her into my side and kiss her temple before saying, "I don't intend to."

Maxine's dark eyes open wide and her mouth gapes as someone clutches at my shoulder. The hard squeeze is familiar and annoying.

I turn to face Walt, keeping Angelica tucked into my side. "Walter."

He holds out a hand to shake mine and I reciprocate, but when he leans in for Angelica it takes all my willpower not to push him away from her.

Instead, she takes the lead, extending her hand before his mouth graces her cheek.

"Walter," she repeats the way I said his name. "Merry Christmas." Despite the tight salutation, her rejection is clear. Back off.

I want to kiss her right in front of him again for holding him off.

However, I'm not certain I'm much better than Walt. Angelica and I didn't discuss boundaries or limits. Kissing her earlier wasn't in our unspoken contract. However, I do need her to come across as my girlfriend, which means touching me.

As if reading my mind, she wraps herself around my side and pats my chest. "I could really use a drink, *baby*." Her tone is edgy. "You worked up quite a thirst in me earlier."

Sweet Father Time. What the fuck?

My head swivels in her direction. Our faces are so close I need to pull back to see her better. Her eyes twinkle, playful and mischievous.

I'd like to make her pay for that little dig, but the comment also builds the necessary illusion with Walt.

Hell, for the rest of the evening, Angelica applies just the right layer of appropriate innuendo, making the board fall in love with her. More importantly, they believe that I'm devoted to her.

Eventually, dinner is served, dessert offered, and music begins. Unfortunately, the tunes are ragtag oldies, and only the older people in attendance are dancing. Mainly, the wives. As I'm sucked into another conversation with several members of the board, I watch Angelica talking to Maxine near our table. Her head tips back and she laughs at something Maxine said. Something that is certain to be a jab at me.

Walt approaches the two women.

"Excuse me," I mutter mid-sentence on Martin's chatter about another major department store that has shut its doors.

Setting down my drink on a random table, I near the triangle of Walt, Maxine, and Angelica, just as Walt asks Angelica, "May I have the next dance?"

The old man hasn't even danced with his wife, and he wants to dance with my date? I don't think so.

Extending my hand toward Angelica, I cut off any response. "Actually, Walt, I have the next one." And every other one after that.

As the music shifts from something fast-paced to the deep wail of a diva, Angelica sets her hand in mine, and I silently lead her to the dance floor.

I twirl her around, watching the long hem of her dress flare before I draw her close to me.

"You know, if you peed in a circle around me, it might have made it more obvious. Yellow snow and all." She grimaces.

"Yeah, well, I don't trust Walt." I'd glance over Angelica's head to glare at the old guy, but I don't want to focus on him when I have this beautiful creature in my arms.

Glancing at her, I catch her peering up at me. "This was one of my parents' favorite songs," she says quietly.

I tilt my head, unable to recognize the tune.

"Etta James. "At Last"," Angelica clarifies.

Ah. "My father loved blues and jazz." And because of that, I hated the music. The throaty songs. The raspy tenors. Saxophone. Harmonica. Piano. "He was part of a band when he was young."

Angelica arches a brow. "Anything I've heard of."

I shake my head. "Probably not. Colt45 was their original name. They regrouped after Tucker quit and became The Chrome Teardrops."

Angelica continues to watch me. "Why did he quit?"

I swallow thickly. "My mother was pregnant." Not the entire story, but enough of the truth for right now.

Sensing that's all I'll say, Angelica settles in, and we spin in slow circles to the lyrics about lovers finally found and loneliness being over.

I'm not certain loneliness ever really disappears, but for the past twenty-four hours, I haven't felt the constant brick of emptiness in my gut. I've simply enjoyed my time with Angelica.

Pulling back, our eyes meet, and I stare at the flicker in hers. The warmth and mirth inside them.

I bet she never gets lonely.

"Why didn't you have a date for your brother's wedding?" I'd heard her partner say he'd take her. A woman like Angelica should have men lining up to date her. Hell, she should already have that one man in her life, worshipping her.

She shrugs. "Just haven't found the one. At last." She wrinkles her nose, playing off the song and brushing off my question.

"What about you?" she asks. "You've dated hundreds of women. You could have easily found someone else to pretend with you tonight."

Respectable, I'd told her. I needed someone the board didn't know or recognize, but the situation also called for more. I didn't know what that more was or why I felt she had it, but I didn't think I could pull this off with anyone other than her.

"I didn't want anyone else." Honestly, I didn't. I only wanted one person by my side for this party, and she is in my arms.

Still staring at one another, the song fades and almost instantly another one begins. Angelica steps out of my embrace and starts moving her body in jutting, jerking motions, pausing occasionally at the staggered beat of the new song.

"Oh, God. No."

"Oh, goddess, yes," Angelica smiles, her grin growing three sizes right in front of me while those blue eyes dance.

"Not . . ."

"Yes." Angelica continues moving, smoothing out her motions, while holding her fist in front of her mouth and singing along to a Taylor Swift tune.

Suddenly, I'm a fan, as I watch Angelica spin, tossing her hair over her shoulder, and mouthing the words in my direction. The most prominent of those terms being the song's title, "Lover".

I'm hyperaware of eyes on us. Or rather, on her, making an intriguing spectacle of herself while hammering in that I'm her . . . lover.

With a sharp bark, resembling a laugh, I step closer to her and pull her into me with her back to my front. We sway side to side for the rest of the song.

"Has anyone ever told you you are a temptress?"

"Never," she breathes out, replacing the song title with the singular word.

"Well, I'm telling you. You're delectable."

Angelica spins in my arms. "Chocolate mints are delectable. I am just . . ." She sweeps a hand down her front without realizing she's only emphasizing my point.

She is a chocolate mint, and I want to devour her.

When the song ends, Maxine saunters over to us, waving a sprig of mistletoe in her hand. My assistant looks rather tipsy.

"Oh no," Angelica teases, holding out her hand and waving them at Maxine. "Shoo."

I bite my inner cheek. She's so fucking adorable.

Maxine, however, is wily like me and steps closer to Angelica, holding the mistletoe like she's dangling a treat in front of a pup.

Angelica laughs harder and tucks into me like I'll protect her from a piece of greenery with white berries tied by a red bow.

Instead, I cup Angelica's cheek and tip back her head. Our eyes meet, and Taylor Swift's song echoes through my head about lovers and lights on and saying someone is mine.

Stroking my thumb over her soft skin, I brush over the freckles covered by a dusting of makeup. Then I swipe at the corner of her lip, erasing the cover-up so I can see that freckle that draws my attention over and over again.

“Kiss the girl,” Maxine playfully barks, and while I want to snap this isn’t a Disney fairy tale, there isn’t anything else I want more than to kiss Angelica again.

When our mouths meet, the kiss is soft like the one we initially shared. The one that quickly turned more intense. Not hurried but a slow hunger, like a deep ache in my belly, where I knew I had to savor every sip of her or that ache would grow to a gut-wrenching pain.

I took my time again, plucking at her lower lip and teasing the upper one, eventually dipping my tongue to the corner of her mouth, as if claiming that freckle.

Angelica’s breath hitches, and then she bests me once again, nipping my lower lip. Not hard. Not enough to draw blood, but enough to make an impression. Like everything else about her, she’s getting in my head and underneath my skin, and when I pull back, startled by the claiming bite, our gazes lock again.

Something new is in her eyes. Sweetness and joy, but a little bit of playful mischief, and it hits me hard in the chest—

I don’t deserve her.

Not like this.

I don’t want to pretend with her. Like she demanded last night—*stop acting*. Stop playing a part. Maybe I can do it in front of this crowd, in front of the board, but not with her. Not when it’s us.

Like breaking the surface of a frigid lake, sound rushes around me. The whoops and cheers of our audience brings our position back to me. We’re standing in the middle of a dance floor, encouraged to kiss by a weak collection of leaves and a co-worker.

If I ever even entertained there being an Angelica and me, I’ve blown my chance by asking her to participate in this farce.

Deciding our appearance has been noted long enough, I nod at the faceless crowd around us, slip my arm around Angelica, and lead her wordlessly into the hallway, guiding us back to our room.

I'm done pretending for one night.

chapter 15

[Angelica]

If I thought Jude was going to ravish me after his possessive behavior earlier in the pool and then again throughout the evening's party, I get a cold dose of reality when we enter our room.

He doesn't touch me.

The switch in him is almost mercurial.

With full-on anxiety, I ask him to unzip my dress. Earlier, I had to call the front desk to send someone to help me zip it up, which is the real reason I was late. I didn't want to call Jude and ask him to come back to the room. I was afraid if he did, I might pounce on him.

Him and his damn suggestion that I'd need my phone near the shower again.

He hadn't been wrong, though, and another moment of self-pleasure took the edge off. Twice in less than twelve hours was like a Christmas miracle.

With my back to Jude, I sense his hesitation. The warmth of his breath against my neck as I hold up my hair. The long exhale from his chest. Then thick fingers brush along the expanse of skin exposed above the zipper on the wide-necked dress before he grips the top of the dress with pinched fingers and uses his other hand to lower the zipper.

The lazy drag down my back is like the gentle pull of stage curtains. A slow revelation of pale skin. But if I thought Jude would dance his fingers down my spine, he doesn't. There is no encore to our earlier actions where the dance floor kiss was almost as powerful as the hot tub one.

For a second, I simply stand still, holding up my hair with one hand while clutching the front of my dress with the other, anticipation nearly killing me.

When I turn to face Jude, holding the dress to my chest, I silently beg him to make a move, knowing I can't. I want Jude to be into this as much as me.

For just a moment, those icy eyes are cold. His smile is tight, like he's slipped into character again. I have no doubt a man like Jude can have sex without emotion in the act.

Unfortunately, I cannot, so I drop my gaze.

Almost instantly, Jude's eyes shift. The ice melts away a little bit until he almost looks . . . stricken. Like the last thing he wants to see is me naked, despite flirtatious words and seductive actions.

Reality strikes like the cold rush of falling between cracks in ice. He only kissed me for show. In front of a board member. In the middle of his party.

Embarrassment mixed with a pinch of shame fills me, and my tongue ties when I try to speak.

"I'll just be—"

"It's not that I—" he cuts me off.

"We don't have to—"

"I want to—"

"*But*." I can almost see the word between us, like an iron security gate lowered for protection. Is he protecting his heart? Or mine?

Unrequited desire is the worst. The naughty person list should have a column for it.

But. One simple statement that says so much.

Without another word, I turn for the bathroom, blinking back the sudden sting in my eyes.

I don't know what I was thinking, anyway. I can't get involved with Jude. One night would wreck me. I should be *grateful* he doesn't want me, which is all kinds of wrong to consider.

When I come out of the bathroom, I slip my dress onto a hanger and hang it back in the closet while Jude sneaks into the bathroom. I help myself to the bed and lie back, staring up at the ceiling. Despite feeling tipsy earlier, I'm suddenly stone sober and wide awake . . . with disappointment.

When Jude returns to the bedroom, he stares down at the floor where he slept last night. His pile of folded blankets and a pillow are still on the boudoir chair.

His hand squeezes at his lower back. Whether he's done that for affect or absentmindedly, I don't know, but I sigh heavily.

"When my mother was young . . . too young. She was involved with a married man. He was almost twenty-five years older than her. And he got her pregnant."

I prop up on my elbows to get a better look at Jude, who continues to stare at the floor.

"My dad . . . Tucker . . . the former rock star . . . wasn't the father. *His* father was the man who went after my mom." He finally glances at me, but I'm confused as I process the relationship.

"Tucker was asked by his grandfather, my great-grandfather, to marry my mom, because she was the daughter of a prominent business associate of Ashford's."

Jude is quiet for another second. "If it appears like I pissed a circle around you, as you so eloquently put it, it's because Walt's behavior reminds me of what my father, the sperm donor, did. How I was conceived."

He swallows thickly. Despite his eyes toward me, he doesn't see me. He's lost in his head. Everything in me wants to give that lost boy inside him a huge hug, but I don't move.

Instead, I speak. "I appreciate you looking out for me, but trust me, I'm not interested in married men or older men or men like Walt."

"I'm not certain my mom was interested either."

The quiet admission is a blow to my belly, and I swallow thickly. "I'm so sorry, Jude." What more can I say? There's no excuse for his biological father's behavior or the sadness in Jude's eyes.

"I appreciate you sharing this with me." His honesty is raw, and his voice rough. Like he might not tell many people his secrets.

"For the longest time, I blamed my dad . . . Tucker . . . for my mother being miserable. For her having the affair she later had. But then I learned the truth and I was so . . . angry."

I hear it in his voice, even now.

"I'm not a good guy, Angelica. Not a great man, and I don't want to hurt you."

"You won't," I state, licking my lips, feeling his rejection once again. He's wrong about himself. He's nothing like the man who impregnated his mom.

"I've been born and bred by selfish men." His eyes narrow, and he looks away from me. "Well, Tucker didn't turn out to be selfish, but that's another story."

One I'm certain Jude doesn't want to share tonight as he bends with the intention of lowering to the floor.

"Just sleep in the bed." I can keep my hands to myself as he's certainly going to keep his hands to himself.

Jude halts his movements in that bent-over position and stares at me. Those cold eyes melt a little. The urge to hug him returns, but I recall how stiff Jude was when Sabrina hugged him. Maybe he doesn't like hugs. Or maybe . . . he isn't used to them.

Either way, we don't need to touch. I grab one of the pillows from the pile next to mine and set it between me and the opposite side of the bed.

"Pillow wall. Nothing passes," I state, like when my younger sister and I shared a bed.

Jude hesitates a second as he stands to his full height. His eyes are suddenly wild, like when Sabrina gave him that awkward hug in the hospital, and he didn't know how to respond.

Eventually, he kneels at the end of the bed and crawls up it. The prowl shouldn't look so sexy. The slink of his body. The hug of his boxer briefs. That tattoo on his side.

Dragging my gaze away, I fall to my back again while Jude flips to his before reaching for the lamp and turning off the light. We're plunged into darkness, and silence falls heavily around us, the weight thicker than the pillow between us.

Eventually, he clears his throat. "Thank you for listening. And being here with me."

"Of course." I smile, but the motion feels forced. "That's what a fake girlfriend does."

"Yeah. A fake one," Jude replies, his voice quiet, sleepy almost.

After several long minutes of silence, I assume he is sleeping when he clears his throat. "Can I ask you something?"

"Sure," I whisper to the dark ceiling, before holding my breath.

"Do you think people can change?"

I roll my head on my pillow, struggling to make out Jude's form in the darkness. "Absolutely. Why?"

He doesn't respond at first, then says, "Something strange happened to me. When I had the heart attack."

Stress cardiomyopathy, I want to correct, but I bite back the words.

"I heard something. Felt something."

I roll my lips, holding my breath.

"Like a voice spoke to me." He pauses. "Asking me not to leave her."

"Who?" I whisper, not because I need to know who she is, but to learn if he knows it was me.

"I don't know. I think she was an angel." He chuffs, dismissive but low. "But that's silly, right?"

"Anything is possible, Jude."

He is quiet another minute. But I can almost hear the gears of thought clicking from his side of the bed. Questions churning. Emotions concerning.

"She didn't kiss me, but it almost felt like she did." His voice is so quiet, I'm not certain he intends for me to hear him, but I do.

"Like she was giving her breath to me." The confusion in his voice is evident. Like he's baffled by what he's saying, by what happened to him.

"Like she wanted me to live and brought me back so I could."

I lick my lips before I speak. "Maybe she did want you to live."

His head turns in my direction. "But not as I was. Not like those greedy bastards with old school ideas and a fixation on money."

"Perhaps," I offer.

He shifts once more. With my eyes adjusting to the dark, I see he's on his side, facing me. His hand slips over the pillow and his fingers brush the inside of my elbow.

"The whole idea is a bit ludicrous, though. Scrooge didn't really change after those three ghosts visited him, right?"

"I think he did," I state, recalling how *A Christmas Carol* is all about transformation. In an effort to lighten the moment, I add, "And I thought you didn't watch that stuff."

"Don't you remember it being required reading back at Immaculate Academy?"

I chuckle. "I'm surprised you remember."

Silence fills the room again until Jude's fingers brush along my inner arm. "I'm sorry we weren't friends in high school."

My damn eyes start to burn again, and I blink at the threat of tears. The apology is decades late and not really necessary, but the sincerity in Jude's words is like a needle through my heart. A good needle, stitching up a hole.

"Thank you, Jude. I'm sorry we weren't friends as well." Because Jude could have used a friend back then. A real one. Someone who supported him so he didn't slip on frozen ice.

Or didn't suffer a broken heart.

chapter 16

[Jude]

My alarm goes off at an ungodly hour, and I wake with a start. Disoriented at first, I glance around the dark room while sensing the warm skin beneath my palm. I slept the entire night with my hand tucked around Angelica's arm.

"What time is it?" she mumbles, her voice groggy and rough when she first speaks in the morning. My head makes a mental note of the sound. My dick is already aware of her presence.

I'm a fucking idiot.

Who turns down an offer of sex from the sexiest woman he's ever met? One looking at me with soft, eager eyes, silently begging me to make a move on her.

I might have turned down lesser women because I'm an ass, but turning down Angelica took me to a new stratosphere of asshole-ishness.

She wanted me. I want her.

Still, I didn't act. I couldn't do it. Not with thoughts of Walt, and then my father in my head, lumping us all together as men who take advantage of women. Innocent, beautiful women.

My frozen heart went cold for good reasons last night.

I didn't want to hurt her as I said. But I was too late, noticing the sense of rejection in her eyes. The disappointment she felt was so evident. Better to let her down gently, than to shatter her.

Then I went and told her that fucking angel story. She probably thinks I'm a loon.

"Jude?"

"Yeah?" Her voice suggests she's waiting on an answer about the time. It also breaks into my thoughts, which registers the annoying ring of my alarm.

I quickly shift and stretch for my phone, hitting the off button on the alarm, which illuminates the screen and the time.

"Four-thirty," I answer.

She needs to return to Chicago by eight for her breakfast with Santa commitment. She explained to me how her Gran volunteered her to host the event at her Gran's church, where Angelica isn't a patron or a parent.

"It's fine," she'd said, explaining how she was voluntold more than asked to participate. Something in her voice hinted she wasn't actually fine about her participation, but she'd power through the morning.

Angelica peels herself upright and swings her legs over the side of the bed. As the room is still dark, I can't make out her features other than a hint of her wild hair. She stretches her arms above her head, and I hear her yawn.

She's so uninhibited and refreshing. And I still cannot believe I didn't have sex with her.

What was I thinking?

Then again, I was thinking exactly what I admitted. I didn't want to hurt her. We were becoming friends, if only on a surface level. Still, she was more genuine than any friend I'd had in the past or present, although my current collection is selective and small.

"I only need the bathroom for a few minutes. My bag is mostly packed, so I can be ready in fifteen minutes, if that works? We can grab coffee on the go."

"Yep." I bend my knee upward, hoping to disguise my morning wood, which stands tall and proud, and admonishing about my choices. He considers them poor ones. I consider them smart.

I didn't want to take advantage of our *fake* situation. Especially when sleeping with her might have been a little too real for a pretendship.

Angelica is quiet as we gather our things, circling one another in the hotel room. We grab weak coffee from the front lobby before checking out and hit the road, where Angelica remains equally quiet in the car.

Normally, I don't mind the silence, but I'm coming out of my skin. My thoughts are a blizzard of scenes. A replay of ice skating and hot tubbing. Heated kisses and simple touches. The look on her face when I turned down sex. The fact I told her about my near-death experience.

"Do you think the board believes I'm your girlfriend?" Her question startles me after nearly an hour of silence.

"Absolutely. They loved you."

"But will it help you?" she asks.

"Definitely." My hope was to show the board that I can commit. One woman. One profitable store. I wasn't wayward; I was dedicated. Angelica made it easy, and she made the board members easily believe I had changed.

"You really sold yourself to Ed Marksman and his wife, Catherine. They were eating up that line you gave them about volunteering at the children's hospital. Working with The Giving Tree."

Catherine Marksman was practically drooling with pride when she learned that Angelica volunteered to help collect and distribute toys for hospital-bound children during the holiday season. I'd forgotten that the Marksmans had founded the program because one of their now-adult children had been hospitalized as a child.

"I wasn't trying to sell myself." Her tone rings with disgust while giving me a quick glance. "It wasn't a line."

"Well, they loved it."

But how did I feel about her volunteerism? Her natural instinct to be so good? She was selfless even with her holiday plate full. Her brother's wedding. Her grandmother's shopping. The breakfast with Santa. She puts others above herself.

Even me. She attended this party, giving up two nights, last minute, to be my date. To help me show the board I'm a changed man. But am I changing? Was I turning over that leaf I promised to flip, or was I just twiddling it between my fingers?

Something cold and ugly unfurls inside me. A combination of irritation that she's so good and a twinge of shame that I'm not.

Angelica adjusts in her seat, like she's suddenly uncomfortable in the heated leather passenger seat. She addresses the windshield when she next speaks. "Have you ever volunteered anywhere? Does Ashford's have community service opportunities?"

"Of course, we do." Only, I can't recall a single event off the top of my head. As the minutes tick by while I try to think of one, the sudden chill coming from her side of the car is disorienting. That twinge of shame flares stronger, along with my agitation.

What did it matter if I volunteered anywhere or if Ashford's had community causes?

"You should try it sometime," Angelica says.

I grunt.

"It's rather rewarding. To give, instead of receive. To volunteer, instead of being asked."

"Like you were voluntold by your gran to host this godawful early breakfast?" The words are too harsh, too cutting, but the sting inside me causes me to strike back.

I risk a glance at her when I sense her shifting again. "I'd do anything for my gran."

"Like host an event when you don't have a child or a stake in the church."

"There isn't an endgame here."

"You just mentioned a sense of giving rather than receiving. That sounds endgame to me." My hands tighten on the steering wheel, anger surging.

Angelica is quiet another minute before she pulls out her phone. Staring at the screen, she says, "I've been thinking about something. About what you said last night."

"What did I say?" I snap, knowing I said too much. Told her about my parents, then told her about that stupid angel. "You won't tell anyone about my parents, right?" *Shit*. I should have had her sign an NDA. Then again, I didn't know I'd be opening my mouth and pulling skeletons out of my closet like it's Halloween instead of Christmas.

Her head swivels in my direction again. "Of course not. That was personal and private, and—"

"Between a *fake* girlfriend and boyfriend," I interject, aware of the itchy agitation in my throat.

"I was going to say, between us. You and me." Something about her voice turns my head one more time.

She looks down at her lap, staring at her phone once again, before adding, "It felt like something real."

Silence fills my car, making the already tight space feel even constricting. I don't like the growing tension.

"What did I say?" I snap. "That you've been thinking about?"

"Your question about Scrooge and transformation."

I snort. "What about it?"

"Maybe you don't believe in change because you haven't lived change yet."

"What do you mean?" My brows pinch while I tighten my grasp on the steering wheel once more.

"You don't believe Ebenezer Scrooge transformed after his night with the spirits, but he did. He gave money to a kid to buy the largest goose in the town. He made amends with his nephew, Fred, and recognized Bob Cratchit's worth. And he showed compassion toward Tiny Tim."

I shift uncomfortably in my seat. "Then he ran down the street like a lunatic wishing a Merry Christmas to all, and to all, a good night."

"The first part of your statement was in *It's a Wonderful Life* when George Bailey runs home to his wife because he's had an epiphany about his life. And the second part is from "A Visit From Saint Nicholas" a poem about Christmas Eve."

I chuff, puckering my lips as I glare at her. "You know what I mean. Scrooge probably had a momentary reaction, then slipped back into his old miserly ways."

Angelica stares back at me, but I return my gaze to the dark road in front of us, suddenly not liking the path of this conversation.

"Maybe you need a little practice. Or you might return to your miserly ways." Under her breath, she adds, "Or miserable ones."

"What was that?" I counter, although I heard her as if she spoke directly to me. When she doesn't answer, I add, "And you think volunteering is good practice?"

"It's a start."

Her thumbs start typing on her phone, and my annoyance further grows. Who the fuck could she be talking to this early in the morning?

"What's so important over there?"

"I'm making you a list."

"A list?" I parrot, then mock. "One you need me to check twice?"

She ignores me, lifting her head once a few seconds later and staring out the windshield, before she returns to her aggressive typing. When her fingers stop moving, she stares down at her phone, presumably reading whatever she's written.

"I've made a list of the things Scrooge did immediately after his night with the ghosts." She pauses, while still gazing at her phone, then reads off her interpretation.

Her list is a repeat of what she'd previously mentioned. "I don't need a fucking English Lit lesson."

She smiles, unfazed by my tone. "You need a wake-up call. Here it is." She wiggles her phone in the air. "I'm going to text this to you. Think about ways you can do things like Scrooge did. Then maybe, just maybe, you'll feel like a changed man."

"There's nothing wrong with who I am," I defend.

But wasn't that the crux of things? I'd asked her if she believed people could change, because something happened to me. I feel different, unsettled, anxious for . . . something I can't quite explain to myself, let alone to her. Now, she's turning that confession into an assignment.

Fuck that.

While white-knuckling the steering wheel, a notification pings on my phone, announcing the arrival of her list.

I need coffee before I can tackle this shit. Real coffee. Not the fake stuff. Like a fake girlfriend telling me how to change my reality.

"You're right, Jude. There isn't anything wrong with you. But you . . . the real you . . . is buried somewhere inside you, waiting to be a better you."

I'd told her last night I wasn't a great man. Not even a good man. I didn't see how I could transform into a better one. I wasn't a fucking butterfly.

And I hate that she's turning what I said against me.

"So, what's on the list?" My back teeth snap as my jaw tightens. I don't even know why I ask. I'm going to ignore the list and delete it from my phone. Still, curiosity has me in a chokehold.

"Just read it later." Her voice is too cheerful, like she's really proud of herself for coming up with something special.

There's a list for good boys and girls. A list for the bad ones. And the list of ways to make a change.

I huff again and press my elbow to the edge of my driver's side door, resting my temple against my raised, fisted knuckles because I suddenly have a headache. Coffee is the only solution for this discussion.

Eventually, Angelica dozes with her head against the opposite window, and I'm grateful for the silence.

Don't you leave me, Jude. The voice whispers through my head again.

I sneak a glance at Angelica, wondering if she's playing with me by whispering in her sleep.

Ruling out the absurdity, I think about that voice and remember again the promise I'd made to turn over a new leaf. Flip the page on the old me and start a new chapter. A better one.

"Fuck," I quietly exhale. Maybe she's right. Maybe I do need help.

As we pull up in front of her apartment building, Angelica slowly rouses, glancing out her window before sitting up straighter. She stretches her arms forward and curls her back before looking at me. Those blue eyes remind me of my mother's favorite porcelain coffee set, matching the roundness of the saucers and the brightness of the cups.

God, I feel obsessed with the morning liquid gold right now, and if I only had a cup, I might be able to think straight.

Instead, I struggle for words. "Angelica, I—"

She startles me by quickly shifting in her seat and reaching for my jaw. Her thumb strokes along the bristly layer of hair that has grown thicker overnight. Her palm is warm from being tucked into her coat pocket. Her touch is soothing.

"Jude." She smiles hesitantly. "I'm not a very good liar, and while we might have pulled off a fake relationship with your board, I don't want to lie to my family. I've made a mistake wishing for a date to my brother's wedding."

"What?" I blink, not sure I fully comprehend. This sounds an awful lot like she's breaking up with me, when we aren't even officially together.

"I won't need you as a date for my brother's wedding after all. In fact, I've decided I don't need a date period." She removes her hand from my jaw, and I want to beg her to put it back.

Just give me a minute to think.

"But we had a deal."

She wrinkles her nose. "And deals can be broken, especially fake ones."

"But, I can be there for you." I said that I would, and I plan to follow through.

"But . . . I don't need you to be." She sets a quick kiss on my cheek before popping open her door. A cold blast of crisp winter morning air fills the car as she hops out, and I follow from my side, reaching the trunk as it springs open.

Where is this rejection coming from? Is this because I didn't have sex with her? That can't be the reason. So, what just happened here?

Instead of asking these pertinent questions, I reach for her bag at the same time she does.

"Allow me." It's the least I can do after she just broke things off. I don't know why I'm upset. We aren't breaking up. We weren't anything to one another. She's been a means to an end.

My chest clenches, knowing that isn't true.

What did she say about lying? The other night, she said pretending was like covering the truth.

The truth is, I don't want there to be an end between us. Not yet.

"I got it." She smiles weakly, meeting my eyes only briefly while taking the bag from me and pulling up the handle on the rolling case.

I step to the back passenger door, where her dress is hanging inside.

Angelica shakes her head. "Maybe you could donate it to a good cause. I won't be wearing it again." She sounds sad, almost disappointed, like never wearing the dress again is disheartening.

Or is that disappointment about me?

"Take care of yourself, Jude. You and that precious heart of yours." She smiles again, but her eyes are cloudy. "Live a good life."

I've been living a good life. I've had a great life. Travel and parties. Dinners and dates.

But good isn't what she means. She means live a *better* life.

One that isn't full of extravagance, wealth, and hanger-ons telling me only what I want to hear. She means a better life than the lonely life I've been leading.

But I don't need this shit. *She's* breaking up with me. My fake girlfriend is stomping on my weak heart.

"Yeah. You, too."

I watch as she walks through the small courtyard and disappears through the entry door without a glance back in my direction.

Yeah, fuck this, Angel.

I slam my car door shut, pound my hand on the steering wheel, and tear from the curb with a heavy screech from my tires.

I don't need a better life. I don't want to volunteer or give up my time. I certainly don't wish to donate a thousand-dollar dress to a charity.

When I get home, I toss my bag on the entryway floor and head for the coffee machine. My head is suddenly pounding. My heart races. Caffeine might be the last thing the ticker needs. Maybe I should just start day-drinking. A strong whiskey might calm me down.

Only as I open the fridge, a white bakery bag stares back at me. One that I've been holding onto for a week. Each day since I've returned from the hospital, I've treated myself to one chocolate mint. The truffle-like candy was a secret reward. I'd been alive another day. Plus, eating only one a day prolonged their existence.

Hastily, I reach for the bag, ripping the top of the folded-over sack open to find the bag empty. I'd eaten the last one on Friday before I picked up Angelica and must have absentmindedly returned the bag to the refrigerator after my silent wish to pull off a fake relationship to appease my board members.

A fake relationship with a real woman.

A beautiful woman.

One who visited me in the hospital and brought me chocolates.

One who agreed to a deal but has broken the pact. Selflessly taking nothing in return for being my date. Not even keeping the dress. She could have sold it on one of those repurposed dress sites herself. She could have kept the money.

Angrily, I crumble the bag into a tight, waxy-paper snowball before tossing it toward my trash bin.

I miss the shot.

What the fuck?

Next, I whip my phone out of my pocket. The text notification from her practically glares at me. My thumb hovers over the message before eventually pressing it. Her list fills the screen.

Where can you make a meaningful donation?

How can you gift time?

Who do you need to make amends with?

Who deserves an apology from you?

How can you show compassion for another?

I slam the phone face down on the countertop and brace my hands wide on the edge. Hanging my head, I curse again.

I don't need this.

Then I flip the phone over and read through the list one more time, noticing one important question is missing.

A question I can't quite form yet but have an answer to already.

The one thing Scrooge didn't get in the end . . . the girl.

My eyes close. My chest pinches. I flatten my palm over my left pec, feeling my heart galloping. I catch the time on my watch.

"Fuck it," I shout to the empty room, then snag my keys off the quartz and stomp to the front door, telling myself I'm heading out for coffee.

Screw waiting for the machine.

Back in my car, I ask my phone for a certain church's address, then punch it into my GPS, and fifteen minutes later, I'm parked on a side street in a northside neighborhood, without having gotten any coffee.

chapter 17

[Angelica]

To cry over a fake relationship breakup would be ridiculous, so I bolster my inner strength, allowing only a brief wallow for the loss of what could have been.

The hope that Jude was different.

The wish that his kisses meant something.

The desire to be his friend.

Letting out a deep breath, I tamp down my disappointment. I've been disappointed before, so I recognize the sensation, but Jude doesn't warrant the sluggish energy.

I'd done the right thing. Among all the other reasons I could list for Jude and me not being compatible, top of the list is that I wouldn't be able to explain him to my family. How could I be attracted to a man so clearly self-absorbed he didn't give of his time or offer apologies. My family just wouldn't believe I'd be interested in him.

And like I told Jude, I didn't want to lie to the most important people in my life.

Physically, I was drawn to him. He even had rare moments of playfulness and humor that also endeared him to me.

But one laugh and one afternoon do not turn a lie into a truth.

The truth is *I* could fall for Jude. His sad soul spoke to mine, but I was also smart. He wouldn't be good for me, and I was trying to live my best life.

Even if it was lonely.

On that note, I check my phone as I gather my things for breakfast with Santa.

I'd gotten a few texts yesterday and quickly tackled them before powering down my phone for the evening to focus on Jude's party.

How many red tablecloths do we need again?

Erin Cumbers can no longer volunteer.

Is Nick Santos confirmed as Santa? Want to share his number with me so I can double-check?

I chuckled at the last one. Some women are ruthless in their pursuits, even though Nick Santos is a happily married man. He plays our Santa each year because he does such a convincing job in the role, but the moms among the parent volunteers know he's a local fireman.

Mix fireman with naughty Santa fetish, and, well . . .

Thank goodness, his wife, Holliday, is good-natured about the lust for her husband.

She once told a woman *her* chimney is the only one Nick goes down on, and I might have laughed a little too hard at Holliday putting that aggressive cougar in her place.

When Holliday is the first person I see upon arriving at the church community room, I'm relieved. I need a second to get my head into the spirit. The spirit of hosting two hundred families with eager children hungry to see Santa.

The lovely blonde gives me a concerned look. "Girl, you do not look well."

"I'm fine," I lie, waving my hand to dismiss her concern. I will be fine. This morning's activity is the distraction I need to wipe away the question in Jude's eyes. Did he really not see our incompatibility? Plus, Jude needs to work on himself, and I am not a life coach.

Seriously, what was I thinking by making a list of self-improvement questions based on a classic Christmas tale about transformation and giving it to him like an assignment?

Beauty and the Beast might have been a better study of change. However, neither reference matters. Jude didn't *need* me anymore. My part in his act was complete. He should be relieved. He's off the hook and doesn't need to attend a stupid wedding days before Christmas.

I inhale to calm my racing thoughts.

"Well, put me to work," Holliday says, continuing to give me a puzzled look, like her mom-senses know something isn't right, but as my friend, she won't pry.

"Follow me to the kitchen?"

Holliday has already put in time volunteering when her children were younger. Now, she's present more to keep the cougar-moms in line around her husband, but she'll be happy to have something to do. Nick is a good sport about the extra attention. Holliday is a freakin' saint.

Once inside the industrial-sized kitchen, I check my iPad for the list of things to be done. The community center is already set up with tables and chairs, and a crew of people arrived last night to decorate the tables with disposable tablecloths and plastic wear.

This morning, mini donuts will be placed on each table along with a carafe of coffee and a pitcher of juice. For now, coffee is brewing, hot water is boiling for tea, and containers of juice and cartons of milk are ready for distribution. Making scrambled eggs and sausage will be up soon, and I glance toward the commercial-grade stove where a volunteer dad leads a team of other men who will assembly-line cook the protein portion of breakfast.

While glancing at the group of men, the kitchen door swings open.

A man walks in looking a little lost and I'm frozen in place as I take him in. Like viewing an animal outside its natural habitat, he looks confused, almost frightened. His hair is mussed up. His dark jeans, thin sweater in dark gray, and the hint of a white tee peeking out of the collar sets him apart from the other men in the space.

"Who is that?" Holliday whispers beside me.

"Jude." My voice cracks and I clear my throat, trying his name a second time, a little louder. "Jude Ashford."

Holliday is looking at me, but I cannot pull my gaze from Jude. How uncomfortable he looks. How good-looking he is.

As if he heard me state his name, his head turns in my direction, and his eyes catch on mine. He offers a puzzled smirk, like he's been caught where he shouldn't be. Then he rounds the stainless steel worktable and stalks toward me.

"Oh my," Holliday whispers, her head swiveling from Jude to me and back.

When he finally stands in front of me, I'm tongue-tied by his sudden, unexpected presence. We stare at one another, as if an entire conversation is happening with our eyes, but I can't interpret a single word because I'm flabbergasted by him standing here. In the kitchen of a church community room.

Eventually, Holliday softly clears her throat and sticks out her hand. "Hi. I'm Holliday Santos."

"Jude Ashford," he says, reciprocating her greeting, snapping his attention briefly from me to her.

"What are you doing here?" I ask.

"I'm just going to . . . yeah . . ." Holliday points with both her hands and steps away from Jude and me.

"Thought maybe I could give of my time." He slips his hands into his pockets and glances around the kitchen.

"Jude." I sigh, certain I've insulted him. Or maybe . . . I've inspired him.

Jude tips up his chin and shrugs. "I've got to start somewhere." His voice is quiet while his icy eyes meet mine again. "Tell me what to do."

The plea holds a double meaning, but I don't want to psychoanalyze him again. Maybe I'd been too harsh earlier. Then again, he's standing here.

Technically, he shouldn't be. We have screenings for our volunteers, and he isn't a parent, nor a member of this church, but I'm not about to turn Jude away when I'd accused him of never giving of his time.

"Okay. Cooking or dishes?"

"Cooking, I guess." He glances at the loosely formed assembly line of men. Some are mixing eggs in a bowl before passing them to another who pours the mixture onto the sizzling griddle, while other men open packages of sausage and place them on cooking sheets.

I walk Jude over to the lead dad and introduce them, explaining how Jude is an extra set of hands. When I make to step away, Jude stops me by saying, "Where are you going?"

"I have other areas to supervise. This kitchen is in capable hands." I wink at the dad, then excuse myself.

Stepping into the short hallway that leads to the community room, Holliday nearly knocks me over.

"Holy peppermint sticks! Who is that?" Her voice lowers on the question as if someone might hear us when we are the only two standing in the short hall.

"His name is Jude," I remind her. "We . . . we went to high school together."

"And you recently reunited?" Holliday arches a brow.

"Something like that." I sheepishly glance away.

"Something *more* than that," Holliday chuckles.

"Not more," I argue, holding my head a little higher.

"Girl, the way his eyes latched onto you, I could feel the burn standing beside you."

"I know his eyes are a bit icy, but—"

"Icy?" Holliday interjects. "They were fire. Pure flames. And he wants to heat your chimney."

My face heats to inferno level. "He does not."

"He certainly does."

"Who does what?" The deep masculine voice behind me turns my head, and I'm met with the dark eyes of our resident Santa, Nick.

"Angelica has an admirer," Holliday explains to her hot husband.

"Admirer?" I counter. "What is this? 1940?"

"Nope. 2025, and that man wants to eat you alive."

Nick snorts at his wife's brazen comment before wrapping his arm around her shoulder and pressing a kiss to her temple. "Behave."

She wraps her arm around his back and pats his chest. "We need Miss Angelica to misbehave a little bit. With him." She hitches her thumb toward the kitchen.

Suddenly, a loud clanging comes from the enclosed area and a muffled shout. All three of us race for the swing door, entering the kitchen with haste, where we find a bowl of cracked eggs dripping off the worktable and onto the floor. Jude is holding up his hand, blood dripping from his palm.

"Get him away from the food," I demand, dropping my iPad on the nearest counter as I rush toward Jude and pull him toward a sink. I instantly hit the cold water, adding in the hot, and checking the temp before forcing Jude's hand beneath the faucet.

"What happened?" I ask softly.

"Stupid." Jude shakes his head. "I was using a knife to slice open a package of sausage and cut my hand. Overreacting, I hit the nearest bowl with my elbow and sent the eggs flying."

Jude glances over his shoulder, noticing the crew of people working to clean up the mess and disinfect the worktable.

"Fuck," Jude mutters as he turns his head back toward the sink and closes his eyes. "I made a damn mess of things."

I focus on rinsing his palm and inspecting the cut when I say, "As long as you are okay."

"But you're mad."

"I'm not mad." I lift my head, meeting his eyes. What is there to be mad about?

"Disappointed."

"Disappointed?" I question next, tilting my head.

"You know, like spilt milk. I spilled the eggs." His eyes are focused on mine, as if trying to read me, searching for something.

I shrug. "I mean, it sucks that the eggs are a lost cause, but your hand is more important." I glance back at his palm, noticing the cut runs clean. Industrial-grade brown paper towels aren't soft, or particularly absorbent, but will have to do until I can find the first aid kit. With a wad in my hand, I press it into Jude's palm.

"Hold this." I force his fingers to fist around the clump of paper towels.

Thankfully, the kit appears on the counter beside the sink, and I glance up, giving Holliday a grateful look. "Thank you."

She nods and steps back, and I inspect the kit for antiseptic ointment and a large bandage.

"I'm useless," Jude whispers.

My head snaps upright at the downtrodden tone. "Don't say that."

"But I ruined it."

"You ruined nothing, Jude. They're eggs. We have more."

"I'll pay for them."

"No need." I try to reassure him, wondering where this sudden vulnerability is coming from. This man exudes confidence, so there is no reason to be upset about a dozen eggs.

"Angelica," he states, eyes locking on mine.

"Jude." I exhale. "What's really going on here?"

I reach for his palm and remove the wad of paper towels. Instantly, his hand bleeds again, but I don't think he needs stitches. I dab at the wound with fresh paper towels and apply a healthy layer of antiseptic ointment.

"When I was a kid, my mother would go ballistic if I spilled something. Milk at the table. Dropped a cookie on the floor. Anything that soiled the counter or carpet." Jude shakes his head, watching me work on his palm. "And I've spent years in therapy discussing the aftereffects. How accidents happen, especially child ones, but I can still remember how mad she'd get. Angry. Disappointed. Because I wasn't perfect. I was useless."

Useless in his mother's social media portrayal of a perfect family.

"That's awful, Jude." Not that I want to speak ill of the dead but it's a terrible thing to make a child feel incompetent over spilled milk. Not to mention, Jude still carries these triggers as an adult.

"And this . . ." I point at his palm. "Was an accident. Which happened because you were trying to be useful."

I reach for a large bandage and place it over the cut.

"But now I'm of no use in this kitchen."

"I'll find you another job." I smooth over the bandage, then place my hand on top of his. "And I'm thankful that you're here."

Jude scoffs.

With his hand still beneath mine, I squeeze. "I don't want any of that."

"What?"

With his gaze lowered to where my hand covers his, I reach for his chin, lifting his face back toward me. We all have vulnerabilities but somehow seeing them on such a confident man softens my heart toward him. I imagine the courage it must have taken to come here. To step out of his pristine palace and his comfort zone, and give up whatever he had planned for a Sunday morning in December.

"Why are you really here, Jude?" If helping out a small church community breakfast is his answer, so be it, but Holliday's words ring through my ears like the toll of church bells.

He wants to eat you alive.

Could that be true? Is Jude here for me?

"I wanted to help." His icy eyes hold firmly on mine, but I drop my gaze, realizing we are still holding hands.

Gently tugging my hand free, I say, "Right. Okay. Let's get you something to do outside the kitchen, then."

I'm still happy he's present, but my chest aches for the sad child inside him who was made to feel like accidents were casualties.

And a part of me wishes Jude was here for me.

+++

"You have a boyfriend?" My sister corners me before I reach the hallway leading to the kitchen while my arms are full of a tray of coffee mugs.

"What?"

Christmas has red hair like me, but she colors it to a vibrant scarlet shade, which matches the signature color of the holiday season and adds to the mystique of her name. She's attending breakfast with her three boys.

"That holiday hottie is telling everyone he's your boyfriend." She points.

"Gran taught us it's not polite to point," I scold her while still turning toward the community room and following the direction of my sister's finger, which is aimed at Jude, who is pouring coffee and smiling broadly at a seated mom surrounded by three kids. One hanging off her shoulder, one on her lap, and one seated beside her.

He glances in our direction as if he can sense he's being watched. Quickly, I look at my sister. Her blue eyes are wide. Her smile is deep, but hesitant.

"When did this happen?"

"Nothing's happened." I don't have time to give my sister details, like I normally would, because one kiss and a weekend away does not make Jude Ashford my boyfriend. *He* was only pretending for the sake of his board members.

I spin for the kitchen, but Christmas does not let up. She follows me. Her boys are seated at a table with a single-mom friend of hers.

"Angelica," she groans, as I rush into the kitchen and set the tray of mugs near the dishwasher.

"Chrissy," I counter as she hates her full name, especially at this time of year.

"Why would he say he's your boyfriend if he's not?" She stops right beside me. Her hands work faster than I can speak, and I watch as my younger sister takes over, lifting mugs, rinsing them, and then setting them in the dishwasher.

"What are you doing?" I chuckle.

Christmas glances down at her hands like she hadn't even noticed that she'd taken over filling the dishwasher. "I don't even know most days." She sounds weary, and I want to ask if this is about her husband, but she holds up a hand.

"But we're talking about you."

"But . . . we don't need to talk about me," I argue, gently pushing her out of the way and taking control of the coffee mugs.

"Let's start with how hot he is," she continues as if I didn't just suggest the topic should be closed. "Where did you meet him?"

"Not answering," I say, forcing the hot water pressure to high as if that will drown out my sister's questions.

"And how is he so good-looking? He must have a ridiculous moisturizing regimen."

"It's called Neutrogena."

Both Christmas and I shift, glancing at the man standing close behind us.

"Over the counter. Any pharmacy or Target sells it."

Something tells me Jude doesn't shop in a Target or use the famous facial cleanser, but still, he's humoring my sister, who is almost simpering beside me. Dreamy best describes her wide eyes.

"Stop that," I snap, and Christmas turns her attention toward me.

"What? I'm allowed to look."

"Not at your sister's boyfriend," Jude defends, and I swear I could kiss him. Not that my sister has ever stolen my boyfriend, or lusted after the rare ones I've had, but the way Jude refuses to let my sister ogle him, like he really belongs to me, has my pulse racing.

Feeling chastised, Christmas holds her head higher. "You're right. I'm Christmas, by the way. Angelica's sister." She extends her hand, and Jude glances at me first before shaking hers, like he wants my permission to touch her, which is all kinds of strange and a little bit hot.

Then I remember the single mom in the community room and Jude's smile at her.

I turn away while Jude introduces himself to my sister.

"I guess I'll be seeing more of you," Christmas says it like she'd love to see more of Jude's body, but I know she doesn't mean it that way. Not after Jude just put her in her place. She's acting so weird.

When she steps away, I apologize. "Sorry about that. That was just . . . not like her."

"So that was your sister," he states, like he's checking off a list. "Next comes Dane and then Beau, the brother getting married."

Nope, not happening. "I've let you off the hook. Be happy. Take the win."

His brows severely pinch. "By forfeit, and I'm not letting you quit."

"Deals can be broken. Let's just say coming here today makes up for whatever guilt you are feeling. Consider us even."

"This isn't a date, Angel." Jude steps closer to me, swiping back a strand of hair that's come loose from my ponytail. "And our deal was a date for a date."

Actually, our deal turned into a two-night stay for two dates, but po-tay-to, pa-tah-to.

“Well, whatever this *was*, we can be done.”

Jude lets his finger glide down the side of my neck, watching the trail he makes. My body trembles beneath the tender touch.

“I don’t want to be done,” he quietly says. “And whatever this is . . .” He pauses to glance at my eyes. “Is me trying to make a better impression on you than the one you have.”

My breath hitches, and my gaze drops to his mouth. A mug slips from my hand into the stainless-steel sink, bouncing against the side.

Jude chuckles. “Back to work, little elf.” The fingers along my neck drift over my shoulder before he spins for a fresh coffee carafe and heads for the five-gallon percolator to refill the container.

With a wink in my direction, he exits the kitchen, leaving me stupefied.

Why would Jude Ashford want to impress me?

chapter 18

[Angelica]

After breakfast with Santa, Jude quietly excuses himself while I'm in the middle of a final inspection of the kitchen. He stayed to help the cleanup crew pick up and dispose of trash, and he folded tables and chairs, assisting in collecting both items and returning them to the storage closet.

Three days have passed since then, and I haven't heard from him. Deep down, I'd hoped I might, but logic told me I wouldn't.

I picked up an extra shift on Monday, then worked my regular two days, and went to the bar with Maddix afterward. I hadn't been feeling great, so I told Maddix one drink was my limit. O'Malley's is our regular stop and the location of last week's A Snowball's Chance fundraiser.

Sitting beside me at the bar, Maddix says, "I can't believe you missed the fundraiser."

"I told you, I wasn't feeling well." The lie was the excuse I used because I didn't want the guys knowing I'd agreed to go on a date with a previous patient. Even if it was a fake date.

Karma seems to be catching up with me, though, as my throat is itchy and my face has that tingly the-flu-is-coming-for-you sensation. Even with a flu shot, I get a severe cold at least once a year.

Tis the season.

Still, I'm able to swallow down a beer I probably shouldn't be drinking.

"Ever get a date for Beau's wedding?" Maddix teases while I stare mindlessly up at the television behind the bar playing a holiday movie on mute with subtitles.

"Yeah, but it isn't going to work out."

"What? You haven't even gone out with the guy," Maddix prods.

"And I shouldn't." I squint, swallowing down the lie, because I have already gone out with Jude, so to speak. We had a rather incredible two nights when I think back on the time. Our fake relationship felt real in rare moments. That kiss certainly felt real. But his silence means he's accepted our broken deal. I'll probably never see Jude Ashford again.

For some silly reason, my eyes blur while reading the subtitles on the television screen, and I rapidly blink back the threat of tears. I'd never be able to explain them to my partner.

Maddix is quiet beside me a second before he says, "I'm still available to go with you."

"Nah." I sigh, lifting my beer for a sip, before turning toward Maddix and offering a weak smile. "I can handle Aunt Gertie and Gran on my own."

Any one of the guys would have stood up as my stand-in, but my family would have seen through their attendance. Friends. And that failure would be added to my list of lacking accomplishments. I couldn't even find a date for a family wedding, other than a pity date with a friend.

I'll just tackle their disappointment. How so-and-so is a doctor. And Sally Lou Whoever is a nurse. How I am reckless, racing around in ambulances, rushing into situations that might be dangerous. Emergency medicine isn't for the faint of heart.

However, my job isn't always a battlefield. It can be filled with sweet elderly people in need, innocent accidents, and the occasional asshole retailer.

Only, he wasn't an asshole. Not really.

"Hey, Angelica. Thanks for the donation." Zebb Scroggs's kind voice has me turning on my stool and facing the former football player-turned-firefighter. "Didn't know you made that kind of money driving ambulances. I'm definitely in the wrong division in the department."

He's teasing because he has more money than anyone in our respective departments. His warm smile confirms the jest, but I'm confused.

"What donation?"

"The one for A Snowball's Chance." His dark brows pinch, his eyes questioning me a second.

"Oh, yeah. Sure." I pledged a hundred bucks, which isn't chump change, but doesn't warrant the grateful enthusiasm coming from Zebb.

"How much did she give?" Maddix asks.

"Dude," I grunt, lifting my beer for another sip. *None of your business.*

"Half a million dollars."

Because my glass has just reached my lips, I exhale sharply, then inhale too deeply. The first action causes me to spit across the bar, like a loose fire hose, spraying beer everywhere. The other causes me to choke on a nearly nonexistent swallow.

"What?" I spin toward Zebb, slamming my beer mug down and swiping the back of my hand over my mouth like I haven't been bred with manners.

Zebb leans his six-three form a little closer to me. "Know anyone with that kind of money?"

I lower my head, averting my gaze. Only one person, but it couldn't have been him, could it? He wouldn't have.

"I know a guy," Zebb continues. "Real dick. Used to be my wife's boss."

My head snaps upward. Zebb's wife, Eva, worked at Ashford's a while ago. A long while ago.

"Didn't she work for Ashford's?" Maddix interjects, like he's read my mind.

I don't look at him.

Zebb continues. "After she helped raise their sales for eight consecutive years, he accused her of shorting a cash drawer, essentially stealing from the company."

Slowly, my head bounces, like a Santa bobblehead springing forward and back. Sounds like the man *I* know.

When I finally look directly at Zebb, his dark eyes lock on mine. "I don't want to see you get hurt, so be careful around him."

"Nothing to worry about," I admit, straightening my back and letting out a long sigh. "He's already gone from my life."

Haven't heard from him since Sunday morning; don't expect to hear from him again.

"Are we talking about that Jude Ashford guy?" Maddix grunts. "We got a call on him about . . ."

I risk a glance at my partner, whose eyes suddenly narrow, putting two and two together.

"I didn't know he was *in* your life."

I swipe my hands like brushing cookie crumbs off them, signifying how I'm done with Jude. And done with this conversation. Only, sourness fills my belly like I've eaten too much raw dough.

Jude's donation was generous, but what does it mean? When did he do it? And why?

I spin back for my beer, apologizing to Sullivan, the bartender, for making a mess. Lifting my glass, I take one whiff of the pale ale and decide I'm not thirsty after all. My throat is really scratchy.

Along with my heart.

+++

While I'd had full intention of storming into Ashford's and demanding what the hell Jude thought he was doing, I decided a donation was a donation, and Zebb's foundation could use the money.

Also, I was officially sick. Fever. Chills. Headache. Stuffy nose. Sore throat. And as much as I didn't think Jude would be sick, I still felt obligated to inform him of my plight. The flu was no joke. Other viral diseases were even worse.

Sometime in the middle of the night, I sent him what I considered an obligatory text.

Hey. Just wanted to let you know I'm sick. I hope I didn't pass anything on to you.

I hit send before re-reading the text that sounds like I'm warning him about an STD, and I'd love to delete the message, but I'm too tired to care.

Instead, I power through a second message.

Thanks for the generous donation to A Snowball's Chance. The foundation will put it to good use.

I click off my phone, snuggle deeper into my bed, and fall back asleep until the hammering in my head becomes too much.

"Holy snowballs," I whimper as I clutch at my skull and curse the rattling at the front door, which happens to match the thumping in my head. As my family members all have a key to my place, I'm assuming the urgency is from a misplaced delivery person.

Sometimes a food service pops into the building and knocks on the wrong apartment.

When the *thump-thump-thump* continues, I peel myself out of bed, wrap the duvet around me, and shuffle to the front door.

"No one's home," I attempt to holler, though the sound is closer to a bark.

"Angel?" A pause. "Angelica, open up."

Not by the hair of my chinny-chin-chin, but then the voice registers.

Jude?

Slowly, I step forward, twist the deadbolt, unlatch a second upper lock and turn the knob. I'd say he's a sight for sore eyes, but my eyelids are heavy. The walk to the door took all my energy. I don't even ask why he's here, I just turn for my living room, stumble to the couch, and collapse onto the three cushions.

"Holy shit. What's wrong with you?"

"Hi, Jude. Great to see you again. Thanks for the donation. Get out." Only the words all sort of roll together, and I'm not even certain any of them came out of my mouth.

He doesn't respond, but after a minute his cold hand covers my forehead, and I snuggle into the touch despite a shiver that runs down my spine.

"Hmm. That feels nice," I purr.

"You're burning up."

"Yep. I'm hot." I attempt to smile, giggling at my own joke. I'm a hot *mess*. I haven't showered and a funky smell is coming off me.

Wait. *What day is it?*

"Friday," Jude answers, because I guess I asked out loud.

"Friday," I whisper, like it's the greatest day of the week, but I work odd hours, so I don't really have weekends. More like midweeks. Sometimes Mondays.

And it's been twenty-four hours since I've messaged Jude.

"How did this happen?" he asks as if people schedule getting sick.

"You know the old adage, don't go out in the cold with wet hair. Mine might have been damp this past weekend." When I'd taken a shower and then we went for a walk. Then, we stayed outside in the cold, ice skating. However, that isn't exactly how one catches the common cold or the flu.

Jude is quiet a second before his cool hand comes to my head again. "We need to cool you down."

Suddenly, I'm up in the air, pressed into Jude's chest. He sniffs. "And you kind of stink."

"You stink, too," I argue. "Like something expensive. And sexy." I smile to myself, digging my nose into his shirt.

Wait. Jude isn't wearing a suit. Maybe *he's* not feeling well. Maybe I'm delirious. Maybe this is all a dream. With my eyes closed, I hum again, hoping the dream doesn't end. I'm in Jude's arms. He's taking care of me. He cares *about* me.

The next thing I know, Jude is helping me sit up on the edge of my bed and he's removing the blanket around me.

"If you wanted to get me naked, you lost your chance," I grumble.

"I wanted to see you naked, but I didn't want to lose a chance at something more with you."

Something more? Like what? If I ask this out loud, Jude doesn't answer.

"I'm gonna help you get undressed, but I promise not to look."

"Yep. Don't look. I wouldn't want to tempt you." I laugh. No, I think I cackle. "Don't want you to fall in love with me."

Jude snorts. "I don't know what love is."

That's so sad. Jude is so sad.

He grunts.

Oops. *Did that slip out of my mouth?*

Jude removes the sweatshirt I'm wearing and then reaches for the waistband of my pajama pants. I fall back on the bed, instantly closing my eyes as he tugs the flannel pants down my legs. Braless and in day-old panties, I can't look at him, and he doesn't appear to look at me.

He exits my room for the adjoining bathroom, where I hear water fill the tub.

When Jude returns, he takes my hands, pulling me upright, and then I'm in his arms again, floating through the air while tethered to him before he sets me on my feet beside the tub. He turns me to face the tiled enclosure.

"Slip off your panties."

As I do so, I sense Jude stepping backward but keeping his hand at my waist, so I don't faceplant into the porcelain edge. When I stand upright, I fling my underwear over my shoulder at him. He chuckles and holds out a hand, guiding me to lower into the tub with my back to him, but eventually, I twist and dissolve into the warm water and mounds of bubbles.

I close my eyes and sense Jude kneeling beside the tub. He reaches for the pile of hair on top of my head and finger-combs the greasy tangles.

"You don't need to—"

"Slip lower," Jude orders, his voice low, tight even, like he's holding something back. But I'm too tired to read him. "Get your hair wet."

I do as he asks, dipping deeper into the warm water and dousing my hair. When I scoot back upright, I keep my eyes closed and hear the pop of my shampoo bottle being opened.

"What are you doing?" I mumble, flipping open only one eye to spy on him.

He doesn't answer. Instead, he simply lathers up his hands and starts massaging my head.

Holy Santa. He's washing my hair.

I could argue that my hair is too gross to touch, but the tender pressure of his fingertips against my scalp keeps my mouth shut and my eyes closed. Jude really takes his time, scrubbing gently near my temples and stroking up and down near my nape. When he's finished, I dunk again to rinse the suds.

When I glance at Jude, he's watching my face, his eyes roving over my cheeks. He inhales. Exhales. Then his gaze drops to my lips.

Kissing him is the last thing on my mind, so I close my eyes once more and sink into the warm water.

Jude takes a seat on the closed toilet lid until I'm sweaty and spent.

"I need to get out," I whisper.

"I've got you." He holds up an outstretched towel, keeping his head turned as I stand, then he blindly wraps it around me. Covered by only the towel, he picks me up again and carries me back to my bed. He slips a clean T-shirt over my head while I wiggle out of the damp terrycloth. I collapse back into fresh sheets.

When did he do this?

"You rest. I'll make you some soup."

"Do you even know how to make soup?" I tease, turning away from him and curling into myself.

"I can read a label."

I scoff, but smile, hugging the covers to my chest. Before Jude leaves my room, he takes the broad-toothed comb I use for my curls and gently combs through the fresh tangle of them.

I drift back to sleep, deciding this is a really nice dream.

Jude Ashford might be a decent guy after all.

chapter 19

[Jude]

Angelica is sick, and I am fucking scared. I've never taken care of anyone in my life, except myself, so I do what I always do when I don't know what to do.

"Hi, Jude."

"Julia." I breathe a sigh of relief after hearing my younger sister's voice. The quiet redhead who turned into a spunky wife and mother of three is my answer for anything I don't know.

"How are you in trouble now?" she laughs.

"Why would you think I'm in trouble?" I grouse.

"Because it's mid-morning on a Friday and you'd never call me this early without it meaning trouble," she teases.

"I'm not in trouble." Not exactly. "But I am with a sick friend, and I've tried everything I know to help her. Warm bath. Soup. Rest."

Silence fills the phone.

"Julia?"

"I'm sorry. I'm just trying to unpack that sentence. Friend. Sick. You help. *Her*." Julia's voice shifts. "How is Sabrina?"

My sister has met my previous on-again, off-again friend-with-benefits, and she does not approve, although she'd never outright say that. Her tone when referencing Sabrina implies her opinion, although Julia is the least opinionated person I've ever known.

"It's not Sabrina." I scrub my hand down my face as I stand in Angelica's living room, looking into the gloomy courtyard of her apartment complex. I should have taken her to my place, but I was afraid to move her. She's hardly moved other than flipping from one side of the bed to the other and sitting up for only a few sips of soup and half a piece of toast.

"Oh." Pause. "*Oh*."

"Don't *oh* me right now," I snap. "I need to know what to do."

Silence fills the phone again, but I can practically hear the smile in my sister's voice when she eventually says, "This is new."

"Yes. It's new."

"No, I mean, that tremor in your voice. You must really care about this one."

"Her name is Angelica."

"Angelica," Julia whispers, like she worships the name.

"Don't say it like that."

"I'm only repeating you. It's beautiful."

"She's beautiful," I grunt, swiping over my hair and cupping the back of my neck.

"Oh, Jude." The sigh in my sister's voice is too much. It's almost as if she's proud of me for some reason.

"Look, are you going to help me or not?"

She laughs outright at my distress. "Okay. Here's what to do."

I quickly make a list, finding I've already done most of what she tells me.

"Monitor her fever, and if she still has it tomorrow, I'd take her to an urgent care."

Urgent care? That sounds serious.

"Does Dad know about Angelica?"

"Of course not." Once again, my tone is too harsh. Julia isn't the issue. My racing heart is. I want to take care of Angelica. I want her to feel better. And then, we need to talk.

As the quiet lingers between Julia and me, I swallow down my pride and ask a question that's been on my mind.

"Do you think it's too late for Tucker and me to have a relationship?" I'd taken to calling our dad Tucker once I learned about the convoluted relationship we have.

"No, Jude. I don't think it's too late." Again, a smile fills her voice. This one sounds motherly, which is ironic considering she's younger than me. But Julia has always been my rock. I never faulted her for being the true child of our parents. My once-shy and innocent little sister until she surprised us all and went off to California.

I could ask Julia how to fix the divide between Tucker and me, but I only have one concern right now. When I hear the bathroom door close, I turn toward the open doorway to Angelica's bedroom.

"I've got to go."

"I'm proud of you, Jude. You actually sound like you're growing up."

"Funny."

"No more lost boy for you," she teases, as if I'm Peter Pan, which is something she teased me about as a child. Never wanting to grow up. Always causing mischief. Only I was more like Captain Hook, grumpy and angry. Envious.

"Yeah, yeah. Gotta go," I state again.

"I love you, Jude."

My shoulders relax a little. "Love you, too, cupcake," I tease, using her husband's nickname for her.

The line goes dead with my sister's chuckle echoing in my ear.

Returning to my nursemaid duties, I check on my patient. When I enter Angelica's bedroom, she's exiting the bathroom. Her body is hunched forward like it took all her effort to walk the few steps.

"I'm so cold again," she grumbles, climbing back into her bed and bringing her covers up to her chin. She visibly trembles, although her forehead feels warm.

"We've got to get that fever down."

Angelica hums while her eyes close.

I do the only thing I can think of next. I strip out of my clothes, down to my boxer briefs, and climb into the bed behind her, tugging her back to my chest.

"What are you doing?" The rough grumble sounds like it takes all her energy to speak.

"Warming you up." I wrap my arm over her waist and tug her tighter to my chest. I tuck my knees behind hers and press them upward, like she's sitting in my lap. I set her cold feet on top of mine, touching every place I can so the heat of my body seeps into hers.

"If you wanted to get in bed with me, all you had to do was ask," she mutters.

"And if you wanted to see me again, you didn't need to play sick. You could have called." Not that she's faking this illness. But why hadn't she called me sooner?

She scoffs, snuggling deeper into me. I press my lips to the back of her hair. She smells like sugar and spice again, but also warm and dewy from the fever. I slip my arm beneath her oversized T-shirt so we are skin to skin as much as we can be. She settles into the added warmth against her belly.

"I'm sorry you're sick." It's all my fault. Wet hair and a cold walk. Prolonged exposure while ice skating. I should have taken better care of her.

"It's not your fault I feel bad," she says, her voice still quiet and sleepy.

"But I want you to feel better," I mutter to her neck. *I want to make everything better.*

"Just a few more days," she murmurs, like she knows exactly how long she'll be ill.

A few more days. I close my eyes, curious if she'd like another day with me.

I'd like more than another day with her.

+ + +

By late afternoon, Angelica is complaining about being too hot and scooting out of my grasp. Surprisingly, I'd fallen asleep as well, and I roll to my back as she moves away from me.

"How are you feeling?" I ask, as she lies on her back as well and kicks her legs out from underneath the covers.

"Hot." She rolls her head on the pillow to look at me.

I have several comebacks, but instead, I blurt something very ill-timed. "Let me take you to your brother's wedding."

Angelica shifts her head for a better look at me. "Jude." She sighs. "You don't need to do that."

"I don't want you to think I'm selfish. You were my date. Now let me be yours."

She shakes her head and turns to face the ceiling again. "That wouldn't be the reason I'd consider you selfish."

I shift to my side and prop up on my elbow. "Then explain it to me."

Her head whips back in my direction. "Why does my opinion matter?"

Because you matter to me. For reasons I cannot explain, what she thinks of me has struck a chord.

"I'd just like to know what my offenses are." I tip my chin, bracing for a list of infractions. "Why did you change your mind about dating me?"

"It was one date, Jude."

"Two," I remind her. A rehearsal dinner *and* the wedding.

She exhales heavily. "When you suggested that my volunteering set you in the good graces of your board, it diminished the work."

"I—" I'm cut off as she looks away from me. "I'm sorry." However, the apology is too late.

"Volunteering time. It's on the list," I state.

She rolls her head back in my direction. "You read the list?" Her large eyes are still fever-riddled but beautiful when she blinks at me.

I shrug, dropping my gaze to her arm that rests on top of the covers. Her skin is so pale, so soft.

"I'm trying to *do* the list," I admit, keeping my eyes focused on the crease of her elbow.

"Really?" Her excited trill has me briefly meeting her eyes, but just as quickly, I look away again, feeling my face heat.

"Want to tell me what you've done so far?" Her eyes are expectant, blue flames of hope. *Hope for me?*

I fall to my back and tick off on my fingers. "I gave of my time at the breakfast with Santa."

"And how did that make you feel?"

I turn my head on the pillow and narrow my eyes. "Are you my shrink now?"

She waves her hand and gives me a soft smile. "Fine. Continue."

"I donated money." A Snowball's Chance. She already knows this one.

I'm not ready to admit that I might have cheated a little bit, and I've put purchasing her Christmas presents on the list. It kind of matched up with Scrooge tossing coins at the boy and telling him to purchase the biggest goose. While I'd initially told myself the purchases were made in gratitude for her saving my life, I actually enjoyed the time we spent together as she carefully selected items for each of her family members. Her love for them was obvious in every decision she made.

Did I think I was reformed? Did I like giving shit away? Donating money. Paying for others. *Not particularly.* But it had not been as bad as I thought it might be. In fact, it had been kind of nice.

I shiver at the thought.

What has been miserable were the days of silence between us since the breakfast with Santa. Why hadn't she called me? She never answered that question, and when she didn't answer any of my phone calls on Thursday after her midnight announcement about being sick, I stormed her apartment on Friday morning wanting answers.

Staring at her beside me, I still have questions. But the biggest ones on my mind center around her. Does she believe in me? Could she be proud of me? Does she see a change?

As for her question—*why her?*—I didn't have an answer, but I had an inkling it had to do with that feminine voice asking me not to leave.

Someone needed me. So far, the need had been my time and my money. The bigger items on the list were still up for consideration.

"I'm proud of you, Jude," she says, her voice soft.

And I turn my head again, certain she's joking. But the gleam in her enticing eyes and the soft curve of her lip, highlighting my favorite freckle, is all the reassurance I desire.

"It's a step," I admit.

"Never gonna skate, if you don't put on the skates."

"'You always miss one hundred percent of the shots you don't take.' Wayne Gretsky. Hockey great," I explain.

Angelica chuckles, which leads to a short coughing attack. As she presses herself upright to a seated position, I sit up as well and reach over her for her water bottle on the opposite side of the bed. This causes me to lean against her. My chest brushes over her covered breasts. She tracks my retreat over her body and drops her gaze to my bare chest.

"What does that tattoo mean?" she asks, still struggling to clear her throat.

I hand over her water and remain sitting. The blankets pool over my lap, while I glance down at the elaborate design. I raise my arm so she can better see the ink.

The image is an intricate clock, like the one outside Ashford's. Surrounding the large timepiece is a rose vine. Some flowers are in full bloom, others are only buds. On one portion of the clock, the flowers are wilting while another is only a vine of thorns.

"The clock is Ashford's signature piece. The roses symbolize the seasons."

Angelica stares at my hand as I stroke around the ink. Something inside me wants her to trace the cycle. Run her fingertips from spring to summer to fall to winter.

"The thorny vine is closest to your heart."

"Winter is my favorite season."

"It's also my last name," she states, arching a brow. Maybe there is deeper meaning to the tattoo after all. A subliminal message I hadn't even known I'd imprinted on myself.

"Fancy that," I tease.

"So grim, though," she counters about the coldest season of the year. But she continues to stare at the tattoo while drinking from her water bottle. When she pulls the bottle from her mouth, her lips are moist, and she swipes at them with her thumb.

I might actually be jealous of drops of water.

"So, it wasn't a fever dream," she whispers, dipping her gaze to the blankets over my lap.

"What wasn't a dream?"

"You climbing into bed to heat me up. Or you running a bath for me. Or washing my hair." Her gaze leaps to my face, while the hesitation in her voice suggests she isn't certain any of those things really happened.

"Not a dream," I admit.

"For a minute there, I thought I was having my own *Christmas Carol* moment."

"Oh yeah. What ghosts haunt you?"

Her eyes remain fixated on my face. "Only friendly ones." She takes another sip of her water. "Thank you for being here, Jude. Thank you for taking care of me."

A strange sensation that can be called nothing other than warm and fuzzy fills my chest. I'm not certain I've ever felt whatever this tickle is inside me. I almost feel giddy, and then I want to slap myself.

However, my sister was right. This is new, and I must admit, it feels incredible to be genuinely appreciated. To take care of someone else's needs.

I wouldn't say I'm fully reformed, but I'm getting there.

Like learning to skate again, I’m still a bit wobbly.

chapter 20

[Jude]

The next day while Angelica sleeps, I attempt to work, but my mind continually wanders. I take a second glance around her apartment. The rug covering the hardwood flooring. The abundant pillows on her couch. The worn leather chair. She even has a small Christmas tree strung with real popcorn and dried cranberries. It doesn't contain any ornaments, but the simplicity of it is beautiful. A string of lights hangs around the window.

Her place is comfortable, cozy even, which is something I hadn't considered yesterday. Her one-bedroom apartment is a home compared to my place on the upper floors of a downtown high-rise.

I'm easily distracted by the floating shelves on one wall near her television, which holds a myriad of framed photographs. Close-ups of children. Laughing adults. A couple in black and white. A pair of older women.

Eventually, I stand to further inspect the images.

With my hands behind my back, I stare at each and every image as if I'm viewing fine art in a gallery instead of candid photos.

I note the close-up of the children. Some of the boys have a mischievous twinkle to their eyes, while one of the girls has the same. Each face looks relaxed, content, well-loved. Their smiles appear genuine.

Next, I stare at the adults, easily distinguishing Angelica, her sister Christmas, brother Dane, and assume the final male is her brother Beau. In one picture, they are laughing with large grins and their heads tipped backward. Whatever was said or done to prompt such a photo was truly funny, but the attractive part of the image is that they appear to genuinely enjoy one another.

The pair of older women must be her Aunt Gertie and her grandmother. The two have their heads together, like a couple of teenagers. The image is rather sweet.

Finally, I focus on the black and white image of a couple on their wedding day. They're dancing with their foreheads touching. Her eyes are closed. He appears to be looking at her. I'll never be able to meet Angelica's parents, and yet looking at this image, the love within them radiates outward, unlike the wedding portrait of my parents, where they both look stiff and uncomfortable.

Heck, I couldn't recall a single photograph that was spontaneous for my family. Nothing was unplanned. Photos were taken, and then re-taken, if our smiles weren't just right. With our perfected smiles, we always had a slightly stilted expression.

"My dad liked to stare at my mother."

I don't turn my head but catch Angelica out of the corner of my eye leaning against the door jamb to her bedroom, tipping her head to the side. She's wearing a dark green pajama set today. Silky pants and a complementary top with three buttons.

"When he got caught by one of us, he'd always say our mother was the most beautiful creature he'd ever seen."

Hearing the soft smile in her voice, I turn my head, noting a hint of sadness in the curve of her lips.

Turning back to the photographs, I say, "You all look like you genuinely like one another."

Angelica chuckles. "We do. Most days."

She steps closer, pointing out her nephews and nieces by name, then her siblings, and finally confirming her aunt and grandmother.

"My grandmother was a quiet woman," I admit. "My grandfather was stern. A miser, I suppose one would call him."

A person who hoards wealth and spends as little as possible.

I wouldn't say I've inherited that trait, although I've inherited plenty of other things from the patriarchal line of my family.

"I've told you that Tucker isn't really my dad. His father was my father, which made my grandfather my great-grandfather."

Essentially, my dad was my brother, and it was so fucking complicated.

I continue to stare at the image of Angelica's grandmother. Her smile is warm and kind. Her sister beside her has a glint of mischief in her eyes, like that of her great-niece and several great-nephews.

"What I didn't mention is how Tucker has brothers, which makes them my brothers." I turn my head, hands still behind my back to witness the expected shock on Angelica's face from revealing another secret without an NDA.

Why was I telling this woman everything? The answer comes quickly. Because I'd like to share. I'd like to unburden this load I bear with her.

Angelica doesn't look shocked, only sad. Sad for me. I could rage at her pity, but instead, I drink it in. While I've never wanted anyone to feel sorry for me, ever, no one has had the opportunity because of the secrets I keep deep within me. The ones we've never openly shared although Tucker and his brother, Mach, own a business together and refer to one another as brothers all the time.

"My *father* had a set of male twins a little younger than Tucker with another young woman," I clarify of the list of bastard children my father bore. "And another child somewhere out there, who is a full-fledged adult by now, who is between them and me. Tucker was his only legitimate son."

The list of adulterous acts is daunting.

Angelica doesn't speak. Her head remains tipped against the jamb, arms crossed loosely over her chest.

She's so beautiful, and if she looks like her mother, which is difficult to tell from this image, I understand her father's fascination. Angelica is the most beautiful creature I've ever seen.

But I pull my gaze from her and stare, almost blindly, at this wall of photographs.

"I'm sorry you aren't close to any of them," Angelica begins. "But there is always time for a relationship, if you want to put in the effort."

Make amends. It's on the list, but I don't think she realizes how difficult that would truly be.

"How are you feeling?" I ask, abruptly changing the subject.

"Would you hate me if I said I'd love a cheeseburger the size of my head?" She chuckles at her admission, and I glance back at her.

"Something tells me I could never hate you," I admit. Something tells me I could *love* her, but love is skiing during an avalanche, dangerous and inevitably it could suffocate you.

I shrug. "I could eat a cheeseburger."

Her gaze blatantly roams up and down my body, before she chuffs. "When have you ever eaten a cheeseburger?"

"Were you just checking me out?" I laugh, turning my body toward her. "Get a good look?"

Her face turns a sweet shade of pink, punctuating those freckles across her cheeks, but the one I concentrate on near the corner of her lip is like the North Star in the sky leading me home.

"Don't worry," I add. "I enjoy the view, too." I keep my eyes on her a second before scanning down her body, letting my gaze trace the outline of her form. Those smaller breasts and wider hips. The curves and dips in all the right places.

"You said you didn't look earlier." She straightens from the door jamb.

"I didn't." But I cross my fingers behind my back while I speak because I might have gotten a tiny peek. More like an unintentional flash, but I quickly held back from taking a fuller glance. I've seen the outline of her body before, in that one-piece bathing suit while we were in the hot tub. It didn't leave much to the imagination but left enough that I've been wondering what she'd look like all laid out and naked on my bed, her alabaster skin contrasting with my dark sheets.

As we continue to stare at one another, blood rushes through my body to places it shouldn't be rushing. I clear my throat and swipe a hand over my hair to cup the back of my neck.

"So, cheeseburgers?"

"You don't need to feed me." She draws a circle with her toe on the rug and lowers her head.

"I need to eat." My hunger is the perfect argument. "How about a movie, too?"

"You want to watch a movie?" Her reddish brows lift.

"Why are you acting like I don't do anything human? Eat cheeseburgers and watch movies."

"I don't know." Her shoulders fall. "I guess I just kind of see you above the mundane with your suits and your top-floor office. Watching a movie and eating a burger must seem kind of boring." She wrinkles her nose like she still can't believe I'd do something so simple.

I could chastise her for being a little judgmental but instead I say, "Let me show you that I'm not really that complex of a man." I'd really like her to see me as something other than someone on some unattainable mountain peak. "I'll even let you pick the movie."

"Any movie?" she teases, tweaking one brow again.

"Any movie," I agree.

"You might regret that," she continues, stepping around me for the remote near the television.

"I regret nothing," I counter.

"Ever been to a drive-in movie?" She adorably tilts her head sideways.

"Random." I laugh, the sound sharp and quick, and foreign feeling. I glance toward the window, noticing snow lightly falling. "And a bit cold for one tonight."

"Just answer the question." Her mouth curls in the most delicious way.

"An Ashford only attends red carpet events and movie premieres," I mock myself, recalling how I told her an Ashford only skis and snowboards.

She laughs next, the sound loud and cheery, before she points at me. "See. Complex."

But she doesn't seem to mind as we order cheeseburgers and fries, and wade through two Christmas rom-coms, before she picks a slightly spicier holiday movie, and I'm having serious concerns about the complexity of my feelings and my ability to hold back from what I want with this woman.

chapter 21

[Angelica]

We've watched two movies before this one, and within minutes of those shows, Jude spoiled the plot by predicting the outcomes. Of course, the couple would end up together and experience their first kiss with only five minutes remaining in the film, but I wanted to enjoy the *known* without his interpretation. Still, it was funny how easily he guessed the storyline correctly.

My head is pillowed at the far end of the sofa, and here we are tangled, but not tangled, sharing space like it had always been ours. Jude's head is at the opposite end of the couch, his legs stretched and tucked around me. My feet are perched on his chest.

It is oddly intimate. Strangely comfortable. And nothing like how he typically was. Jude, in his suits, crisp and self-contained, is always slightly removed. This is different. This is him, relaxed and quiet, and letting me rest against him like it is completely normal. I like it more than I mean to. I like him like this more than I should.

And it isn't awkward. Not at all. Not until that scene comes on. Then suddenly, I am too aware of the shape of him beneath my heels, the quiet way he breathes, and the warm line of his thigh pressing against my side. The closeness that had felt safe now feels charged, and I don't dare move.

A viewer couldn't even see all the details of the couple's bodies, but you knew from their movements and moans exactly what they were doing. Pressing my thighs together, I rub my knees against one another in the slightest motion, while Judd holds my feet captive in his hands.

"Easy there," he chuckles, catching onto my not-so-subtle squirm. "Getting turned on?"

"Shut up," I whimper, unable to look at him, while attempting to playfully kick at his chest.

Jude tightens his grip on my feet, pinning them against his firm pecs. "Is that what you want? A romp in a barn with a cowboy?"

"Who says 'romp'?" I twist only my head to glance at him, while he tugs off a sock from one of my feet and lifts my bare toes toward his mouth.

"You won't?" I shriek.

"Wouldn't I?" He nips at my big toe. "Now tell me . . . a cowboy in a barn?"

How about a millionaire in my apartment? But I don't dare mention it.

Jude tugs the other sock off my opposite foot and bites my other big toe.

"Gross." I gag, while surprisingly aroused.

In a sudden shift, Jude crouched over me, and I'm on my back staring up at him. I choke out, "What are you doing?"

He presses pause on the remote without breaking his focus from me.

"You had a *situation* last weekend." He arches one of his perfectly sculpted brows. "And you let an audiobook help you out."

"A situation?" I choke. "Is that what people call it nowadays?" The urgent desire to get off, to release tension, to imagine what it would feel like to have his hands on me.

He tugs the blanket between us out of the way, then returns to all fours over me, ignoring my sarcasm.

"Now . . . you're allowing a movie to work you up." Those icy eyes of his are pure fire. Sparks practically fly out of them. The gleam is mesmerizing.

"When I'm right here." His voice drops, low and arousing. "Let me be the one to give you what you need."

"And what do I need?" In my head, I'm stronger than my voice conveys because I'm nearly hyperventilating with him over me. His expensive cologne is intoxicating. The temptation to kiss him is overwhelming.

"You tell me." His gaze narrows in on the corner of my lip before shifting back to my eyes.

"You probably shouldn't kiss me," I warn, licking my lips.

Jude gently cups the front of my throat, and I swallow against the cuff of his palm. The icy touch is gone, and in its place is warmth that spreads around my neck like a comforting scarf.

"You don't want me to kiss you?" Jude continues to stare at my lips, rolling his own like he's holding them back from taking what they want.

"I don't think you should kiss my mouth," I clarify, swallowing again underneath his palm holding my neck. "Because I've been sick."

While I feel so much better than I did, I unfortunately can't seem to shut off the practical, medical side of my brain, which is whispering about lingering germs, while the other half is screaming for me to lift my head and take what I want from him.

Jude quickly removes his hand and kneels back. Concern instantly mars his edgy features. "You said you felt better."

"I do feel better." I swallow one more time. "Just not my mouth."

Slowly, he leans forward, eyes locked on mine. "But I can kiss you in other places?"

I hold his gaze another second before slowly shrugging. Like the *slowest* shrug. More like a shoulder wink.

Jude's hand is suddenly back on my throat, turning my head to expose the side of my neck. He runs his nose along my flesh, sending goosebumps across my skin. I shiver as the tip of his nose crests the edge of my ear.

"Are you giving me permission to kiss you anywhere I wish?" His voice is almost sinister while wildly seductive at the same time.

"Yes," I whisper.

His mouth latches onto the side of my throat before the final *S* hisses from my tongue. He sucks long and deep, moving along my jugular like a vampire seeking his first bite.

I've read Twilight too many times.

"Tell me. Did the narrator of your book say I want to kiss you everywhere?" His voice drops to the perfect rugged tenor, and goosebumps break out on my flesh.

He shoves aside the loose collar of my pajama top and sucks on my collarbone. His tongue is a gentle lash and slow lick, and my hips move of their own accord, needing connection or friction or just something more.

"Oh God," I whimper, my entire body lighting up with anticipation. We probably shouldn't be doing this. I've been sick. He isn't my boyfriend. But every cell in my body wants to feel his touch, experience his caress.

He works down my chest. "Did your narrator say show me those pretty tits. I want them in my mouth. Swirl my tongue over your tight nipples." He unbuttons the large buttons on my silky pajama shirt as he talks, and all thoughts fly out of my head, other than he'd make a damn good audiobook actor.

Jude spreads my shirt wide, humming at the lack of a bra beneath the shirt that matches my pants. Then runs his tongue over one breast, circling my tight nipple before sucking deeply at it, acting out exactly what he suggested.

Again, I cry out quietly, arching toward him and spreading my fingers through his hair.

"The prettiest," he groans at the sharp, wet peaks, blowing on one before traveling to the other, teasing it in the same manner.

"Jude," I whimper, shivering as he moves down my body, pressing kisses to my midsection.

"That's right. *Jude*. I'm here. I'm the one who's going to take care of you." He reaches the top of my waistband. "And I'm the one who wants you to show me that sweet pussy. Gonna let me spread you wide, use my fingers, my mouth, my tongue, angel? Lift."

Without answering him, I lift my hips for his ease in removing my pants.

"No panties?" His head pops up and those typically cold eyes are deep wells of desire.

"I need to do laundry," I admit, embarrassed.

"Lucky me," he mutters, glancing back at the strip of hair on my mound while he pulls my pants further down my legs.

Jude settles between my thighs, wrapping my legs over his shoulders. Once there, he stares at where I'm anxious for his touch.

"It's my fingers touching you," he murmurs, swiping through slick folds and quickly finding that triggering nub.

"My fingers filling you." One easily glides inside me and my back bows.

I whimper at the sweet intrusion, full but not satisfied with only one finger.

As if reading my thoughts, he pulls back and adds a second, watching my face as they disappear inside me.

"So eager." With his eyes still focused on my face, he lowers and flicks his tongue where I'm most sensitive.

My hips flinch. My thighs clench.

"Gonna be my tongue that licks this sweetness. Makes a mess of you." Then he dives in.

It's been so long since I've been in this *situation*, that I've almost forgotten how sensitive I am, how easily I can be aroused, how much I've missed this kind of intimacy.

Only, Jude isn't particularly gentle. He sucks my lower lips before flicking my clit like a man on a mission. One determined to drag me up a mountain and dangle me over the peaked top, like I'm hanging by a rope off an imaginary sleigh, when all I want is to travel down the other side, chasing the high of racing. Eventually, I totter over the edge, barreling down the opposite slope, feeling my blood rush to the center of my being.

"Jude," I cry out, loud and shocked at how quickly he brought me to this point. Then I simply enjoy the ride as he doesn't relent, twirling and swirling, and blowing on that trigger spot like a private blizzard.

Which winds me up for a second coming, literally.

"Jude?" I question, as he continues to lick and lap, squeezing at my backside with his firm hands, and tipping up my hips, like I'm a treat he'd like a second helping of.

My fingers fist in the shortness of his hair as my body preps for another spin. The spiral is a little slower but no less intense when I finally crest a new hill and whiz over it, sailing down another curve of arousal.

"Jude." His name is one long syllable, punctuated by the hitch in my breath near the end. My hips sag. My backside rests in his hands. I flip my arm over my eyes, hiding them in the crease of my elbow.

What the hell just happened to me?

Jude Ashford happened to me, that's what. He's acted out a fantasy, making it a reality, and I just came twice in a matter of minutes.

A full-on kiss is pressed to where I'm swollen and soaked, and then Jude lifts his upper body, forcing my legs to fall from his shoulders. He tugs my arm free from my face.

When his eyes connect with mine, they remain bright, almost wild. Nothing like that moment they closed off in the inn a week ago. Where I'd been willing to give him my body, but he seemed turned off by the possibility. He didn't want to have sex with me.

What changed?

I wanted a chance at something more.

He'd said that, right? But what had he meant?

Judd slowly folds upward to his knees again, staring down at where I'm the mess he promised to make of me.

"Tell me I'm better than any audiobook or a movie." While his tone is demanding, his expression is sheepish, like he needs this confidence booster when he's the most confident person I've ever known.

"You know what I love best about an audiobook or a movie?" I counter, not admitting to anything quite yet. "You can always re-listen to a book or re-watch a movie, and have a totally different experience the second time."

He drops to his hands, giving my breasts a quick glance before meeting my eyes again.

"Are you saying you need a do-over to decide if that was good?"

I chuckle. "Oh, no, I'd say it was plenty good. Five stars." More like seven in heaven, but that's not a rating.

Judd slowly smiles. The corner of his mouth twitches, and that apostrophe pops, like it has possession of his lips. His wicked mouth, which just brought me two orgasms in mere minutes.

I run my hand over his cheek. "I'd return the favor . . ."

He catches my meaning, then grabs my wrist and turns my hand so he can press a kiss into my palm.

"Always a chance for a re-listen or a re-watch, right?" he mutters to the inside of my hand.

I laugh again, embarrassed that I'd said such a thing, but don't miss the implication.

Is he suggesting we have more than tonight together? Hope feels like too much to ask for.

Instead, I slip from the couch and quickly use the bathroom. When I return to the living room, the movie is still paused, and I take a seat on *my* end of the couch. Jude leans forward, grips my ankles, and repositions us in our original entanglement. He reaches for the blanket on the floor and tosses it over both of us, and we settle in for the not-so-surprising conclusion of another holiday movie.

chapter 22

[Angelica]

Sunday morning is the breakfast with Santa at Ashford's, so I'm not surprised when Jude is gone, and I awake on the couch, tucked underneath the throw blanket.

I flip to my back and stare at a crack in my ceiling, replaying all that happened over the weekend, but specifically what happened last night.

The shift in his eyes from icicle chill to hot springs. The drop in his voice, seductive and low, enticing as he spelled out what he'd do to me. And then what he did. His fingers. His tongue. His mouth.

I tug the blanket over my mouth and scream into it, whacking my heels into the couch cushion, like a teenager. My smile is almost too wide and my face flushes.

What did I do? And why do I want more? The answer comes quickly. Jude.

The way he took care of me this weekend, when no one else ever does. I'm confident in my ability to care for myself, but it was a pleasant and welcome surprise to have someone else here for me. The most surprising thing was learning that Jude read the list I made him. He's attempting to complete it. He's willing to change. Not for anyone but himself.

Reaching for my phone on the coffee table, I open the original list I made for him and check off what he's already completed. Hope blossoms in my chest that Jude can do this. Transformation is inevitable.

On that positive note, I spring from the couch. I have laundry to do before I head to Gran's.

Cookie baking is on the agenda for the day.

Gran has three cookie exchanges to attend, requiring that she bring three dozen cookies to each. She also selects this date and considers it an annual cookie bakeoff, which includes the entire family. She doesn't always wear her glasses while baking, swearing she knows every recipe by heart; however, her memory isn't the best either, and a few too many times, flour has been substituted for sugar. Or cayenne pepper for cinnamon.

Hence, the need for my supervision.

Her three-story building consists of a garden apartment; the raised, first floor flat, and the second level, where my sister lives. Gran's official address is the middle floor, where her front door is open, allowing Christmas's boys to run from the upper level to the lower one, like they are already hyped up on cookies.

"Gran," I call out, entering her apartment. Instantly, I am hit with a wave of nostalgia, both joyful and melancholy, while standing in her dated living room. Decades of holidays have been held in this space. The doors from one floor to another were always open, allowing the family to meander from one place to another, but this apartment was the prime gathering spot. Holiday dinners were served here. Birthdays celebrated. Presents unwrapped.

Riotous laughter pulls me like a magnet through the dining room toward the kitchen.

When I reach the arched entry, I stumble to a halt. The countertop is littered with bowls and ingredients. Flour. Sugar. Food coloring. Sprinkle packages. The round table to the right of the U-shape of cabinets and appliances is covered with a plastic tablecloth decorated with giant holly leaves and red berries.

However, what stops me short is the man on one side of the table.

"Jude?" What the heck is he doing here?

"Angelica, why didn't you tell us this fine man had entered your life?"

I blink at my Aunt Gertie, wearing her stylish, dark-framed glasses that are a little too large for her petite face. Her white hair is pinned up on the back of her head, and she has bright red lipstick on despite it being a Sunday morning with no place for her to go. And she's smiling up at Jude, who is nearly a foot taller than her short stature, like he invented Santa Claus.

Gran sidles up beside me. She is everything opposite her sister, standing a little taller, a little broader, but no less mischievous in her own way. Her gray hair is cut in a sharp, chin-length bob.

"You didn't tell me you had a boyfriend."

I sigh heavily, instantly miffed. I haven't told anyone because I *don't* have a boyfriend, and this is precisely what I wanted to avoid—lying to my family.

Glaring at the man of the moment, his icy eyes stare back at me, not a trace of chagrin that he's crashing cookie baking. He's dressed in a suit again, making him look sorely out of place in my grandmother's kitchen with her scuffed linoleum flooring and scratched, wooden cabinets.

Jude circles the table, stepping into my space.

"What are you doing?" I whisper, glancing around him, catching the eyes of my entire family staring at Jude's back before busying themselves again.

"When my girlfriend uses an excuse of baking cookies to get out of breakfast plans, I have to see what's all the fuss." He smugly glances over his shoulder, causing me to catch a second round of my family eavesdropping, paused in positions that should be motions, like holding flour over a measuring cup or slicing through butter sticks.

"Can you say stalker much? Plus, you didn't invite me to breakfast. And how did you even know where my grandmother lives?" I could add a final argument . . . *and I'm not your girlfriend.*

Then I think back over the past few days. How Jude has taken care of me, both when I was sick and when I was horny. Who does those kinds of things?

A friend, I guess. A friend . . . with benefits.

Jude's mouth pops open, then clamps shut. His forehead pinches like he doesn't recall that he *didn't* actually invite me to the special event at Ashford's. And he's not about to explain the creepy way he knows where my grandmother lives.

Instead, I grip Jude's suit coat lapel and tug him into Gran's living room, away from my nosy family.

"Jude," I grunt, then lower my voice. "I am not your girlfriend."

Before he can comment, thundering footsteps clamber up the half flight of stairs to Gran's open doorway, and my brother Beau skips into the room. Literally skips, despite his mid-thirties age. He even looks younger than he is, with blond hair he colors for a beach-bum effect, which plays off his tall, lean stature.

"Never fear, Beau is here." He waves his arms to further announce himself, although the only ones present for his entrance are Jude and me.

Belle, his petite fiancée, follows him. "Beau, you didn't hold the main door for me." The brunette graduate student carries a paper grocery bag that looks heavy, and Beau spins to face her.

"I'm sorry, snookums." He takes the bag from her hands, presses a kiss to her forehead, like she's a child, and then rushes off toward the kitchen.

Belle gives me a sheepish wave and scampers after him.

"Ah. Beau and Belle." Jude watches the adoring couple as they head for the chaos of the kitchen.

"Jude," I redirect his attention. "You aren't answering my question. What are you doing here?"

He exhales and swipes a hand through his hair, looking a little unsettled. Mussing up his hair, which results in a sexy finger combing, but I don't allow myself to get distracted.

I lick my lips to tamp down the effect, but Jude's eyes fix on my mouth.

"I wanted to see you." The answer is simple enough and shouldn't have a strange effect on me. Like blowing a warm breath on cool glass and watching the vapor spread. My insides heat as well.

"You just saw me this morning," I state, without adding how he snuck out when he didn't need to slink.

"Look, you've been sick, and you work too hard." He waves toward the living room like the space is evidence of all I've been doing this holiday season. "Let me help you."

"Make cookies?" I clarify. "With my family."

Jude shrugs, hanging his head. He practically kicks at the worn carpeting, like he really wants to participate in baking cookies, which doesn't make any sense. He's a busy man. He even had plans on a Sunday morning, and I didn't barge into his schedule. Didn't disrupt his calendar of events.

I don't even know why I'm so worked up, but I cross my arms and glare at him.

Which is the position I'm in when Beau re-enters the living room.

"Angie," he says a little too loudly. "My beautiful sister, Angelica. Queen of organization and family functions."

Oh boy.

"Have you found us a wedding venue yet?"

"Venue?" I choke. "You said you were looking for a restaurant. One that holds twenty people."

Beau slides up to me, wraps his arm around my shoulders, and tugs me tightly into his side. "And now I need space for fifty. Belle's family is slowly getting on board with the wedding, and we need to expand our horizons." He waves his hand outward like a snowy landscape is in front of us.

He tips up his chin at Jude, finally noticing him. "What's up?"

As the youngest child in our four pack, this is typical Beau. He needs to be the center of attention, and he needs everything done for him. It's a wonder he's as successful as he is.

He extends his hand to Jude. "Beau. Her favorite brother."

Not exactly the truth.

"Jude Ashford," Jude counters, his jaw tight. His smile is a pinched one, not even the practiced pleasant one. "Her boyfriend."

Beau squeals like a teenage girl, lifting his hands in front of his lips and doing a little two-step jig.

"Sister's got a boyfriend," he sings while pinching my cheeks.

I close my eyes with embarrassment before quickly pulling away from his fingers and punching his stomach, to which he exaggerates the effect and calls out to Gran.

"Gran, Angie hit me." He pouts.

"Beau, quick picking on your sister," Gran hollers back, knowing the truth.

"Rude." He winks at Jude. "But I still love you, Gran."

Beau claps his hands once, and with both hands joined, he points at me. "Venue. Wedding. Ten days."

"Beau," I sigh, exasperated by him. "We aren't going to find a—"

"You could use the Oak Room."

Beau swivels his head toward Jude while I blink at the suggestion.

"The Oak Room?" Beau echoes. "As in *the* Oak Room in Ashford's." Beau narrows his eyes as things begin to click in his youthful brain.

"Ashford. Like *the* Ashford's," Beau adds.

"Yes," I snap. "We've established the Oak Room and Ashford's." I point at Jude. "But the answer is no."

No. Absolutely not to Beau getting married or throwing a reception in that beautiful oak-paneled room with high ceilings and floor-to-ceiling windows.

"Why not?" Beau asks innocently.

"What's wrong with the Oak Room?" Jude questions, his voice growing tighter.

"Nothing is wrong with the Oak Room. It's perfect." I address Jude first, then turn to Beau. "But you still aren't getting it for your wedding."

Beau pouts. "But why?"

"Because . . ." I stammer, scrambling to come up with a reasonable excuse when deep down I know the reason.

"Because . . ." I try again, shifting my gaze from Beau to Jude and back, still struggling. A cold sweat breaks out on my neck.

"Perfect. Then it's settled." Beau pats Jude on the shoulder. "Thanks, man."

However, Jude isn't looking at Beau but watching me. With those intense eyes on me, my own begin to burn, and I spin away from both men, rushing for the open front door and thumping down the half-flight of stairs. I could push out into the cold December air. The chill might be refreshing, numbing even, which is what I need right now, when I consider my younger brother might get married in a place that holds no meaning to him.

And all the meaning to me.

chapter 23

[Jude]

With Angelica's abrupt exit, I follow her, watching her indecision in the building entryway about rushing into the cold December morning, before she breaks left and thunders down another half-flight of stairs to the garden level. With only two doors on this floor, the one swinging shut from the force of her entrance is my clue to where she went.

The laundry room has a distinct scent of Tide laundry detergent with a hint of bleach, but the fragrance that draws my attention is the sugar and spice scent from the woman with her back to me. Her arms are spread wide, and she leans over the washer, hanging her head. The hunch of her shoulder does something to me. Like all I want to do is pull her into my arms, wrap them around her, and keep her safe from whatever is hurting her, because something hurts.

The panic in her eyes as she struggled to give a reason why her brother could not use The Oak Room for his wedding spoke volumes.

"Want to tell me what that was all about?" I softly ask, coming up close behind her but not touching her yet.

She shakes my head, holding her position, keeping her back to me.

"*Is* something wrong with The Oak Room?' I ask, repeating my question from upstairs, with apprehension. What doesn't she like about the place?

"No," she chokes out, sniffling with her response.

I sense my brows lifting in surprise then crashing back over my eyes, troubled by her tears. Like someone has ripped open my chest. Like sawing the fresh cut at the base of a Christmas tree. I hate that she's crying.

"Angel," I whisper, no longer able to keep the distance. I step closer and spread my arms as well, covering her hands with mine and bringing my cheek near to her ear.

"Nothing is wrong with The Oak Room?" I clarify.

She shakes her head, which is still lowered. Her shoulders softly rise and fall as she sniffs again.

"But you don't want your brother to have his wedding in my restaurant?"

I'm clearly missing something, and I brush my cheek against her ear until my lips are right there.

"Tell me," I whisper. Not like the seductive bastard I was last night, but like the concerned man I am today. The worried *boyfriend*, if we were acting. But this isn't an act. In the quiet of this basement laundry room, we're all alone, no audience, no witnesses, and I want to know what's bothering her. What's troubling her heart.

Gently, I slip my hand around her throat and tip her head back so she rests it on my shoulder. From the corner of my eye, I watch her close hers.

"It's not fair," she whispers.

"What's not fair, angel?" I keep my voice low, soothing, because I want to calm her.

"Beau always gets what he wants." She exhales heavily, letting the weight of her body completely rest against mine.

Sadly, I understand. As much as I love my younger sister, I'd grown up thinking she was the spoiled one. She had the love of both our mother and our dad, *her* father.

"I'm being silly, right?" She shrugs against me. "At thirty-seven, what do I care if my younger brother still gets everything. The girl he wants. A spontaneous wedding. A holiday one at that." She pauses and licks her lips. "And the venue of my dreams."

"What?" I whisper, slow and low, and totally stunned. I must have misheard her. Yet despite a ccrtain tightness in my chest and a sudden cotton ball in my throat, I ask, "You want to get married in the Oak Room?"

She closes her eyes again, like she instantly regrets the admission, when I don't want her regretting anything between us. Not truths or touches or secrets for just us.

Suddenly, I can envision it. Her standing in a white dress near the antique mullioned floor-to-ceiling windows. A stream of sunlight beams into the room, highlighting that red hair, which is pulled back at the top but loose and wild down her back like she's a Celtic queen. Her cheeks are rosy; her lips red, and that freckle is on display. *My* freckle, brightened by her smile.

And who the fuck is her groom?

I only see red. Not the vibrant, joyful color of the holiday but scorching, angry crimson.

I haven't been able to stop thinking about Angelica. Not since the moment my eyes opened on that stretcher, and she was the first thing I saw. Those summer-blue eyes. That rope of hair. And that freckle. She's infiltrated my waking moments, like this morning when I woke early and just stared at her. And, my sleeping ones, when a vivid dream of touching her again, filling her with more than my fingers and tongue, woke me.

And I'll be fucking damned to Santa's permanent naughty list for my next thoughts, but I cannot get them out of my head.

"When are you planning to get married?" With my hand still on her throat, I stroke my thumb along her neck, feeling for her pulse, finding she's settled the tears, but her blood begins to pump at the talk of a wedding. Her wedding.

My voice is rough as I struggle to remain calm, but my pulse accelerates the more I envision her waiting on a groom. Some faceless twat who won't appreciate her. Her ability to sacrifice for others. Her lack of care for herself first. He won't put her first in his life.

But I will.

The thought hits so hard, I still my thumb.

"Only in my head," she whispers, and it takes me a second to jump back to the question I'd asked her.

Relief washes through me like a slow trickling river. One released after being frozen for the winter.

With that awakening, also comes snark. "You just tell me what the date is, and The Oak Room is yours."

She can have that beautiful room with its crystal chandelier and ballroom-like setting on one condition.

"Why?" she chuckles, but the sound is bitter, contrasting her typically cheery voice. "Because we're friends? Because I saved your life?"

The twinge of sarcasm hammers home my condition. Not because we're friends. Not because she saved my life. Because I cannot stand the thought of her marrying someone.

Anyone.

Other than me.

I don't have the slightest idea where the thought comes from. I don't believe in love or commitment. But I also don't take the time to unpack this sudden scratch clawing at my chest, at the thought of her with someone else.

I don't answer her questions, reasoning why I'd give her the room for a wedding.

Instead, I state my demand, “The only condition is that I be your date.”

Angelica pulls her head off my shoulder and spins to face me. I don’t move back, remaining in her space. Her breasts brush my chest as I lean forward, setting my hands back on the washing machine behind her.

“That doesn’t make any sense,” she begins. Her saucer-like eyes ping back and forth between mine. “I wouldn’t need a date for my own wedding. My date would be my groom.”

I let her answer linger between us.

Yep, I’ll be her permanent date to weddings. Her brothers or hers . . . I won’t be choosy.

“Jude.” Her brows form a deep V between them while that soft voice crushes all my resolve.

I’m talked out, and I need her not to ask any more questions because I don’t have answers. Not yet. I cannot explain myself, so I do another thing I haven’t been able to stop thinking about.

I kiss her. Take those lips that have made a permanent impression on mine, leaving me hungry for more. I want to feel her tongue against mine, and I slip mine forward to do just that, savoring the sweetness in how they tangle together.

Last night she wouldn’t let me kiss her, but today I cannot help myself.

Sweet relief, like that cold river running faster, fills me again when she gives in and kisses me back. I lean forward, pressing the sudden hard length of my cock against her, dipping my knees the slightest bit to line us up.

She gasps in my mouth, and I grip her hips, lifting her on top of the washing machine to better line us up.

I don't want her thinking about her brother's wedding. Or her own. I only want her thinking about me and what I can do for her. What I want to do with her.

"Let me touch you again," I beg. The plea rings in my ear like church bells on Christmas morning.

"Here?" she chokes against my lips.

"Here," I murmur, slipping my hand between her thighs and directly against her center, which is warm and damp through her leggings. She wraps her legs around the backs of mine, drawing me closer to her.

Dragging her back off the washer, I spin her to face the machine and press my throbbing dick against the firmness of her ass. I slip my hand around her waist, dipping it inside her leggings while kissing the side of her neck, sucking at where that pulse beats strongest.

That river of relief rushes through me, turning into wild, relentless rapids, jostling me over the rocks of my feelings for this woman and dipping me into new territory. A territory where she is mine for real.

Last night was not pretend.

Right now isn't pretend either.

When my fingers meet the slickness of her warm heat, we both sigh.

"Have you been thinking about last night?" I murmur into the skin along her neck. "I have."

She hums.

"Are you wet thinking about it now?" I continue. "Is it the idea of getting married that gets you drenched?"

She doesn't answer, but her mouth falls open as I slip a finger into her.

"See yourself in a white dress." I purr against her neck. "But you aren't innocent, are you, my angel?"

She slowly shakes her head, whether dismissing the vision of her in a dress or her innocence, I can't tell. I don't care. *I* see her in white, looking radiant and loved with a secret inside her.

"You want your future husband to sneak beneath that dress and finger you like this, don't you?" I slip a second finger into her, feeling the heat of her channel and the sweetness of her essence coat my fingers.

Her hips buck back, and I lean forward, wedging my hardness more firmly against her, pinning her to a washing machine.

Not the most romantic location to touch her, nor the most secluded, as her family is present up half a flight of stairs. But I cannot resist her.

"Jude," she whimpers as her knees slightly bang on the metal machine, and I rock forward, trapping my hand inside her panties, my fingers deep within her.

She clenches around my fingers. My hand is damp from the mess I'm making of her. And I am here for it. For her soft cries and her body tightening, and her giving me another sweet orgasm.

"You lit up pretty quickly last night," I remind her, bringing up my own memories of my tongue skating over her folds and slicing into her precious pussy. My mouth waters again at the musky taste of her that mingled with her sugar and spice scent.

"Let me see how colorful you can be again," I groan at the side of her throat, because she is light in the darkness. The promise of longer days after winter ends. The bright bulbs glistening on evergreens. The face of an angel after a near-death experience.

When she finally releases, we both exhale, while my dick seeps in my suit pants. Angelica grinds back against me while I dig deeper, more firmly inside her, feeling her hug my fingers in her snug heat and coat my hand in her sticky sweetness.

When I eventually pull them free from her, instantly missing her warmth, I bring my fingers to my lips, sucking them into my mouth. She tilts her head to watch me over her shoulder.

“Last night, you mentioned how re-listening to an audiobook or re-watching a movie always allows for another interpretation.”

I draw my fingers deep within my mouth to suck every drop of her from them. “I know what my second impression is of you on my tongue.” I hum as I release one finger but suck the first one another round. “Still delicious.”

Angelica lowers her head toward the washing machine and chuckles. “You’re so bad, Jude.”

“I thought I was complex.”

Straightening, she turns to face me. “Maybe not as complex as I thought.” Her eyes narrow, forehead furrowing as she watches me suck my finger.

“Well, if you were my wife . . .” I pause and shove my hand in my pocket, adjusting my dick, which is cursing me for getting her off again but not finding my own relief. “The only thing I’d want to watch on repeat is your expression when you come.”

I lean closer to her, forcing her to arch her back a little bit over the washing machine.

“For now, though, I’m going to settle for visions of you coming in my head and the taste of you on my tongue, while we make cookies with your family.”

Her eyes widen, brows lifting before she turns her head like it has suddenly occurred to her where we are.

I pinch her chin to bring her attention back to me and kiss her quickly one more time, rushing to invade her mouth with my tongue before pulling back and pressing away from the washer.

Smoothing my hand down my shirt and adjusting my belt buckle, I add, "Oh, and you can get to me about that wedding date. The one in The Oak Room."

With that, I spin on my hard-soled shoes, leaving her to wonder if the date I mean is actually a number on the calendar, or a physical date, where I'm the man standing across from her.

chapter 24

[Angelica]

I need a minute to wrap my head around what just happened.

The equation of Jude being my date to my own wedding equals him as my groom, which makes no sense. None. It would never happen.

Yet, I still can't get out of my head all he said. Me in white. And my faceless future husband doing salacious things to me beneath my dress.

I shiver at the thought and grip the washing machine behind me to steady myself. My legs are already shaky after what he just did to me. His fingers were ruthless yet delectable. He'd gone so deep and touched me in a way I've never been touched. Something inside me triggered an orgasm that brought stars to my eyes.

Jude was so bad, in the most complex and delicious way.

Speaking of delicious, I need to get back upstairs to cookie baking and act like nothing just happened in this laundry room.

Trouble is, I'm horrible at pretending.

As I enter the kitchen, I catch the tail end of Jude telling Beau, "Sorry, man, but that date in The Oak Room is unavailable. We're actually completely booked for the season."

When Jude notices me just inside the kitchen, he winks. That flip of his eyelid shouldn't do funny things to my insides. Neither should the way he talks dirty to me or touches me.

But as he watches me, that funny feeling flutters faster and I place my hand on my belly in an attempt to settle down.

"Alright, fancy pants, suit coat off, shirt sleeves up," Aunt Gertie demands, staring at Jude.

Most of my female family members are mesmerized by him as he slowly shrugs off his coat and then meticulously rolls his shirt sleeves up to his elbows.

Christmas bumps into my shoulder and hums. "He's sex on a peppermint stick."

"You're married." I turn on her.

"Which means I'm taken, not blind."

Jude steps over to the sink to wash his hands, and I watch Aunt Gertie pick up Jude's suit coat and bring it to her nose.

Stepping forward, I snag the jacket from her hands. "Aunt Gertie, why don't you grab the flour?"

I spin for the dining room to set Jude's coat on the back of a chair, but not before taking my own whiff, inhaling his expensive scent.

Within minutes of returning to the crowded kitchen, Christmas is pulling sugar cookie dough from the refrigerator. Panic sets in as I know Gran can mess up the recipe.

"Don't worry," Christmas says near me. "I made the dough last night."

Hunks of dough are broken off from the giant balls and distributed. When one is handed to Jude, he stares at it like he isn't certain what to do. I step closer to him as he focuses on the clump in his hand.

"I've never actually made cookies." His voice is low, so only I can hear. "All the images on my mother's social media were staged. The cut-outs had to be perfect. The decorations like a master baker had made them. Kids in the kitchen were messy." He glances up at me with sadness and fear in his eyes. Like he's afraid he'll fail here, like a repeat of when he'd spilled the bowl of eggs during the breakfast with Santa.

"I'll help you," I say, placing my hand on his forearm, finding his skin no longer so cold but warm beneath my hand. Stepping in front of him, I take the dough from his hands.

"First, you need flour." I point to the giant container and watch as Jude dumps an exorbitant amount on the plastic tablecloth, noticing that Christmas did the same thing.

"Next, you spread it." There's no reason for my voice to drop, but I take Jude's hand and place it right in the flour, forcing the downy whiteness to spread. When he picks up his hand, he stares at the powder still on his palm.

"Okay, now we drop the dough in the flour and roll it." I lean forward, stretching over the table for a rolling pin. Bringing it closer to me, I take Jude's powdered hand, wrap it around the wooden cylinder, and guide him to stroke it, intending to coat the roller with the excess flour.

My gaze leaps to Aunt Gertie, who is watching Jude's action like he's doing something sexual.

"Okay," I say a little too loudly. "Now we roll the dough."

I hand Jude the roller and place my hands over his, and together we flatten the dough.

"Just like that," I mutter. "You're doing great," I encourage, all the while being hyper aware of Jude's closeness at my back and the way the roller moves back and forth, rocking Jude's body ever so slightly into mine.

"Now who's the bad one?" he eventually whispers near my ear, his breath tickling my neck and reminding me of his hand on it, his thumb stroking over my pulse point, and eventually his mouth sucking at me there.

"Pick a cutter," I state, finding my voice tight, strained almost, when we finally have the dough spread out.

Is it hot in here? How can I be getting turned on with my family in the room? I tug at the collar of my sweater.

"You okay there, Angelica?" Christmas asks from across the table.

I glare back at her. "I'm fine." But I'm certain my cheeks are rosy and my eyes wild.

Jude leans around me to pick a cutter from the middle of the table. "What the heck is this one?"

"A grinch," one of my nephews states.

"Fitting," Jude mumbles before pressing the form into the dough.

But when the cookie is eventually baked and decorated by Jude himself, he's rather proud.

I'm proud of him, too. He didn't complain about the flour on his suit pants or the chaotic noise of my family.

"You okay?" I asked him at one point.

"It's just so bizarre," he admitted. "No one is fighting or complaining or demanding a reshoot."

He means the staged photo shoots of his younger cookie-baking experience.

I focused on the side of Jude's beautiful face. The puzzlement and wonder frosted in his expression, and my heart crumbled like a few of the cookies we'd made. He's missed out on so much. Things he didn't even know he'd missed. Things he hadn't known were possible. Love and laughter, even happy bickering, among a family. I wanted to wrap him in a hug.

And in this case, the only one taking pictures is my Aunt Gertie, who has an unhealthy obsession with her phone camera and is using it to capture every moment.

Or hot men baking cookies.

On more than one occasion, Gran had to tell Gertie she'd take her phone away from her. I caught Gran's eye, who nodded at Jude. Thank goodness Aunt Gertie didn't understand the internet or how to upload images to social media.

Eventually, the air was permeated with scents of vanilla and peppermint. Flour and brightly colored sugar is everywhere. Frosting overdecorates cookies and drips onto the table.

Christmas's three boys were out of control, doped up by a sugar buzz. My brother, Dane's twin girls were polar opposites of each other. The shier one wanted everything to be perfect; the wilder one deciding the more candy on a cookie, the better.

And in the middle of it all was Jude, silently observing, like he was taking notes.

My family didn't leave him out of the mix but blended him in as if he'd always been here. A part of us. A member of the family.

The thought was doing strange things to my head. *Weren't we pretending to date?*

"Uncle Beau is sucking Belle's face again," the oldest of my nephews eventually announces to the crowded kitchen, sometime after dinner, which was delivered pizzas.

Gran rushes out of the room to separate the couple while Gertie reaches for her cell phone. "Just going to capture the moment."

Our cookie baking is winding down.

With Dane and the twins long gone and Christmas wrangling her boys upstairs for a bath, I glance around the kitchen, which looks like holiday elves had a rage party.

"I guess I should get to cleaning up."

The countertops don't have a stitch of vacant space. The table is covered in remnants of flour and colored sugar. The candy-sprinkle containers and bowls of dried frosting add to the mayhem.

"I can stay, too," Jude offers, but he can't fight a tight yawn.

"You need to work tomorrow," I remind him.

"So do you," he states.

It strikes me how much we know about one another in such a short period of time. Where we each live. Our work schedules. We both work odd hours and any day of the week, although he has more liberty than I do, and I need to make up for missed shifts when I'd called off sick.

"When can I see you next?" he says, stepping close to me and brushing back hairs that have come loose from my braid.

"Jude," I whisper, lowering my head. "We don't need to do this."

"Do what?" he asks, slipping his hands into his pants pockets, which have a dusting of flour near the edge.

"This." I point between us. "Pretend."

"Pretend?" he parrots.

"The boyfriend-girlfriend thing." I exhale heavily. He made quite an impression on my family, and I'll have to pick up the pieces eventually, explaining how Jude wasn't ever really my boyfriend. But for now, he's fitting in. "My family loves you. You can be my date for Beau's wedding."

My voice isn't convincing. I mean, I want him to be my date for Beau's wedding. But I also want him to be more. However, all that talk in the laundry room was just talk. Flirty words while getting me off, distracting me from the issue at hand. Beau's wedding. Which I still don't have a venue for.

"We don't need to keep up the ruse outside of them."

"Ruse?" Jude takes another step closer to me, forcing me back into the side of the refrigerator. Brushing loose curls around my ear again, he strokes down the side of my neck, and I close my eyes.

"Does this feel like pretend?"

Isn't that the issue? Everything is starting to feel a little too real. The way we meshed on my couch last night. The way he blended with my family. The way he kisses me.

"I don't know," I whisper, swallowing against the goosebumps breaking out on my skin. "Isn't it?"

Jude's expression hardens, and he drops his hand. His eyes slowly restore to that icy glare. His brows pinch like he's deep in thought.

"What about when my fingers were inside you earlier? Did that feel fake?"

I couldn't possibly fake how my body responds to his. The way I clenched around his fingers. The way I drenched his hand.

"What about last night?" he continues, lowering his voice and leaning his forehead closer to mine, but not close enough to meet. "You didn't taste like pretend on my tongue." He pauses a beat. "In fact, you tasted better than anything I've ever tasted before."

My cheeks feel like they are sunburned as he stares at my mouth.

"Jude," I whisper. "What are we doing? I'm not your type, and you aren't mine."

The second I say the words, I know I'm wrong. He could be everything to me.

"I'm not?" He abruptly stands taller, a deep line forming between his brows. He suddenly looks wounded, like I've pierced his heart or ripped it out of his chest. He even covers his left pec and rubs over it a second before asking, "What makes me not good enough for you?"

My eyes go wide. That's not what I'm saying. "I never said you aren't good enough. You're plenty good."

He's trying so hard to complete the assignment I gave him. The list. He donated a crazy amount of money to A Snowball's Chance and gave of his time last weekend at the breakfast. He's different. I can see it now.

"But not good *enough*," he counters, his voice like acid. "You want me to be better."

I don't *want* anything from him. I want him to want to be better for himself. Less extravagance and more joy. Less loneliness and more love.

"Yeah, I get it," he states, though he clearly doesn't because I'm not explaining myself well.

He takes a giant step back, putting more space between us, and bumps into the edge of the table.

"Everything is always pretend. Never as it seems. Just like Santa Claus, it's all a lie." His voice rises.

I gasp at the same time I hear, "Santa isn't real?"

With shock, Jude and I both turn our heads toward my youngest nephew, who is standing in the kitchen archway in winter pajamas and with wet hair. *Crap*.

"Devin, what are you doing down here?" I rush to pick him up, pressing a kiss to his temple, catching a sharp whiff of baby shampoo on him, while I glance at Jude.

He closes his eyes, the expression on his face reading, *Fuck!*

"He just said Santa was a lie." Devin's little voice trembles.

"He said Santa likes pie," I try to deflect.

"Mommy says lying is bad," he replies, fixated as young children can be.

Shit, shit, shit. My sister is going to kill me for this one, but I can't take my eyes off Jude, who looks devastated, and I can't decide if it's from our discussion or the sudden crush of a child's beliefs.

"I'm sorry," Jude mumbles, eventually opening his eyes, which are back to their icicle gaze. I don't like that I'm the reason for the sudden, distant coldness in his eyes when they were starting to thaw over the past few days, growing warmer, like puddles of hope.

He brushes past me, and I spin toward the dining room as he rips a container of cookies with his name written on it like he is part of the family off the table.

"Jude. Wait," I call after him, but he doesn't turn around.

"Maggie," he states aloofly, addressing Gran, who stands at the opposite end of the dining room as he passes her.

"Christmas," I hear him say next, knowing my sister must be near the open living room door, seeking her escape-artist child.

"The day has been a pleasure," he states, sounding like a robot, reminding me how he suddenly shut down the day we'd been shopping.

When moments of fun collided with a hasty exit.

Like the exit he's making right now.

"What the hell happened?" Aunt Gertie's voice startles me, and I spin to find her standing in the back exit. The space leads out of Gran's kitchen to a set of enclosed stairs, like a fire escape. Every apartment building in Chicago has two entrances and exits for fire safety.

I cling to Devin for another second until Christmas enters the dining room.

"Devin," she groans.

The boy lunges toward his mother, who holds out her hands for him.

"That man said Santa is a lie." His tiny voice quivers as he lays his head on Christmas's shoulder.

Christmas glares at me. "What man?"

"Mr. Jude"

What the fuck? Christmas mouths at me over the shoulder of her sleepy boy's head.

"He didn't say Santa was a lie." I try to reroute while smoothing my hand down my nephew's little back. "He said Santa likes pie."

I'm a terrible liar.

Christmas raises her brows, her expression once again saying, *what the fuck?*

I mouth, *I'm sorry*. I don't think quickly on my feet, especially when I'm tired from standing on them all day. My back aches. Who knew making Christmas cookies could have such an effect?

Gran stands behind Christmas. "You know Santa doesn't come to little boys who aren't in bed when they are supposed to be." Her intention to distract Devin works as he lifts his head, glancing at his great-grandmother with wild eyes, before he cups his mother's cheeks.

"Mama, I need to get to bed. Quick, quick." He wiggles in Christmas's arm, like he isn't the least bit tired.

"Alright, alright," she says excitedly, playing along with her son's sudden urge to race to bed.

Before she departs, she spares me one final glance. One that says, *we'll talk about this later*. Like she's *my* mother as well.

As they exit the dining room, Gertie speaks. "Think Santa will make me come if I go to bed when I'm supposed to?"

"Gertrude!" Gran turns on her sister.

I spin to face my great-aunt, who is lifting a bottle of wine to her lips and wiggling her brows. She takes a quick sip right out of the container.

"You've raised a bunch of horn dogs, Maggie," she counters to her sister. "I deserve some fun as well."

"Horn dogs?" I snort.

"I have proof," she teases, lifting her phone with her other hand. Holding her screen face out is an image of me against the fridge with Jude in front of me. His hand is at my throat.

"Aunt Gertie," I bark.

"Gertrude Marie, what did I tell you about taking photos of people?" Gran admonishes her sister.

"You said I could not take photos of *random* people." After Gertie figured out the camera on her phone, she'd snap pictures of good-looking men walking down the street or in a restaurant, like most tourists take photos of the scenery. While she tried to play innocent old lady if men caught her, one time a man didn't take too kindly to his image being captured without his permission, and Gran had to explain to Gertie, for the tenth time, it wasn't legal to photograph someone without their consent.

"And this is family." She jiggles the phone in her hand, like taking our photos without permission does not fall into the no-consent category. We might complain, but we aren't going to file a lawsuit against her. Or so she thinks.

I snatch the phone from her, prepared to delete the image. But first, I pause to stare at it. Gertie's angle is surprisingly good. While Jude blocks me for the most part, you still see a sliver of my face in reaction to his question.

Does this feel fake?

I'm staring up at him. My eyes are wide. My cheeks rosy. I look . . . turned on. Whenever he does that throat thing, I strangely am, and I don't recognize my reaction.

I also don't recognize me in this image. The way I'm looking at him. I wish Gertie had caught his face, so I had a second glance at Jude. A redo, for a second impression. Because somehow, I've misjudged Jude. I've *hurt* him.

He looked so wounded when he claimed I didn't think he was good enough. Then he shut down. His expression grew hard, and his eyes closed off, like a red alert for a blizzard warning. He froze me out.

His Santa-is-a-lie comment was not intended for little ears. How many times have we, as adults in my family, had to double-check ourselves when talking about the white-bearded man around any of the kids? I don't believe Jude is so cruel he'd ruin Christmas for children.

I brush my thumb over the image once, then seek the trash can icon to delete it from Gertie's phone.

Without a word, I hand the phone back to her. My aged aunt stares at me.

"Keep up on that protective skin." Her voice turns harder than her typically teasing tone. She winks. "You don't want wrinkles."

By wrinkles, she means a lapse in judgment. Falling in love again.

I love my aunt. She's flirty and fun, and gives no fucks, but her reckless behavior hides a deeply scarred woman. One still aching from a decades-old betrayal.

Which I completely understand.

I've also worked hard to guard myself against *it* ever happening again. I don't have one-night stands or chase men or take random photos of ones I ogle. I don't drink straight from the bottle of wine or cry late at night. Been there, done that.

Most of all, I don't want to harbor bitterness in my gut like she has. Her heart was shattered once upon a time. Mine, too. The difference is, I patched mine back together. I still choose love over everything else. I *want* to love again.

I'm just pickier this time.

"Are you ready to discuss why you didn't mention you have a boyfriend?" Gran says, stepping up to my side.

"I don't have—" I freeze at the hopeful expression on Gran's face. Unlike her sister, Gran experienced the love of a lifetime until Gramps passed a few years ago. She has always believed in second chances at love, and she's held her breath with every date I've been on in the last decade, hopeful that love has found me again. Or rather, that I've found it.

When I consider her question, it also gives me pause. While Jude might not be my boyfriend, something *is* happening between us. Maybe it isn't as formal as relationship labels. Maybe we are just building a friendship. One that might include some benefits.

Only I don't do friends-with-benefits, so I'm confused.

Does it feel like pretend to you? His finger stroking along my neck is turning into my new favorite move. His eyes were the thing that caught me off guard. They didn't look like ice caps as much as clear pools, allowing me to see inside him, but I hadn't looked hard enough.

I didn't know how to pretend to touch someone, but I worried Jude did. All those broken-hearted girls in high school. The ones he so easily discarded. I even think of Sabrina, and how he so casually said he didn't care about her anymore.

Hadn't that been my experience? People fall in love and then stumble out of it.

I promised myself I'd never project my fears on another person. I had a protective skin, sure, like Gertie called the necessary shield to her heart. But I've been wanting to shed that layer for a long time. Too long.

Noticing Gran is still staring at me, waiting for some kind of explanation, I clear my throat.

"We're still new. No formal declarations or labels yet," I offer, along with a tight smile. One I'm certain Gran can see right through, but she doesn't press.

"Declarations?" Gertie snorts, pulling the bottle from her lips like she'd just taken another drink. "Write your own declaration." Her voice sobers while deepening to poorly imitate a masculine tone.

"I do solemnly swear that I can take care of myself and provide my own orgasms— Hey!"

Gertie cries out as Gran swipes the bottle of wine from her hands. "I think that's enough of that."

Then to both our surprise, Gran takes a drink directly from the bottle.

"Gran." I chuckle.

"Thatta girl," Gertie encourages.

"Yes, well, this girl has a kitchen to tackle."

Her comment pulls me back to the current state of the other room. Disaster.

"I'll help clean up," I offer, holding back a heavy sigh when I recall the mess. When I make chocolates in my apartment, I clean as I go. Gran has always been the opposite, saying not to fuss.

Cleaning the kitchen while baking is like shoveling snow during a blizzard, she'd say.

As I step toward the kitchen, Gran lays her hand on my forearm. "Sweetie, go home."

"I can help."

She's already shaking her head. "You worked tirelessly today, and I appreciate you."

I chuckle as Gran has picked up the modern phrase for praise.

"Now," Gran continues. "I just want some quiet." Without mentioning it, her statement implies having great-grandkids is wonderful, in theory. In practice, the mayhem is a lot.

"Cleaning the kitchen won't take me long."

When Gran has something on her mind, she says, *it's nothing cleaning a dish won't solve*. The expression was her way of explaining how handwashing dishes cleared her thoughts.

In this case, I worry about what might be on Gran's mind.

"Let me help," I say again. "Many hands work faster, or something like that." I wasn't as good as Gran with wisdom off the cuff.

"And too many cooks in the kitchen can spoil a pie. Or cookies." She glances at the multiple plastic containers of cookies covering her dining room table.

"At least let me put these in the freezer." Gran has an upright freezer down in the laundry room, and she will save most of her cookie collection for distribution to friends.

"I'll do it tomorrow." She pats my arm, punctuating her request. She wants me to let it go.

"If you're sure?" I hesitate, taking another peek toward the kitchen where I can see the mess splayed out on the kitchen table from where I stand.

Gran raises the bottle of wine in her hand a little higher. "I'm sure. Plus, I have Gertie to help me."

"Me? I was hoping if I went to bed, Santa might visit me early." She wiggles her brows.

In so many ways, I wish I was like my great aunt with her carefree attitude and the ease with which she lets things roll off her tongue.

Still, I recognize the coverup, and I don't ever want to appear as broken as I know she is.

I also don't want to break someone else, which has my thoughts returning to Jude.

As much as Gran wants me to go home, I have a stop to make before I do.

chapter 25

[Jude]

The entire way home, I stew.

What are we doing? she'd asked. I thought we were getting to know each other better. Building on whatever this strange connection is between us.

Hell, hours earlier today, I practically asked her to marry me. When I don't trust the institution. My experience has taught me to distrust marriage.

Does this feel like pretend? I'd asked her. Maybe we'd started out with that intention. The fake-date exchange. But something has shifted. Something I want to explore, and yet somehow, I've misread the situation.

An audiobook narrator is fictional. An actor goes through motions. But the softness of her pleas? My name on her lips which drove me wild? Her body's response to my touch was not an act.

She said she wasn't my type, but she was wrong. She is exactly what I need. Who I want.

As for me being her type, maybe she wasn't wrong there, but how can I prove to her that I want to be? I want to be someone she's proud of and excited about. Someone she wants to see again and again.

Even though she mentioned attending her brother's wedding, she didn't sound convinced my attendance was what she really wanted. This was no longer about a square deal. This was about feeling something. Something strong and overwhelming and unfamiliar, but something I wanted to embrace.

Slamming my hand on the steering wheel, I maneuver into the private parking garage of my building and make the silent climb in the elevator to my condo. Once inside my place, the loneliness is almost too much. It's quiet compared to the chaos of Angelica's grandmother's kitchen. It's empty and hollow, like my heart feels right now.

I head to the shower, needing to wash off the scent of sugar and spice, and baking cookies.

I'm just stepping out of the shower when I hear a sharp rapping on my front door. Strange, considering the building is secure, and I don't interact with my neighbors. Typically, I'd ignore the sound. Whomever is on the other side of the door will get the hint and go away.

But something draws me to my entryway. Maybe it's the insistence of the knock. Maybe I'm just curious.

After peering through the security hole, I yank open the door and exhale a confused breath.

"Angelica?"

"I'm sorry," she blurts.

"How did you get up here?" I glance into the hallway. She is familiar with where I live because of her first responder position. This building is an icon in Chicago, but getting up to my floor involves being buzzed up or being on a list.

She sheepishly shrugs. "I can be persuasive without being in retail."

I'd smile at the joke if I weren't still so confused. Instead, I open the door wider, inviting her in.

I don't miss how her gaze leaps to my naked chest and the low-slung towel around my waist. My wet hair should confirm I'd been in the shower.

She enters my spacious living room, where the city is on display through the wall-to-wall windows. Pinpricks of light dot various buildings along Lake Shore Drive. The stars are out there somewhere over Lake Michigan. One of the reasons I love this place is the view of the water during daylight.

A butter-soft leather couch faces the windows, and Angelica stops behind it. I lean against the back. Spreading my hands wide, bracing them on the support, I cross my ankles and hang my head, waiting for her to speak. She came to me.

Don't you leave me, Jude. The quiet command still makes no sense, but it is a reminder that I promised myself I'd turn over a new leaf. That leaf feels like an autumn one right now. Crunchy and brown, and crushed underneath someone's foot.

And I shouldn't have left her grandmother's place the way I did.

"I wasn't fair earlier."

My head pops up and I watch as she licks her lips.

"The past few days have just been a lot. I'm not used to someone taking care of me like you did when I was sick. And then hanging out with my family was new, too. I meant what I said; they really adored you."

But does she adore me?

She waves toward me, while her brows crease. "And this morning got a little intense. I've just been in my head."

The laundry room and wedding plans.

"I never meant to imply you weren't good enough as you are, Jude. Or even suggest you need to be a different person. You have changed. I've seen it."

Has she? I turn my head, staring at a dark piece of art over a false mantel. The image is abstract and disturbing, like the artist was mad while creating it, and simply smeared the paint over the canvas. I instantly connected with it. Angry. Bitter. Spoiled.

But holding those negative feelings up as a shield has been exhausting.

"I do want to change." I slowly turn my head back toward her. "I *am* changing." Maybe the ways have been small. Maybe it's more of a feeling than something physical. I can't describe it, and I don't want to try to quantify it for her.

This wasn't about her. After the heart attack, I felt different. Felt something for the first time in a long time. Something strange, almost itchy, like I'm coming out of my skin most days, but when I am around her, everything feels right. Calmer. Peaceful.

Today had been a surprisingly great day. Her family was so . . . real. It had been fascinating to watch, to participate in their chaos, witness their love for each other. It made me both happy and envious. I want what they have.

"I'm not pretending with you," I blurt. I'm through pretending. Holding back emotions. Struggling with feelings. Putting up an act.

"Okay." She nods, rolling her lips inward like she has more to say but stopping herself.

Silence weaves between us before she asks, "Can I hug you now?"

I stiffen for a second, uncertain I've ever been asked. I hardly remember the last time someone willingly hugged me. Or I hugged someone back.

With a sharp nod, I invite her toward me, but keep my arms locked around my bare chest.

When Angelica steps closer to me, she gently pulls them apart. Because I don't know what to do with them, I set my hands on the back of the couch again, fisting them on either side of my hips. For some reason, I'm sweating.

Angelica doesn't falter.

My feet uncross like they have a will of their own and she steps between them, forcing my legs further apart as she settles into the cradle between them. Her hands come to my chest first. Her touch is like a hot iron on my skin, branding me. My heart races as she takes her time to skim up my pecs and around my shoulders. Slowly, ever so slowly, she presses her body against mine, tightening her arms around my neck. Her cheek meets my ear as she tips up on her toes to match my slightly seated height.

We awkwardly stand like this for a solid minute. The longest minute of my life, if I'm honest, and I inhale her sugar and spice scent. A loose hair of hers tickles my jaw.

When I sense her ready to pull away, I finally react. My arms wrap around her back, and I tug her tighter to me, feel her settle against my chest, like she's melting into me. She shifts her head and smiles against my neck.

"That's it, Jude," she whispers near my ear, like when she was coaching me to ice skate.

I continue to hold her, feeling my shoulders start to relax, and my arms loosen from their stiffness. I hold firm, but not so awkwardly. Even my legs begin to mellow, releasing from their stiff stance, like beams holding up a building.

We stand like this another minute as Angelica cups the back of my head, and I slide my hand up to her nape. Slowly, I turn my face into the space between her throat and shoulder, inhaling and exhaling like the nurses taught me.

Only, my heart doesn't stop racing.

When I feel Angelica pull back, I don't want to let go, but I don't want to force her to hold on longer than she desires.

Lowering my arms, I catch her hips as she leans back and slides her hands down my chest again. She watches the path her palms take. I watch as well, liking how her delicate fingers look against my skin. Loving the feel of them against my flesh.

"I've never seen you so casual," she teases about my towel-only attire.

"You've seen me in my underwear. Doesn't get any more laid-back than that."

She chuckles. "You are a bit shameless."

"But you like it." Cautiously, I glance at her, meeting those soft, flaming eyes.

She gently plucks at a few chest hairs. "Yeah. I like it."

The smile slowly forming on my lips feels strange, almost too large for my mouth, and I dig my teeth into my lower lip as if I can stop the unfurling spread.

But when Angelica smiles back, my grin is inevitable. Like a fool, I suddenly feel like I can't stop smiling.

Angelica covers my hands on her hips with hers, and I expect her to push me away. Instead, she holds onto them and steps away from me.

"I'm tired, Jude. And it's late." She stands tall, but something in the set of her shoulders suggests she's nervous. "And since we've already slept together . . ."

I arch a brow, prepared to make a joke, but the flickering gleam in her eyes stops me. Without another word, she tugs at my hands and takes another step backward, urging me to rise, and follow her.

She helps herself down my hallway, as if she knows where she's going, as if she's been here a thousand times before.

With her confidence shored up, she spins to face the last door of the long hallway and leads me into my bedroom.

chapter 26

[Angelica]

My intention wasn't to have sex with him. Jude still looked like he was hurting. For a minute there, I thought he might combust from my hug. I didn't miss his hands fisted at his sides, like he hated the embrace. He was so tense.

But when I finally decided to stop torturing him, he began to relax. He slipped his arms around my back and held tight, like I was a buoy in rough seas. I don't know how long we clung to one another, but once my body settled against his, my eyes drifted shut.

It was late. I was exhausted. And Jude was comfortable.

I should have left. Another twenty minutes, and I'd be home in my own bed, but I didn't want to leave him. Not yet. My argument was that we'd already shared a bed once, I didn't see why we couldn't share a bed again.

Once inside his room, I didn't know what to do next. I didn't have a plan.

Thankfully, Jude takes the lead. He pulls a fresh T-shirt from a drawer and hands it to me. "You can sleep in this. Bathroom's in there."

"Thanks." Stepping into the smaller room he pointed toward, which is the size of my entire kitchen, I quickly take care of business. Undress, use the facility, and swipe some toothpaste on my finger to brush my teeth. Not the best bedtime routine, but not the worst either.

When I return to his bedroom, Jude is already in his bed, boxer briefs on, lying flat on his back. A lamp beside the bed illuminates the room. He watches me as I circle the bed and climb beneath the covers. His sheets feel decadent and rich.

Mirroring Jude's position, I lie on my back as Jude stretches for the lamp, clicking it off. I flinch even though I anticipate the darkness. Jude shifts to his side, facing me, and I turn only my head.

When his fingers touch my arm, delicately stroking up and down the length, my eyelids feel heavy again.

"When I was a kid and I couldn't sleep, my mom would tickle my arm like that."

Jude doesn't respond.

"That feels nice," I whisper, my voice sleepy.

Another minute passes, and I sink further into the bed.

"I don't know how to go slow," Jude finally says, his voice low, before he stops tickling my arm and cups my hand, bringing it up to his lips to kiss the tips of my fingers.

"But I'm trying," he adds.

I stare at him as best I can in the dimly lit room. An orange glow from the city lights, stories below, reflects into the clouds outside the wall-to-wall windows, casting a dull glow in his room.

With my head turned toward him, I say, "Who says you have to go slow?"

I'm not certain who moves first, but suddenly, our mouths press together, and hands roam. Our bodies draw together like puzzle pieces, and that crackling sensation of cold air crystalizing on glass tickles over my skin at the sudden contact. Our arms wrap around each other. Our legs entwine. I'm hyper aware of the coarseness of his against the smoothness of mine.

Our mouths continue to meet, discovering one another, although we've kissed before. This is different. This is Jude unleashed and me untethered, both of us riding out the storm of whatever this is between us.

He rolls me to my back, pinning me beneath his weight. His hands seek mine, and he lifts both my arms over my head.

We stay like this for a long minute with our mouths still joined, searching for more. His weight feels so good over me and my hips shift, legs spreading wider, welcoming him into the cradle between my thighs.

"Angelica," he moans as he shifts his lower half, and I'm met by his hard length against my soft center.

With nothing more than my thin panties and his fitted boxer briefs between us, I feel everything. The length and solidness and the heat of his tip when he meets the dampness of my own underwear. He rocks forward, and I tip my head back, momentarily breaking our kiss.

"Jude," I cry out. I'm suddenly wide awake and wanting everything. My arms struggle in his grasp over my head.

"Need something, angel?"

He kisses me before I can answer.

You, I want to shout. For better or worse. I want to feel him naked and raw against me.

Instead, I let the subtle jolt of my lower half express all that I desire. With my clit practically kissing his tip, I moan in desperation.

Jude continues to pin my hands above my head, locking my wrists into one of his hands while the other travels down the underside of my arm. Trailing down the sensitive length of skin, my existing need for him blooms into a desperate desire. He reaches for the hem of his shirt on me and pushes it upward so he can cup a breast. I cry out again at the sudden pinch he gives my sharp nipple. My hips buck, and I wrap one leg around his lower back, opening myself wider.

He breaks our kiss and moves quickly down my neck where he nips at the juncture of it and my shoulder before dropping even lower to my breast.

Jude sucks, sharp and quick. When he pops off the tender swell, I let out a little yip. He moves down to my belly before he releases my wrists, and I clutch at his hair as his head lowers for where I want him most.

When he reaches my panties, which are soaked, he swipes his tongue over the damp silk. Then he hums against where I'm most sensitive.

"You smell like sugar and spice, even down here." Hooking his fingers into the waistband of my underwear, he slides them down my thighs to just below my knees, then forces my knees wide again, which rolls the underwear to my ankles.

Jude settles in once more. With the first lick, my lower half bows off the bed, but Jude uses those broad hands of his to hold my hips still, keeping me once again pinned to the bed. His tongue does wicked things, sliding through slick folds and twirling against that trigger point.

My legs begin to shake. Holding me in place only adds to the climb. The spiral up and up and up a steep mountain until I've reached the summit where Jude likes to dangle me on the pinnacle before setting me free.

I scream his name as I come hard and fast, barreling back down the other side of that mountain in a rush I've never felt before.

Jude continues to hold my hips, driving his tongue deeper, prolonging the ride as I moan and hum and toss my head from side to side until I'm wrung out and collapse back to the bed.

I quickly catch my breath as Jude's fingers enter me, sliding in and out in a lazy motion.

"I want to feel all this wetness dripping down my dick."

"Yes," I whisper.

Jude presses up to his knees and one-handedly shoves down his boxer briefs. His fingers still only momentarily inside me, and then he's on top of me again. The weight of his shaft glides back and forth in the wetness he's made before his tip catches on my clit.

Jude cups my shins and presses them to my chest, holding my legs up and wide. I'm on display in a way I never have been, and he settles his thickness against me once more, sliding his hard cock back and forth through the soaked creases.

"You feel so good," he strains, his voice as tight as his grip on my legs.

When his tip notches at my entrance, we both freeze. His blue eyes are reflected in the dull light and sparkle like ice crystals. Quickly, he releases my legs and stretches for the nightstand beside his bed.

I hear the telltale sound of a rip and then watch as Jude covers his length. He settles back between my thighs, but keeps his arms extended while his hardness lies against my clit.

"This still okay?"

"More than okay," I whisper, holding on his eyes before he glances where we meet. He grips his dick and lines it up, then slowly dips inside me.

Jude is big. Bigger than anyone I've ever experienced, and I appreciate the time he takes to slowly fill me. Once he's to the hilt, he pauses.

"I just need a second." His voice comes heavy and ragged while he hangs his head, still braced on extended arms.

I reach up and cup his jaw. "You won't break me," I whisper.

"But I want to." His head pops up and he stares down at me. "I want to shatter you in the best way."

That shouldn't turn me on as much as it does. "Break away," I whisper, wanting him to do his worst.

"Angel," he groans as he pulls back until only his tip rests inside me. Then he drives home again, a little quicker, a little sharper.

When I puff out a breath, he does it again and again, taking his time to tease and torture. Back and forth he moves while I cling to him. My hands cup his face first, pulling him down to kiss me until we can't keep the connection.

Then, I wrap my arms around his slick back, nails scratching down his spine. The move causes Jude to react. His head pops up, and his hips move faster.

"Do you like that?" I tease, drawing my nails back up his back.

"Fuck," he grunts, moving even faster. His hips snap forward and mine snap back, each of us meeting the other thrust for thrust.

"You feel so good." He sounds almost surprised, but I'm not. Not that I didn't think Jude would be talented in this area, but his expertise surpasses my fantasies. The reality is so much better than what I'd imagined in my head.

Eventually, he brings his hand between us, catching his thumb on my clit.

"What are you . . ." My breath hitches as I quickly discover what he's doing and wonder how no one has ever done this to me before.

His skilled thumb circles my clit, and his hard length dips in and out, and I feel the familiar climb only this man creates.

"Jude," I cry out in warning.

"Yeah, sweetheart," he grunts. "Come for me. Come all over me. Mark me as yours."

The command is deep and shattering as he promised. I break into a million little pieces, scattering in the wind like drifts of snow across a flat field. Weightless and breathless, I come again, wrapped around him.

Jude rocks even faster, driving even deeper, until he abruptly halts. He flings his head back, and I stare at the vein on his neck, pulsing in rhythm with another spot on him.

When Jude collapses over me, he brings the hand that touched me to the top of my head as if cocooning me beneath him. His inhales are rapid, and his chest presses against mine, before he rolls us to our sides.

He swipes his hand over my hair, holding it back while he stares at me.

"Why did that feel like another epiphany?"

"I don't know." I chuckle, feeling strangely the same way.

Jude Ashford just ruined me.

"From the moment I met you, I've had this pull to you," Jude says, his voice low as he continues to smooth back my hair.

"It's called transference," I tease, feeling something rise in my chest. A fear that things are moving too fast, when I'm the one who told him he didn't need to go slow. "You *think* you're attracted to me because I saved you."

Transference happens in many ways, but it's mainly when someone hurt believes they love someone who helped. Patients with doctors. Victims with first responders.

It's one reason I warned Jude not to fall in love with me. He'd fall under a false perception, not actual attraction.

Jude chuffs. "Oh, there is no doubt I'm attracted to you, but it's not because you saved me."

"Really?" I arch a brow, both curious and teasing. Desperate to keep the moment light.

"Really." He bops my nose before he lowers his gaze to my lips. "And I'm most attracted to this spot right here."

He sets his fingertip just below my lower lip, off to the left.

"Why there?" I question with a nervous laugh.

"Because you have a freckle that I've claimed as mine. Like the North Star in the sky, leading me—"

He abruptly stops, and I hold my breath, waiting on that final word.

Instead, he leans forward and presses a soft kiss to that spot just below my lip.

I shouldn't like that out of the freckles I've always considered a nuisance, he's claimed one as his own. "That was beautiful. Thank you."

"You're beautiful," he says before giving me another quick kiss and rolling from the bed to dispose of the condom.

When he returns, he presses me away from him, then settles his front to my back, lining himself up with me everywhere he can, like he did when I was sick.

And we fall asleep for a short winter nap.

+ + +

Morning comes too quickly. Like snapshots on Aunt Gertie's phone, I flip through the captured moments of the past few days. Jude in my place; me in his. His hands on my skin and his kiss on my lips. It's all been so much so fast, and I don't want to get ahead of myself, but I can't seem to slow the rapid roll of wanting more with Jude.

Like he said, he's not pretending.

I couldn't fake these blooming feelings if I tried.

He's so different than I first thought. The selfish, distant man is more open-minded than I'd initially given him credit. He's changing right in front of my eyes.

Like I told him, I see him wanting to do better, putting in effort to be better, and the trait is endearing.

He's still as complex as ever, especially with all that talk of being my groom.

With that thought, I roll my head on the pillow and watch him rest. He looks less intense as he sleeps. Not so hard, but also not completely soft. He's just . . . Jude.

Beautiful on the outside, complex on the inside, a perfect blend like my chocolate mints.

On that note, I slowly slink from Jude's bed. After missing days of work, I don't want to be late, and I need to make a quick trip home. Tiptoeing around Jude's room, I collect my underwear and yesterday's clothing before stepping into his bathroom. Every sound is too loud. The toilet flushing. The water running. Even braiding my hair somehow feels noisy.

When I re-enter Jude's room, he jackknifes upright, lifting one knee and wrapping both arms around it.

"Where are you going?"

"I'm on shift today, and I need to go home to get my uniform." As I hadn't planned a sleepover, or a night of unforgettable sex, I need a few minutes before I head to the firehouse.

Jude hums, running his hand over his head and mussing up the already rumpled hair. He looks well-rested while freshly fucked, and I fight a smile, knowing I did that to him.

At least for one night.

"Maybe you should bring that uniform with you the next time. We can re-enact the day I had the heart attack."

"A broken heart," I correct, both a little thrilled at the mention of a next time, then crushed when I remember what Jude was probably doing when he had the stress episode.

He brushes off my correction and continues to give me that twitchy smile, which grows a little wider.

"You could pretend to be my angel. Maybe kiss me this time."

The reminder of what I'd actually done, but haven't owned up to yet, slaps my cheeks.

"Yeah." I choke. "Pretend." *Pretend to do something I already did.*

"You okay?" Jude tilts his head, staring at my face, which I'm certain gives me away.

"I'm good. It's just early. I need coffee." I roll my eyes and tug at the quick braid I made of my hair.

Jude tosses back the sheet over his lap and slips from the bed, prowling toward me with a seductive gleam in his eyes. He cups my jaw and gives me a quick kiss.

"Would you be interested in attending a hockey game with me sometime?"

"Sure." He knows I'm not a hockey fan, but he's asking me to do something with him. Something that interests him.

"How about Tuesday night?"

"Let me check my schedule and get back to you." I'm supposed to have holiday-escape drinks with a few girls this week.

Jude's face falls a little bit, but he quickly gives me one of his practiced smiles. Because I don't like the look, I run my thumb along his lips, intending to loosen them. Instead, he leans forward and kisses me with a broad sweep of his tongue.

A hockey game feels very dating-ish, but I don't mention it. We established last night that we aren't pretending. We are friends.

Maybe a date is a benefit.

chapter 27

[Jude]

When I pick Angelica up at her place, I'm nervous, which is ridiculous. It's not like I've never had a date. I've attended plenty of charity events and expensive dinners, but this somehow felt different.

The hockey game was personal. I loved the sport and was an excellent armchair player for someone who never learned to skate well.

I also had something for her, but I didn't know how she'd feel about it.

When she opens her door, she's wearing an off-the-shoulder sweater that hangs long over her curvy form with a pair of black leggings and knee-high boots. I'd skip the game and beg her to keep the boots on and remove the rest if the game didn't suddenly feel like an important step in proving myself to her.

I could go on a regular date, especially with someone I enjoyed being around.

"You look . . . casual," she teases as she leans back and gestures for me to enter her place. I'm wearing jeans and a long-sleeved shirt with Chicago's professional hockey team logo on the front. Underneath, I wear a second shirt because I don't want to take my jacket into the stadium.

"And you look beautiful," I state, leaning forward to kiss my favorite freckle.

When I pull back, we just stare at one another a second, fighting smiles and failing.

"I have something for you." I hold up the item, clutched in my sweaty palm.

"Since I knew you weren't really a fan of hockey, I didn't think you'd have anything to wear to the game, so I brought you this."

I hold up the old hockey uniform, a replica of the Chicago favorites.

"Ashford," she reads the back of the jersey that was customized with my name. The number nine is stitched underneath.

"My mom gave me this back when I was in college, and I just thought . . ." I watch her face, morph from confusion to something softer.

"You don't have to—" Suddenly, it feels like a silly thing, a stupid ask.

"I'd love to wear it." She reaches for the jersey and runs her fingertips over my name on the back. "Can I wear it tonight?"

Sheepishly, I admit, "I was hoping you would."

Right in front of me, she whips off her sweater, exposing a red tank top, and then slips the jersey over her head.

Fuck. She looks hot.

Spinning to give me her back, she asks, "What do you think?"

I think I like my name on her a little too much, and it makes me wonder if she'd ever attend a softball game with me in the summer. I play in a sixteen-inch summer league. But summer feels like a long way away from winter.

"I think you look like the ultimate fan."

She beams a smile at me, and I reach for her, needing another kiss before we leave.

When we finally arrive at the stadium, I'm leading her to our seats when I hear someone call my name.

"Ashford."

With my hand on Angelica's back, I glance over my shoulder at a man from that summer league softball team.

"Fitz," I hold out a hand and shake his. The dark-haired, dark-eyed man instantly captures Angelica's attention.

"Fitz, this is Angelica Winter. Angelica, Fitz Carlucci." His real name is Leonardo, but his dad goes by Leo, so Fitz goes by a shortened version of his middle name.

"Carlucci," Angelica gasps. "As in the restaurant?"

"Yeah," Fitz chuckles, good-natured and easy about his famous name.

Carlucci's is a famous Italian restaurant in the city and seeing Angelica's excitement about meeting this restaurant entrepreneur makes me add Carlucci's to my list of places to take her in the future.

But I have another reason for Angelica to meet Fitz.

"This is the woman I told you about. The one needing a place for her brother's wedding."

Angelica's head swivels toward me. The concourse in the stadium is crowded, and this isn't exactly how I planned to introduce her to my idea.

"You're trying to secure Carlucci's for my brother's wedding?" Her voice rises with hope, and I hate to dash that enthusiasm.

Fitz does it for me. "Whoa, whoa, whoa. Carlucci's books out months in advance." He chuckles again. "But we just opened a new brewery in November, and the event space on the second floor is available."

Angelica looks wide-eyed between Fitz and me. "So, you have space for a December twenty-third wedding?" she clarifies.

"An entire party room at your disposal, beautiful." He winks at Angelica, and I'd throat punch him if he weren't making her beam the way she is. Beam, while she's looking at me.

"Really?" she asks me, like she needs my approval.

"Really." I nod at Fitz.

"Here." He reaches into his back pocket and pulls out a black card with embossed gold writing. His name and a phone number. "Don't share that with anyone. Call me tomorrow, though, and we can discuss the particulars."

"Thank you." Her voice is wistful with relief while still a little shocked.

"Now," Fitz pats my shoulder. "Enough business. See you in the box." He nods at Angelica and heads toward the ramp for the upper levels.

"What just happened here?" Angelica asks, mouth gaping while staring at the black business card.

"You have a place to host Beau's wedding," I state.

"What did you do?" she whispers, lifting her head and gazing up at me with confusion.

I scrub at the back of my neck. "I, uh . . . I'm on a summer league softball team with a few other businessmen. We do favors for one another." I might be a member of one of the elite business networking clubs in the city as well but the guys on the team are the men I feel more comfortable asking for something personal.

"What will I owe the man?" She chuckles, the sound still full of shock. "My first born?"

"I'll probably owe him *mine*, but I've pulled in a favor. He owes me one."

"For what?"

Those innocent wide eyes do not want to know. Let's just say I have friends in not all the best places, and I respect their privacy.

With a name like Carlucci, Angelica shouldn't be asking me for details.

Realization slowly dawns on her. "Never mind." She hugs the business card to her chest. "But thank you, Jude. This is . . . what do I owe you for this?"

Staring at her, with that smile aimed at me, she doesn't owe me a thing. This isn't another one-for-one exchange.

"Just your company tonight." I swipe my finger down her nose.

"Your friend mentioned a box." She tilts her head, implying the private, personal way to watch a game.

"Our group collectively owns a box, but I bought us regular tickets for tonight." Regular seats. Regular dates. Trying to be a regular guy. "I just wanted it to be us tonight." I stare at her, hoping she isn't disappointed. Lots of people foam at the mouth over box seats, which include a private room and cushioned stadium seats, along with a full-service bar and food.

"I like that," she says, still giving me a smile, and I wrap my arm around her in relief.

After pressing a kiss to her head, I ask, "Now, what would you like to eat? We have your typical fried foods, or burgers, or hot dogs."

"I love all of the above," she hums, glancing up at me from under my arm.

Next to that freckle, her smile might be something I love above all else.

+++

When we sit in the seats I purchased, our beers and bratwurst balanced in our laps, the energy of a stadium packed with hockey fans is contagious. Angelica really gets into the game, whooping at good plays and catcalling at the referees for the bad ones. She's a ball of energy, and I'm loving every second of it.

During a break between the first and second period, she brings up the box seats. "I feel kind of bad that you're missing out on your friends."

She hadn't missed me checking my phone twice before powering it off. Fitz is blowing up my phone over the fact I brought a woman to a game when I never bring someone with me.

When he called her a stunner, it was time to turn off the device.

"I can see them another time," I admit, just enjoying the time with her.

But after a break between the second and third period, we're caught in the hallway after I waited for Angelica to exit the bathroom.

"Come up, man," Fitz begs, squeezing at my shoulder. "We haven't seen you in a while."

I hang my head. The group knows the holidays are my busy season. Still, I glance at Angelica.

"Think you'd be up for one drink?" I ask, almost hoping she says no. I don't want to share her with them. Not yet.

"Okay." She shrugs, slipping her arm around my elbow. "Besides, I've never been in a box before."

"Never?"

"Definitely a first."

Leading her toward the box seats, I wonder how many other firsts I can give her.

Once we reach the private box, someone calls out, "Scrooge," and I'm suddenly the center of attention along with Angelica.

I introduce her to the president of a prominent local bank and the part-owner of a professional sports team before Fitz circles over to us.

"How does *Fitz* fit with Carlucci?" she teases.

"Fitzgerald. I'm part Irish, part Italian."

Angelica whistles. "Quite the combination."

Fitz laughs. "My dad always says it was my mother's fault. No woman fought with him half as much as her. And he loved it." He waves a hand in the air, like *can you believe it?*

I can believe it. Not that Angelica and I fight, but we're opposites in so many ways. I think that's another thing I like about her.

As she spins to chat with someone's wife, Fitz leans into me. "Stunner, man, like I said."

"Off limits," I warn him, feeling a flare of the evil green eye.

"Got that memo the second you introduced her. You never bring women with you."

"Never had someone to bring before."

Fitz hums, knowing I just said more than I actually said.

"Nice uniform she's wearing," he jokes, arching a dark bushy brow.

"Fuck off," I snap, but my irritation only goes throat deep because deeper inside me is the pride that she's wearing my old jersey and everything about that says she belongs with me.

The Clara-Nutcracker thing.

"So the real question is, how did a beauty like you end up with a beast like this guy?" someone nearby asks.

I turn toward Angelica.

She glances at me, slipping her hand into mine. I'm distracted by the possessive touch and stare down at our hands, linking our fingers together.

"I saved his life," she begins.

A few gasps lift my head, and I meet Angelica's bright, playful eyes. "He had a broken heart."

Additional sounds of surprise have me facing the closest group and clarify, "I had a heart attack."

Our little gathering goes quiet, before erupting into a barrage of animated questions.

"What the fuck, man?" Fitz practically shouts.

"Why didn't you tell us?" someone else asks.

"What's this about a broken heart?" another interjects.

"He had a stress cardiomyopathy incident," Angelica explains, to which more questions explode like popcorn in a concession stand machine.

The bank president seems to know what Angelica is talking about and goes into a detailed explanation about how he suffered the same thing once.

"Thank you for that," I whisper with sarcasm, leaning down to kiss her shoulder.

"Should I have told them how we exchanged dates instead?"

Her eyes focus on my face as I slowly lift my head. "These people obviously care about you, Jude."

I shrug. *Is it obvious?*

"Seriously," Fitz clutches my shoulder, pulling my attention from Angelica again. "You should have reached out to one of us."

"I'm fine. There isn't anything anyone could have done for me." But looking back at Angelica, I decide my statement might not be correct.

She's done more than she'll ever know for me.

chapter 28

[Angelica]

We finish out the rest of the game in the box section, finding a thread of commonality in being sports fans. While we don't spend a long time with these people who are clearly Jude's friends on some level, what strikes me most is that they are just men, like the firehouse guys. They might have bigger wallets, but they talk about the same things. Sports. Mortgages. Women. And aging.

When the game ends, we shuffle along with the masses to the parking lot. Jude wraps his arm over my shoulders, and I lean into his side.

"Have fun?" His question is hesitant, like he's worried I didn't.

"Loved it," I admit. It was a great night. A great date. Between a light buzz and the laughter of the evening, plus all the little touches Jude has been giving me, I'm not ready for the night to end.

"Come over?" he asks me, pressing a kiss into the side of my head, before we reach his car.

Relief washes through me. "I thought you'd never ask," I tease.

By the time we enter his high-rise condo, he's already kissed me silly in the elevator.

Once inside his place, I push him against the hallway wall.

"What the hell?" His voice is sharp, and my confidence falters. But as I lean into Jude, taking his mouth with mine, he settles in. His lips curl against mine, and I pull back to witness a crooked smile.

"Where is this coming from?" He chuckles. The sound is so honest.

"Watching hockey, I guess. I never realized how much I might like it. Something so primitive about checking a guy into the boards." I hold my arm against Jude's chest like I'm doing it to him. "Don't even get me started on those warm-up moves."

"What warm-up moves?"

"The one where the guys are on their knees, holding their upper body off the ice, but their lower body dips and thrusts toward it. The way those hips move . . ." I hum and chew at my lower lip.

"You like that move, huh?" He arches a brow, the curl of his mouth almost sinister, seductive.

I hum and reach for his belt to answer his question.

"Whoa," he says, as I unbuckle it with a little too much force.

"Want me to stop?" I glance up at him. The entire night is catching up with me. Jude asking me to attend the game with him. The fact he bought separate tickets for us to be alone. He called in a favor to help me with my brother's wedding. Then he shared his small group of friends with me. The whole experience opened my eyes to who he truly is.

Quiet and kind. Thoughtful, not boastful. Possibly shy. Definitely an extraverted introvert.

"Is Santa's favorite color red?"

I tilt my head. "What's your favorite color?"

His eyes widen. "Are we really doing this now?" He glances down to where his belt dangles open and my fingers are on the button holding his jeans closed.

"Just figured your favorite color is something a girlfriend should know. Fake or not."

Jude stares at me a minute before his hands clasp my face and he kisses me. The connection is so powerful. I'm walked across the short width of his entryway and pressed into the opposite wall.

Never in my life has a kiss felt so claiming. His tongue practically etches his name on mine. His heart hammers in his chest beneath my palms, telling me he's just as affected as I am by this moment. But I push him away, because this moment is mine.

As I press against his chest, he takes a step back to the other side of the entryway.

"Green," he says.

I tilt my head again.

"My favorite color is green."

I lean into Jude once more, kissing him quickly before lowering to the floor and working at his zipper.

"Angelica." His voice cracks.

Glancing at him, I don't think I've ever seen Jude so vulnerable.

"Let me please you," I whisper, my confidence faltering another step. It's been a long time since I've done this, but I want to do it to him.

He cups my jaw, holding his gaze on my face. "You already do."

Dammit. His words empower me more, and I boldly tug at his jeans and boxer briefs, lowering them over his hips, while watching his thick shaft spring from the confines. When I wrap my hand about the base, Jude hisses. With a firm squeeze, I aim the tip toward my mouth and lick the slit, seeping with desire.

"Fuck."

Peering up at him, I watch him tip back his head. He holds the hem of his shirt up against his washboard abs, and I take a second to admire the ripple of his belly and the dark hairs leading to the massive length in my hand.

Opening wide, I suck at the tip, popping off only momentarily before taking more of him into my mouth. As he taps the back of my throat, Jude collects my hair and wraps it around his fist, lifting it off my neck. He gently holds the back of my head, rocking ever so slightly into the warmth of my mouth. I suck and lick and savor the salty maleness of him.

"This feels so good, angel," he groans before abruptly pulling free.

"Why stop?" Did I do this wrong?

"I want more of you." Jude reaches down for my hips and tugs me upward from my crouched position until I'm wrapping my legs around his waist. He carries me like this to his living room and sets me on the low table in front of his couch. Quickly, he removes my knee-high boots and pulls me to stand to remove my leggings and underwear.

When I reach for his jersey, he stops me. "Leave it on."

The request gives me pause, and I glance down at the uniform. Vulnerability slams into me.

"How many other girls have you told to do the same thing?" I shouldn't ask. It's ruining the mood and bringing down my empowered woman vibe. But something deep inside me needs to know.

"Zero."

I tip my head, not certain I believe him. With Jude seated on the couch and me standing over him, his eyes shift. The cold icy glare so natural to him melts to clear pools again.

"I swear on my sister." He makes an X over his heart. "I have never *touched* a girl wearing that jersey because no girl has ever worn it before you. No one."

He licks his lips and adds, "I didn't bring women here. In case you haven't noticed, I'm a private person. Cautious about who I bring close to me."

He leans forward and runs his hands up the back of my thighs.

"And I want you closer."

My heart nearly does a back flip in my chest as he tugs me onto his lap.

While straddling him, he tugs off his two shirts, then lifts me just enough to shove down his boxer briefs and jeans.

From the back pocket, he removes another square packet and rips the edge with his teeth. I watch as he rolls it down his length, then holds the base, making the length stand tall and proud and eager for me.

"Ride me." His voice is so low, so deep, I almost don't recognize it.

Still, I hold his shoulder and climb over his lap, resting my entrance at the tip. With my other hand, I hold up the edge of his jersey.

Jude brings his other hand to my lower belly and stretches his thumb for my clit. "Hang here a second."

As I balance on the edge of him, he circles that sensitive nub, making certain I'm ready to take him.

No concerns here.

I release his shoulder and nudge his hand away. I just want to feel him slide into me, and once his hand is free, I lower.

"Oh shit," Jude mutters, watching himself disappear. He doesn't take his eyes off the spot until I'm as full of him as I can get.

His head snaps upright, and he looks me in the face. "You are so beautiful." He pulls forward to kiss me, bracketing my jaw in his hands again, and for a beat we stay in this position. Him buried inside me while we kiss. When I feel him jerk within me, I pull back, needing to move. The tension is building, and I'm ready to continue the climb.

With one hand back on his shoulder, and the other holding up the edge of his jersey, I do as he asked, and ride. Up and down, my slickness coats him, and I move faster and faster until he pins me to his lap. I rock forward and back, letting my clit kiss his pelvic bone.

"Holy . . . *holy* . . ." I cry, lost in the sensation.

"That's it, angel. Fucking ride my cock."

"Jude," I cry out.

"That's right. And you don't want holy *holy*, you want bad." His jaw snaps. His fingers dig into my hips.

"My good girl wants the naughty list," he continues. "And she wants it with me."

"Yes," I call out, tipping my head back a second as I pump over him.

"Let me feel it, angel. Want to feel you dripping down my balls."

"Oh God," I whimper, hearing the slick mess we're making. Then my breath hitches. "Jude?"

I glance down between us like I don't know what my body is doing.

"Touch yourself."

My head pops up, and I stare at him. I've never done that with someone.

His fingers press harder at my hips, tugging at the sides of his jersey to keep it raised just enough so he can see where we are connected.

"Let me see it."

Hesitantly, I lower my hand to my clit, rubbing small circles where I need attention while I glide up and down on him. Then I scissor my fingers, feeling him slide between them. I squeeze his gliding length before returning to myself.

"Holy shit." Jude barks, like I've surprised him. Then his voice strains, "Get there, sweetheart."

"Jude," I cry one more time, removing my hand and slamming down on him, rubbing against that delicious bone of his again, before I snap. Like a Christmas cracker, I come unraveled, exploding over Jude like colorful strings of ribbon and bits of confetti. My mouth hangs open and my head tips forward as I rocket and crash, collapsing over him a second.

Jude rocks us forward. Up and off the couch we go, as he slips free from me. He spins and sets me back on the couch on my knees, facing away from him. He wedges my legs apart as he crawls up behind me, pressing me gently forward to bend over the back of his sofa.

"I want to read my name on your back while I fuck you."

"Jesus." I shouldn't like the sound of that, but as he surges into me, stealing my breath, I thrust backward, drawing him deeper. As if I can't get him deep enough.

"Green," he shouts, and I turn my head, wondering why he's calling out the color.

"Nine," he grunts next, and I glance down at his jersey, noting the number.

He leans forward without breaking his rhythm. "And I've newly developed a taste for chocolate mints made by a beautiful creature named Angelica."

It hits me in this precarious position, that he's just told me his favorite color, number, and food.

"Why?" I gasp, cutting off the rest of my thought. Why is he telling me these things?

He surges into me one more time, before leaning forward and whispering toward my ear. "Because these are things my girlfriend should know."

He doesn't clarify fake or not. He simply pulls back and begins a relentless rhythm that I embrace as I cling to the back of the couch.

His hands clutch at my hips again, certain to leave marks, if not the imprint of him as he drives into me.

"So. Good." He grunts before releasing one hip and awkwardly smoothing down his jersey against my back.

His name is on display. His number as well.

"Angelica," he shouts, then stills inside me, where I feel him jolt and jerk. He collapses forward, resting his forehead between my shoulder blades and slipping his hands around to my lower belly, pressing gently at it, as if he can feel himself inside me.

When he slowly lifts, he's gentle as he slips out of me. I fold to one side, sliding down the cushion to sit.

Jude reaches for me, lifting me into the air and presses a kiss to my temple.

"Let's shower."

Within minutes, we begin round two.

chapter 29

[Angelica]

On Friday, I have plans to meet up with some of the girls. It's been too long since we've gotten together. Christmas is less than a week away, and everyone is busy, but also needs a break from the chaos. For me, between the anxiety over Beau's wedding, and my work schedule, plus my newfound interest in Jude, I could use some time to process what the heck we are doing.

Holiday Escape, they dubbed the evening, because everything feels like it needs a theme this time of year.

For the moms in our gathering—Holliday Santos and Eva Scroggs—a night out during the busiest time of the year for mothers is a necessity.

For the single girls in our group, which includes me and an emergency room nurse friend named Noelle Darling, we just want to have fun.

Originally, we were supposed to go to a country bar, which are few and far between in a major metropolis, and line dance. Eventually, we settled on O'Malley's as the other girls just wanted to drink.

"I don't want to do anything that involves exerting energy other than lifting my glass of wine," Holliday says once we settle in a back booth.

Since O'Malley's is kind of my after-work spot with the guys, I wasn't as thrilled to be here. Still, Seamus O'Malley, the owner, treats the first responders who frequent his place with respect. Our first round is on the house.

"So . . ." Holliday breaks in as soon as our drinks arrive. "What's the word with the boyfriend?" She wiggles her brows at me.

"You have a boyfriend?" Eva asks. The brunette beauty is married to Zebb, who hosted A Snowman's Chance fundraiser. She's embraced being a bonus mom while she and Zebb have two additional children.

"Not exactly." I lift my cranberry vodka for a sip, noticing immediately that it doesn't rival the fancy cocktail I had at Jude's holiday party in Wisconsin.

"What exactly is it then?" Noelle asks. She has red hair like me, although hers isn't as vibrant as mine. More subtle, bordering on acorn brown. We met about a year ago when she was new to Chicago, and she's come out with me on occasion to get some girl time. She's in a relationship that she's hoping will be taken to the next level any day now. I've only heard about the lawyer-boyfriend, but I've never met him.

"I . . . I don't know." I consider how Jude mentioned *girlfriend* the other night. The things a girlfriend should know about him. *Green. Nine. Chocolate mints*. But it all feels too much, too soon. We're past the faking-it part. We agree we aren't pretending.

But we're still undefined, which is what I say next.

"Undefined?" Eva questions.

"Do we need a definition?" I counter. All of us are near or past forty and declaring someone my boyfriend feels almost juvenile. Still, if Jude and I were to continue, I'd like a commitment between us.

My insecurities almost got in the way the other night. The idea of Jude being with other girls in his old uniform struck a chord. Swearing on his sister drove home the truth in his eyes. I was a first for him.

Noelle chuckles. "Speaking as someone without labels on her relationship, as long as you are the only one he is fucking, I think you are safe."

Am I the only one? I think I am. We've video-chatted the nights we haven't been together. It would be pretty difficult to keep up a relationship with someone else while talking with me.

Then again, I've been burned before, and I should know better. The things I don't see are the things that should worry me.

Still, I want to be confident in where Jude and I are. We don't need to plan out a future. Maybe this is just a winter fling. An I-date-him, he-dates-me thing to get us through the holidays. One of my favorite holiday movies involves a couple who agrees to be each other's plus one to all the holidays throughout the year.

With Noelle's statement, we round into sharing some of the worst situations we've been in with men in the past. For Holliday, her ex turned out to suck. Eva claims she'd been too busy for relationships. Noelle already told the group about her previous relationship. I mention my past failure.

"Well, here's to sour dates in the past and only sweet sex in our future," Noelle announces when we've gone a round with our sucky tales.

"Here, here," Holliday taps the table.

To our surprise, a round of shots is delivered to the table.

"What's this?" Eva asks, lifting the small glass and giving it a whiff.

"Fireball. Compliments of the chief." The young waitress points in the direction of Brock Scroggs, Zebb's older brother.

"Ah," Eva cries out, standing from our table and approaching her brother-in-law and the woman with him. Eva drags her over to us.

"Ladies, do you remember Pear?"

Pear Claus is our battalion chief's daughter and Brock's forever girlfriend, and we should have thought to include her in our gathering.

"Join us," I say, pointing to a chair at the nearest table.

"I don't want to intrude, but Brock was noticing y'all looked a little serious. He said you needed some Fireball to burn down the glum faces."

Brock was a party man prior to meeting Pear. He was a constant troublemaker within the department. Eventually, there was an issue with my brother, Dane. As pals, they worked it out, but Cap, our battalion chief, was still pissed, and he sent Brock on a retreat. Getting snowed in with Cap's daughter was probably the last thing Cap expected to happen. Now, the two are the cutest couple.

"Still, take a seat," Eva encourages and points at Brock, implying he should send over one more shot.

"Fireballs at the ready," Noelle shouts once we each have a shot, and then we down the cinnamon-burn in one go.

Laughter is restored to our table, and the fun continues until the guys crash O'Malley's. An additional table is drawn up to the booth, and musical chairs happen as couples drift together. Zebb and Eva. Brock and Pear. Nick and Holliday. Noelle and I are left alone, until my brother Dane slides in beside Noelle, laying his attention on her a bit thick, considering she has a man, and he isn't officially divorced yet.

Despite the music and laughter, everyone looks all cozied up, and I feel like the odd woman out again.

I can't help thinking about Jude. He should be here with me.

I give in and message him.

Girls' night suddenly feels like a distraction I'm done pretending I need.

chapter 30

[Jude]

O'Malley's on the northside is the last place I expected to go on a Friday. As the last official weekend before the holiday, Ashford's has been a madhouse. As much as I could use a drink, I hadn't intended to go out and deal with people, but when Angelica messaged me, I couldn't refuse.

Knowing this place is more of a firefighter's bar, I try to downplay my appearance, wearing jeans and a green waffle-weave Henley. As I approach the bar, the familiar itch of playing a role comes over me. Who will I need to pretend to be for her friends?

I didn't want to think that way, but old habits die hard.

I've also been struggling with the rest of the items on her list. I hadn't forgotten about it.

Ask forgiveness and *make amends* were the most difficult.

As I wander through the bar, because Angelica said she was in the back at a booth joined with a table, I don't immediately see her.

However, I do see someone else I hadn't expected to ever see again.

"Miss Nazar," I address Eva Nazar, my former top manager, who quit the day after Christmas a few years ago.

"Mr. Ashford." Her jaw is tight as she greets me in return.

At the mention of my name, Angelica appears over the back of the booth. She's tucked into the corner facing the wall, which explains why I didn't see her.

"Mr. Ashford?" Angelica glances from Eva to me and back.

To Angelica, it probably appears silly that a woman older than me addressed me so formally, but Eva was always the epitome of professionalism. And even if I was younger than her, I was her boss, and therefore, she addressed me as such.

All eyes are suddenly on me. Instantly, I recognize Eva's husband. Zebb is a former football star from our high school, although a few years older than me. He went on to play professionally, and I followed his career. When I looked further into A Snowball's Chance, before making a donation, I learned more about his involvement with the charity. He *is* the charity.

His eyes focus on me as he slides his arm around his wife's shoulders. If he could leap over this table and strangle me, I bet he would.

I swallow, knowing I'd hold my own, but I don't want to fight him.

My gaze swings to Angelica. She hadn't told me she was friends with Eva. Or maybe Zebb is her friend, as a fellow in the department. I hadn't really put two and two together that they might work in the same firehouse.

I also recognize Dane, Angelica's brother.

"Hey man, what's up?" He lifts his hand in greeting, but the tension around the table becomes thick as an iceberg.

I'm intruding.

Everything in me wants to shout that I'd been invited. And for half a second, I worry Angelica did this on purpose. She set me up to feel uncomfortable around this collection of people.

Especially with a woman I falsely accused of stealing from Ashford's.

I didn't really believe she'd short a register, but she was on security tape having sex in one of our fitting rooms. Highly inappropriate. But as I'd been guilty of the same act a time or two in the past, I couldn't really fault her.

I had already faulted her, and she quit.

Suddenly, this seems like a moment.

"Eva, could I have a word?"

"How about two words?" Zebb states, glaring at me.

"Zebb," Eva says, lowering her gaze and swiping her long hair around her ear. The diamond on her finger flashes at me.

She looks so much happier than when she worked for me.

Taking a deep breath, I glance at Angelica, still perched on her knees and staring at me over the back of the high booth. Her gaze bounces from me to Eva, and I wonder if she knows the story. Focusing on Angelica a second, I count to four on an inhale and another set of four on the exhale. I find that freckle. My freckle.

Then I turn back to Eva. "Eva," I begin, licking my lips while fisting my hands at my side. "I'm sorry."

Her eyes widen.

"I'm sorry I doubted you when you'd been one of our best employees. And I'm sorry I suggested we let you go for that incident in the fitting room."

"What incident?" Angelica asks, her voice rising as she glares at her friend.

But Eva and Zebb share a look, and Eva's face turns pink.

I roll my lips before saying, "Can you forgive me?"

My heart is hammering. If there was ever a moment a second stress cardiomyopathy incident might strike, this is it. My ribs begin to tighten as if caving in on my insides. I unflex my hands, stretching my fingers, before pulling them back to fists.

Please forgive me.

"Of course," Eva says, glancing at Zebb a second before looking back at me. "It was a long time ago." She waves a dismissive hand. "And, you did me a favor. Leaving Ashford's was the wake up call I needed to start my own little shop."

My shoulders slowly lower. I loosen my fists. She's letting me off too easily, but most of all, I'm glad she found another path.

"I'd love to see it," I admit. Retailers love to check out other retailers. Although I won't be doing it because I consider Eva competition. I'd just like to visit her shop.

"You're welcome at any time," Eva says, offering me a hesitant smile.

"Let me out," Angelica says, her voice carrying over the group, and I turn in her direction.

The person in a chair near the booth moves, and the person in the booth scoots out, and Angelica walks across the bench on her knees, with her coat and her purse suddenly in her hands, before stepping away from her friends.

Standing right in front of me, so close I want to pull her in for a hug when I'm not that guy, she says to me, "Let's get out of here."

Taking my hand, she leads me out of the bar and onto the sidewalk. Snow is lightly falling, and I glance up at the dark sky.

"I'm so proud of you, Jude."

When I gaze down at her, her face might as well be the moon, illuminating the heavens. Her smile is wide. Those eyes of hers are flames of light.

"I'm kind of proud of me, too," I admit, though I tremble just a little bit. The rush of adrenaline is slowly settling in my system.

"For a minute there, you almost gave me a heart attack." She slaps her hand above her left breast. "I thought you and Eva . . ."

"Oh no. God, no." I shake my head. Eva is beautiful, but she has nothing on the angel in front of me.

Angelica wrinkles her nose. "Your fitting rooms, Jude? Really?"

Guess I won't be telling how I lost my virginity any time soon. But it doesn't matter what happened before.

"I checked another thing off the list."

"You did?" She tilts her head.

"Ask forgiveness."

Slowly, she smiles. "You're really taking the list seriously."

I'm taking you seriously. And if I want to make a better impression . . . be better . . . I need to change.

I want to change.

"Still up for a drink?" I ask.

She hesitates. "There's another bar down the street."

"Perfect." I hook her arm in mine and let her lead the way.

chapter 31

[Angelica]

"How was your night?" Jude asks, once we squeeze through another crowded bar and find a single stool near the bar.

Jude suggests I sit while he leans against the counter, similar to our position during his holiday party. Nearly three weeks ago, yet it feels like forever has passed.

"Strange," I admit, picking up the Fireball Surprise he ordered me after learning about the round of shots and the disappointing cranberry vodka.

The drink has a little kick to it, but it feels good going down. The hint of cinnamon fits the season, not to mention I feel a little spicy tonight.

"How so?" He tilts his head. He's so good looking, and green *is* a good color on him.

"I really wanted the girls' night." I need someone to talk to about my feelings, which are pinging all over the place when it comes to Jude. "But somehow we got on the topic of ex-es and—"

"You have an ex?" Jude stands a little taller. His eyes focus on my face before dropping to my hand for some reason.

"Not an ex, like I've been married. More like an ex, because I was supposed to get married, and then it didn't happen."

Jude continues to stare at me, waiting out a story that's a decade old and one I don't like to discuss. But I think about how far Jude has come, opening up about himself. Tonight, he looked especially vulnerable as he apologized to Eva in front of an entire group. Eva was gracious, letting Jude off the hook rather easily. The relief in Jude's face had been instant.

"The long short story is I was engaged. But I shouldn't have been engaged. We'd been together for almost ten years. Lived together for a while. Talked about purchasing a house one day. And having kids." Lots of kids.

"We got engaged, thinking it was what we should do to get us out of a rut. Unfortunately, as much as we'd talked about that house and those kids, we couldn't see it happening between us." We, with an emphasis more on he.

I sit up, inhaling deeply, and reach for my drink to take another sip.

Jude watches me intently. He leans against the bar top again.

"We both thought being engaged would bring us closer, but it didn't."

Still holding my glass, I stare down at the amber liquid. "Between my parents' death and the separation from Ian, I have an irrational fear about people leaving me."

I say irrational, because my parents died, and Ian and I fell out of love. Still, I don't like feeling like I've been left behind.

Don't you leave me, Jude. My request hadn't fallen into the same category as losing my parents or breaking things off with Ian, but somehow that declaration has grown into something.

I don't want to lose him next.

"Eventually, I learned he slept with someone during our decade-long romance. I forgave him, because we were over." The betrayal still stung, though.

Jude watches me when he says, "You're a bigger person than I would have been. I can't stand infidelity, and I would have burned his house down."

I chuckle at the thought. Since I'm in the fire department, I know guys who would have willingly set Ian's place on fire. The house he eventually bought without me.

"He's married now. She was a single mom with two kids." I sigh, recalling the first time I saw him after hearing the news. He looked happier than I'd seen him in years, but he said the same about me. We'd been holding each other back, and I never wanted to be in that kind of relationship again.

Jude's brows pinch. "Why are you so good?"

"Because I've accepted that life is short. It can be taken from you in an instant, and I don't want to spend my time dwelling on things that didn't happen, or can't happen, or *did* happen. I don't want to let regret rule my life." And turn me into Aunt Gertie.

Jude sips the straight whiskey he ordered, taking a moment to question my thought process, probably.

"For so long, I've let bitterness pin me down," he admits, staring down at the glass he set back on the counter. Then he looks up at me. "But now I want to be free from that bite."

He snaps his jaw to emphasize his point.

I chuckle at the antics. "You're getting there, Jude."

"Am I?"

"How do you feel after apologizing to Eva?" I lift my glass again. The Fireball ingredient is slowly taking effect, warming my throat and making my insides feel gooey.

"Like my heart might have grown a size or two," he teases.

"See, there's hope for you yet."

"You won't give up hoping for me, will you?" He glances back at his glass on the bar before giving me a sheepish gaze.

"Never." There is always the opportunity to turn your life around. It's why I forgave Ian. It's why I moved on.

"Still want that house and those kids?" he asks, arching a brow.

"One day."

Our eyes remain locked on one another.

"Favorite color?" he asks.

I laugh softly. "Orange."

He puffs out his bottom lip. "Interesting. And number?"

Having never really considered it, I answer, "I think I'm partial to nine."

The corner of his mouth curls. That apostrophe-like dimple pops forward. If he can claim my freckle as his, can I gain possession of that divot?

"And food?"

I sigh with a smile. "I like all food." I slap my thigh, as if proving my point.

Jude snorts, the sound easy and light, compared to the range of derisive noises he can make.

"Let's go back to that favorite number. How do you feel about a six in front of the nine?"

"Sixty-nine?" I question before the number registers.

"Exactly," Jude says, holding those clear eyes on me, letting me see exactly what he's thinking.

"Come over," I state in the same way he said it only two nights ago. Not so much as a question but a command.

"I thought you'd never ask," Jude says, taking my drink from my hand, tossing a hundred-dollar bill on the bar, and leading me out into the cold.

+ + +

The morning after our rather adventurous night, Jude finds me in my kitchen. It's early, but I have a full weekend ahead of me.

As I slowly melt semi-sweet chocolate over boiling hot water, Jude approaches me from behind. I sense his closeness while saying, "Good morning." As I can't stop stirring for a second, or the chocolate might burn, I hold my position, facing the stove and swirling melting chocolate in the pot.

Jude hesitates, and for half a second, nervous energy wavers off him. He sets his hands on my hips first.

I smile to myself, remaining quiet, while Jude figures out whatever he's trying to figure out.

He steps closer and presses a kiss to my shoulder before slowly, very slowly, wrapping his arms around me. He remains stiff, almost as if he's anxious about hugging me.

Running my free hand along his forearm over my waist, I lean into his chest and feel him relax behind me. His chin comes to rest on my shoulder as we stay like this while I continue stirring the chocolate.

"Whatcha doing?" he murmurs near my ear.

"Making my famous chocolate mints." I don't tell him that I bake when I'm stressed. Beau's wedding is coming together. The holiday seems set. Yet, I feel off today. Like I'm forgetting something.

"Famous, huh?"

"Well, famous one day." I smile again as I stare at the creamy chocolate mix.

"I like that kind of confidence." He kisses the side of my neck and continues holding me.

Sadly, I don't think Jude has been hugged enough in his lifetime, and it's made him skittish to give or receive something so simple as a hug.

So, I continue to stroke his arm, keeping him pinned to my back and holding me while I work.

"Why do I feel like I'm being let in on a secret?"

"You are," I tease, the seriousness intended in my voice is disguised beneath laughter.

"Can I help?" His question is almost as anxious as his embrace.

"Of course." I pause, then pull one of his hands forward. "First lesson, keep stirring."

I make his hand take over the stirring I'd been doing.

"Slow," I whisper as he goes a bit too fast.

He hums over my shoulder. "I told you I don't know how to go slow."

I feel his smile against the side of my neck.

"And you also told me you'd try."

While the twirl of his wrist, he moves the chocolate around the pot, and says, "But I don't want to go too slow."

He kisses the side of my neck, like it's the reassurance I need that we haven't leapt too quickly into whatever is happening between us.

"Timing is of the essence," I state once the chocolate looks smooth. "We need to get the rest of the ingredients together."

Jude stands back, and I turn off the stove, moving the pot to a back burner. Then, I hand Jude a whisk and show him how to cream butter.

"You have to really beat it," I say, and Jude chokes.

"Oh, honey, you have no idea how good I am at that."

I snort at the sexual innuendo. "Have a lot of practice, do you?"

"The past month has been the worst," he teases.

"Oh really," I arch a brow as he continues to work the butter to a creamy pulp, and I sift in powdered sugar.

"I met this angel and she fucking haunts my dreams."

"Haunts, you say?" I tweak a brow again, as Jude chews at his lower lip, really concentrating on the butter and sugar combination.

"She's all I think about."

I still for a second, staring at his profile. "Is she like the ghost of Christmas present or something?"

"Apparently, she's the past I missed and the present I'm enjoying." He doesn't look at me, his jaw tightening with the admission. "I think I'd like her to be the Christmas future as well."

"But you don't celebrate Christmas," I say too quickly before realizing he's using Christmas metaphorically.

He doesn't correct me.

With Jude still stirring the butter and sugar, I crack eggs into the bowl and watch the yolky mixture blend with the other ingredients.

Eventually, I still his hand and nod at the extracts, vanilla and peppermint, on the counter. "Want to do the honors?"

He glances up at me. The icy gaze is gone again, leaving only clear blue pools of hesitation. It's always shocking how he's so confident in some manners and cautious in the simple ones.

"It's an exact science," I tell him. "You just measure and pour."

"All my life, I've worked with exactness. Right school. Right friends. Right clothes, job, money."

I nod. "Well, with baking you can't really fuck around and find out. What you'll end up with is a mess. So in this case, exactness matters."

Is this why Jude has been so wild in other ways? Women. Trips. Events. He's been trying to break a mold while living within a glass dome.

We reach for the measuring spoons at the same time, but while Jude halts, I cup his hand.

"I'm right here. I won't let you mess up." Not the chocolates. Not his life.

He's checked another thing off his list, and I couldn't be prouder of him. In fact, last night I learned how very proud of him I am with his face between my thighs and mine over his dick.

I shiver a little at the quick memory, then get back to work.

"You've got this, Jude." Because he has me, for as long as he needs me. As long as he wants me.

He measures out the vanilla, and then the peppermint, with shaky hands. When all is ready, the chocolate is cooled enough to add the other ingredients, then I show Jude how to drop the mixture into the candy forms.

"It will take about four hours to set but overnight is really best."

"Four hours," Jude pretends to look at his silver watch, which isn't on his wrist, but on my nightstand like it belongs there. "Plenty of time to practice exactness."

There's something different in his eyes once again. The icy shards that turn to clear liquid now look warmer, like a summer sky. One threatening to give me a sunburn but promising I'll enjoy the heat.

He lifts me by my hips and sets me on the short counter between my kitchen and living room, making me his pre-breakfast delicacy.

chapter 32

[Angelica]

"Do you have plans tonight?" Jude asks me after breakfast.

I shrug, leaning closer to him. We're sitting on the two barstools that fit at my short counter between the kitchen and the living room.

"Depends," I reply.

"On?"

"On what you want to do."

That twitchy smile of his slowly continues to a full, soft grin. "Yeah?"

I don't answer, just continue to watch him.

"I feel like our date the other night got interrupted by the guys in the sky box."

I offer him reassurance. "I had fun."

"But I still wanted it to just be us," he hangs his head a second, picking at a piece of bacon on his plate. "And with Beau not having a rehearsal dinner, I feel like I owe you a better date."

The brewery is now set as Beau's wedding venue, which feels very appropriate for my laidback brother. With the small number of attendees, a rehearsal dinner would be like a second wedding, and we only need one. We'll wing the processional the day of the celebration.

But what doesn't sit right is Jude thinking he owes me something.

"You don't owe me anything. I'd say we're definitely even, if we need to be."

Jude lifts his head, hearing the irritation in my voice.

"We don't need to be even," he counters. "But I still want to do this."

I'm curious what *this* is.

"Okay," I hesitate.

"Be ready by seven?"

I agree, and then Jude and I go our separate ways for the day.

+++

When Jude picks me up, it's started to snow outside, although he's already told me we'll be inside.

He drives us to the Ravenswood neighborhood, where old warehouses along the train tracks have been converted to a variety of spaces for entertainment.

"What is this place?" I ask of the rather nondescript building with classic red brick that's difficult to appreciate in the dark.

Jude only smiles as he uses a main code to enter the outer door, then leads us up a floor and uses another code to enter a large room. The space is big enough to hold roughly thirty classic cars roped off with red velvet loops near the front of each vehicle, suggesting one can look but not touch. The cars range from a 1920 mobster-looking sedan to the most current Corvette.

Several walls contain metal automotive signs from historical gas stations and iconic highways. An antique gas pump dominates one corner of the room.

A focal point of the room is a 1950-something, cherry red, Chevy pickup truck, complete with wood slats on the back, like it's from an orchard or a Christmas tree farm. Or maybe, it even belonged to Santa Claus. The truck is separated from the rest of the collection and parked in the middle of the space, as if highlighting its uniqueness.

I'm not a car enthusiast, but the collection is impressive.

"Where are we?" I ask, spinning in a slow circle, just taking it all in.

"A guy from the softball team owns this place. He didn't have space at his house for his *babies*, so he stores them up here, and rents the place for corporate parties and wedding receptions."

Tonight, though, we're the only people present.

"And we're here because . . ." I'm not complaining about our being alone, I'm just confused.

"You asked me once if I'd ever been to a drive-in, and I told you no."

"Okay?" I glance around the space again, taking in the shiny chrome and vibrant paint jobs on most of the cars.

"Since you'd never been to a hockey game, and that was a first for you, I thought I'd take you to the drive-in, which would be a first for me."

Still puzzled, I say, "Here?"

"Here." He holds out his hand, pointing toward that cherry red beast in the center of the space. Walking over to it, Jude follows, then leads me to the driver's side. He opens the door, exposing a beautiful red leather bench seat with a picnic basket pushed up against the passenger door.

"Hop in."

I do as he asks, and then he slides in after me, closing the door. From this seat, I see a large movie screen opposite the hood.

"Jude," I whisper, suddenly excited by the prospect of what's happening here.

He leans across me for the picnic basket, exposing a red and white striped box of popcorn, a variety of candies, and a thermos.

"We have movie theatre popcorn, a selection of chocolates, and mulled wine." He shakes the thermos.

"Jude," I whisper again, unable to find the words. This is so romantic.

Jude reaches for a remote on the dashboard, and the lights in the warehouse dim. It's then that I notice strings upon strings of white Christmas lights overhead, dangling from the ceiling like stars.

Jude sets his arm behind me on the bench seat and twists, aiming the remote out the back window where a projector apparently clicks on and the movie screen lights up.

How the Grinch Stole Christmas begins playing on the screen, and I laugh, clapping my hands together. "Are you serious?" But my voice is tickled.

"At the drive-in, there's typically a double feature. Or a short film before the featured show. I figured we could watch this one first."

I shift beside him. "This is the sweetest, Jude." I can hardly contain my smile, and I lean toward him, kissing him, soft and sweet, taking my time to savor his mouth until the first word from the narrator.

Pulling back, I offer him another wide grin.

"Is this the part where you try to seduce me and I don't need to question it," I tease.

His brows hitch. "Does this feel like a seduction? We don't have to do anything other than watch the movies."

"It feels romantic," I admit, maybe a bit wistful, watching Jude's face morph from serious intention to something softer, almost vulnerable. Like he hadn't considered how romantic this might be.

While the movie plays, Jude pours each of us a mug of mulled wine and points out the variety of candy.

"Mint M&Ms, please," I exclaim, excited to see the seasonal candy in the mix.

"You and your mint chocolates," he teases, selecting a package of Mikes and Ikes.

When the first movie ends, I'm warm from the wine and sharing the confined space with Jude. He shrugs out of his jacket, and I do the same, but Jude pulls a plaid blanket from behind the seat and settles it over our laps.

The space isn't cold, but it's not overly warm either, but snuggled beneath his arm, tucked inside this truck, I'm cozy.

The next movie begins after a brief commercial with dancing hot dogs and singing sodas about visiting the concession stand.

I laugh while Jude combs his fingers through my hair.

When the words *A Christmas Carol* highlight the screen, I shift to look at Jude.

"You didn't?"

"I did." He curls a long spiral of my hair around his finger. "Figured it was my theme this year."

"I love it." I snuggle back into his side, setting my head on his shoulder, accepting I might be in love with Jude. After such a short time, my heart is nearly bursting, three sizes too large for my chest.

As the movie plays, Jude and I occasionally kiss, until the kissing turns to making out, then heavy petting, and finally each of us has our hands down the other's pants until we're shoving the picnic basket to the floor and Jude lays me back on the bench seat.

We have sex while the movie plays on and miss the transformational moments for Ebenezer Scrooge, having our own life-altering moment in the cab of the truck.

chapter 33

[Jude]

Angelica volunteers for The Giving Tree, so I carve out an hour to attend the children's hospital gift-giving event to surprise her.

Who surprises me is Ed Marksman. I'd forgotten again how the Marksmans were involved in the charity.

"Jude," the Ashford's board member addresses me with shock as I enter the toy collection room where Ed is dressed like Santa Claus.

With the call of my name, Angelica turns from whatever she's doing and stares at me with equal surprise. She sets down the wrapped gift in her hand and approaches, walking right into me for a hug, which I return. Hugging her has become easier and easier.

"What are you doing here?" she questions, pulling back while giving me a large grin.

"I thought I'd surprise you. And help." I glance up as Ed's brows pinch.

With my arm around Angelica, I say, "Put me to work." I'm strangely excited to be here today but equally anxious. I'm not great around kids, which was proven by calling Santa a lie and making Angelica's four-year-old nephew question the man in red.

Still, I want to give volunteering another try. I hadn't done enough during Angelica's breakfast with Santa.

"Okay. We've sorted the presents into categories. Ed is our Santa." Angelica smiles at him. "The rest of us just need to get into our elf costumes."

"What?" I snap.

"Santa needs helpers." Angelica pats my chest, then steps over to a closet and removes several hangers with elf costumes stored in clear dry-cleaning bags.

"You might need to mix and match to find the right combination for you."

Combination? Combination of what?

Quickly, I learn the getup includes tights beneath a short dress-like outfit with a belt around the waist and a felt hat.

I look like Will Ferrel in *Elf* but feel like Jim Carey in *The Grinch*. I look ridiculous and feel even sillier, but Angelica continues to beam at me.

"You might be the sexiest elf I've ever seen."

Well, fuck.

And she's the sexiest elf I've ever seen. Who knew a pink, felt dress with candy cane striped stockings and an elf cap could be such a turn on? Some role-playing might be in our future.

Taking the stack of presents Angelica hands me, I follow her as she follows Santa Ed. We enter room after room where Ed or Angelica know each child by name, like they actually work for the North Pole.

I'd only allotted an hour, but ninety minutes in, I don't have the heart to leave. These kids are incredible. So small in such big hospital beds, and yet happiness is bigger than the entire building. The smiles on their faces are miles wide, and their laughter is nearly contagious.

On top of it all is watching Angelica interact with them. She's so good, taking a few minutes to chat or tease a child. Offering a hug where it's permissible or a blowing a kiss like she's elf queen where it's not. The kids adore her.

I adore her.

And I'm grateful I've stayed when the last hospital room becomes a challenge.

The girl sitting up in the hospital bed stares suspiciously at Ed. From the expression on her face, it's evident she doesn't believe Ed is Santa. Her blue eyes are almost too wide, and her cheeks are rosy. She doesn't have a single strand of hair on her head. She looks rather young, and a nurse is present but not a parent.

"Ho, ho, ho," Ed begins, but the girl crosses her arms and falls back against the raised bed.

"Save it, Santa."

"Oh, ho, ho," Ed chuckles. "Don't tell me we have a little grinch on our hands?"

"I'm not a grinch," she counters, but with her arms crossed and a pout prevalent, she's definitely looking like a familiar green character.

I glance at the nurse, who stands close to the side of the bed. "Lulu, you promised. No sass today."

"And Mommy promised she'd be here, but she isn't." The little girl doesn't bat an eye as she makes her argument, but her lower lip trembles.

The entire point of The Giving Tree is to provide a gift for a child who is hospital-bound, but a hospital-bound child without a parent is a whole other level of heartache. And I don't expect the pinch in my chest. The one relating to this lonely girl.

"What's with the lip, sassy pants?" I tease.

"Jude," Ed admonishes while Angelica gasps.

"Your name is Jude. What kind of name is Jude for an elf?"

"A cool name for the coolest elf in all of North Pole land." The statement is stilted, making me sound uncool, but the comment does the trick.

"Sounds dumb."

"You're dumb," I counter.

"Jude," Angelica shrieks.

But I see the twitch. The way the corner of Lulu's lip starts to curl. Arguing with a child is a skill; fighting with a sibling is an art, and from somewhcre in my brain, a disagreement with Julia comes forward. One where only those you really care about can get away with calling you a name.

"Your pants are sassy," I comment, keeping my eyes on the young girl.

"Your name isn't classy."

"Good one." I step forward and hold out my fist. To my surprise, she bumps mine with her rounded knuckles.

"I take back what I said. You're rather smart."

"And you smell like fart."

"Lulu," the nurse scolds, but Lulu breaks into a fit of giggles.

"Alright, girl with the sass in her pants, are you going to take this present or what?" I hold out the last gift, which Ed was supposed to pass to the child.

When she reaches forward, I tug it back, teasing her once more.

She laughs again, and I press the present toward her one more time. This time, I let her take it from my hands.

"Well, open it." I urge, glancing at my watch like I haven't got all day.

Hesitantly, she asks, "What is it?"

"That's classified information, miss. You'll need to open the gift and find out for yourself, should you choose to accept the mission."

She stares at me like I've lost her, and I don't care as long as she keeps smiling. She takes her time to open the present, like she's savoring every pluck of tape and rip of paper until finally the toy is exposed.

In her hands, she holds a doll that looks just like her only with long blonde hair and a pink bow tied on top of her head.

"How did you know?" she glances up at me, her lower lip quivering again.

I hitch my thumb toward Ed. "Wasn't me. It was all him."

Ed really has been remarkable today, and I'm certain my little stunt of calling a sick child dumb will get me cancelled. But seeing the joy on Lulu's face as I help her unwrap the doll from the packaging is worth every second of this experience.

"Alright, Lulu," I begin. "This elf is out of here."

I hold up my hand for a high five, but Lulu shifts among the cords attached to her beneath a nightgown. She holds out her arms, and I glance at the nurse.

With a subtle nod of permission from her, I awkwardly embrace little Lulu.

"Merry Christmas, baby girl," I murmur, recalling what Tucker sometimes called Julia as a child.

"Merry Christmas, big elf."

Releasing her, I catch Angelica watching me. The tears welling in her eyes clash with her soggy smile.

This moment was worth a mountain of presents.

chapter 34

[Angelica]

After Jude volunteered for The Giving Tree, he returned to work, but that night this sexy little elf made a second appearance at his condo wearing the felt pink dress with candy cane tights and let Mr. Grinch have his way with me on his kitchen counter like I was a peppermint treat.

Since that evening, we've been like sleighs passing over the hills and through the dales between his hectic holiday work schedule and mine. First responders almost never have holidays off. Still, Cap is considerate with the team and what time we want off most. Christmas Day is my top priority, so I can witness my nieces and nephews experiencing Santa Claus. That means, sometimes I need to work the evening shift or a double on Christmas Eve, which is the case for me this year.

But first, I need to get through Beau's wedding, which is another crux in this already frantic season.

I worked the day shift, so I didn't have much time to set up for Beau's Wednesday-at-six wedding during one of the most chaotic weeks of the year. Thankfully, the brewery crew set up square wooden tables and chairs for dining and left a small space on the dance floor for the ceremonial arch. To everyone's shock, Beau wanted to keep the tradition of not seeing his future wife on their wedding day before they met at the altar. This also meant Beau was conspicuously absent from setting up for his own ceremony.

Christmas and I rushed around setting poinsettia plants on the tables as centerpieces along with votive candles. An elaborate evergreen garland arch was made by my creative sister, complete with pinecones and white fairy lights. The room would be dimmed for the ceremony and then brightened for the buffet dinner.

"Think we should tell him poinsettias are actually a funeral flower," I mutter to my sister, who has been grumbling along with me about Beau's absence.

"It's his funeral," she jokes about the shackle of marriage.

We like Belle, but this rushed wedding doesn't sit right with either of us. However, it's Beau's life, and he's always been the spoiled, wild card in the family.

After a sweaty race to finalize decorating and check in with the kitchen, which is preparing their first party since opening, I rush to a small room off the second-floor party space to dress. The space is more like a cleared-out storage closet, but has a gold-framed, floor-length mirror in it.

Suspiciously, I'd found the green velvet dress Jude purchased for his board member party hung in my closet after I'd been sick. While I'd told him to donate it to a worthy cause or resell it, seeing it in my closet again, I didn't have the heart to part with such a precious item myself.

As Belle was allowing wedding party attendants to wear whatever they wished, as long as it was green for photos, the formal dress from Jude's Christmas party was perfect.

I've basically taken a deodorant shower followed by a perfume spritz before Gran enters the room.

Our eyes meet in the floor-length mirror.

"Not going to be fair that you show up the bride," she says warmly, staring at me in the floor-length, off-the-shoulder dress. "You look as beautiful as your mother did on her wedding day."

"Gran," I whisper, as my throat clogs. Unfortunately, it isn't *my* wedding day. The thought is punctuated as I run my hands down the soft emerald-green velvet over my belly.

"I knew it would happen for you," she adds, stepping closer to me and cupping my shoulders. Our gazes hold through the mirror, and I worry Gran is having a moment. A forgetful one.

"It's Beau's day," I remind her.

She smiles slowly. "Yes, it is, but you're still going to steal his breath."

"Beau?" I question, deciding Gran has really lost it. Maybe she needs to sit down for a minute. Her memory is always a concern.

Gran shakes her head. Her white-haired bob doesn't move thanks to the hairspray on it. She's dolled up in a dark green dress as well.

"Jude, sweetie." Her brows pinch like I'm the silly one.

"Gran," I mutter again, holding her gaze. "It was only pretend." I swallow the lump in my throat. The lie I've been telling my family.

Her brows crease with confusion.

"It should be pretend, but I think . . . I think I've skipped right past pretending and crashed into something more." Something earth-shattering and scary because it feels so real. I wring my hands, and Gran covers them with her own.

However, a date for a date was our agreement, and as there hasn't been any discussion about *after* Christmas, I'm slipping into the this-is-it-mindset.

After tonight, Jude won't feel obligated to continue whatever it is we are doing together.

While Jude and I shared texts over the past few days, he's worked most nights until midnight, and in the few short days since the night on his kitchen counter, I feel him slipping away from me.

Next to his assistant, I might be the longest relationship Jude has had. Almost one month together.

Then I remember Sabrina and how Jude had been on and off with her for years. I'm not interested in that kind of rollercoaster ride.

"I don't believe it was pretend," Gran begins, but a sharp rap comes to the door.

As Gran calls, "Come in," Dane opens the door and slips into the small space. He lets out a low whistle when he sees me reflected in the mirror, and I spin to face my older brother.

"What do you think?" I curtsy.

Dane hums. "Gonna make the man sweat." He winks at me.

"Is Jude here yet?" My voice rises, too hopeful, too eager.

"Not yet." Dane's face slowly sobers. "Neither is Beau."

"Oh dear," Gran whispers while glancing at her gold bracelet watch.

"Yeah." Dane sighs.

"I'll kill him if he doesn't show." When I think of all the planning and rushing to gather wedding necessities, especially the favor Jude called in for this place, which ended up being free minus the food and a minimum bar tab . . .

"He'll be here," Gran states, but she doesn't sound convincing.

It'd be so like Beau to flake out *on his own wedding*.

The door rushes opens, nearly hitting Dane's broad shoulders, and he steps back as Christmas slides into the tight space, then closes the door behind her.

"Where the hell is Beau?" she snaps, as she collapses against the closed door and tips back her head before righting it to glare at Dane.

"How the fuck should I know?" Dane counters.

"Language, young man," Gran says to her nearly forty-year-old grandson.

"I knew we should have put a leash on him today," Christmas states.

Dane snorts.

"Where are the boys?" I ask Christmas. For that fact, where are Dane's girls?

"I'm letting them run wild around the party room," she deadpans, then sighs. "Actually, Kevin showed up. He can *act* like their father for thirty seconds."

I'm not touching that comment with a ten-foot peppermint stick. Not today, at least.

Dane is clicking on his phone. Christmas and I meet eyes, and then the door opens again, forcing Christmas toward Dane as Beau eeks into the space which is not made for five grown adults. He's wearing a sleek black tux, and his highlighted-blond hair is tame today.

"Are we having a family meeting without me?" he questions, glancing around the room. "It's bad enough there aren't any baby books for me, and now you're hosting a secret society without me."

I bark out a laugh. As if we'd ever exclude him. He wouldn't let us.

"We would never leave you out, honey," Gran says, approaching him.

"Where the fuck have you been?" Dane questions.

"Language," Gran mutters, knowing it's a lost cause.

“Never fear, Beau is here,” our late-to-his-own wedding brother states, but his typically cheerful tone sounds off.

“Now,” Christmas sighs.

Gran reaches for Beau’s cheeks, and he lowers his face to her height, allowing her to cup his jaw. “Another addition to our family. Your parents would be so proud.”

“Yeah,” Beau swallows, and Christmas and I lock gazes once more.

A single word shouldn’t sound so uncertain.

Dane’s phone vibrates with a bridal march ringtone. “Okay, man, time to get this party started.” He claps our youngest brother on the shoulder and reaches for the door, practically pushing Beau out of the closet-like space. Christmas follows while Gran spins toward me.

“Don’t worry, honey. Your miracle is coming.”

Was Beau getting married a miracle?

I wasn’t so sure about a magical moment for me and offer her the same response Beau gave in an equally uncertain tone.

“Yeah.”

chapter 35

[Angelica]

I didn't want to doubt Jude, but when I am lined up to follow Christmas down the make-shift aisle, and I can't see him among the guests gathered in the larger room, my anxiety soars.

He wouldn't have forgotten. Like Dane, he'd set a reminder. I was certain of it.

Still, a cold sweat dampens my pits as I hold a simple bouquet of white roses.

The first refrain of "A Thousand Years" began to play, and Christmas and I are on standby before we walk to our designated positions. Belle's two best friends are in line behind us, gushing over the bride dressed in a strapless white mini dress with an elaborate, poofy veil.

Gertie wondered if Belle had gotten the message that today was her wedding day.

I wasn't here to judge.

I just wanted my date to show up as promised, even though it shouldn't have mattered. I'd told Jude weeks ago I didn't need him to attend. I could face my family on my own, as I'd done for nearly a decade. The questions. The stares. The sympathy in some aunt twice removed or cousin I didn't care about witnessing yet another sibling of mine get married before me, the one who had a long-term relationship that never ended after a broken engagement.

And yet, still, I wanted to show them all that *I* wasn't broken. I could get a date. I had a date.

Only, he wasn't here.

Christmas steps forward on the lyric we'd agreed would lead the bridal party procession.

As I go to take my first step, my elbow is clutched, and I turn my head.

"I'm sorry I'm late."

Tears instantly well in my eyes as I stare at Jude, who looks impeccable in a black suit. *Of course, he does.*

"All that matters is you are here now," I say, uncertain where the words come from as I struggle with a rush of emotions within me.

This hasn't been real, right? A seasonal fling, perhaps. But the relief I feel at Jude's sudden presence is instant forgiveness.

"See you inside," he says, tipping his head in the direction of the dining room.

"I'll be the one in green." I shrug. "Well, one of many," I note.

"My favorite color," he admits, letting his gaze roam down my body. "On my favorite person."

While I want to throw myself at him, making out with him when I should be walking down the aisle isn't the time, and a throat clearing behind me reminds me what I need to be doing.

With one foot in front of the other, I proceed to the corner of the room set up with the pine-scented garland and take my spot. I should be watching for Belle to make her grand entrance, but I can't take my eyes off Jude as he stands toward the back of the room.

Beau opted for guests to be seated at the tables instead of chairs in rows on the dance floor for the ceremony. The garland arch will be moved back against a black-painted brick wall and used as a photo prop once the ceremony is over.

Suddenly, "Drunk on a Plane" begins, and the guests shift as Belle makes her entrance.

I glance at Christmas beside me, who only shrugs. "It's how they met, remember?"

Shaking my head, Jude and I gaze at one another across the room. His crooked smile suggests he's enjoying this spectacle, and I decide to soak in the moment.

All *my* favorite people are gathered in one place.

Jude included.

+++

Like champagne, weddings can be bubbling with happiness. Or a predictable headache, the one you'll experience after too much of the fizzy sensation.

Thankfully, Beau and Belle's ceremony is short. The drinks start to flow. Dinner is a buffet of bar foods. Other than the high-top sweetheart table where Beau and Belle are seated, the rest of the room is open seating. As I've waited for most guests to go through the buffet line, I'm quick to learn we've run out of most items, especially the cheeseburger sliders I'd been focusing on as my personal reward for throwing together this last-minute wedding.

I'm starving and my first bride's-choice candy cane martini has slunk through my bloodstream rather easily.

Disappointed, I take my mostly-empty plate to a table in the back corner where Jude is seated.

"You aren't eating?" he questions as I sit.

My feet ache in the thin, strappy gold heels I'm wearing, and I kick them off underneath the table.

"I'm starving, but they've run out of food." My shoulders sag as I fall back in the wooden folding chair. "I'll just drink my body weight in martinis. That will fill me up."

Jude stares at me a second, then stands. "I'll be right back."

I have no idea where he's going, and I don't ask. The weight of this wedding is hitting me in the chest. A sense of finality rests there. All my siblings are married, although Dane is getting divorced and I don't know what's happening with my sister and her estranged husband. How are we all such a mess? We had loving parents as a prime example of what marriage should look like. How could we each be so bad at picking partners?

My gaze leaps to Beau and Belle. I hate to admit it, and I'd *never* say it aloud, but I give their marriage less than a year. Meeting because they were drunk on a plane. Announcing their wedding at Thanksgiving. Getting married weeks later. Their age difference. Their *everything* difference. I didn't want to be a skeptic, but I didn't see them lasting.

None of us Winter siblings had a perfect track record for long-term relationships.

Your miracle is coming, Gran said.

Poor Gran. She didn't understand. She and Gramps had been another example of a devoted marriage. One where the big things were important, but the little things mattered most, like—

A set of three cheeseburger sliders and a heap of fries on a plate is set in front of me.

I look up as Jude takes a seat beside me and shifts his chair closer to mine.

"Eat." He nods at the plate, and I nearly cry again because of this man.

"What did you do?" I whisper.

He simply nods toward the plate again.

Sitting up straighter, I reach for one mini-cheeseburger and bite into it. Instantly, I close my eyes and hum.

"That is so good." The simple reward I anticipated for throwing this wedding together.

Jude's hand comes to my thigh beneath the table. He chuckles.

Turning my head toward him, I remind him, "I told you I love food."

His mouth pops open like he intends to speak, then he slaps his lips shut. He swallows thickly, like whatever he was about to say is choking him. With those clear blue eyes on me, he shifts in his seat. The hand on my thigh is removed, and he rests his left arm on the back of my chair. He sits sideways and settles his right hand on my thigh instead.

He tips up his chin toward the burger still in my hands. "Eat."

I take another bite while Jude slips his hand around my thigh beneath the table.

"Jude," I whisper in warning.

"Scoot to the edge of the chair."

I swallow the lump of cheeseburger in my mouth and do as he commands. With my backside near the edge of the seat, it's easy for Jude to force my legs apart, forcing the slit in my dress to spread open underneath the table. His warm hand glides against exposed skin.

"What are you doing?" I ask, placing the final bite of the small cheeseburger in my mouth.

"Getting jealous of the sounds you make while devouring that slider."

For some reason, the comment spurs me to reach for the second one and take another hasty bite. With my gaze fixed on Jude, I purr around the combination of soft bun, melting cheese, and warm meat.

And Jude's hand rushes up my thigh toward my center.

Slamming my thighs together, I trap his hand between them.

"What are you *doing*?" I hiss as my eyes widen a second, and then I glance around the room.

"I'd never let anyone watch the things I want to do to you," he confirms. "All anyone sees right now is my girl enjoying a mini cheeseburger while her boyfriend watches her eat."

My head swivels in his direction. I've set the slider back on my plate, and I stare at him. His hand is still trapped between my thighs.

"Be a good girl, and open wide for me." He nods toward the small burger on my plate, but his fingers twitch between my thighs.

Slowly, I spread my legs and reach for the partially-eaten slider. My fingers tremble as I lift the small burger, when I'm now hungry for something other than food.

Jude takes his time to slide his hand all the way up my leg, meeting the damp slip of fabric over where I ache for him.

"So wet," he hums. "Tell me it's me and not that burger soaking your panties."

"Jude." I choke on a laugh when he nudges the scrap of material to the side and easily slips a finger into me.

I lower my hands, nearly dropping the slider on my plate. I clutch at the edge of the table and spread my legs to the corners of the seat underneath it.

Jude rewards me with a second finger.

"Oh God," I mutter, lowering my eyelids while glancing around the room again.

Jude slides his fingers in and out, taking my essence from wet to a mess.

"Jude," I whimper.

"The first night you wore this dress, I wanted to fuck you so badly."

My head turns in his direction, remembering he hadn't touched me. He'd turned me down.

"You stole my breath that night. Entered that party like a girl boss, and all I could think about was she's mine. Like Clara receiving that nutcracker."

"*The Nutcracker*?" I choke. Not exactly a reference I'd use as *he's* the one toying with me right now. His strokes remain slow, methodical, and torturing. I spread my legs wider, as if it will bring him deeper. He passes his thumb over my clit, and my eyes shutter closed.

"Keep those eyes open," he demands. "We don't want someone innocently noticing. Only I can know what you look like when you come. When you make a mess on my fingers beneath this table."

"Jesus," I groan.

Jude leans closer to me, pressing a soft kiss to my exposed shoulder, then casually sits up like he doesn't have his hand between my thighs and his fingers buried inside me. He swipes over my clit again, this time more intentional.

"Take another bite of food," he commands.

I blindly stare down at my plate. A meal, hot and fresh, and made for me at his request. I pick up the final bite and guide it toward my mouth just as Jude applies more pressure on my clit. My eyes close on their own as my breath hitches.

"You're doing so good," he encourages, while I falter, holding the slider mid-air while the intensity of his fingers increases.

"Bite," he groans, and I place the final piece in my mouth, chewing slowly as Jude works me faster. His fingers glide deeper, curling inside me, and I gasp despite the food in my mouth.

He scoots a little closer, and his fingers from the hand on the back of my chair tickle my exposed shoulder.

"You know what I'd really like to do," Jude continues. "Place you on my lap, facing this room. Spread you wide and finish you off with my cock buried deep inside you."

I nearly choke on the burger in my mouth.

"Would you like that, naughty girl?"

I don't answer him. I can't. I'm afraid to move, but my hips rock subtly beneath the table. I clutch the edge of my seat and tip my hips. The angle shifts how Jude is touching me. He easily reaches something deep inside while his thumb works circular magic.

"Jude," I whisper, knowing I'm so close to the edge, and it's more than balancing on this seat.

"Easy there, sweetheart. I'm right here." He practically purrs as he leans closer once more and kisses the side of my neck. The touch is featherlight, but his words at my ear are hot and hard.

"Come, my angel. You're turned on by the thought of being on my lap, stroking my currently hard dick with your slick pussy and—"

My mouth falls open as I pitch forward. Slamming my elbows on the table and covering my lips with shaky hands, I sit straighter and ride Jude's fingers. My orgasm hits like *The Polar Express* gliding out of control on an ice-covered lake. Hard and fast, I spiral toward a climax that ends all too quickly, screeching to a halt.

I'm not done with Jude. We need that small empty storage room.

Still, I practically sag against the table, and Jude strokes his other hand up my back, beneath my hair to cup my nape.

"Such a naughty girl." He chuckles before pressing a kiss to my shoulder again. "Letting me finger fuck you at a family wedding."

I turn my head to witness that sly smile of his grow to a full grin.

"Why would you do that?" he asks, a little too late for regret.

Why *did* I do this? His question might be rhetorical, but I have an answer.

"Because I trust you." I trusted him to be here for me, and he showed. I trust him not to let my family see what he's done to me beneath the table.

And I'm trusting him not to break my heart.

His eyes widen as he slowly removes his fingers and sits straighter in his seat. He takes his arm from the back of my chair and straightens his suit coat. With that same hand, he picks up a fry and chews while watching me. Then he takes the hand previously touching me, and sucks at his fingers, like they contain the salty residue of greasy fries.

Oh, he's good. The bad take on what he's doing would only be caught by a trained eye, but like I thought, I've trusted him not to expose us. Not to expose me and what he's just done.

"Now what?" I joke, the sound almost bitter. Because what I'd really love is for us to slip into that small closet-like space and finish this little snack in the position he just suggested.

I'd ride him reverse cowgirl like a woman on Santa's lap.

Please, Santa, can I have another. I only want orgasms given by him.

He snorts. "Now, you finish eating that last slider while I mentally talk down my dick. Then we'll dance, knowing you still ache for me." He leans close once more. "Don't worry, angel. I ache for you, too."

He kisses me quickly, then reaches for another fry and pops it into his mouth, smiling like a Dr. Seuss character pleased with the places he takes me.

chapter 36

[Jude]

I'd almost fucked up.

When she told me she loved food, I almost said *I love you.* Which I never say to anyone, other than my sister, and even then, it's a shortened version.

I don't know what's come over me other than a foreboding feeling that the wedding is my last night with Angelica.

A date for a date. Yet, somehow, we've turned into so much more.

Work has been hectic, to say the least, and the late nights and early mornings didn't leave me much spare time to foster whatever is between Angelica and me. Because there definitely is something happening between us. Something I'd like to continue to explore, but I didn't know how.

Thankfully, before I said something foolish, I did something sexy and dirty. To my surprise, Angelica went along with it.

Because I trust you.

Fuck. The statement was equal to saying she loved me, which would not, could not happen. We had a deal.

Deals are meant to be broken, she once said. *Even fake ones.*

I wasn't worried about breaking a deal as much as her breaking my heart.

I've never really listened to wedding vows, but I listened wholeheartedly to Beau and Belle's. Love, honor, and respect. Good times and bad. Sickness and health. Until death parts them.

I want to do all those things with Angelica. I wanted to be good enough, but I still didn't feel that I was.

I'd fallen for her. Hard and fast, and rather completely, and it scared the fuck out of me that she might not feel the same way in return. I needed to end things before she ended them for us.

Still, I wanted one more night.

In *A Christmas Carol*, Ebenezer Scrooge is visited by three ghosts on Christmas Eve. The experience transforms him, and his changes begin on Christmas Day.

My epiphany happened the day after Thanksgiving because of a heart attack, and the bargain I made to an angel.

Being that I'm still a devil inside, though, I intend to steal one more night.

Christmas Eve, we are open for those late-night, last-minute shoppers, however, our doors close at eleven. I'll be here until midnight. While most might think I'm sitting up in my tower office, punching numbers into a spread sheet, and tallying Ashford's profits, I'm not. I'm thinking about one hot, redheaded EMT.

911. I text her.

What's wrong? Angelica had to work a double today to make up for her shift change on December twenty-third. She already explained the holiday scheduling of the department, and how she always takes Christmas Eve night to give parents time to do their thing for their kids.

Possible heart attack.

I rock back in my comfy desk chair, knowing I shouldn't be joking about a health scare with an emergency medical technician.

Jude, you need to call 911 for real.

A pause.

I'll do it for you.

NO!

No ambulance.

Only you.

Another pause follows before three dots pop up and disappear.

This isn't funny. What's going on?

A broken heart.

The ticker is tightening in my chest. She's my only solution. Just one more night. Christmas will be my reset like it always is. A day where I do nothing but drink my weight in whiskey and stare at mindless television, attempting to unwind from the hustle and bustle of the season.

Meet me at Ashford's State Street entrance. Midnight.

Last night, Angelica did sit on my lap like a woman on Santa. Her green velvet dress was pooled at her waist, blanketing where we were connected. I held her in a way she faced my wall-to-wall windows. Our reflection mingled with the winter night's glow from the city streets of Chicago, and we watched as I entered her.

The vision was enough to beg for another night, and tonight's plan evolved last minute.

Close to midnight, I head to the first-floor entrance and wait. Security is present in the building but has confirmed that Ashford's is empty, minus our overnight cleaning crew.

I've requested that no one enter the seventh floor. The Oak Room specifically.

When Angelica finally arrives, she looks skeptical and exhausted, as she only got off shift about a half-hour ago. For a second, I reconsider. Between the hectic holiday, Beau's wedding, and her job, plus a late night of incredible sex, she looks like she's been run ragged.

She also looks beautiful with her hair in a wide braid and her uniform still on.

I open the front door and invite Angelica in, leaving the security guard to secure the entrance.

"Jude, are you sure you are okay?" She scans me from top to toe.

Admittedly, I like her concern.

"No chest aches? No heart palpitations? What about fluttering?" She reaches for my wrist like she's about to check my pulse.

I chuckle and catch her hand with mine, lifting it to kiss her palm. "I'm hoping for all of the above."

First, I have something to show her. Keeping her hand in mine, I lead her toward the escalators. I asked maintenance to leave them running a few minutes longer.

"What is this all about?" she questions, taking in the dim lights and noticing the emptiness within the department store.

"Special VIP tour." I nod like I didn't just make that up.

Angelica only stares back at me. Those soft blue eyes are wide and suspicious as we take the first escalator upward. Then the next. Eventually, she relaxes into the ride up six stories up to the seventh floor.

Once there, I place my hand on her back and lead her toward The Oak Room.

The lights are off in the entryway except for the exit signs. The dining room is dark as well, except for the giant two-story Christmas tree lit in the center.

"Wow," Angelica whispers, staring up at the tree decorated in white lights and countless ornaments that glitter and glow from the silver and gold sprinkled on each of them.

Slowly, she lowers her head and looks at me like she did that day when I caught her staring at the glass dome in the center of the building. A second dome is in this room, but unable to be easily seen because of the towering tree.

"It's so beautiful," she continues to whisper, as if in awe.

"I knew you'd like it." Angelica loves Christmas despite the rat-race of it, and I wanted to give her this one peaceful moment before tomorrow morning, which I'm certain will be filled with squealing children in her gran's cozy home.

I almost wish I could be there.

With her head lowered, she glances back toward the room, noticing the pile of pillows and blankets spread beneath the tree.

"What's that?" Her voice catches as if she knows what it is but still asks.

"A midnight picnic."

Her hands clasp in front of her chest, and she dips her head. "Did you do all this for me?"

"I thought you could use a silent night before all the noise, noise, noise tomorrow," I tease, and wave in the direction of the chilled champagne bucket and a three-tiered tray with chocolates and strawberries, plus whipped cream.

Angelica slowly walks toward the nest I've made, and I follow, watching the sway of her hips and how the light of the tree reflects off her hair, highlighting the multiple colors within the red braid.

My chest does ache. She's so beautiful, and I imagine her freckle, sight unseen.

My freckle.

When she stands beside the spread duvet, her brows pinch. "Did you open these fresh from the store?"

I shrug. The housewares department will forgive me. The items will only be used once.

Angelica bends forward to unlace her boots, and I toe off my shoes. My suit coat was removed hours ago, and my shirt sleeves are rolled to my elbows. I hold out my hand like I'm helping her step into a hot tub or a boat, or a sleigh of blankets.

We fold down to the pillows, and I reach for the champagne chilling in a stainless-steel bucket then pour each of us a glass.

Handing a flute to her, I hold up mine. "Merry Christmas, angel."

"Merry Christmas, Jude." She tilts her head. "I thought you didn't celebrate?"

I don't. But am I?

I chuff and lift my glass for a bubbly sip. I'm a man used to the finer things in life. Champagne. Fast cars. Expensive suits. But I've found more comfort and joy in a woman with a cozy apartment, a tempting freckle, and a loving extended family.

The champagne suddenly tastes bitter on my tongue, but I ignore it. Instead, I reach for a strawberry and hold it out for Angelica to take a bite. The fruit is huge, and red juice drips down her chin.

Nothing holds me back. I lunge for her, licking up the dribble and then thrusting my tongue into her mouth. The action nearly knocks her over, and she chuckles against my mouth.

"Whoa. Slow down." She swipes at her lips while I lean back.

"I've told you I don't know how to go slow." But I also told her I wouldn't ever love her.

Could she love me?

Angelica reaches around me and drags the tiered dessert-stand closer to us. She picks up a chocolate and holds it out to me. I take a hearty bite.

Her brow tips like she wants my assessment.

"Not as good as yours."

"You're a charmer." She giggles.

Am I? Does she find me charming? Does she want to keep me?

The thought is too heavy, and I reach for a strawberry again, swiping it through the cream before holding it out for her mouth again. She leans forward for a bite, but I pull the fruit back.

"Tease." Her eyes gleam in the glow of the Christmas tree.

I snort. "You're the tease." With her hair and her smile and her ease. I push the strawberry toward her again and watch as she takes another sensuous bite. She doesn't realize how seductive she is. And with a drop of cream on her lip, I attack again, licking at the spot and then kissing her deeply once more.

She doesn't laugh this time or pull back. Instead, she melts into the kiss until I'm pressing her backward. Once she's on her back, I slowly unbutton her uniform shirt, revealing a tank top underneath. The shirt must go. The tank as well.

"Jude," she glances over her shoulder, like someone will see us.

I tug her upright to remove her tops. "There's no one here. Just you and me tonight."

She glances back at me and then removes her uniform shirt on her own. I take over next, reaching for the hem of her tank and pulling it over her head, then pop off her bra and press her down again. Reaching for another strawberry, I swipe through the whipped cream once more and then paint a white streak down her neck.

Angelica tips back her head, and I lick at the sticky sweetness before releasing her and biting into the strawberry. My mouth fills with sweet nectar, and I lean forward to sip at one peaked nipple before moving to the other. Angelica's hands come to my head, combing over the short hair and cupping the back of my neck.

I want to rush, while I want to savor every second I have left with her.

Like those spirits that visited dear old Scrooge, I'm afraid she'll disappear when morning arrives. So, I take my time removing her pants, and eventually her panties, all the while painting her body with a combination of whipped cream and fresh strawberries.

Eventually, I drag the tip of the final fruit between her legs, which she easily spreads for me.

"You wouldn't." Her voice catches as the cold point of the strawberry nudges against her entrance.

"Wouldn't I?" I love a good dare, but I sense her hesitation. Fruit is a hard limit.

Instead, I dip the strawberry in the cream and use it to spread the whipped stuff over her sensitive folds. Then I take a final bite of the strawberry and swallow before climbing between her legs and devouring her, licking and lapping at the sweet mess I've made of her.

Angelica moans and squirms at the combination of cold cream and warm tongue, and I pin her thighs, keeping her open and wide.

When she finally bursts against my mouth, she cries out. "Oh, Jude." Her voice is like a song, and I continue to feast, driving my tongue deeper, demanding a second serving from her.

She breaks again, hailing my name one more time, before I kiss her lower lips, and pull back.

With rapid strength she sits upright. "My turn."

"Nope." I catch her hand on my waistband. "Tonight, you're all mine."

However, I let her undress me, taking my time to kiss her in between her unbuttoning my shirt, popping the clasp on my slacks, and eventually, removing everything.

Pressing her to her back again, I climb over her, blanketing her for a second, while enjoying the taste of her mouth. Sticky cream and sweet strawberries mingle with the flavor of her on my tongue.

Eventually, I hold myself at her entrance, swiping my tip through where she's hot and needy. I just want to feel that wetness for a moment. She's so wet and warm, and too quickly, I'm sucked forward as if she's pulling me inside her.

I freeze with just the tip wedged between her slick lower lips.

"Angelica?"

"Please," she whispers, like she wants to feel me as much as I want to feel her. Raw and bare and real.

The color orange and the number nine and a girl who likes all foods. These are a few of her favorite things. She is my favorite person, like I told her only yesterday.

"Are you sure?" My dick is begging for entrance, but I won't do anything without her permission. We already know each other's health history, and she's on the pill.

"I'm sure."

Angelica slides her hand over my shoulder and down my arm, around my elbow until she catches my wrist. Then she tugs at my hand and links our fingers.

For a second, I just stare at where our fingers fold together, clasping one another. Like that hug she gave me weeks ago, I'm frozen. No . . . spellbound.

She lifts our hands and kisses my knuckles before settling our collective hands against her chest.

I slide into her with all the patience I can muster. My heart hammers. The palpitations she was concerned about earlier begin in earnest. Who knew flutterings were a real thing? While one part of me moves as slowly as I can, another space inside me races as if I'm skiing down a steep hill. A slippery slope right into love.

Ignoring the thought, I glide into her warmth, melting from both the snug fit and the raw heat, and my heart patters faster.

"Angelica," I grit, knowing I can't last at this pace. The lazy rhythm where I feel everything. Her and me and us joined together.

As I settle to the hilt, she slides one foot up over my calf and behind my knee, then up my hamstring to my ass. Every brush is another electrifying sensation. A prickle of heat like I've never felt before. The melting of my heart, which has frozen for too long.

I swipe back a loose hair stuck to her cheek and kiss her forehead, lingering there a second as I try to settle the tightening of my rib cage and the racing of my pulse.

Then Angelica tips up her hips, and I pull back, slow, purposeful, torturous, but awe-inspiring.

So fucking . . . real.

Glancing down at her, my soul screams *Mine*. I'm a fucking toy soldier desperate for this human to claim me as hers.

"Angelica," I whisper.

"I'm right here, Jude."

The words could mean anything. They shouldn't sound like the *something more* I've been seeking this entire season.

Desperate to push away my fear that she doesn't mean it—she isn't mine to keep—I pick up the pace, taking her a little harder while still slow. A little deeper while still struggling with patience. The sound of us coming together is like a tabernacle choir of slapping skin on skin and moans with moans.

I can't fucking take it because I know what this moment means.

We're making love and I've never done this before. Never felt this way.

I'm certain I'm having a second stress cardiomyopathy incident. My heart is shattering, and yet I can't stop. I don't want to stop. Not us or her.

As I slowly drag my dick through the heat of her channel before surging forward, I feel every spark of her warmth and squeeze of her attempts to keep me inside her, filling her.

I release her head and reach for her clit, but she pushes at my wrist.

"My turn," she whispers, eyes locking on mine for a second. It's too much. The heat in them. The hope.

I can't look. Instead, I kiss her hard and deep, like my hips flex. Angelica wraps both her legs around my waist, clinging to me as we ebb and flow like a sleigh up and over snow-covered hills. Up we lift and down we fall, until finally, I can't take it anymore.

I clutch her hip and drive faster, snapping my hips in response and tapping her deeper. Her head tips back and she calls out my name, like she's begging me to hurry.

Don't you leave me, Jude.

It whispers through my head one more time, and I race to reach whoever it is that needs me. Wanting it to be her. My angel. My Angelica.

Her mouth falls open and her eyes roll back, and she lets out a surprised cry, as her body tightens. Her pussy squeezes me as she falls over the cliff while I continue to climb, climb, climb, and then crack, spilling inside her.

"Fuck," I grunt as the release is like angels singing and bells tolling, and I don't know what the fuck is happening to me. Collapsing over her, I breathe in her scent, forcing my senses to memorize the fragrance.

Sugar and spice and sex. Us.

I roll to the side, taking her with me, and we stay wrapped around one another until I pass out, dreaming of her over me, begging me not to leave, and leaning in for a kiss to pull me back from endless darkness.

chapter 37

[Jude]

I wake with a jolt.

Rolling my head side to side, I sense I'm alone. A blanket covers my still naked body, and I sit upright, prepared to call out Angelica's name until I notice her uniform and shoes are gone.

Falling back to the pillows, I comb my hands into my hair and hold them at the top of my head. Staring up at the ceiling, just past the star on the top of the two-story tree, faint light seeps through the glass dome.

Morning?

I pull back my left arm and check the silver watch on my wrist.

Officially, Christmas.

Although wasn't it already Christmas last night at midnight? When I said I didn't celebrate the holiday, and yet I did, making love to a beautiful woman, who has clearly disappeared this morning.

I turn my head toward the pillow where she slept and find a small package, wrapped in green paper with a red ribbon on top.

Slowly sitting upright again, I pick up the box, hesitating with it in my hand like I'm holding an explosive instead of a gift.

Maybe it is meant to implode my heart because I don't receive many gifts.

Pulling at the ribbon, it easily releases. I flip the square package and unwrap it with care, like I want to save the pretty paper. Once unwrapped, I flip the box and pull off the lid.

Inside is a pocket-sized copy of *A Christmas Carol*. When I pick it up, something falls out. A flat silver disc with a rudimentary angel on it. One complete with wings and wild hair and a long flowing dress.

Flipping over the silver medal, the back reads: a pocket angel.

I softly smile as I run my thumb over the raised design and then thumb through the hand-sized novel.

Instantly, I find a written inscription.

To the man who had a change of heart and changed mine along with his.

Here is an angel to always guide you out of the dark and remind you to live.

Fuck. My eyes burn and my throat thickens. I didn't understand.

How could she leave me such a sentimental gift, but be gone?

Reaching for my phone, the first notification I see is from Angelica.

Spend Christmas with me.

I can almost hear the soft command in her voice, like when she invited me to go home with her only last weekend after I apologized to Eva in the bar.

Quickly, I scroll to the transformation list Angelica made me.

Where can you make a meaningful donation?

How can you gift time?

Who do you need to make amends with?

Who deserves an apology from you?

How can you show compassion for another?

A circle with a check mark ticks off what I've completed.

Donate money. Check.

Gift time. Check.

Apologize. Check.

Show compassion. Check.

What remains is making amends. But with whom? My family immediately comes to mind, and I send Julia a text wishing her and Chopper and the kids: **Merry Christmas**.

While chatting on the phone with her the other day, I let it slip that I'd had a heart attack, and my sister went batshit crazy on me for not mentioning it sooner. She was so angry, she hung up without saying she loved me.

Perhaps she's who I need to make amends with. Especially when she doesn't immediately respond to my text, which isn't like her. Then I remember California is hours behind Chicago, and if first light is cracking here, her family is hopefully still snug in their beds.

My thoughts then drift back to Angelica's invitation.

Spend Christmas with me.

But I don't celebrate this day. Slowly, I rise from the blanket nest and redress in yesterday's clothing. I need a shower and a stiff drink. My own bed is calling as well.

I head to my office, to collect a few things, but once I'm there I stand still and pull out my phone one more time.

Spend Christmas with me.

Glancing around my cold, empty office, where I'm alone on Christmas morning, it hits me that this cannot be it. This cannot be my entire world. This is not living my life.

I feel that itchy sensation again. That feeling under my skin, drawing me somewhere, toward someone.

Don't you leave me, Jude?

"I won't," I whisper to the room. "I won't let you go."

Rushing to the elevator, I repeatedly poke the down button, as if it will make the lift rise faster. Impatience gets to me, and I race for the escalators next, knowing the descent on the automatic stairs could take even longer.

I skip steps, hanging on the railing, like I did as a child, as if it will propel me faster down seven flights.

I'm running across the red carpet, about to cross where it intersects, when I stop.

Looking upward, I stand directly beneath the glass ceiling seven stories overhead. I tip my head further back and stare at the dome window arching toward the sky that I've seen a thousand times in my life.

And as I stand perfectly still, the light slowly illuminates the glass panes and spreads over the angles, forming a slow kaleidoscope of light against the west wall. The longer I stand, the brighter the window grows and the wider the stretch of light cascades down along the wall, bouncing off the gold railings around each level, reflecting like a prism.

While I still can't define what Angelica sees in that rounded ceiling, I admit I feel something inside me. Something warm and longing, almost poking against my rib cage like it wants to be set free. Like it's stretching the iron bars around my heart and reaching through the cracks, hoping to expand my chest.

I take a deep breath and find it easier than I would have thought to breathe, considering the ache.

Blood rushes through my veins, and my pulse pounds in my ears, and yet I'm not afraid.

This isn't stress or shattering or an attack.

This is something more.

My lips curl, exposing my teeth, until my mouth opens and I laugh. Loud and echo-y in the emptiness of the store, where I'm suddenly reminded that I'm standing here alone.

All alone on Christmas in my legacy.

A building that proudly displays my name but has sucked the soul out of me.

A place that has taught me to chase bottom lines and top sales and the black on a spreadsheet.

The strangest sensation fills my eyes. They burn and itch and then water, and I pinch the bridge of my nose, blinking at the foreign dampness, and swallowing the thickness in my throat.

Because the one thing I've never chased: the girl. And love.

Ebenezar Scrooge didn't get his girl in the end because too much time had passed. She married some other guy. The nameless, faceless one, who probably never put her first.

That will not be me.

A plan instantly forms. A new deal for Angelica. A better one.

A better me.

And I will not spend another minute without her.

chapter 38

[Jude]

As the sun has just risen, it's early when I enter my condo for a quick shower and change before I rush to Angelica's to discover an explosion of bags and boxes and wrapped Christmas presents.

"What the fuck?" I mutter, scanning the typically empty space that is cluttered by the pile of gifts, oversized bags near the entrance, and a double stack of pizza boxes on the kitchen island.

I'd question if I've been robbed, but this looks more like an invasion.

Tossing my keys on the kitchen island, I swipe a hand through my hair and prepare to storm down the hallway when the guest bedroom door opens.

A timid child exits and stares at me. I stare back at a miniature version of Julia. A little girl who looks exactly like her mother did when she was that age.

Despite the shock, I squat to my niece's level. "Hi, Lollipop." I don't expect her to approach me. I haven't seen her often enough in the four years of her life. Lolly Rochelle Paige has wild curly hair, reminding me of a certain someone who snuck out of Ashford's this morning.

"Are you Santa Claus?" She eyes me with suspicion. "You don't look like Santa Claus."

I bite my lower lip, fighting a smile. "No. I'm your Uncle Jude."

"Hey, Jude," a masculine voice sings, and I glance further down the hallway to see the sleepy father of this little one exiting my bedroom. My brother-in-law loves to sing the song I'm named after, like it's a joke, when he bears the nickname for a motorcycle.

In the name of Christmas, what the . . .

"Chopper." I slowly stand to greet the heavily tattooed man wearing a white T-shirt and gray sweatpants, who scoops up his daughter, pressing kisses to her neck, which causes her to squeal. He carries her to the end of the hallway, but not into the open space of the living room and kitchen.

"Did you peek?" Chopper questions. "What did Mama say? No peeking. You need to come get her and me first."

Slowly, I glance at the presents, realizing that my sister and her family have invaded my home, bringing their Santa duties with them, for Christmas.

"What the fuck?"

Chopper gives me a scathing look as I finish speaking, while Lolly quips, "He said a bad word, Daddy."

"He did say a bad word." Chopper continues to glare at me. He'd be scary if I didn't know he's a teddy bear for my sister and their kids. "I bet Santa didn't bring him any presents."

"But Santa brought me presents. Right, Daddy?" she squeezes her father's cheeks to gain his attention.

"I bet Santa brought you lots of presents." Chopper rubs his nose against hers, and she giggles again.

"And I bet . . . Uncle Jude would like to know how Santa got here." I arch a brow at my brother-in-law.

"He drove his sleigh," Lolly explains, like I don't know the details.

Chopper shifts Lolly to his hip. "And a delayed flight from L.A." Chopper narrows his eyes one more time, imparting the situation.

My sister brought her family to me on one of the busiest days for travel in an airport.

Behind Chopper, who still holds Lolly in the tunnel of the hallway, my sister approaches her husband and wraps her arms around him from the back. Chopper shifts to kiss her.

"Merry Christmas," she says softly to him.

"Merry Christmas, cupcake."

Lolly giggles again and reaches for her mother.

"I'll get the boys," he comments, before sparing me another glance, threatening me to be nice to his wife.

I don't need the warning.

With Lolly on Julia's hip, twinning in a way, my sister stares at me. "Don't be mad."

"I'm not," I admit, glancing back at the pile of presents and sighing heavily. Despite the exhale, I'm not upset. In fact, I feel strangely lighter, almost pleased that she is present.

"You scared me," she whispers.

My head swings back in her direction. Instantly, I realize what I've done. The heart attack. My sister has always been a worrywart, and she might have been afraid she'd lose me in an instant, like we lost our mom.

"I'm not going anywhere," I weakly attempt to reassure her. I pat my chest. "Made of steel."

If only that were true, because it aches this morning. While I feel like my heart fills my chest, it also feels strangely empty. Like an inflated balloon.

"You know I've always doubted that," Julia says about my heart, hitching Lolly higher on her hip.

I finally approach my sister. "But you've never doubted me, and that's all that matters." Standing right in front of her, I stroke a shaky hand down Lolly's wild curls. She tucks her head into my sister's shoulder, and I pull back.

Julia watches me. Her brows pinching at something she sees in my face.

"I'm sorry," I blurt, to distract her. "For making you concerned."

"I know you are." She slowly smiles. "And as your penance, we are here to celebrate Christmas." She jostles Lolly on her hip and bops her on the nose before looking back at me. "We are just waiting on—"

A sharp knock comes to my front door, and I turn to face it before spinning back for my sister.

"Perfect timing. Can you get that?" Julia adds.

"What the hell is going on?"

Julia tries to give me a stern glare, but stoicism isn't possible on her freckled cheeks.

Spinning toward the front door, I curse the building security. They exist so random people cannot enter the inner building without permission, and I only have two people on my admission list.

Julia and Angelica.

My blood rushes through my veins as hope sores. Maybe she's come to me.

But when I open the door, I come face to face with a familiar-looking man and the sunshine of his life beside him.

"Dad?"

chapter 39

[Angelica]

I hate that I snuck out of Ashford's, but when I heard soft voices and light music, I panicked.

I slipped into my uniform and slunk down seven flights of stairs until I reached the first floor. Thankfully, the same security guard was present at the State Street entrance to let me out of Ashford's.

"Merry Christmas," I muttered to the poor man working an overnight shift on Christmas Eve.

I'd been there. Knew someone had to do it. First responders like me. And medical staff. And security personnel.

I took an Uber back to the fire department to retrieve my car with blurry eyes both from exhaustion and an aching heart.

I couldn't shake this sudden foreboding sensation that last night Jude was telling me goodbye, when I only wanted to keep saying hello to him over and over again.

The way Jude clung to me. The way he took his time. His patience was unparalleled considering he never goes slow. Every sexual encounter with him has been a rush, but last night, time stood still.

In that stillness, I felt him slipping away.

And because I'm a glutton for punishment, I invited Jude to spend the day with me, somehow knowing he won't accept the invitation. Sensing I was pushing him too far.

A man can only change so much.

Once home and showered, I pull up the invitation for Jude to spend Christmas at Gran's, seeing it's been read, but not responded to. The pit of my stomach feels like I've eaten an entire fruit cake.

When I get to Gran's, it's still early, but her living room is an explosion of gifts, from big to small, and everything in between. While the packages are wrapped in brightly colored paper decorated with snowmen, reindeer, and elves, I envision every present I purchased for Gran and Gertie. The gifts I picked out myself . . . while shopping with Jude.

Hardly a month has passed since that day, and yet, it feels like a lifetime ago.

Our story will be one I tell in the future: *The Month I Loved a Grinch.*

Because I'd fallen in love with Jude Ashford. The new Jude. The one no longer a spoiled, aloof teenager, nor a short-sighted businessman, but the one who transformed into something more.

The one who embraced my family while baking cookies and donated half a million dollars because I missed a fundraiser. The one who took care of me when I was sick and paid for all my Christmas presents. The man who made a little girl smile in a hospital bed and kissed me like it wasn't pretend.

He felt something, right? Something more. Last night certainly felt extra.

As I sit on Gran's worn couch, I hear the rumble of feet racing down the stairs from Christmas's apartment above. Gran and Gertie stumble from the kitchen, each holding a cup of ambition as they'll need it to get through the chaos of the next few hours.

Dane will be here later with his girls.

Beau and Belle are off on their honeymoon.

And while I'm not alone, loneliness blankets me.

I wish Jude was here.

+ + +

The next few hours pass in the chaos only Christmas brings.

Squeals of delight. Pressure to immediately put items together. "Do you have batteries?" is said three times because *someone* forgot to purchase them. The pile of wrapping paper grows like a building blizzard.

Once the kids are content, Gran and I head to the kitchen, where I start making breakfast. Every movement is labored. Every motion rote.

Pancake making. Bacon sizzling. Coffee brewing.

"What's wrong with you?" Christmas asks, finally entering the epicenter of Gran's home.

"Nothing," I lie.

"Santa doesn't come to those who tell a lie," my sister teases.

"Santa already came," I mutter, and the one thing I wanted didn't arrive.

"What's Jude doing today?" she asks, reaching for the coffee pot and pouring herself another mug.

"He doesn't celebrate." I sigh, whisking the ingredients for pancake batter faster.

"What do you mean he doesn't celebrate?" Gran asks, from somewhere behind me.

I glance over my shoulder to see Gran and Gertie sitting at the kitchen table, which already holds a stack of plates and silverware for dinner later today. A roast will go in the oven soon. Mashed potatoes were previously made, frozen, and were now defrosting on the countertop. The green bean casserole needs to be made. Rolls, too. Salad.

"Angelica," Christmas says, pulling me from the ever-present list of things to do. "What do you mean Jude doesn't celebrate?"

She eyes me suspiciously.

"He just doesn't believe in the day, I guess. Retail is a hard industry, and the season sucks the energy out of him." I shrug, although I don't firmly know Jude's reason for not participating in this holiday.

Her brows furrow.

"That's nonsense," Gertie says from her seat at the round table. "There's always a reason to celebrate a day, Christmas or otherwise."

"Well, I guess, he goes with otherwise and not Christmas." I don't know why I'm suddenly defensive. He has a right to peace and quiet and to be alone.

Suddenly, it hits me.

Jude will be alone. All alone. What will he do today? How will he pass the time?

I spin to face Gran. "He's going to be alone," I whisper.

Gran sits straighter, reading something in my face. "Invite him to come here."

"I did," I admit, my throat clogging with the reminder he didn't accept the invitation.

The kitchen is silent for a minute before Gertie says, "Well, if he won't join the party, the party should join him."

"Gertie," I groan. "I can't invade Jude's space." He doesn't want to be with me today.

But then what was last night? The romantic setup. The chocolate and champagne. The strawberries and cream he'd painted over my body.

A shiver ripples up my spine.

Did he want to be alone? Or was last night his quiet plea to be with someone? To celebrate with me?

"Gran . . ." Suddenly, I'm setting down the pancake bowl and swiping my hands on a dishtowel. "I think I need . . . I should . . . I might . . ."

"We're right there with you." Gran is the first to jump up from the table. Opening the fridge, she's already pulling out the butcher-paper wrapped roast and the bag of fresh green beans.

"What are you doing?" I chuckle anxiously.

"If he won't come here for Christmas, we'll take Christmas to him."

I glance at my sister who hollers toward her sons. "Everyone pick two items and then get dressed. We're going on a holiday adventure."

"This is crazy," I state, staring at my sister and then turning toward Gran.

"Any crazier than Beau getting married two days ago to a girl he met while drunk on a plane?" Christmas snorts, patting my shoulder.

Beau is always going to one-up the rest of us.

And I watch as my family goes into snowstorm mode, packing up our meal, and gathering the boys and their new toys, before we head out to Christmas's van in hopes of restoring the holiday for Jude.

chapter 40

[Jude]

I stare at my father a moment too long before Mae, his wife, clears her throat. She's a beautiful brunette woman, close to my dad's age, and everything opposite my mother. A little carefree; a lot lighthearted, and she makes my dad smile like I've never seen before.

"Surprise," Mae says, making jazz hands from where they stand in the hallway.

"Merry Christmas, son," Tucker says, hesitantly.

I've been ambushed, and they know it.

Julia!

Still, I know my sister did this out of love. Fear and love. Fear she'd lose me and love.

Don't you leave me, Jude.

My guardian angel was not my sister, but Julia has been a steady force for most of my life, and I appreciate what she's trying to do. I accept it.

"Merry Christmas, Dad." My voice is rough as I step back and wave for them to enter my place.

As soon as Tucker and Mae enter, Lolly breaks free of Julia and races for them.

"Boppa," she cries out. "Mimi."

Like a punch to the gut, I realize that Julia's children have only ever known Mae. She is their grandmother, not our mom. Another thought hits. She'll be better at the position.

And in our mix and match of family, nothing follows a straight line.

With Lolly in Tucker's arms, she says, "Can we open presents now?"

"Yes, we can open presents now," Julia confirms as Chopper enters the living room with their oldest boy, Charlie, beside him, and their second son, Ransom, in his arms, who looks like he'd rather continue sleeping as his head lies on his father's shoulder.

"Santa came to Uncle Jude's," Lolly confirms for everyone.

Suddenly, I realize I don't have a single present for any of them.

I sent gifts to Julia, Chopper, and the kids, but I don't even know what was sent. I had my assistant pick out items, sparing no expense. As for Tucker and Mae, I hadn't sent a gift to them. Ever.

My head hangs in shame. "I don't have anything for everyone."

Mae steps closer to me. "That doesn't matter. Christmas isn't about gifts. It's about gathering together." She offers me a soft, warm smile.

I miss my mother, but she was always cold, always standoffish. As that's all I'd known, that's how I thought it should be. My mother's image in front of others was more important than compassion in her home. She'd been everything I'd turned into and no one I wanted to be anymore.

The tenderness in Mae's eyes reminds me of Angelica, but I ignore the pinch behind my rib cage.

The next hours pass in a whirlwind of unwrapping presents. Brightly colored paper is made into balls and tossed across the room. Gadgets and gizmos, with instructions and batteries required, fill my living room floor. The kids squealed with excitement, and the adults *ooh-ed* and *aah-ed.*

And it all felt so foreign.

This was nothing like the stilted holiday I'd had as a kid. The formal attire and photo opportunities. The neat piles of used paper and the tight smiles over gifts 'donated' by sponsors to meet Mother's influencer image. The awkward silences between the gift exchange and the family dinner.

This was different.

I stare at my sister, animated and bright, adoring her children as they marvel at what they believe Santa brought them. I glance at Tucker, smiling just as wide, his arm casually around Mae, who leans forward, equally excited by every gift *her* grandchildren open.

How did they do it? How did they let the past go?

Suddenly, I'm too warm and I stand, stalking toward the kitchen, needing at least the island between me and them. Hell, I've needed most of the country to separate us, like them in California and me, here, alone.

My stomach turns again. Because I didn't want to be alone.

"You okay?" Tucker says behind me, and I busy my hands, pouring coffee from the machine my sister must have set last night.

"Yeah," I mutter toward the coffee pot. "It's just a lot." I hate admitting weakness, but I find I'm too weak to resist.

Tucker is suddenly beside me, hip leaning against the countertop. I slowly glance up at him. His hair is fully gray now. The lines near his eyes tell a story. The concern in them puzzles me.

One day, I'll look like him, but not really.

"You feeling okay?" His voice is hesitant, like he knows any minute, I'll snap. I'll bark a sharp retort or a lashing comment.

I hate you. How many times did I say that to him when I was younger?

"I just feel . . ." I sigh, risking a glance at him again before looking back at the hot liquid in my coffee mug. "A little untethered."

Tucker remains quiet.

"Displaced, actually."

"Displaced?" he questions, and I look firmly at him.

"Yeah. Actually, my entire life I've felt displaced." Not so much as a stranger or an outsider, just somewhere, or rather, someone, no one wanted. Learning I wasn't Tucker's son and that we shared a father. Learning how my mother had been a young girl taken advantage of. The reality made me sick.

"A product of . . ." I couldn't say the word, and I swallow thickly. *What is wrong with me?* Blinking at the burn in my eyes for the second time today, I recognize that earlier the wetness was tears, but I don't want to admit that I'd been crying. I'd been overcome with something I couldn't define.

And I don't know why I'm taking this sharp turn down memory lane.

Quickly, Tucker cups my neck, and I pull back instinctually, but he doesn't let go. He squeezes gently, holding me still.

"You are a product of love." His tone is tight. His words determined. "*I* love you."

Despite.

He leaves off the quantifying word.

Despite my dickishness over the years. Despite missing holidays and birthdays. Despite trying to sabotage his relationship with Mae, because I couldn't see him happy if I was unhappy. Despite the accusations that he never loved my mother, and the hurtful pride I tossed at him when I inherited the family business.

As if reading all of this in my eyes, Tucker reiterates. "I love you. *As your dad*." Not my father. Not the man who produced me, but the man who raised me as his own.

I nod, still unable to find the right words to say back. Words that don't feel big enough for a man who has taken my shit over and over again and still stands in front of me offering his love.

"I'm sorry." I swallow thickly, knowing an apology is weak and long overdue. "I've been so . . . wrong."

About everything. Him. Mom. I don't know how to make amends.

It's never too late, Angelica had said.

Tucker simply nods, easily accepting my contrition. Too easily, but I don't have the energy to argue.

"Now, how are you feeling?"

"About apologizing?" I arch a brow. I am not about to psychoanalyze my feelings while still rolling in the uncertainty of them.

Tucker chuckles. "I meant after the heart attack." His brows pinch again, concern marring those lines near his eyes. "Why didn't you call me?"

Because I'm selfish? Because I didn't want him to know? Because I didn't want him to worry?

Because I didn't think he'd care.

"It wasn't a heart attack," I admit, shrugging. "It was a broken heart."

Tucker slowly softens his hand on my neck and pats over my chest with his other hand. "What happened?"

"Stress."

His brows rise. He knows the pressure of running Ashford's. It's one reason he skipped out on *wanting* the place.

"But you're okay now?" His voice is still hesitant, still troubled. Still concerned . . . because he does care.

Slowly, I shake my head. "Actually." I roll my lips. "I've met someone. And I think I fucked up."

I glance toward the living room where Chopper and Julia continue to open complicatedly sealed packages, and Mae is trying to help, but I'm certain their ears are tuned in my direction.

"I met someone," I announce a little louder. "But I . . ." *I fucked up*. And I should be there right now.

Mae spins on the couch, glancing over the back at me, and smiles. She's such a good woman, and I've done her wrong as well.

I have more apologies to share, but the next one goes to Angelica. I need my angel.

Glancing around my place, there isn't a stitch of holiday cheer. Not a tree. Not a decoration. Nothing to entice Angelica to come to me. I need to go to her.

"I have to go somewhere, but I promise I'll be back." I reach for my keys on the kitchen island. I'm still wearing yesterday's clothing, and smell of Angelica and I together, and that's exactly what I want.

Her and me.

Rushing to the front door, I sense my family staring at my back as I pull it open with force, and halt.

Like a crowd of carolers, a family stands in the hallway outside my door.

Christmas and her boys. Maggie and Gertie.

And at the center of them all is Angelica.

My angel.

chapter 41

[Angelica]

I hold my breath as Jude stares at me. Knowing he might be angry. Knowing he might push me away. But his typically icy eyes are clear, and he's evidently going somewhere.

"Angelica?" he breathes out my name in surprise and relief. At least, I hope it's relief. It sounds like relief. A little breathy. A little eager.

Still, I don't move.

"Merry Christmas, holiday hottie," Gertie states, pushing forward and helping herself to enter Jude's place.

"Gertrude," Gran groans before addressing Jude. "Merry Christmas, Jude. We don't mean to intrude."

"Yes, we do," Gertie calls over her shoulder. "Oh, look, the party has already started."

I glance around Jude. "You have . . . guests?" I swallow at the thought. Is another woman in there? Already? I don't want to believe it. Even if he's Jude, he can't possibly work that fast, can he?

Instantly, I'm jerked against Jude's chest. His arms wrap around me like a vise clamp. I'm so stunned, I don't respond. My arms hang limply at my sides. My throat tightens. Just as quickly, he releases me and addresses Gran and Christmas.

"Please, come in."

But Jude holds me back by a hand on my belly. Once my family enters his place, he reaches behind him and shuts the door, closing us off in the hallway. He gently presses me across the space until I'm flat against the wall opposite his door.

"You left."

"I'm sorry," I whisper, straining to keep my emotions in check. "I panicked." Maybe Jude could get caught naked in his store, but I didn't want to be found in a compromising position.

He nods, leaning over me by pressing his hand above my head.

"Don't leave me like that, ever again. You aren't the only one with abandonment issues."

I've never heard Jude so vulnerable, but I'm on shaky ground as well.

"Don't you leave me, Jude."

He stares at me for a second. Those icy eyes are clear pools today, but he's unblinking as he pushes himself off the wall.

"What?" he whispers as he crosses his arms. "What did you say?"

"Last night felt like goodbye." I meet his stare. My own eyes water. "Are you saying goodbye, Jude?"

"No." His voice hardens, and I watch his throat roll. "No, absolutely not." His eyes search my face. "But I want you to repeat what you just said. Exactly as you said it."

I give him a questioning gaze before I state, "Last night—"

"Not that. The other statement. Don't you . . ."

"Don't you leave me, Jude?"

Our eyes remain locked on one another before he whispers, "It was you, wasn't it?"

I chew at my lower lip, knowing exactly what he means.

"You are the angel."

"No angel," I whisper.

"Yes. An angel who begged me not to leave her." He pauses as his brows lift.

I dig harder at my lip.

"You brought me back."

"Back from what?"

Jude watches me for a long moment before he laughs. The sound abrupt and sharp. Then he laughs harder.

"Oh my God, it's been you all along." His hands cup my jaw. "Why didn't you tell me?" His expression returns to a pensive gaze. The same vulnerable one he gave me when he asked me not to leave ever again.

"Transference, like I told you. I didn't want you to *think* you'd fallen for me under a false pretense. Or some sense of obligation."

He chuckles while shaking his head, then presses his forehead against mine. "Angelica." He exhales my name again. The sound once more like relief. "No obligation. No false pretense. Only love."

Then, he kisses me, and as our lips meet, I melt beneath him. The warmth of his mouth. The tenderness of his hands. The desire in his taste.

"Because I've fallen. Fallen hard and fast and so deeply in love with you, angel," Jude whispers against my mouth.

The wind knocks out of me. "Really?" I whisper, emotion clogging my throat.

"Really," Jude says, his twitch of a smile no longer present. Only a blinding grin, emphasizing that apostrophe at the corner of his mouth.

"I love you, too."

Jude's smile grows even wider before his mouth is on mine again. We kiss like we have all day. A snow day. A holiday.

Suddenly, Jude's front door flies open behind him.

"Gertrude," I hear Christmas groan.

"Just capturing a moment," Gertie says.

"I want every moment with you," Jude mutters against my lips, ignoring my great aunt behind him. "Strings attached. No . . . ribbons. And bows. I want to wrap you up and unwrap you and keep you all the same."

I chuckle against his mouth, giddy with the thought of him tying me up, but even more ecstatic that he wants to keep me like I want to keep him.

"Aunt Angelica is making out in the hallway," a small boy's voice announces behind Jude, but we don't stop smiling at one another.

"Bunch of horn dogs, Maggie," Gertie tsks, but I can hear the approval in her voice.

"Want to meet my family?" Jude asks me.

"Your family is here?"

Jude nods. "They're staging an intervention."

"I'm so sorry. We can go. I can round up my clan and—"

Jude covers my lips with one single finger. "Why *are* you here?"

"I didn't want you to be alone. I don't want you to ever *feel* alone again." I will be here for him. Me, and my family, and apparently, his.

"You gave me an angel for my pocket, but I want the real Angelica by my side."

"Yes," I whisper.

"Time to cook the roast beast," Gran announces, letting out a rare whoop and dragging her sister away from the door. "I'll close the door so you two can make out in private."

"Oh God," I mutter, tipping my head into Jude's chest.

He chuckles above me and kisses the back of my head. "Later. Let's make a date of it. Make out in my room in an hour?"

"A date for a date," I arch a brow, reminded of our initial agreement.

"All the dates, including holidays."

I chuckle and tip up on my toes to kiss Jude one more time before he leads me into his condo.

When we approach the living room, he wraps his arms around me from behind and settles his chin on my shoulder.

"Tucker. Mae." He points toward his father who is a stunning man in his sixties and the lovely brunette with a purple streak of hair beside him.

"My pain in the ass sister, Julia." He points at her, while love fills his voice. "Her husband, Chopper, and their rugrats, Charlie, Ransom, and Lolly."

Jude kisses the side of my neck and stands taller.

"Family. This is my girlfriend, Angelica. Her favorite color is orange, favorite number nine, and she loves . . . me."

I twist to look up at him over my shoulder, where I'm met with the warmest gaze I've ever seen from Jude.

"And I love her."

epilogue

The first week of January

With a new year comes the dreaded board meeting. The one in which the directors want to vote on my competency as the president of Ashford's. When anarchy ensues, the leader isn't typically present for the coup, but these older men want me to witness their power.

As I sit at the head of the large oval table, I stare at the men who once knew my great-grandfather. Many of them were between his older age and the 'youth' of my grandfather. All of them made their fortunes in retail.

Sitting on pins and needles, I refuse to be washed up in my thirties, but Angelica reminded me that new books are written all the time. Maybe mine had a moral.

The value in life doesn't come from a store. Not the things you purchase or own. Not how you spend your money. Time is the commodity. And value comes from the people in your life.

Family. Love.

As I teeter on the possibility of losing my legacy, the door to the conference room opens, and Tucker enters.

"Dad?" I whisper. He hasn't attended one of these meetings in years, often voting by proxy. Beside him is my uncle, Mach. Since he moved to West Virginia a few years ago, we haven't been as close, but I've always admired him. Always thought I'd be him. A single man to his core.

Then he fell in love in his forties and moved to the south.

I have him beat by a decade on the love front.

Tucker takes a seat next to Ed Marksman, with Mach on his other side. I stare at both men while Walt calls the meeting to order.

Most of what he says is drowned out as he drones on about my unnecessary expenditures, my delinquent behavior, my reckless attitude, like I'm fifteen, not thirty-five.

Finally, voting is called, and the men begin to raise their hands in favor of removing me. There are nine of us, typically my favorite number.

To my surprise, Joseph Banks doesn't raise his hand. Neither does Ed Marksman. Or Tucker. Or Mach. Four against four, which leaves me with the deciding vote.

My hand rests in my lap.

Walt stares around the room, betrayal evident on his face.

"Now that *that* vote is completed. I propose a new one. The removal of Walt Wittiker for sexual inappropriateness and sexual harassment toward women and two men in this company."

"I beg your pardon," the older man snaps like he's swallowed an entire Christmas goose.

"You can beg me to have you escorted out of here. After the official vote."

But I'm no longer messing around with men like Walt. If the board doesn't vote him out, the lawsuits that are about to hit will.

Hands go up, favoring eight over one.

I punch the button on my phone for security. Then call Maxine.

"Mr. Wittiker will be escorted from the building."

"Right." Her efficient tone holds a smile, and I glance toward the opposite end of the table where Mach . . . and my dad . . . give me a reassuring grin as well.

A true vote of confidence from both of them.

+++

"We need a vacation," I tell Angelica as we sit inside my soaker tub. Her back is to my front.

In January, the weather in Chicago is frightful. The polar vortex causes temperatures to dip to negative twenty-five degrees Fahrenheit. And a blizzard shuts down the city.

"Isn't that how you got in trouble in the first place?" she laughs.

Her hair is piled on top of her head, allowing me to kiss her neck.

"I was thinking more like a family trip. Visit California. See Michigan." Julia lives out west; Mae and Dad share a place in the mitten state.

Angelica shifts to look up at me. "That sounds wonderful."

Since the Christmas intervention, in which her family merged almost seamlessly with mine, I've been having weekly check-ins with Tucker. Nothing too deep. Just a chat. We have a long road to travel, but I'm willing to ride the path.

I don't believe Scrooge changed everything about himself in a day.

But with my *girlfriend* at my side, I'm willing to weather storms and climb mountains.

I'm still getting used to the term, but I can already think of another one I want her to use.

Visions of her in white, standing by the floor to ceiling windows in the Oak Room still haunt me. A good haunting.

Angelica shifts again, resting her head back on my shoulder. She strokes her fingers over my forearm like she says her mom used to do to her. The motion is soothing, comforting.

With the most hectic retail season behind me, I have about six months to prepare for the next run. Christmas enthusiasm starts earlier and earlier every year, but I'm not going to let the hype steal the season from me again.

"So . . . a vacation," Angelica hums. "Road trip?"

I chuckle, knowing that's how Tucker met Mae. I'm not as adverse to flying as he is.

"Whatever you want, angel."

Angelica leans forward and spins, straddling me within seconds.

"Whatever I want, huh? Is this like *I can have anything I want from Ashford's*?" She laughs, reminding us both of how I'd once given her the same offer. Knowing she isn't a material girl, I don't even take her question seriously.

"As long as what you want is me."

Leaning down, she kisses me, soft and too sweet. I cup the front of her throat as she pulls back.

"Always," she whispers.

"Sold." Then I smile, and she watches the divot by my mouth. An apostrophe on my smile she calls it. She claimed it as hers like I've claimed that freckle near the corner of her lips.

Angelica laughs again, but I cut off the sound, swallowing it, savoring it.

And falling more in love with her every second we are together.

She saved my life with a kiss.

I stole her heart in return and the grinch still deep down inside me plans to keep it.

In the end, this scrooge gets the girl.

+++

Thank you for taking the time to read ELF-ish.

Please consider writing a review on major sales channels where ebooks and paperbacks are sold and discussed.

Want more of Angelica and Jude? BONUS.

If you loved this holiday hottie, you might also enjoy THE HOLIDAY POST, when a globetrotting toy-mogul and a single mom become reluctant roommates after he crashes in their small town during the holidays.

Flip the page for a sample.

OR

Start at the beginning of the Holiday Hotties with SCROOGE-ish, where SHE hates the holidays and HE's out to prove it's the most wonderful time of the year.

Flip the page for a sample.

season's greetings

Titles can be tough for authors. Many of us have a process on how to choose the right one. For me, I like to have a title before I even set fingertips to keyboard. A title guides my story.

Before publishing, this book had a title change, which is something I rarely do.

Initially, this holiday romance should have been titled *Grinch-ish* keeping with the grumpy/naughty theme of the Holiday Hotties, in *Scrooge-ish*, *Naughty*-ish, and *Grouch-ish*.

Hopefully, you see the pattern.

However, the word grinch, while recognized as a noun for a person who is mean-spirited and unfriendly, is also protected with something like fifty-four trademarks that relate to Dr. Seuss and his tale, *How the Grinch Stole Christmas*.

I really wanted *Grinch-ish*, but I also really don't want to be sued.

Thank you to my reader group, Loving L.B. (Dunbar), for coming up with title alternatives. While *Humbug-ish* was my favorite (I'll be tucking it away for future use), it just didn't fit Angelica and Jude once I started writing their story.

Jude is too selfish and Angelica too elfish.

This Holiday Hottie is a combination of several Christmas-centric stories. *A Christmas Carol* and the redemption of Scrooge; the possessive nature of Clara (and the Nutcracker) in *The Nutcracker*; and of course, Dr. Seuss's famous Christmas tale, about a creature who feels like an outlier, lacks compassion, and ultimately, is lonely.

Ho, ho, ho, my wannabe hero!

A person desperate for light in the darkness of loneliness, and love. Love. Love. Love.

I *love* a good redemption romance. I hope you've loved it, too.

On that note, may this holiday season be full of that light you deserve, and the love you desire, and maybe a few chocolate mints, and some strawberries and cream.

Happy holidays –

L.B.

The Holiday Post Sample

1
[Saint]

December 4
20 days until Christmas Eve

Fuck! I was lost. Late and lost.

"Da is going to kill me," I mutter to no one as I continue my death grip on the leather-wrapped steering wheel of my forest-green Aston Martin DBX707. The car is a total luxury.

And one not built for snow.

About an hour ago, the wind picked up and the snow swirled, and I'd hiked my baby girl into high gear, like I could outrun the weather.

I have, on occasion, but that's a different story for a different time.

My GPS went out around the time the weather kicked in, the snow changing from pretty, dancing flakes, like the inside of a snow globe, to vengeful crystals of ice, angrily pelting my car.

My subscription radio service went out at roughly the same time, and I switched to a regular FM station, hoping for a local weather update.

No such luck.

Certain I'd made a wrong turn because the road grew narrower and curvier, I could hardly make out the blacktop that should have been in front of me. Instead, it was snow, snow, and more snow, obscuring my windshield, blanketing the road, and weighing heavily on the thick trees surrounding my highway path.

Yep, definitely lost.

Eventually, I break through the trees, and a vague emptiness appears on my right, as if nothing exists over there.

"Am I on a cliff?" Squinting to better see through the barrage of flakes and the dark night reflected back at me by the sports car's headlights, my breath catches.

"Is that the fucking ocean?"

I'd been crossing through Maine on my way to Bangor, the final destination of a three-month cross-country road trip. I could have ended the trip in Chicago, where I'd been visiting my brother Nick, or grabbed a flight from New York, but I'd wanted to continue the journey in my beautiful green machine until the last possible minute, and the last minute meant from Bangor to a private plane in Nova Scotia to take me home.

North. The place was waiting for me.

Only, I don't appear to be anywhere near Bangor, possibly not headed north, nor south, as I'd hit the edge of the Atlantic Ocean. Trees tower to my left, water is somewhere to my right, and I pray I don't end up in it. Neither myself nor my car desire a winter dip in that certain-to-be freezing water.

With brief thoughts of icebergs and polar bears and the state of the polar cap, I mutter aloud another thought. "Do not let me die in snow."

My entire life I've battled frozen temperatures and frigid nights, and I've survived fifty years of the wintery mix Jack Frost tosses into the air.

"Snow will not be the end of me," I vow, again to no one as I am alone in my green machine.

Always without a partner at my side in this adventure called life. Been that way for fifty years as well. There'd been plenty of women in my life, but not *the* woman. The right woman. The one who would understand what I do. Believe in me. Accept me.

With my chest pressed to the steering wheel, my hands are covered in leather driving gloves and perfectly placed at midnight. Narrowing my eyes, I'm certain I've seen something dash into the road.

Blinking rapidly, I pray out loud again, "Don't be a deer." Or worse, a reindeer. Those beasts can cause some serious damage to a vehicle. I don't want to think about what they'd do to a human inside a low-to-the-ground sports car. Then again, caribou are not common in Maine.

With my thoughts scrambling once again, two bright eyes flicker to life in my headlights, blinding me like an old-fashioned camera bulb. The level of the pair is too low for a deer. Plus, the dark, furry patches around each eye, outlined by white fur on a large, round head suggest that this four-legged creature is a Saint Bernard.

In the middle of the road.

Instinctively, I swerve left, hopeful the big dog goes right, but as my car starts to tailspin, I'm worried it isn't going to matter which way the dog runs, if he even ran.

Why the fuck was he sitting in the middle of the road during a godawful snowstorm?

All these thoughts continue to whirl in my head in the blink of an eye as my car spins in a circle at high speed, while feeling like slow motion, until I come to an abrupt stop, jolting me side to side inside the Martin. The thud on the right side of the car means impact with something solid and sturdy.

Closing my eyes as the air bag deploys, punching me in the face, I hold my breath, wincing at the sting in my nose and the burn in my eyes at the swift release of protection. Taking a moment to catch my breath, I keep my eyes closed.

Please let the dog be safe.

As the airbag deflates, I slowly crane my neck to the right. The front side of my car is pressed up against something circular and firm. A tree, perhaps.

Oh fuck, not my car. Not my sweet baby girl green machine.

Reaching for my phone, I notice there is no reception. Probably due to the storm. And now I have no way to call for roadside assistance, not that anyone would find me in this blizzardy mess right now anyway.

Squinting into the darkness, my headlights are the only illumination.

Tilting my head forward, I correct my assessment about a tree, deciding instead that I might have hit a utility pole.

Great, just great . . .

Only as I narrow my gaze, resting my forearms on the steering wheel, over the burst airbag, I see that I've hit a pole of some sort. A mile marker, maybe.

Either way, I'm off the road a bit, and now, I'm not only late and lost, I'm stuck.

And the dog.

Quickly, I glance out the front windshield, slanting my eyes.

"You have got to be kidding me," I glower.

With a heavy press against the driver's side door, I force the opening into the fierce wind. Bracing myself for the cold, I slowly stand, using my gloved hand as eye protection and the door as a shield as I holler over the top of the window.

"What the hell are you thinking?" I shout at the giant Saint Bernard, who looks at me with a puppy dog gaze despite his grown size. The expression suggests I'm the stupid one.

Not to mention, he appears to be in the exact same spot he was sitting only moments ago, having shifted his body to face my new direction. Not a scrape or scratch on him, thankfully. Also, apparently, not a single care that a blizzard rages around us.

"Come here," I call out to him, stepping to the side of the open door and waving toward the warmth of the car, which will quickly be lost the longer it takes this beast to hop inside.

He's lucky I didn't hit him. He might not be so lucky a second round, especially as he continues to stare back at me with those large, melancholy eyes like I'm the one he feels sorry for.

With a quick, sharp whistle, one that demands he follow my command and works on other animals in my care when I want their attention, I motion toward the car again.

This gentle giant, however, does not move.

He turns his large head slowly, like he's heard someone call him. He pauses a second as if listening, then lazily lugs the lower half of his large body upward and sluggishly runs off, back toward the trees.

Having no idea where I am, I lean into the wicked wind, stepping forward as best I can to both assess the damage to my car and hope the post my baby girl is now wrapped around will give a hint to my location.

First, I glance at the way my front right tire bends in the wrong direction and the front fender panel kisses the post, offering it a hug I'd prefer it not give. Next, I glance up at a sign attached to the post and narrow my eyes once again against the blinding wind and bitter cold to read it.

Welcome to Hideaway Harbor.

"Well, this certainly has been quite the greeting."

Continue reading THE HOLIDAY POST.

The Holiday Post

Scrooge-ish Sample

chapter 1

I hate Christmas.

I don't know who thought every female must love shopping, wrapping, baking and hosting—as commercialized on nearly every holiday advertisement—but if those things are supposed to be coded into my DNA, I'm missing it.

And my hatred is exacerbated each year by gifts given more from obligation than love, well wishes without heart behind them, and family.

Don't get me wrong. I know Christmas isn't about gifts. The season wasn't born in a store, and I believe that kindness can be found in a word or smile just as much as a deed, but something is always missing for me.

Somewhere along the way, I stopped caring about this holiday.

Maybe it was when certain people stopped caring about me.

Refer back to reference three above: Family.

What's the worst is I work in retail, where the happiest time of the year is accentuated by the beep-beep of chip scanners, the screaming emotional meltdown of children, and annoying, selfish customers. I'm in management at Ashford's, a top-end department store in downtown Chicago, open seven days a week because my boss is an asshole.

I work a lot of hours, volunteering to fill in for others because they have families, or family emergencies, or friends with families who have emergencies, and more work for me means more money toward my dream. It also means less time facing reality.

I don't have a life.

And I'm lonely.

But no worries. It's late Wednesday, Thanksgiving Eve, which has somehow become a thing on the night before an American holiday, and I'm working.

"What are you still doing here?" Zaleya asks me as I hand over two bulging bags of random clothes to some older woman who has no idea what she's just purchased for her grandchildren. Cha-ching, cha-ching, though…

"I'm working."

"But you were off at six and now it's eight." Zaleya Stone is a curvy brunette with a huge heart and an infectious smile. She's excellent with difficult customers and a dream to work with.

"Eight. Six. They both have a little, swirly circle at the bottom of them." I shrug giving Zaleya a smile. The Ashford's smile. The I'm-happy-to-work-here-even-though-I'm-really-miserable-but-need-the-money smile.

"Ev-a," Zaleya draws out my name. At least she says it correctly. Ev-ah, like Evan without an -n. Not Eve-ah, or even Evie, or Eve, or whatever name Jude Ashford likes to say when he grows frustrated in a management meeting and can't remember my name despite eight years working here and making top manager three years in a row. Jude is younger than me and the owner of the entire company. He's also hot which makes him even more annoying, but I'm not into the cougar-thing.

"You have a thing tonight," Zaleya reminds me although I really don't want the reminder. I mean, who celebrates twenty-two years since high school graduation? We were supposed to have a twentieth in 2020, when a world pandemic hit, and the celebration had to be cancelled. Then the alumni organization wanted to host a glorious twenty-one the following year, only the planning committee members contracted COVID from each other. Gossip on the street, though, is the cancellation was because a set of former high school sweethearts and two former jocks leading the planning had a four-way one weekend that ended a marriage and a business partnership. It was a scandalous situation the high school couldn't allow affiliated with the reputation and prestige of good old Immaculate Academy.

"Oh, I'm not going." I force another smile as I nod at the next customer to step forward. I shouldn't be working a register, but the floor is busy despite being the night before Thanksgiving. We're running a door-buster deal this evening as a jumpstart on Black Friday's five a.m. opening time. We used to open late night on Thanksgiving, but we've canceled that extra evening of potential revenue. To be closed on a national holiday actually felt rather compassionate which wasn't my thing.

I've been told I'm selfish and unfeeling, according to my last three attempts at relationships. And while I tend to agree with that assessment, I stopped caring a long time ago.

"You have to go," Zaleya admonishes me.

"I don't have to do anything." I ring up a female customer's purchase, hoping she isn't intending to wear the two items purchased in combination.

Zaleya nudges me out of the way before the next customer steps forward, swipes her team member card through the register, and logs me off the system. Somehow, she's overridden the program and clocks me out of work.

"I could write you up for insubordination and unethical practices." I narrow my eyes at her, without any heat in my threat. Zaleya is older than me by almost two decades, but under me as an assistant manager.

"One day that veneer is going to slip, and you'll realize a real softy lives beneath that tight leather skirt and take no prisoners heels." Zaleya winks.

"Don't you mean others will realize . . . and also, you're wrong. Nothing soft here." I pat my belly, which actually does jiggle a little and grumbles, reminding me I haven't eaten all day.

"Yeah, well, eat some peppermint bark or a Christmas cookie . . . or five. And put some roast beast on those bones." She eyes me up and down, and I marvel at her use of a Grinch reference.

I like Zaleya. She reminds me of the mother I never had, which doesn't make sense as my mother is still around. Can't have a memory of someone who didn't exist, though. Mom left on Christmas Eve, when I was ten, and Dad cancelled the holiday that year. And most years after that. Zaleya is more like a mentor, or a guardian angel, if I believed in such a thing. She's just an overall nice person, and I hate her a little for her good cheer. But not really.

Zaleya nudges me out of the register station. "Get going. I predict great things from this evening."

+++

By eight-thirty, Zaleya catches me still lingering in my meager office on the upper floors of Ashford's. The flagship store is the last remaining Ashford's. The company was bought out, and all but the landmark location was converted to the other conglomerate's brand. Gossip around the water cooler, so to speak, is that Jude inherited the single store, instead of the brand going to his father. As the sole family member who owns Ashford's, I've heard words like spoiled, entitled, and ungrateful for his inheritance used to reference him. On a side note, we don't have water coolers because Jude is too cheap to pay for such a service for his employees.

"Eva." Zaleya's motherly tone is both admonishing and chagrin.

"It's too late to go."

"It's only eight-thirty. You young things are just getting started at this hour."

I'm no longer young. I'll be turning forty this December.

"I'm not dressed."

Zaleya eyes my outfit, taking in the leather pencil skirt in bright red I'm wearing. I'd worn it in an effort to appear holiday-cheery when I'm not.

"You look gorgeous."

"I'm too old to attend these things. I mean, who goes to high school reunions, really? Jocks who can't let go of state championships two decades-old and still wear their high school rings. Nerds who want to show everyone they made it financially. The pimply kid who wants to prove he was a supermodel underneath his skin. The homecoming queen who popped out three kids before thirty and is divorced from her second husband."

Zaleya stares at me.

"Where does that put me?" Not jock. Not geek. Just your average girl in high school. Good grades, clean-cut, and boring.

"It puts you attending. Not to prove anything to them but to allow yourself a night out on the town among people you once knew."

"But that's my point. I don't know these people anymore. I hardly knew them twenty-two years ago."

"Just go. 'Tis the season." Zaleya waves a hand above her head. "Magic is in the air."

"The season doesn't officially begin until tomorrow, when Santa drives his sleigh before Ashford's in the parade." Sarcasm fills my voice. I don't believe in Santa any more than I believe in magic.

Zaleya puts her hands on her hips. "Honey, Christmas lives all the year through."

Jiminy Cricket, she sounds like a holiday card.

"Who knows? Maybe an old boyfriend will be there." Zaleya wiggles her brows.

I snort.

"Or a boy of former interest." Her voice hitches, gushing with innuendo.

I huff.

But someone does come to mind.

Someone I deny myself the chance to remember, as I'm certain he's forgotten me.

Continue reading SCROOGE-ish.

Scrooge-ish direct

More by L.B. Dunbar

Sterling Falls

Seven small-town siblings muddle their way through love over 40.

Sterling Heat
Sterling Brick
Sterling Streak
Sterling Clay
Sterling Fight
Sterling Touch
Sterling Stone

Chicago Anchors

When your eyes are on the silver fox coach, more than the ball.

Elevator Pitch
Catch the Kiss

Parentmoon

When the mother of the groom goes head-to-head with the single father of the bride.

Holiday Hotties (Christmas novellas)

Holiday novellas certain to heat the season.

Scrooge-ish
Naughty-ish
Grouch-ish
Elf-ish

Hideaway Harbor

Where four small town sisters find love later in life.

The Holiday Post

Road Trips & Romance

Three sisters. Three destinations. All second chances at love over 40.

Hauling Ashe
Merging Wright
Rhode Trip

Lakeside Cottage

Four friends. Four summers. Shenanigans and love happen at the lake.

ELF-ish

Living at 40
Loving at 40
Learning at 40
Letting Go at 40

The Silver Foxes of Blue Ridge
Small mountain town, silver foxes. Brothers seeking love over 40.
Silver Brewer
Silver Player
Silver Mayor
Silver Biker

Sexy Silver Foxes
When sexy silver foxes meet the feisty vixens of their dreams.
After Care
Midlife Crisis
Restored Dreams
Second Chance
Wine&Dine

Collision novellas
A spin-off from After Care – the younger set/rock stars
Collide
Caught

The Sex Education of M.E.
The original sexy silver fox.
When a widowed professor decides she'd like to date again, and a local fireman volunteers to give her lessons.

The Heart Collection
Small town, big hearts - stories of family and love.
Speak from the Heart
Read with your Heart
Look with your Heart
Fight from the Heart
View with your Heart

A Heart Collection Spin-off

The Heart Remembers

BOOKS IN OTHER AUTHOR WORLDS

Smartypants Romance (an imprint of Penny Reid)

Tales of the Winters sisters set in Green Valley.

Love in Due Time

Love in Deed

Love in a Pickle

The World of True North (an imprint of Sarina Bowen)

Welcome to Vermont! And the Busy Bean Café.

Cowboy

Studfinder

THE EARLY YEARS

The Legendary Rock Star Series

A classic tale with a modern twist of rockstar romance and suspense.

Paradise Stories

MMA romance. Two brothers. One fight.

The Island Duet

Intrigue and suspense. The island knows what you've done.

Modern Descendants – writing as elda lore

Magical realism. Modern myths of Greek gods.

About the Author

www.lbdunbar.com

L.B. Dunbar loves sexy silver foxes, second chances, and small towns. If you enjoy older characters in your romance reads, including a hero with a little silver in his scruff and a heroine rediscovering her worth, then welcome to romance for those over 40. L.B. Dunbar's signature works include women and men in their prime taking another turn at love and happily ever after. She's a *USA TODAY* Bestseller as well as #1 Bestseller on Amazon in Later in Life Romance with her Sterling Falls, Lakeside Cottage, and Road Trips & Romance series. L.B. lives in Chicago with her own sexy silver fox.

To get all the scoop about the self-proclaimed queen of silver fox romance, join her on Facebook at Loving L.B. or receive her weekly newsletter, Love Notes.

+++

Connect with L.B. Dunbar

www.ingramcontent.com/pod-product-compliance
Lightning Source LLC
Chambersburg PA
CBHW060853210726
48293CB00006B/1779

9781956337686